River Without End

PAMELA JEKEL

River Without End

A Novel of the Suwannee

KENSINGTON BOOKS
http://www.kensingtonbooks.com

Excerpted from *Neither Wolf nor Dog* by Kent Nerburn © 1994. Reprinted with permission of New World Library, San Rafael, CA 94903.

Excerpted from *Light a Distant Fire* by Lucia St. Clair Robson, © 1988. Reprinted with permission of Ballantine Books, NY.

Excerpted from *The Okefenokee Swamp* by Franklin Russell and the Editors of Time-Life Books, © 1973. Reprinted with permission of Random House, Inc., NY.

KENSINGTON BOOKS are published by

Kensington Publishing Corp.
850 Third Avenue
New York, NY 10022

Copyright © 1997 by Pamela Jekel, Inc.

Kensington and the K logo Reg. U.S. Pat. & TM Off.

Library of Congress Card Catalog Number: 96-079078
ISBN 1-57566-172-1

First Printing: June, 1997
10 9 8 7 6 5 4 3 2 1

Printed in the United States of America

for my only child, Leah Justine,

> my truest mirror,
> my favorite angel,
> my highest hope.

Now, at three, you ask me, "Are you my very best friend?" and I always say, "I am your very best friend." The day may come, my daughter, when you cease to ask the question, but regardless, I shall ever know the answer. Yes, dearest one, soul of my soul, always and ever after.

SUWANNEE

Way down upon de Swanee ribber, far, far away
Dere's wha my heart is turning ebber,
Dere's wha de old folks stay.
All up and down de whole creations,
Sadly I roam,
Still longing for de old plantation,
And for de old folks at home.
All de world am sad and dreary,
Ebry where I roam,
Oh! darkeys, how my heart grows weary,
Far from de old folks at home.

Stephen Foster, "Old Folks At Home,"
1851, Firth, Pond, & Co.

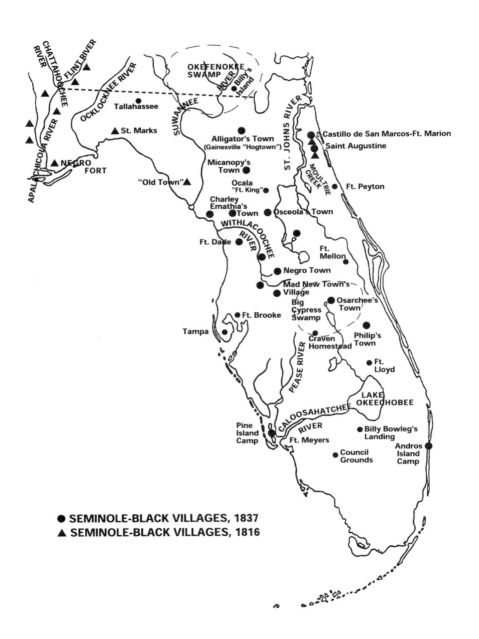

CHATTAHOOCHEE RIVER

FLINT RIVER

OCKLOCKNEE RIVER

▲
▲
▲
▲

● Tallahassee

SUWANNEE

OKEFENOKEE SWAMP

RIVER

Billy's Island

▲ St. Marks

Alligator's Town
(Gainesville "Hogtown")

ST. JOHNS RIVER

Castillo de San Marcos-Ft. Marion

▲▲ Saint Augustine

APALACHICOLA RIVER

▲ NEGRO FORT

"Old Town" ▲

Micanopy's Town ●

Ocala "Ft. King" ●

MOULTRIE CREEK

Ft. Peyton

Charley Emathia's Town ●

WITHLACOOCHEE

RIVER

Osceola's Town ●

Ft. Dade ●

Ft. Mellon ●

Negro Town ●

Mad New Town's ● Village

Big Cypress Swamp

Osarchee's Town ●

● Ft. Brooke

Tampa ●

PEASE RIVER

Craven Homestead ●

Philip's Town ●

Ft. Lloyd ●

LAKE OKEECHOBEE

Pine Island Camp ●

CALOOSAHATCHEE RIVER

● Ft. Meyers

● Billy Bowleg's Landing

Council Grounds ●

Andros Island Camp ●

● SEMINOLE-BLACK VILLAGES, 1837
▲ SEMINOLE-BLACK VILLAGES, 1816

Prologue

*D*eep in the belly of Georgia lies a place so remote from all things civilized, at once so wild and also suffused with a queer antique quiet, that it has drawn the outcast, the runaway, and the scalawag since man first stumbled upon its dark, tangled paths. Okefenokee or "trembling earth" it was since the first Indians named it; the Swamp it was to a handful of intruders for a century, and finally, as civilization attempted to contain and thus maintain it, the Okefenokee National Wildlife Refuge it has been for some twenty-five years: more than four hundred thousand acres, the largest wetlands in the United States.

Once the Atlantic covered most of Florida and southeastern Georgia, but the land rose and the ocean receded, leaving an impounded saltwater marsh. Over millennia, rains sweetened the waters, aquatic plants invaded and prospered, and decayed vegetation became peat. Cypress, gum, and bay grew high and dense, and birds flocked to the swamp, thriving in its insect-rich habitat. In places, the marsh opened up to the light, and maiden cane swayed like broad fields of Kansas wheat. In others where the eerie wilderness was dense with Ogeechee tupelo and only the splash of a bowfin or the bellow of an alligator broke the silence, the Okefenokee was at its most primeval. The waters, the muck, and the rushes teemed with life from the lowest forms on up the scale of evolution, and it was easy to believe that it was from these untrammeled swamps that life first emerged from the sea to colonize the land.

From the bowels of the swamp, a dark green river was born, twisting its way 265 miles across the Florida panhandle to the Gulf of Mexico. The Suwannee, the Seminoles named it, after an early and beloved chieftainess. Or perhaps its name came from a corruption of the Spanish name for the river,

San Juanito. Whatever the source of its name, and though a dozen different kinds of men have tried to own it, the Suwannee has remained largely undisturbed and undeveloped, as though it carried the mood of the Okefenokee in every ripple.

Before America, Spanish soldiers splashed across its fords, but the missions they left behind soon disappeared. Seminole Indians and gator hunters roamed its banks, and moonshiners set up furtive kingdoms in its swamps, but the Suwannee gradually overwhelmed all traces of early settlement.

During the Second Seminole War of 1835, the army floated steamboats up the Suwannee and after the Indians were vanquished, people came from all over the world to sample the crystal-clear mineral springs which nourished the river on its journey to the Gulf. Once, small plantations crowned its banks, while planters tried to compete with the larger, more successful plunderings of cotton and sugar farther to the north. Once, the wealthy played in transparent pools where shells gleamed twenty feet below the surface, but now, nothing remains of these resorts and those plantations but the massive stone walls built round the springs to keep the tannin-dark river water from flooding in.

Mostly, the swamp has dictated what the region would be to man, for the swamp and its wilderness have ruled the Suwannee longer than any trespasser, any invader ever could.

The Suwannee is one of America's most romantic, most mysterious rivers, a river road of history and legends, swamps and springs, the forgotten, the disappeared, and the solitary. And in the spring when a million white water lilies, yellow-spiked neverwets, and green clusters of floating hearts transfigure the dark surface of the water, and time stops to listen to the whisper of cattail and the elusive call of a low-flying blue heron, it is one of America's most beautiful.

1790

In the east, the faint light of early morning came filtering through the dense canopy of trees, and the sky turned from pitch-black to a less absolute black, tinged with the palest green. The relative quiet of the night was broken then, and the deep, coughing grunt of a black bear hunting breakfast came from the thicket. A cluster of white egrets rose to the air from their nests in the canopy, beating the heavy air with their wings, and their chuckling calls seemed to mock those who lay on the damp ground below.

Black John rose slowly up from the wet swamp grass and stared blearily at the growing light from the east. "We got to move on," he said quietly. He put his hand to the small of his back and pressed back the stiffness. Threescore years and sleeping out on the cold dirt, 'twas nothing but God's grace he could walk at all, he reminded himself.

The five prone bodies at his feet began to stir and rise at his soft words. They did not need to be called twice.

"Bear or painter?" Simon asked, listening to the departing thrash of the creature.

"I 'spect a bear," Black John said, moving painfully to the water's edge and squatting to take a drink. His knees snapped and cracked like lightwood put to the torch.

"He were close," Susan murmured. She joined Black John at the water, but she kept one eye at the trees behind her.

"Swamp playin' tricks on your ears," Black John said with more confidence than he felt. "Could be, ol' marster bear more'n a mile off."

All of them came to the water now, five black bodies in ragtag raiment, two women, three men, none of them moving too spry, he saw, except Susan, and her barely a woman, by his guess.

Old Abby peered into the swamp water, swirling it slightly with her cane. " 'Pears to be movin' west."

"That a fact," Simon said morosely. "Look to me like it don' move at all."

"Away from the sun," she said stubbornly, ignoring him.

"An' we got to do the same," Black John said firmly, rising from the water and appraising his followers. Peter and Simon seemed rested enough; Joseph looked as weary as death. He'd had hard use from his master; he might not make it to the Gulf at all.

Black John tried to keep the worry from his voice. "We got to make least a mile 'for we stop for 'visions."

" 'Tain't hardly worth stoppin'," Peter grumbled. "Nothin' left but a speck o' meal an' a smear o' grease—"

"I eat your part then," Susan said cheerfully. "An' you can go on back an' 'vision with the rest o' the niggers."

Peter glared at her, but he fell in behind Joseph in his usual place in the line after Old Abby, and Black John turned his straggling band downriver, searching for the widest bank, the shallowest water, in this labyrinth of tangled green jungle.

The six runaway slaves had come to the fringes of the swamp only two days before, and they had no sense of how deep they must go within its dense heart of more than four hundred thousand acres before they came out on the other side. From two Georgian plantations they had escaped, led forth by Black John, goaded by Old Abby, the most ancient among them, following the dream of the Suwannee.

"Suwannee take us to freedom," Black John had told them, one by one, as they came to knock at the door of his cabin. "We jes' follow ol' river to the sea, an' they cain' never track us in that swamp."

But how will we find our way? they asked, what will we eat, and what will they do if they catch us? The questions were always the same, and many who came to ask them never found the courage to come again. But a few did. Five, in fact. And those few came again and again until finally, the plan was resolved.

Black John would lead them from bondage, from out of the despair of the quarters and the depths of their hopelessness. He knew a little of the swamp, for his master had taken him hunting there time and again, though never too deeply within. He said there was game afoot, fish in the waters, and enough frogs to feed them on the way to the sea. "Suwannee one o' the mos' dark an' mystery rivers in the world," he said knowingly, "an' marster don' go there much, an' then none too far. If we keep to Suwannee, we make it to freedom."

"How you know it go to the sea?" Joseph asked.

"Marster tol' me."

"How far you been?" Peter asked.

"Far enough to know what I ain' seen. I can make it to the river, I know that much. An' once we there, we jes' follow the water."

"Is there haunts in there?" Simon asked fearfully. "I hear tell they's jes' waitin' for a body to trespass—"

"That's white folks' tales to spook you," Black John said firmly.

"I hear the water's poison," Joseph murmured.

Old Abby snorted and rolled her eyes in silent derision.

"I drink it, an' I still here to tell it," Black John said. "But if you scared, don' go. Stay here an' shoe the man's horse 'til you drop dead." He added this last in so mild a voice that none could take offense.

"How long you think it take?" Susan asked.

"No tellin'. I study on a month, maybe more. 'Less we get lost, which I don' aim to. But don' go, less you fixed on it. I be goin', no matter. I glad for the comp'ny, but I ain' no Moses."

"I been waitin' all my life for Moses. I ain' never seen him yet," Peter said. "Guess I settle for some rickety ol' nigger who will fetch up frogs 'stead o' manna."

Susan laughed, a low-throated warble of delight. "The Lord done got a good sense o' fun, ain' He? I go with you, ol' Moses."

Black John spoke into the night of the possible dangers ahead, trying to keep them sober. If they were captured, their masters'd likely cut off a foot so they couldn't run again. Or maybe a hand, for thieving themselves from those as which owned them. They might fall into sucking mud and drown, might get set upon by wolves or snakes or bats, might wander for months with only the food God might provide— but for all he said, they would not be sober another moment. The mere promise of freedom made them drunk enough to dare whatever lay ahead.

And so, from the terror of the cabin where her white master came in the night to take her without shame and against her will, Susan stole away on the chosen night to join them. From the field where Simon had been whipped for stealing corn he came, carrying his master's hoe and cane knife, stealing from him one last time. From the stable, where Joseph groomed the master's horse and from the brickyard, where Peter made the master's bricks, they came in the night, looking over their shoulders in fear lest they be taken up before they could flee. And from the Big House, where Old Abby had served the young mistress willingly, until she was sent to the quarters, too old and crooked to be seen by guests anymore, the old woman hobbled. One by one, they all came to be delivered.

Old Abby watched them assemble that last night, peering at them wrathfully over her stinking pipe. She was nigh to sixty, Black John thought, near as old as himself and crippled by the rheumatism. But she could tell the direction of the storm before it blew, could conjure sickness from most any failing body, and had the sharpest eye for evil of any in the quarters. "I be goin' along," she said in a voice that brooked no trespass. "An' when I see my Lord at last, I tell him I seen his hell mos' like, jes' send me 'long to heaven."

"We cain' take no granny with us," Peter said staunchly. He did not know Old Abby well, or he never would have spoken.

"You never make it, if you don'," she said.

Peter snorted and rolled his eyes, silently appealing to Black John, known to be one of the smartest slaves in the county, to put the old woman straight.

"You know, 'tween two, which root to eat an' which to leave be?" Black John asked him genially. "You know how to keep skeeters an' blackflies an' stingin' bugs off your hide? You know, if you get bit by a cottonmouth, how to keep alive? Ol' Abby knows. If she wants to come, she comin'. Need be, we carry her all the way."

"Who gonna' carry who?" Peter asked. "Not you, ol' Moses, that for damn sure. It be me or Simon here who do the carryin'."

"Ain' nobody need to worry," Old Abby said firmly. "If I cain' walk, I die happy where I fall. Better out in freedom than here in mis'ry. 'Sides, if you don' take me, I set up such a holler, they find you gone 'fore you reach the swamp."

Peter glared at her and then at Black John. The old man shrugged. "She be slow, but we cain' go fast anyways. The swamp won' let us."

Susan added, "I cain' go with no passel o' menfolk by myself. Should be some other womenfolk 'longside."

"You aim to protect your good name?" Peter hooted.

"I aim," she said with small dignity, "to do the right thing."

The silence round the cabin was changed by her words right then, Black John felt it at once. They were now bonded to the plan and to each other.

And so, finally, they set off on a black, moonless night, away from the cotton fields of Valdosta, thirty miles to the east, to disappear into the depths of the Okefenokee Swamp.

For five nights, they walked until they reached the river, enclosed in denser forest than any they had seen. The sounds of the creatures around them were terrifying, but they kept on. The snakes became more numerous, blacker and thicker round than a man's arm, and still they kept walking. The mosquitoes and gnats tortured them, stinging their necks, their arms, flying into their mouths and eyes, and they slapped swamp mud on their skin, plaited grass hats for their eyes, and went on. They ran out of provisions and strength, and they killed rabbits and pigeons and endless frogs and still, they talked themselves into going forward.

Black John was right, it was not hard to find the Suwannee. But keeping to it was tougher. He knew, he told them, that this slow, languid river would soon run faster, would widen and deepen and run fresher once away from the tea-dark swamp waters.

"An' will it come at las' to the sea?" Susan asked, over and over.

"Yes, child," Black John reassured her.

"An' what we do there?" Peter wondered.

"What you want. Me, I build me a boat an' sail to Cuba." Black John grinned.

"I go with you," Simon said quickly. " 'Less they catch me an' shoot me down."

"I never go back," Susan said darkly. "I cut my throat first."

"Cut them frog legs instead, sister," Black John said kindly. Susan was not lovely, was all arms and elbows and knees, was a mere girl and useless in most ways, but she was still female. As such, she deserved, he thought, his gentle voice.

They were gathered in a circle round a small fire he had managed to make. Six frogs were laid out next to Old Abby. For two days now, these creatures had made up the better part of their meals. Susan set to her task, and Peter stoked the fire with glum, jabbing pokes.

"Mighty sick o' frogs an' fish," he muttered.

Old Abby snorted. "Best get joy o' them, mister. We still got a mighty long river to walk."

"You think we made five miles today?" Joseph asked quietly.

Black John shook his head slowly. "More like three. But we do better tomorrow. We gettin' seasoned."

Peter slapped at another mosquito. "That good, since we gettin' eat up sure 'nough."

They settled down then for the evening, each to his own thoughts. Black John foraged at the edges of the firelight, careful not to go too far from the safety of the flickering flames, gathering grasses and boughs for their beds. As he brought back an armful to young Susan, she murmured to him softly, "Thank 'ee, John."

He paused for a moment in confusion. There was something subtly different in her tone, and she had never called him that before.

"I reckon," she went on, "when we get to freedom, you want to lose that 'black' from your name. Might as well start now." She smiled at him, and he felt an old warmth seep into his loins, the familiar uncoiling of desire. It had been a long time since he'd felt that old heat, and it left him confused. She was only a green heifer—

"Don' you dream on it?" she asked him. "What you gonna' call yourself, when you free? I 'spect you would."

"Guess you're right," he muttered. "Never thought much on it."

"We got to think on lots o' things we never thought much on before," she said. "Man finds freedom, he got to make a new life."

He glanced at her sharply then, for there was no mistaking her invitation. "Time enough to think on that if we make it," he said firmly, clearing his throat as though he swept out a room.

"Oh, we make it," she said firmly. "You gonna' see to it."

He looked at her then in the firelight. "I be a old man, child. Way past my prime. Could be, you do better to lean on the Lord to get us home."

She laughed gently. "I leaned on the Lord, ol' John. An' He bringed me to you."

"He ain' that foolish," Black John murmured.

Before she could answer him, he heard a sharp crack from the clearing and the rustle of moving brush. He whirled quickly, and the startled cry died in his mouth. Dark shapes moved suddenly on them, man-shapes, more than a half dozen of them, and as rough hands grabbed him, yanked her up sharply, she screamed once in wild fright. A hand clamped over her mouth, and the other sleeping bundles were set upon, pulled upright, and pushed into each other in confused terror.

Now Black John could see in an instant who had attacked, could see in the flurry of firelight and swift movements the long, black hair, the paint, the wild eyes—the savages had them.

In swift moments, the sleeping men were yanked to their feet, their hands tied together, ropes round their necks, each to the other, and their cries stifled. Old Abby was trussed like a sow and thrown on a litter, the men were prodded together with sharp knives, and Susan was surrounded on both sides by tall warriors. She wailed and was cuffed to silence.

Black John saw in the firelight that the brutes were painted as for war, their long hair tied with quills, and the stench of them was strong in the thick, black night. "Seminoles," he said to the others when he could find his voice. "Don' make a sound, an' don' struggle none. Likely, they leave us when they see we got nothin'—"

But before he could say anything more, he was hit smartly across the mouth, a warning for silence. He bowed his head, appalled to feel sharp tears of rage and pain flood his eyes. He felt as helpless as he had the first time he'd been whipped.

He heard rough guttural words, as one savage spoke to another, and the men then moved them into a tight circle, bound their hands and feet, and prepared to stand guard until daylight. Peter, Simon, and Joseph were silent. Susan's whimpering had stopped abruptly. All of them had become mute and somehow, instantly, smaller than they had been. Except for Old Abby, who cursed the savages softly in a steady, determined drone of righteous anger.

*   *   *

In a dry, lowland apron near the Suwannee, where the swamp was not so marshed, a five-foot serpent hunted rabbits at the edge of his territory. He was Talus, a medium-sized Eastern diamondback rattlesnake, *Crotalus adamanteus*, and he was unusually active this warm autumn night. Talus was brown, with a dorsal pattern of dark, yellow-bordered, diamondlike blotches and a brown-and-white tail, a muted coloration which suited him well as he lay in wait on deer paths and rodent trails. He might grow to be ten feet long in a few seasons, if he lived long enough. He planned to do exactly that.

It had only been recently that he had been large enough to take on mature rabbits. Last season, he fed primarily on mice and rats, perhaps a squirrel if he could catch one. But now, he was larger, and he felt his power over every sinuous muscle of his body. Particularly did he feel that power this night. Empty of food and full of restless energy, Talus moved quickly through the brush, almost unable to lie still long enough to capture his prey.

Talus did not recall that he had mated the year before, for his brain was not built for storage of specific stimuli such as that. Had he remembered, he might have also recalled that he had been fortunate enough to have found his first female without any other male about, had mated, and had left her thus alone with no incident. He never saw her again, nor did he give her or any possible get another thought.

But instinct pressed him onward this night, and he left the tortoise burrow where he had been waiting for a rabbit and ventured forth with a strange sense of scattered focus, as though danger loomed unseen, just beyond the reach of his senses to perceive it.

He had not gone far toward the cypress grove when he encountered it. Another male diamondback, also on the hunt. But now Talus understood that this night was less for rabbit than for mating. He coiled rapidly out in the open, once he was certain that the other male had seen him as well. The male approached him warily. Talus could see that they were well matched for size. He stared at his rival, flicking his tongue. Somewhere in the grove was the female, of that he was certain. He flicked his tongue repeatedly, alert to every particle of air which might carry information of warm-blooded prey and the male before him. Now the male coiled close to him, staring intently. Neither snake moved.

Suddenly, Talus lowered his head and moved toward his rival, and the male did the same. The two snakes met and slowly entwined each other, feeling each other's muscle mass, testing each other's strength. With jerking motions, they moved their noses up and down the other's body, bent on discovering what they could without combat. But then, in an instant, Talus moved quickly and tried to throw the other snake off-balance and to the ground, pushing with his body and his neck. He sensed that he was just as strong as his rival, with nearly as much length. He felt the presence of the female, and he was filled with a will to overcome this male and drive him off. This grove was within his territory, he was certain, and he had marked it well with his scent. He thrust again and again with his body, feinting and dodging the pushes and thrusts of the other male, shoving with every muscle to knock the male down onto the ground.

Their combat went on for long moments, and they writhed and twisted and hit each other over and over. An observer would have seen no display of emotion, heat, or ferocity; nor did either snake ever bite or attempt to do more than unbalance the other. Yet the sheer effort of staying upright, of continually thrusting and parrying with each muscle, eventually took its toll. Talus knocked the other male over and finally, finally, his rival did not make an effort to rise again.

Talus watched as the other male crawled slowly away, watched and waited to be sure that he left the grove without a backward glance.

When he was gone, Talus put his nose to the ground and explored very carefully the scent trail of the nearby female. He was exhausted but strangely restless still, and he knew that the long night still held much promise. He began to hunt her avidly.

* * *

It seemed they walked forever. The savages had them up at first light and then on into the new dawn. They stopped twice to gulp water with cupped hands from the river, then were pushed on, stumbling into each other in silent fear. The going was arduous, through the densest undergrowth, where only a deer path cut through the tangled vines, the overhanging canopy, the brush so high that they often could not see the sun. On all sides, the birds, the bugs, the creatures swarmed, as if the swamp were the birthplace of all living things, particularly those things which bit or stung or clawed or screamed. Strange shadows flitted by swiftly, and the captured slaves ducked and winced and stifled gasps of fear as they trod along, their heads down in postures of submission.

Black John kept a wary eye on the savage nearest to him, trying to discover what their fate might be. The man looked wild as any beast, painted with stark black and white and red figures on his face and body, his naked skin glistening from some oil, likely bear from the smell of it. He carried an evil-looking sword, and a sharp knife was tied to his waist. His coarse black hair was braided and festooned with feathers and the small bones of animals. Black John shuddered when he thought what such a man might do to a woman like Susan.

He tried to still his terror, plodding along. He was an old man, after all, he told himself. With any luck and God's mercy, he wouldn't live long under their hands anyway.

Ahead, the brush began to thin somewhat, and they finally came to a clearing in the swamp. It was a vast wet prairie, with raised areas of cypress, gum, and bay trees. A wide lake spread out in the distance. At the edge of the hammock, a village was laid out in a circle, rude open-sided huts made of wood and thatched with palm fronds and grasses. Drying sheds sat in the middle of corn rows, and from everywhere, brown savages came out of their houses and from their work, naked running children, barking dogs, and the slower, more stately advance of the warriors and women, dressed in long skirts, their breasts covered with some sort of bodice made of woven grass. There were several hundred of them, Black John counted grimly.

He glanced at Susan. She was cowering between two of their captors, flinching away at the sight of the savages. Only Old Abby struggled to rise and face them defiantly, but one of the savages casually shoved her back down on the litter, barely glancing in her direction.

Now a more stately cluster of Indians came from behind the savages, obviously the nobility of the tribe. One old man was walking slowly, being led forward by two younger women. He wore a circle of white feathers round his head like a crown, and as he drew near, Black John could see that he was elaborately tattooed over his brown, wizened body. The warriors fell back at his advance, and the two men who held Black John bowed their heads in silent respect.

The old man spoke to them in a soft, clicking tongue, and the crowd hushed to hear his words. One of the warriors, obviously the leader of the capture party, answered back in deference. Black John watched the old one's eyes, certain that he would see their fate there first. Susan began to weep softly to his right, and when he turned to glance at her, she bowed her head in shame. "Don' show your fear," he murmured to her quietly.

When he turned back to watch again, he saw that the old man had observed him carefully. He gestured to Black John, asking the warrior a question. And then to Black John's alarm, he walked slowly closer to him. "You are a slave?" he asked then, his voice rising and trembling slightly with age.

Black John stammered in surprise, "Yessuh! You speak like a white man."

The ancient one smiled, a wry grimace of thin lips. "We know a little of the white man, yes. You run away?"

Black John dropped his eyes. "Yessuh. We aim to make it to the Gulf."

"You will never make it," the old one said firmly. "Not with women."

Susan had moved closer to him, and she watched the exchange with wonder.

"We cain' go back," Black John said then, raising his head and meeting the old man's stare. "They whip us nigh to death for show. You aim to kill us, too?"

"If you were white," he said. "The warriors capture all trespassers on our land, and the whites, we hang. You are not white, however."

"That's surely true enough." Black John shook his head ruefully. "Guess we be the blackest skins in these parts. Were we white, we won' be runnin'." He had the sense, as he had before when he was trying to evade punishment, that the more he talked, the better off he might be.

"The lands you ran from were ours once," the old man said. "Now this"—and here, he gestured widely all round the village—"now this is ours. And we will keep it."

"We jes' aim to get free," Black John said wearily, dropping his head. "Don' figure to take no land in the bargain, an' we won' tell nobody we been here."

The chief spoke then to his people in his own tongue, and they listened raptly, Black John noted, with nary a shuffle of foot nor a child's murmur. Even the dogs were quiet.

"You stay among us," the old man said to Black John. "Work our fields and tend our stock."

"I won' be slave to no savage," Black John said swiftly, before he thought. The sharp intake of breath in the Indians closest to him told him that he had likely guaranteed his death. He glanced at Peter and Simon and saw that their eyes were wide and white with fear. He added, half-apologetically to his comrades behind him, "I druther die first."

But to his amazement, the old man grinned. "Not slave, nigger. Kin. You build your house, you tend your crop. You welcome here."

Black John felt the heavy fear lift from him slowly. "We welcome? To stay an' farm the land?"

"But what 'bout marster?" Joseph asked fearfully. "If we don' make it to the Gulf, he come kotch us, sure 'nough."

"You are safe here," the old one said firmly.

"We be safe here," Black John turned and repeated to them. "Ain' no white man gonna make it so far, not jes' to chase some no-count niggers." He scanned the rest of the faces behind him. The men looked hopeful, fearful, wary—all of which he felt himself. Susan had her head lowered, the perfect picture of submission. No doubt that posture had saved her before, and she knew no other. Only Old Abby looked obdurate and wrathful, glaring at the surrounding Indians the way a rattlesnake glares down an intruder. Black John bent to help her then, and she snorted derisively as she tottered upright.

"How come these brutes know so much 'bout the white man?" she asked loudly. "Why should we trus' them?"

A scattering of small laughter blew through the Seminoles closest to the old woman, and her words were quickly repeated among those listening with delight.

"It is a fair question," the chief answered her. "The whites drove us from our lands to the north many seasons past. When I was only so tall as this one here," he added, gesturing to a young boy closest to him in the crowd. "They drove out the Cherokees, the Choctaws, the Chickasaws, and the Creeks, our brothers, and scattered them to the four winds. We left our brothers and came to the south, to this place which no one else wanted, and we have made it our own. No one else knows this land so well. No one else can find the way through the swamp."

"We did," Old Abby said stubbornly.

"Ay, you did," the old man grinned at her. "And we tracked you for two days before we took you."

She glared at Black John fiercely. "You never saw them."

Black John shook his head slowly.

"I be hungry," Simon said then, quietly.

The old man gestured quickly to a few of the women and nodded. "You will be fed. Go to any *cheke* you wish—"

"What this chickee?" Black John asked.

"Our homes." The old man gestured.

Black John said nothing, amazed. They actually lived in these— these tents. Nothing more than four poles and a grass roof. Quarters were better on the meanest plantation.

"Any woman will give you food," the chief added.

The crowd then dispersed slowly, leaving them alone, just as the old man had promised.

"They got no walls on the houses?" Joseph asked, wonderingly. "What keep out bugs?"

"Same as keep out critters," Old Abby glowered. "Nothing at all."

Black John hunkered down on his heels, gathering the others around him.

"Think they mean it?" Joseph asked. "We can stay an' not be slaves?"

Susan finally spoke softly. "We always be slaves," she said. "They work us if we stay."

"They say we welcome," Peter said. "Anybody gotta work to eat."

"Wonder what they eat?" Simon asked. "Bugs an' gators an' such?"

"They got land an' women an' standin' corn." Peter gestured to the village. "A man could make a life here."

"They don' say nothing 'bout women," Black John said skeptically.

"I gonna' stay," Peter said again. "That ol' man be right. This swamp gonna' kill us, sure."

All of them stared at him wonderingly.

Old Abby put her head in her hands. "That be the trouble with niggers. They don' never keep to their own dreams."

"I be keepin' to 'em," Peter said staunchly. "Here, I be free, an' here I stay."

"I be stayin' too, I reckon," Joseph said. "If I can get some food. I hungry as a bear."

"They say jes' go to any ol' hut, an' they feed you," Susan said suddenly, the first words she had uttered. "Go on then an' get you some o' whatever in those pots. Likely, bugs an' snakes."

But Joseph and Simon and Peter still sat. Hungry as they were, they were reluctant to simply go into a hut, even a hut with no walls, and ask for food.

Old Abby saw their hesitation and laughed. "You be slaves, no matter where you be," she shook her head. "Might as well do it here."

With a furious glare at her, Peter roused the other two and the three of them stalked off to the nearest *cheke*. Black John watched and saw that a Seminole woman welcomed them inside and sat them down at a rude table, placing bowls of something before them. The three men hesitated and then fell to, eating whatever she had given them.

Black John glanced at Old Abby. Clearly, she was not wanting to hobble over to join the men, yet she must be as hungry as the rest of them. He rose wearily to his feet. He put out his hand to Susan. "Come on, gal. We got to eat, no matter what else we gonna' do." He put out the other arm to Old Abby as though she were the old mistress of a fine plantation and walked her to another *cheke* across the pathway. Two women came forth and spoke to them, partly in their native tongue and partly in English. Black John could make out a few of their words, such as food and sit and eat. They put before them three bowls, paying special courtesies to Old Abby.

The old woman looked askance at her bowl. "God almighty. What this?"

Susan poked at it suspiciously with her fingers. No utensils had been offered. "Some sort o' grass, I reckon. Guess they don' jes' build roofs with it, they eat it, too."

Black John took a large mouthful bravely and chewed with gusto. "It be good," he said, swallowing vigorously. "Whatever it be."

The women smiled and brought more bowls filled with steamed carp, chunks of white meat which looked a bit like chicken, and a stew of boiled swamp plants. Most everything was savory enough, and they fed until they were full. Rising and thanking the women, the three

then walked in the direction of the corn crop at the edge of the village.
The men were already gathered there.

"Don' look like enough to feed such as these," Joseph said. "Likely
they got other fields 'round close by?"

"They hunt an' fish," Peter said. "Don' none of 'em look like they
miss too many meals. You gonna' stay?" he asked Black John.

In that moment, Black John knew the answer to that question,
something he had asked himself quietly ever since he realized that he
had a choice. "No," he shook his head slowly. "I goin' on. Y'all stay,
though. That be best."

"What you gonna' do?" Susan asked, moving closer to him.

"What I plan from the start. Make my way to the Gulf an' go on
home."

Old Abby sniffed. "You never make it, old man. This swamp eat
you up alive."

He shrugged. "I think I try, anyways."

Peter, Simon, and Joseph walked off to explore the rest of the village
and the outlying fields. Old Abby hobbled over to a nearby shaded tree
and eased herself down, took out her pipe, and began to smoke. Susan
glanced at Black John and joined the old woman. In moments, the two
of them were leaning back, their eyes closed. Black John walked toward
the largest *cheke*, where he could see the old chief speaking quietly
with his women.

The ancient beckoned him over with a small wave. Black John took
a seat warily.

The old man nodded gravely to him with all courtesy. "Your belly
is content?" he asked.

"I thank 'ee, sir."

The old man studied Black John a moment in silence. "You are not
going to stay," he said. It was not a question.

Black John glanced at him, surprised. But then he shook his head.
"No. But I grateful for the choice."

The chief sighed wearily. "You will be lost, my brother."

"My old woman tell me, too." Black John smiled wryly.

"And the others?"

"Likely, they stay." He appraised the old man carefully. Finally he
asked, "Why you want us, anyhow?"

The chief shrugged. "Strong backs, good workers. These things are
always welcome. Those three"—he gestured to where Peter, Simon,

and Joseph poked around the cornfields—"they will not be warriors, but they can be useful."

"Peter, he work bricks for his marster. He can make a pretty tool, if he's a mind. An' Simon, he make good cotton. Good man with a hoe. That Joseph, he jes' ol' man like me, but he got a good heart, an' he follow 'long what you tell him."

The chief nodded. "These are men we can use." He turned and peered at Black John knowingly. "And the woman?"

"Ol' Abby, she a conjure woman," Black John said. "She know mos' every root an' flower, an' folks come for miles to get her cures. I reckon she more'n pay for her keep."

The old chief waited silently.

Finally, Black John muttered, "The young one, that Susan. She likely make a good breeder."

In the silence which followed, Black John began to relax. The sun was warm, and the air was still. Even the mosquitoes seemed to have gone to shade and silence. "How you come to this place?" he asked the old man.

The chief took up a small bowl of black tea which one of the women had brought and supped it loudly. He gestured for Black John to take up the other and do the same. He took a long swallow and coughed. The brew was bitter and strong. The second swallow seemed to soothe the first, however, and rolled slowly down to his stomach like warm, heavy honey.

"We were of the Creek Nation," the chief began, closing his eyes in reverie. "Our lands were in what the whites now call Georgia, and we were a peaceful people. Many strong warriors and many healthy children. The white traders came to us with their iron hatchets and knives and hoes, and the people wanted these things. They also wanted the pipes and scissors and kettles. The women wanted the pots and pans and mirrors. The warriors wanted the guns and coats and hats. The white men wanted pelts and slaves."

"Y'all kept niggers?" Black John asked in wonder.

The old man shook his head. "We took captives when we made war, and these we sold to the white man. But then the deer ran out, and we could get the axes and guns and pots no other way, save by trading slaves. So we made war on the Cherokee and the Chickasaw and the Choctaw to get the things the people wanted."

"Why your kings allow such as that?"

"We have no kings. That is not our way. What the people wish, the people generally will have. Some wanted to keep from the whites, but more wanted what the white man could trade. We began to fight among ourselves, and we grew weaker. The smallpox came and went, over and over, and we were weaker still."

"I never knew no Indians in Georg'a," Black John said.

"This was a long time past," the old chief said patiently. "As we grew weaker, we began to trade our lands away to the white man, to get the things we wanted. The people could no longer remember the old ways. Could no longer make the cooking baskets or the bows to hunt game. They must have the white man's pots and the white man's rifles, or go hungry. When the whites began to fight each other, the King George-men and the King Washington-men, each came and asked us to fight as well. This, we did, and King Washington thanked us. But once the fighting was over, he asked us to give up more of our lands so that the whites could have more room." He shook his head. "We are a stupid and forgetful people. We should have killed every white trader who trespassed our lands from the start."

"Why you give up your land?" Black John asked. "Marster say, land is the only real power."

"The white man is a sly nibbler," the old chief said. "And sometimes, other tribes signed our lands to the whites, claiming it was theirs to sell. The white man often cannot tell one tribe from another."

"That be true," Black John soberly. "Nor one black man from the other."

"And so we came to the swamp, to get from such troubles. The Spanish here called us '*seminolee*' or the wild ones. At first, we were few. But then others joined us. We have made welcome all who will work in peace."

"How many are you?"

The old man shrugged. "It is hard to say. There are five villages like this one—"

"Five!"

"And more which are not yet villages. Perhaps ten thousand of us."

Black John lowered his head and suppressed his smile. The old man was kind enough, but crazy. Ten thousand Indians in this swamp? He had only a vague idea how much ten thousand of anything might be, but he was certain that there could not be that many Indians in all of the southern lands together, much less in this swamp alone. But if the old man wanted to believe it was so, he would honor his belief.

"When we first came here," the old man continued, almost in a reverie, "I was a young warrior. I had a woman then—"

"You have two now," Black John said, with obvious envy.

The old man laughed, a surprisingly youthful sound from such an ancient chest. "They have me. But then, the land was wild and dark, and the game was plentiful. This place was sacred to the Creeks and full of promise. On this place, the elders told us that a black lake once stood, and the biggest alligators in all the world lived in the bottom of the lake. Then the lake slowly filled in and the cypress and tupelo gum grew large and tangled above it, but it was still a place of sanctuary. Here, we made our first village. Others came later and went farther south. Sometimes, we can hear the earth groan softly in the night, and a hole opens up in the forest floor, and the black mud oozes out, and the old air comes up from the belly of the earth and mixes with the foxfire. Then the old ways are very near again. Sometimes," he added, slowly smiling at Black John, "this land is a place of magic, still."

Crazy as a fox, Black John thought. The old man wanted something, that much was obvious. But if ten thousand savages could live here, surely he could travel through it safe enough. He thought for a long moment. "If I leave, they let me pass?"

The old man shrugged again. "Perhaps."

"Will you give me a pass?"

"A pass?"

"Like my marster. If he need me to go to 'nother plantation, he give me a pass, so patrol don' get me."

"I am master to none," the old man said gently. "And if I made a sign, none could read it."

They had no paper, no writing, and, likely, none could read, Black John thought quickly. "You give me something to show, then, if I be taken?"

The old man thought now. He held out his walking stick. "Take this, nigger. If they take you, tell them Dragging Canoe sends greetings."

Black John took the walking stick and bowed low to the old man. "Thank 'ee, sir," he said solemnly. He rose and held out his hand in friendship. The old man took it firmly, clasped his wrist, and then let him go.

Black John walked back to the shade of the tree where Susan and Old Abby waited. Susan looked up at him with apprehension. "He give you that?" she asked.

Black John nodded.

"You goin', then?"

"Yes," he said gently.

Old Abby shook her head in sorrow. "You never make it alive, fool."

"I go with you," Susan said, standing up suddenly, her face stiff with determination.

Black John stood gazing at this young woman, wondering what he could possibly say to make her content. She was so ripe, so full of promise. Likely some savage would take her to wife, and she would bear sons for the tribe, would soon be unrecognizable from the other women who brought the bowls and tended the huts, except for her darker skin. Or perhaps she would go to Peter's bed. Or Simon's. Her fate was uncertain, but at least she would be safe. "You stay here," he said softly.

"No," she said. "You cain' make me. I don' want to live here with animals. You leave me, an' I follow you in the night. An' I keep on followin' you 'til I find you or die."

He crossed his arms in exasperation. "Why you wan' me?" he asked, his voice louder than he'd intended. "I be a old man!"

"Yep," she nodded vigorously, "old an' crotchety as a old bear. But I goin' with you, old man, an' you cain' boss me off."

Old Abby laughed then, deep in her throat. "Both of you damn fools. If the gators an' snakes don' get you, likely you get lost an' wander 'round, crazy-like, 'til the swamp swallow you up."

"We won' go crazy, if we together," Susan said firmly. She put her hand on Black John's arm and smiled. "You see, old man. I make you young again, like a buck deer."

Her smile made the old warmth flood his belly again, and his mouth turned up in a wry grin, despite his efforts to stop it. "I ain' gonna' carry you," he shook his head, "if you get weary. An' if you fall back, I ain' waitin' on you."

Old Abby chortled. "An' I ain' gettin' no older with de next sunup neither." She rose to her feet and toddled over to the nearest *cheke*. "I hungry again. What else these folk got to eat?"

"When you gonna' go?" Susan asked.

"Soon. You best stay."

"I ain' gonna. The white man gonna take these folks same's they take everythin' else. I see it plain as day. They ain' strong 'nuff to stand agin them." She smiled wisely. "You watch. In five years, white man plantin' cotton here, same's where we come from."

Black John sighed. It was not going to be any easier traveling with

He pulled back his hand to strike Peter, when a voice stayed him. He turned to see the old chief coming forward with his women on both flanks.

"You are ready to depart?" the old man called.

Susan found her voice. "Yessuh," she said firmly. "We want to make the river 'fore dark."

The chief spoke directly to her gently. "I had hoped you might stay. My women find you comely," he added.

She edged closer to Black John. "I be goin'," she said politely. "I thank 'ee kindly, suh."

That was what he wanted, then, Black John noted.

The chief turned his attention to Peter, missing nothing of the tension of his stance. He eyed the man calmly. "It is difficult to say farewell, eh?"

Peter had dropped his hand from Susan. Now he dropped his eyes as well. "She need to stay where she be safe," he muttered.

"That is likely so," the chief said, confidentially, "but women will not be driven to and fro as we would wish, eh?" He rolled his eyes at Peter, inviting him to share the jest. "Consider yourself fortunate, my friend." He indicated his own two companions. "Perhaps you would be so good to take one of mine?" The women and the old man laughed cordially, and Peter smiled reluctantly.

Susan moved behind Black John in that moment and assumed her usual position of invisibility. He was struck by his recollection of what she had said before, of how the Lord sure had a good sense of fun. What could be more ridiculous, he wondered, than this old man and this young gal? But it was to be, evidently. Black John extended his hand to the chief. "I thank 'ee for your welcome."

The old man nodded gravely.

In that moment, Black John felt the true terror of his decision. Suddenly it seemed to him that he was leaving all of the world behind him and venturing into hell. With a woman depending on him, no less. But he shook the old chief's hand like a white man and turned his back to the village.

It was midmorning, by the slant of the sun. He hoped to make the Suwannee by sunset. From there, they would follow the river to the sea.

Part One

1818—1838

"Why must we get out? We are not a threat to you whites! We are so diminished by you already, we are but a shadow on the land," said Osceola.

"Move your shadow," General Clinch replied.

Osceola glared at the man with narrowed eyes. "Better move your sun," he said softly.

(overheard at Fort King, April 23, 1835)

*M*ore and more Creeks fled south into Florida as land speculators and
settlers edged into what had been Creek homelands. When the warriors
fought back, massacring nearly four hundred people at Fort Mims near the
Alabama River, General Andrew Jackson wiped out a thousand Creeks at
Horseshoe Bend and scattered the survivors into the swamp. As punishment
for the rebellion of their brothers, Jackson forced the remaining Creeks to sign
away eight million acres, two-thirds of the entire Creek nation, to the United
States. More Creek refugees joined the Seminoles, including as many slaves as
could escape in the chaos of war.

Florida was a Spanish territory after the War of 1812, and the luxuriant
waters and forests of this most southerly land sheltered thriving Indian villages
from the Georgia border to the Gulf. White masters, hoping to catch their slaves
and any other blacks they could find, roamed the country, clashing with the
Seminoles until General Gaines, under Jackson's command, crossed the Spanish
border with troops to arrest a Seminole chief who had been charged with
harboring escaped slaves. In the skirmish, five Indians were killed, the troops
burned the Indian settlement at Fowltown, and the rest of the Seminoles escaped.
It was the beginning of the First Seminole War.

Andrew Jackson, back in Tennessee and itching to teach the Seminoles the
same lesson he had taught the Creeks, wrote to President James Monroe, "tell
me to take the Floridas and in sixty days it will be accomplished." Slave
owners clamored to Congress, and in March 1818, Jackson invaded Spanish
territory with more than two thousand Tennessee and Georgia militia.

April 1818

Dawn came up clear and cool over the *chekes*, the circle of thatched-roof shelters which made up Mad New Town's camp on the Suwannee. The Seminole chief rose from his hammock early, as was his custom, and stood outside his *cheke*, surveying the sleeping people quietly. Fifteen thatched huts, a mere remnant of what they were once. One hundred and sixty struggling Seminoles, looking for a place to plant their corn in peace.

Mad New Town, or Peter McQueen, as the whites called him, was the oldest male among them and as such, was the leader of the *Mikasuki*, the clans of Red Stick Creeks which had fled the north country into Florida more than one hundred years before. Called by the *Muskogee* Creeks, "the people of a distant fire," his clans were known for their solitary habits. His was the Snake clan, once the largest and most powerful. But now they were much diminished. In fact, Mad New Town could hardly be called a chief at all, he knew, for he had no *micos*, no elders to counsel him as was their custom. He felt that lack keenly these mornings, for he knew he could not save his people.

Some of the wiser elders were agreed. They knew that the white men would keep coming, from the north, from the east, even from the west, where their great ships had anchored in any deep water they could find. Soon, they would build their houses on the widest rivers, so they could plant their cotton, their sugar, and sell their slaves. The elders spoke of visions, dreams they had which told that someday, all the land would be under the white man's plow.

"Except where the land will not allow it," they told each other solemnly. "We must go where they cannot take their wagons, where their plows will not follow."

"We must fight!" the young men replied.

"Well and we shall," the old ones sighed. "But it will not matter in the end. They will take the land, they will take the women, they will take even our children."

"We will put them to death first!" the young men protested, nearly weeping with the thought of their young wives and strong children buried under land which would no longer be theirs.

And then the elders had said nothing. For there was nothing else to say.

Mad New Town knew all of this, as everyone did. But each day must be lived as though another would follow. Now, a movement in the far brush caught his eye, over toward the river. He turned quickly, his breath stilled in his throat. He glanced toward his rifle: there, next to his sister's cot. But before he could move toward it, his eyes still staring toward the river edge, the brush parted. He let out his breath again in a sigh of relieved exasperation. Only his niece's boy, out roaming again. Billy could usually be trusted to wander when he should be doing otherwise, and this morning was no exception. He watched the boy with an appraising eye.

Billy, his sister's grandson, was fourteen winters, and still he showed no promise as a man. He was soft around the edges with small hands and feet, a face more suited to a young girl, and the rounded shoulders of a lad who showed no eagerness to carry the responsibilities of a warrior. Not even as strong as the white trader who had fathered him, perhaps not even as quick and determined as his mother, Peeping, who at least had the courage to get herself and her son this far south, away from the blue jackets.

Billy had been born to Peeping on the banks of the Chattahoochee River, her first and only child. Mad New Town had disapproved of her mating with the Scots trader, as did many of her elders. But like other women these days, she did not heed him. Would have what she wanted, and the man had a sack full of red cloth, iron pots, and gilded mirrors.

He told Ochola, Peeping's mother, that he was shamed by his niece's choice. "Let her remain a maiden rather than take such a man to her bed," he had said in disgust when told the news. But so many of the warriors were gone, and the women needed men, Ochola said sadly. It was better to have children, even half-breed children, than no children at all.

It was just another in a long succession of humiliations at the hands of the whites. For two decades, Mad New Town had seen his comrades divided into factions: some wanted to run, others wanted to stand and fight. Some melted into the swamps and disappeared peaceably, others fought among themselves, sometimes attacking the whites, sometimes banding together in vain appeals to the white man's law courts and newspapers. Nothing had worked. The blue jackets kept coming.

When Billy's father, the mongrel Scot, abandoned Peeping and his son, she went back to her mother's *cheke* at the Talassee settlement on the Tallapoosa River. Old Mad Jackson attacked the village, and they fled south once more, with Ochola leading them. Now they were safe for a time at least, on the Suwannee. But for how long?

Mad New Town took some comfort in their presence. Some pride that his sister, his niece, his grandnephew came to him for protection. What family he had left, he would defend.

His sister stretched and rose from her cot behind him, moving toward the fire even as she re-bound her long gray hair up onto her head again. "You slept well, my brother?" Ochola called softly.

He nodded. Billy came out of the brush now and hurried toward the family's *cheke*, knowing that once his grandmother was up, the morning meal would soon be readied. As usual, his hands were empty.

"If the boy must disturb the rest of others, he at least could bring back food," Mad New Town grumbled aloud. "He is too busy, I suppose, to drop his line into the river."

"Did he disturb you, Uncle?" Peeping asked from behind him.

Both women waited respectfully for his reply.

Mad New Town felt a sharp retort on his tongue, but he repressed it. He shook his head. "I suppose not. My rest is disturbed, no matter."

"You have news?" Peeping asked fearfully. "A runner—?"

He put his hand on her shoulder. She was still looking over her shoulder for another attack by the soldiers. "No, nothing new. You must learn to ignore this old bear's growls, dear heart."

She smiled and hurried to fill his tin cup with strong boiled tea, her hands moving gratefully with relief. He sighed again, closing his eyes in weary pain. Peeping was young enough to take another husband, though her face showed the permanent scars of fear. She did not have her mother's spirit, but she was comely enough. Who, though, would take her to his cot? So many warriors gone, so many more in hiding. Women gone, too, to disease, to the blue jackets, even to white mates. Billy's father, William Powell, was not worthy of her, a half-black scoundrel who made his living selling shoddy goods to the tribes. In other times, she might have been first wife to a chief. But those times were done. Now, the women chose for themselves, often the weakest stock of the white settlers, and so they poisoned the people. As one tainted rivulet sullies the river.

Mad New Town rose and stretched, supping his tea slowly while the women fried the corn cakes and bream. It might be his only meat of the day if they were unable to find game again. "Billy," he called to the boy, "hoe the melons today."

"Will we be here to pick them?" the boy asked. There was no challenge in his voice, but the question rankled.

"Since we cannot know the future, the weeds may grow high as saw grass, eh?" Mad New Town scolded.

"No, but—" the boy glanced at his mother in confusion.

"*Shta,*" his grandmother said firmly. "Be quiet. Do not question your elders. If your great-uncle tells you to do a thing, you will do it." She pointedly patted the pouch she wore always at her waist, the one which held the sharp-toothed gar jaw. Every mother and grandmother carried such a pouch. Billy knew he was too old for a leg or arm scratching, something she had done often enough when he was young and rebellious. But the simple act of her reminding him of the possibility had trained him to obedience.

"Of course, *tustenuggee,*" Billy said softly, using the Seminole word for great warrior. "I will weed them well."

Mad New Town glanced at the boy sharply but sensed no mockery. "And plant the beans as well," he added. "Make the hills high and well back from the river's edge."

Billy nodded, reaching for the *sofkee,* the thin corn gruel his mother handed him. With his other hand, he rummaged under his cot.

Mad New Town knew what he was after, but he stifled a reprimand. Sure enough, Billy got out his worn deerhide ball, the one he had brought with him all the way from the Talassee village. Peeping said he was quite good at the rough-and-tumble game the boys played, that he was a leader among them, and always first to be chosen for any team. Mad New Town wished he could see more of those qualities now.

Billy bounced the ball with one hand while he ate with the other, and then he dropped it and kicked it restlessly in and out of the hut. "Wish we could have a game," he murmured.

"Save your wishes for those things which matter," Mad New Town said. "If we had enough boys for a game, we'd have enough to get the tobacco planted—"

"Go on out now, Billy," his grandmother said then, shooing him off. As the boy wandered away, she said, "You have nothing but sharp words for him, my brother. And yet he may be the only seed of your father left when we are gone. Surely you can find something of pride in him, when you think of that."

Mad New Town glanced at Peeping and smiled. "I told you, pay no mind to this bear, child. It is not the boy, it is this place—" He gestured impatiently round the small encampment. "In the north, we had vast fields and good rivers. The game was thick, and the corn tassled three times each year. Here, the stinging flies feast on us, the snakes are thick and surly, and the water stinks when the sun is on it. May the Maker of Breath turn his heart from the whites," he spit bitterly. "We are a wandering people now. I have only a dozen men to help me, the rest are boys or old men. Too many to feed and not enough to fight for the land. Billy is right. We will not see a harvest this season."

There was a sudden scream from the river, one of the women who had gone for water, and Mad New Town whirled toward the sound of panic, instantly alert and afraid. A bugle clarion split the morning silence, so near that he flinched, and the thrashing of horses through the water came at them like a hundred hissing snakes.

The blue jackets were upon them!

Peeping and Ochola swiftly ran in two directions, away from each other, away from the oncoming rush of the enemy, for they had been through invasion too many times to stop and scream. Peeping gave one desperate call for Billy, but when she could not see him, she ran like a fox. Mad New Town raced away from the hut, grabbing for his weapon, hunching over and taking cover in the thick brush. There was no question of fighting, he knew, for they were too many, they were always too many, but his heart still felt the shame and rage as he fled. He hunkered down, trying to get as small as he could, and he saw that half of the encampment was surrounded in seconds. No one put up a fight, and the soldiers never even dismounted, merely spurring their horses into the brush after those who were running away.

He saw them take half of the men, but some had fled too swiftly to be captured; perhaps ten of them escaped. Their women and children, left defenseless, were quickly shoved into place with the old ones and the children.

In moments, soldiers had more than a hundred people rounded together, and they drove their horses into the *chekes*, toppling them over into the dirt. The people were silent as they were herded; even the children were still as captured deer.

And then from the river came the war chief of the whites, the dreaded *Tsek-sin Chullee Hadjo*, Old Mad Jackson on his gray horse. Mad New Town knew him the moment he saw the man's face. He looked like a predatory hawk with small glinting eyes, his hair a spike of white pinfeathers on his head. Mad New Town saw the long fate of his people in his enemy's face. He knew that Jackson would kill them all, hound them to the ends of the continent, then force them to jump into the sea, if he had to, to rid the land of their vegetable rows, their fishing weirs, their pathetic thatched huts. He felt such a hatred and rage that his temples pounded with it, his hands shook, and he was certain the nearby soldiers would hear his heartbeat shake his chest, but he kept silent. He had no choice.

He knew that behind him, on either side, some of the warriors watched as well. Seared with the same pain and rage and shame, they could do nothing but witness the end of their families, their futures.

Now a troop of soldiers came crashing through the brush from behind him, and he shrank to the ground, belly down like a rabbit. When he eased up once more and peered through the brush, he saw that Peeping and Billy had been taken, along with several dozen more of his people. His throat tightened, and his eyes burned like fire with unshed tears.

General Jackson was sitting his horse quietly, watching from the slight bluff of the river. His captains and war chiefs were barking orders at the soldiers. The people were being tied, neck to neck, each to the other so they could not run. Most of them were barely clothed, and few of them had a single belonging in their hands, much less a weapon of any kind.

Peeping and Billy were pushed into line with the others. The older boys and young men were being separated from their families, near forty of them, some just a few years older than Billy. Mad New Town held his breath, wondering if they would take Billy as well. One soldier eyed the boy carefully, as he stood quietly, close to his mother.

Billy managed to look, in that instant, like a boy barely old enough to hold a bow. The soldier passed him by, and he was tied with the other women and children.

A command rang out from one of the captains, and the hobbled lines moved forward slowly, back up the trail to the north, away from the river. Prodded by the horses and soldiers, the people fell into line silently, filing under the hooded eyes of the general, who sat above them like some eagle watching the schooling of fish in the pool below.

There was an infinitesimal noise behind him, and Mad New Town froze. He turned to see Ochola making her way carefully through the brush in his direction. She had managed to make not a sound, he knew, until she wished to, signaling her arrival. He motioned her forward silently. Together, they watched as what was left of their family was herded away, stumbling slowly and painfully upriver under the poised rifles of blue jackets.

As they moved out of hearing, Ochola whispered, "You must go south."

He knew she was right. He could do nothing for these people, and south was the only direction the Americans were not. He turned to go, suddenly unable to watch his future recede before him. Perhaps he and the other men might find each other before the day was through. It was several moments before he realized that she did not intend to follow.

"What are you doing?" he asked wearily.

"I cannot leave my daughter," she said, and she struck out in the direction the captives had gone, keeping to the brush, moving with her head down and her shoulders hunched. He thought she looked for all the world like a burrowing badger, intent on making a refuge before the sun went down.

He did not have the heart to try to stop her. There was nothing more he could do. Indeed, it seemed to him that he had been telling himself that for half of his life. Certainly since he had seen his first white man. He turned away from her, his eyes blinded with sorrow and rage, and pushed through the brush in the other direction.

*   *   *

Tyto flew across the river, a white shape gliding through the moon-glow, swooping over the water, uttering a twittering call as he neared the large oak. Immediately, the normal night sounds of the swamp were interrupted by a chorus of loud, rasping calls, and another ghostly white shape appeared from the large hole in the oak from which the sounds came. It was late December. Tyto and his mate were hard at work raising their second brood of young for the year.

Tyto was a barn owl, *Tyto alba*, larger than a well-fed crow, buff brown above and white at his breast, underwings, and feet. His face like that of his mate, was heart-shaped, and his eyes were dark and luminous. He carried the third mouse of the night in his beak, handing it deftly to his mate, who turned immediately into the hole and began to tear the meat for their fledglings.

Tyto flew to a nearby branch and preened himself carefully. That last mouse had given him a bit of a tussle, and he knew that the family's fate depended upon his swift wings, his strong claws, and his alert eye. He could not afford a failure, not this night, not a single night for the next moon. Every feather must be in place, for his flight and his attack to be silent.

The noise from within the hollow oak told him that all fledglings were feeding. That was well. In other seasons, when prey had not been so plentiful, they had often lost more than half a brood. His mate laid five eggs, as usual, and sat them for the full moon as always. But when the first egg hatched, that nestling got the first food. And because it was strongest, the next food and the next. If Tyto had been able to catch more mice, the others would have survived. But the flooding of the river had made prey scarce. So many of the mouse tunnels were ravaged by the water; so many of the creatures fled the swamp for higher ground. They raised only one nestling that season. Such was the way of his kind, he knew, and the staggered hatchings ensured that at least one lived. But his mate was saddened by the emptiness of the nest, and she came into season again quickly.

Now, prey was plentiful. All the nestlings would surely live. He cocked his head at the peculiar feeding tumult of the oldest male in the brood, a gracklelike click and hiss which showed him to be dominant. Suddenly, a loud screech rang through the swamp. Tyto ruffled himself and settled again quickly. The oldest nestling was raucous this night, and likely still hungry. He took off again in search of another mouse, his large wings lifting silent and ghostly in the still night air.

Tyto knew that he and his mate were the only nesting pair in this particular place by the Suwannee. He had nested here with this same mate for six years: twelve broods hatched and gone in that time, countless mice, rats, shrews, moles, and voles taken, and not a single fledgling had he seen since. They all had dispersed widely, many of hundreds of miles from their nest. It was well, he knew, for the river gave and took the mice with the seasons, and there were not enough for more hunting pairs.

Not so long as the hawks and the eagles took their share in the daylight hours.

As Tyto flew, his wings made barely a whisper in the air. He turned his facial disk this way and that as he swooped over the forest, locating sounds which escape most predators. He suddenly banked, landing softly on a tuft of grass with feet silent as moccasins. Under his feet, a mouse moved in the burrow. He turned his face to the side so that his hearing was most acute: there, under the grass, a mouse scuttered. He sighted the exit hole to the burrow and shifted his weight so that he could strike. In moments of patience, Tyto was capable of being completely immobile, so that his breast barely moved with his breath. After a long frozen silence, the mouse emerged and now he lanced his beak sharply downward, piercing the small soft body and covering it with one clawed foot at once. Another one taken. He took to wing, banking upward and back toward the oak tree. It was his fourth of the night, had he been able to count. He only knew that he must hunt for many more hours by the moon before he would be finished at dawn. It took nearly a hundred mice or rats to raise one of his fledglings to independence. More than four thousand catches in a single nesting season for his whole brood. He had been gone from the nest for too long. He had no time to stop and rest.

Back with the mouse, he called before reaching the nest and was instantly alarmed that his mate did not readily answer. He stopped at the entrance of the hole and gazed about. The young inside clamored for his catch, but no mate reached up from within its blackness to take the mouse. He moved the mouse from his beak to his claw and glanced about carefully. Below the nest, he saw her, still on the ground. He craned his neck, frozen in fear. Holding the mouse still steadily, he called to her, the soft, high-pitched twittering note that he had used to her in courtship. It was their contact call; the call which maintained their pair bond. She did not move. She did not answer.

Only the fledglings responded, screeching still more raucously for the meat they knew he carried.

Still holding the mouse, Tyto flew down to her side and pushed her with his beak. She was unresponsive. He let go of the mouse with his claw and pushed her harder with his foot. She did not move.

Grabbing up the limp mouse once more, he flew up to the branch and studied the hole for long moments. Then he studied the still form on the ground. His mate was dead. Perhaps she had been attacked, but there was no sign of struggle. If it were man, he would have surely taken her. There was no sign of danger. If it had been a serpent, the creature was gone. He did not understand. But he knew death well enough when he saw it.

The nestlings were louder now and more desperate. Tyto knew nothing else to do but to drop the mouse within the hole. He did so and waited. Normally, his mate tore the rodent into small pieces for the nestlings so that they might feed. At this age of only fourteen nights old, they could not do so for themselves. And Tyto did not have the instinct to do it for them.

The five fledglings inside clamored and screamed for food, ignoring the dead mouse at their feet. Without their mother to feed them, they would die, but Tyto could do nothing to change their fate. Helplessly, he took wing again, off to hunt yet another mouse. He did not know what else to do. He arrived back again at the hole soon enough with a small vole and dropped it again into the nest. Again, the nestlings screamed but did not feed.

Tyto delivered more than a hundred mice to the nest over the next two nights. There was scarcely room for the nestlings themselves, for all the dead prey around them. Still, they screamed for food. By the end of the second night, only the largest male was still alive, and his call was weaker with every passing hour. Tyto watched now and waited outside the nest.

When all was finally silent and the last fledgling had collapsed in starvation, he flew off into the swamp alone.

*   *   *

Ochola followed the captives and the soldiers for a day, staying close enough behind them that the dung of the horses was still steaming as she stepped over it. She did not fear they would capture her as well, for she knew that the white men were careless as they tromped through the brush, never looking to the left or right, never anticipating the least resistance from the forest or from those who might live there.

As dusk came upon the swamp, they had moved the people upriver more than twenty miles, by her reckoning. She knew that the women and the children must be weary, the old ones nearly dead with sadness and fatigue. She waited outside the camp while the soldiers hobbled their horses, set up their tents, and she watched as her people went about the business of trying to make themselves comfortable for the night. Without even blankets or cookpots, they could do little. Finally, when the campfires were high and the travelers resting, she edged closer to the large tent where she knew General Jackson awaited his supper.

A sentry startled as she drew into the light and raised his weapon at her. "Get back to the fires," he said brusquely.

"I, Ochola," the old woman said, drawing herself up with dignity and pointing at her chest. "I come to see Jak-son." She was grateful that she had learned the white tongue from her brother.

The soldier pushed her with the butt of his rifle. "He's not entertaining visitors right now. Get back to your fire, I said."

"I not prisoner," she said firmly. "I come with message. From Peeta Mac-Kween, my brother."

"Not a prisoner, eh?" he snorted. "You will be, quick enough."

She glared at him silently.

The soldier peered at her now more carefully, glancing about with some apprehension. Then, he stepped to her and moved his hands roughly over her body, feeling for weapons. Ignoring her stiffness, her sharp intake of breath, he ran his hands up her legs and yanked on her bound hair. When he had satisfied himself, he spoke quickly to another soldier, who disappeared into Jackson's tent. In a moment, he emerged.

"General'll see you," he said shortly, stepping aside so that she might enter. As she passed him, he too ran his hands over her body as one might a likely mare, but this time, she ignored the trespass.

Ochola knew that in this moment, much would depend on her sureness of step, her boldness of speech. She walked into the tent calmly, her head high, as though she had done so a dozen times before. A man sat at a camp table by a single oil lantern, waiting for her with a bemused expression. His hat was off his head, and in the light, she could see that he was older than she had first thought. His hair was gray and sparse, his beard wispy and thin. On the table close to his hand, a large bowie knife lay gleaming. He gestured to her impatiently. "You have a message for me."

She nodded, standing apart from him so that he would listen well and not be distracted by her closeness. "I come from my brother, Peeta Mac-Kween."

"McQueen is your brother?"

She nodded. "He say, you let women and children go. Keep men. He will give up, him and other warriors."

General Jackson smiled. "And if I do not?"

She shrugged eloquently.

"He will fall upon me with his mighty host and destroy us all?" Now he was grinning.

She said nothing.

Jackson leaned back in his chair, stretching his long legs out more comfortably.

Ochola stood perfectly still and calm, enduring his scrutiny. In her heart, she asked the Maker of Breath to heed her prayers, to soften this demon white man's heart sufficiently to let her daughter and grandson go, and then to split his heart asunder like a tree blasted by autumn lightning.

"So. McQueen will surrender."

She remained silent. She had long ago learned with men that if she were silent, they often answered their own questions.

General Jackson rose slowly, picking up the bowie knife and pacing slowly back and forth before her. He paid her no further mind. Finally he said, "Tell McQueen to come in with his men, and we'll let the women and children go."

"He will not," she said softly. "Women and children go first. Then he will come."

"And what guarantee do I have that he will give himself up if I grant his request?"

"His promise," she said lightly.

Jackson laughed derisively. "His promise! I suppose that is meant to give me great comfort."

"Does Great White Father in Wa-shing-town wish women and children for slaves?" she asked innocently.

Jackson scoffed angrily, sticking the knife into his table. "The Great White Father wants only for the Seminoles to keep their promises to leave the land."

"Well and you take them off it, General," she said calmly. "He be well pleased."

"He shall be," Jackson said defiantly.

She fell into silence once more. She knew that she could outwait him, if the sentries outside would only give her the chance.

Finally, Jackson said, "Tell your brother that I accept his pledge. The women and children will leave in the morning. I expect him to surrender before dark with the rest of his warriors."

She bowed her head submissively. She knew it was what the white man expected. "I tell him." With her heart exulting, she left the tent, ignoring the stares of the soldiers around her. She slipped into the brush and went around the campfires until she could see the small fire around which four women and their children sat, huddled together for comfort. Peeping and Osceola were there. When she saw her daughter and grandson, her eyes watered with relief, but she kept herself calm. It was all she could do not to run to them and whisper the news, that they would be freed in the morning. But she knew that the white man could change his mind a dozen times between now and dawn. She knew, also, that if the other women heard the news, there would be such commotion among them and even in the ranks of the men, now sequestered away from their fires and hobbled like the soldiers' horses, that the general might well regret his decision and capture her as well.

She hunkered down on her heels in the darkness, keeping herself as small and quiet as she could. General Jackson must believe that she took his message back to Mad New Town, somewhere far back behind his lines. She must have the patience of the owl now, to wait and wait, believing that with the light would come release. She prayed silently to her spirit helper, Raven, for help and courage. She had done what she could do for now. If Jackson kept his promise, all would be well.

If he did not, she told herself, she would sneak into his tent, take up his knife, and plunge it into his heart.

The next morning, Ochola watched with excitement and trepidation as the general instructed his soldiers to release the women and children. There was some wailing from the women who were being separated from their men, but everyone realized that once free, the women and children could, at least, do something to salvage their families. Ochola kept hidden until she actually saw the soldiers turn their backs on the women, moving into tighter ranks around the men. If the general saw her, he might understand her trick and realize that not only would her brother never surrender, she would never even ask him to do so.

When Peeping and Billy were slightly apart from a tight cluster of women and children, she emerged from the brush and ran to embrace her daughter.

Peeping gasped when she saw her mother and ran into her arms. "You followed us!" she cried, weeping into the old woman's neck. "Where is Uncle? What will we do?"

Billy stood quietly beside his mother, watching the two women. His eyes were huge and dark, his spine stiff with apprehension. Ochola ignored Peeping's questions for the moment and reached out to pull her grandson closer to her. He was as tall as she was now, at that place between boy and man. She murmured, "Your uncle is not here, and we must leave this place as fast as we can walk. Billy, can you help your mother?"

"Yes," he said quickly, taking his mother's arm. "Come on, before the soldiers change their minds."

Peeping asked, "But what of the others?"

Ochola said, "They will make their way as best they can," she said. She turned and walked swiftly through the brush, pushing forward until she got to the game trail she had followed the night before. Quickly she saw that they would do better to put Billy in front, for he could more easily move the reeds aside for his mother than she could. They walked as fast as they could for several miles before they stopped to rest by the Suwannee.

Peeping lay down on the moss by the river and stared out over the moving water. "What will we do?" she asked no one in particular.

"We need to find a village," Billy said.

"The closest one is deep in the swamp," Ochola said, "two days' walk, by my mind."

"All the men are gone," Peeping said in despair. "Even if we find people, it will be only children and old ones and women. How will we survive?"

"I will take care of you, Mother," Billy said staunchly. "Don't worry."

Peeping reached over and rested her hand on his knee. "You are my heart, Billy. The best part of your father."

Ochola snorted. "The only part worth having," she muttered. "Likely my brother has gone to the south. We can follow him there."

"Wherever Uncle goes, the soldiers will follow," Billy said. "We should go into the swamp where they can't find us."

"We'll starve in the swamp," Peeping said.

Ochola laughed. "You have been with the whites too long. I have forgotten more than you ever knew about how to get food, child. I would not starve, nay even if I could not walk. Billy, see if you can find some snails and crayfish under the river rocks." She watched as the boy obediently scrambled up and began to clamber over the boulders at the side of the river, turning over the lighter ones for small snails and darting creatures. When he was out of hearing, she said to Peeping, "We must keep him from my brother. Mad New Town will be taken again, it is only a matter of time. And next time, they won't let Billy go. He is small for his age, or they might not have done so this time. They think him a child."

"He is, in many ways still," Peeping said.

"Well, and that will not save him again." Ochola took her daughter's hand. "I'll see you safely to the Talassees in the swamp, and then I'm going to leave you."

Peeping looked up, alarmed. "Where will you go?"

"To find my brother. I want to be with him at the end."

"And you think the end is near?"

Ochola nodded grimly. "Old Mad Jackson will have us out of the Floridas or die in the attempt." She grimaced. "He does not look as though he means to die anytime soon."

"When did you see him?" Peeping asked.

"When I went to his tent and begged for your life," Ochola murmured.

Peeping recoiled. "You? My mother? You went to see General Jackson?"

"I told him if he would let you go, my brother would surrender."

"And will he?"

"Never." Ochola grinned happily. "If I know my brother, he will be the last one taken."

"Then we should be with him."

Ochola shook her head firmly. "Billy needs to be with his people, not a roving band of outlaws. He will soon wish to take a wife. How will he find such with my brother, who will now be as a hunted wolf before the guns of the blue jackets? No, you take him to the nearest village and disappear as best you can from the whites."

"Perhaps we should go back to the fort and live among them," Peeping said wistfully. "Life with the whites is not so terrible, after all."

Ochola stiffened. "You must do as you will. You always have. But I will never come among them again."

Billy was coming back now, holding wriggling creatures in his hands and grinning in triumph.

Peeping sighed and rose wearily to hunt for kindling. "Will you tell him or shall I?"

"I will tell him," Ochola said. "He's my only grandson."

Billy came up to them now, dropping on the sand four small crayfish and two snails. "Grandmother, you were right. We could make our own village right here."

She smiled and touched his head. "We must be with our people, Billy. We cannot live on river bugs for long."

"How far do you think they are?" Billy asked, as Peeping brought back an armful of twigs and deadfall.

"Likely, we will find them in two days' walking," Ochola said. "Unless they have gone deeper into the swamp to escape the soldiers."

"We should go now," Billy said. "Right after we eat."

"And so we shall," Ochola said.

Peeping looked at her questioningly. Clearly, she wondered when her mother intended to tell Billy that she would only accompany them to the next village, then leave them there. Ochola frowned slightly, turning away from her daughter, letting her know that she would choose her own time for that telling. Billy needed all the encouragement— and courage—he could find within himself now. She would wait until they were safer.

They walked deeper into the swamp for two days, stopping only to eat what they could find and sleep. Billy caught bullfrogs each night for grilling, and Ochola showed him how to catch fish with a net made of her skirt and branches. Peeping and her mother collected what greens they could find as they moved along the game trails, always going south with the flow of the river.

The swamp seemed to open and welcome them within, Peeping thought as she walked along, her head down, the worries buzzing her head like diligent mud wasps. It was so much easier to live with the whites, she told herself. She could almost disappear among them, find another man perhaps; raising a son alone was not what she had planned for her life.

She watched Billy as he trod along determinedly, his head high and curious, his step eager. It was all he could do not to press his grandmother to hurry, hurry, he wanted to get there, wherever they were going, he didn't care where. And the swamp watched them as they walked, she knew. Listened for their voices and their steps, watched for them to pause. She felt no menace in the trees, the water, the brush, even none in the ever-present buzzing, stinging insects. Here, at least, they would not be held against their will. Although she sometimes wished someone would hold her, whether she wished it or not.

The three walked on and on, deeper into the swamp, following what trails they could find, keeping to the river as best they could. Dense cypress groves hanging with moss kept the sun dim on their shoulders, and hanging vines twisted to the swamp floor like the long tresses of lonely women. High in the canopy above them, they heard birds, squirrels, hawks, and jays. But down where they walked, the air was thick and warm, the gnats and the mosquitoes busy company.

They stopped again at midday, having walked and slept as they could, keeping always to the south or the southwest, following the movement of the sun from morning to dusk. "I think we will come to a village before nightfall," Ochola said. "I have seen more sign now on the trail. We're getting nearer."

"I saw tracks back on the riverbank," Billy said proudly.

Ochola nodded. "More refugees," she said. "Barefoot, moving slowly. Likely looking for frogs."

"You think they're starving, too?" Peeping asked.

"Not starving," Ochola scoffed. "Not eating white bread, neither."

"I miss meat," Billy said.

His grandmother stood up and silently beckoned to him. "It is all around you, if you have the wits to catch it." She took him down to the river and stopped, peering down at the muddy bank closely, her old eyes gleaming. "Here," she said softly, pointing to soft tracks in the mud.

He grinned. A raccoon's small handlike prints were disappearing into the brush. Now that she showed them to him, they were so obvious. She beckoned him to follow, leading him carefully up the bank, casting this way and that like an old hound, finding again the trail as it led up to the base of a wide strangler fig. There, almost hidden, was the raccoon's burrow.

Silently, his grandmother looked about until she found the stick she wanted. She took her large hunting knife, the one which never left the waist of her long skirt, and she cut the branch to make a fork, with two sharpened ends. Then she stood downwind and just away from the hole, gesturing for Billy to move back. She jabbed the stick deep in the hole, twisting it as she pushed, and Billy heard a soft grunt from within.

"Elder Raccoon does not like his rest disturbed," she grinned, twisting harder on the stick, leaning into it with her weight. She struggled to pull the creature, impaled on the stick, from out of the hole, twisting him so that his fur was caught along with his flesh. She drew him forth, a growling, spitting, thirty-pound striped demon, all claws and teeth and rage. With a swift slash, she took her knife and plunged it into his head, pinning him to the ground. After a few spasmodic kicks and jerks, the raccoon was dead.

"Now this will not work for a mink," she said matter-of-factly. "They

will wedge themselves deep while they kill your stick. But Elder Raccoon wants to come out and fight in the open, for he always believes
he will win." She grinned as she wiped the sweat off her brow with
her forearm. "Like the white man."

Billy grinned and picked up the carcass gingerly. There would be
meat, at least, for several nights.

They built their cooking fire and Ochola began to cook the raccoon
and two small fish Billy had caught. The smell of the cooking fish and
the roasted meat wafted upward on the smoke and drifted through the
swamp night. Ochola was turning the spit, when she suddenly froze,
her eyes staring into the darker shadows. *"Shta,"* she whispered. "Be
still."

Peeping was instantly alert and afraid. Billy peered in the direction
his grandmother stared. "What is it?" he whispered.

"Panther," she said softly. "Big male, I am thinking."

"Oh no," Peeping moaned.

"The fire will keep him off," Billy said, reaching to add more wood
to the blaze.

Ochola said nothing, but only stared silently into the darkness. Suddenly, she began to sing a low, keening song of plaintive notes. Low
in her throat, she hummed and crooned, a warble which was half song,
half groan.

"What are you doing?" Peeping asked, half-panicked.

Ochola murmured, *"Huhte-tuh.* Wait a while." She continued to sing.

There was a stirring from the darkness, and then a large sinuous
shape moved into the firelight. Carefully, warily, picking his way like
a cat will in wet grass, a tawny panther slid into the circle of light,
gazed unafraid at Ochola, and laid himself down on his paws, purring
gently. His eyes were slits in the gleam from the fire, his body so large
that it took up more space by the fire than Billy's own.

Peeping froze, silent with wonder. Billy stared first at his grandmother, then at the big cat. Ochola continued to sing, her eyes closed,
her hands weaving softly before her stomach as though she rubbed an
invisible pot.

Billy was so close to the giant cat that he could see the small whisker
patches on his upper lip, the small rounded ears, the wet at the top of
his haunches, as though he had brushed under wet moss just before
he arrived. The cat's purr sounded like low thunder in the swamp, a
curiously comforting noise against the crack and snapple of the fire.

Peeping shifted suddenly, and the cat's eyes flared open. He tensed and watched her guardedly for an instant. But as Ochola continued to moan her private song, as Peeping froze under his gaze, the cat settled back once more, kneading his huge claws into the soft earth rhythmically.

Finally, Ochola finished her song. She lifted her head and opened her eyes, gazing calmly at the huge cat. The panther gazed back at her, taking her measure as clearly. Ochola spoke softly. "We are honored that you come to our fire."

The panther did not move, only his ear twitched forward toward the old woman's speech, to catch the faintest whisper in her voice.

"We would share our poor meal with you," she continued, "if you wish." She gestured to the fish on the spit as though the panther were a visiting chief and could understand every nuance of her welcome.

The cat rose suddenly and stretched his body out, tensing his forepaws and then sniffing lightly at the cooking fish. He did not snatch at it, only inhaled its odor. Then without a glance at Peeping, without seeming to hear Billy's sharp intake of breath, he slid away from the light of the fire as silently as he had come.

Ochola said, "The swamp welcomes us. The great cat came to say as much. We have done the right thing, to come this way."

Peeping let out her pent-up breath in a gasp. "No more singing over the fish, Mother! Next time, it may well be a bear!"

"Well, and if it is, he will make his courtesies like the cat."

With that, Billy hooted aloud, shouted as if he had been holding it in for hours, rocked and held his knees and slapped his feet in helpless, rocking laughter. "Next I want to see you try that on Andrew Jackson, Grandmother!" he finally managed to say, shaking his head and swiping his portion of the fish from off the spit.

Ochola smiled at him. "I did," she said gently. "Now come and tell me what you see." She took him to the closest panther track. "A hound's is smaller, eh?"

"Yes," he said.

"But deeper. Do you see claw marks?"

He shook his head.

"The panther does not leave them, except when he attacks. He hunts always in a straight line, his rear paws go into the tracks of his front paws, and he will return only twice to a kill. Will you remember?"

"I will remember," he said.

In the morning, they started off again. Within several hours, they came to a small rise by the river, where a clustered village sat in a clearing of bay trees. Four hastily erected *chekes* close together, three cooking fires, and what seemed to be no more than a dozen people moving to and fro. Ochola went quickly to the nearest thatched hut, spoke to one of the women, and then gestured to Billy and Peeping.

"We are welcome," she said, nodding to the woman in thanks. "They are of the Fox clan. The woman will share what food she has, and her husband will help us put up a roof when he returns from the fishing."

"Where are the rest of them?" Peeping asked, glancing about the small clearing.

"They have only twenty people here," Ochola said. "They have only just come themselves."

"Do they have any warriors?" Billy asked.

Ochola shrugged. "You can ask the woman yourself," she said, pushing him gently toward the rude table under the thatched hut. "You're going to be neighbors now, after all."

Over a slim supper of boiled greens in fish broth, they learned that Old Mad Jackson had sent his captives to Tennessee. From there, they were to be walked to Oklahoma, the new Indian territory. Jackson then turned his ire on Saint Marks and Pensacola, capturing and burning the cities and shaming the Spaniards, whom he blamed for being too tolerant of the Seminoles in their midst. Whenever he found Seminoles, he rounded them up and sent them west, burning their villages and scourging the soil under their corn rows. Those who escaped trickled south, going deeper and deeper into the Florida wilderness.

"We hear that there are more than five thousand Seminoles going to Oklahoma," the woman said to them. "But my husband will not go, no not if Jackson comes himself and points his pistol at his head."

"How many warriors are here?" Billy asked, his ladle moving steadily to his mouth and back again to his soup.

"Six," the woman said proudly. "My husband is *tustenuggee,* and the others do what he says."

"Six," Ochola repeated, politely ignoring the woman's boast that her husband was a warrior leader. "So few of us are left."

" 'Tis enough," the woman said staunchly. "We will never be taken by the white soldiers."

"Well, and that is what my brother said," Ochola said wryly.

"And so he was right," Peeping snapped back at her. She rose and walked away from the hut with a nod of her head and a brief word of thanks for the woman. She already knew her mother's mind. She would want to leave the next morning. She would not let the grass grow a single day under her shadow.

She watched from a short distance while Billy ate his own soup, glanced longingly at the woman's pot where a bit remained, and then rose and manfully strode off toward the river to inspect this portion of the village's territory. He would want to go with his grandmother, likely. But what would they find the farther south they went? Fewer necessities, fewer folks, farther from the settlements of the whites. More snakes, more insects, more wilderness. No, she told herself, I will go no farther. Let him choose however he will, I am staying here. Or perhaps I am going on north again. But I will follow the old woman no more.

Peeping followed Billy to the river and sat upon the bank, watching him amble delightedly among the water shallows, picking up rocks and peering at what scrambled to escape him. He was young for fourteen years, she knew. No father, no real home, a grandmother and mother for company, these things had kept him a boy. It was time he became a man, but who would teach him what he must learn? General Jackson and his white soldiers? The hollow-eyed warriors hobbled like calves or herded into the white forts at the border? The old chiefs who walked at the head of the long lines of doomed refugees on their way to the new territory? She shook her head angrily. It was a poor time to have a son, that much was certain.

She took a sprig of grass and let a fire ant crawl upon it, watched as it waved its small feelers in her direction, sensing the foe so near. She moved her hand over a hooded pitcher plant, and waited. The pitcher plant was a pretty yellow flower with red veins and pale spots, expanded at the top into an overarching hood. Peeping knew that if she dropped the fire ant into the flower, it would lap up the nectar eagerly and then head for the translucent spots on the lip of the hood, thinking those its exit. It would try and try to get out, finally exhaust itself, and then fall down into the narrow tube of the stalk where the pitcher plant would slowly digest it.

The fire ant scrambled closer to her hand now, desperate to fight her or flee. She jostled the grass stem slightly, watched as the ant struggled to maintain his hold, and dropped him into the waiting pitcher plant. She rose then and called to Billy. There was no sense staying to watch the ant's fate; it was inevitable.

That night, Ochola told Billy that she would be leaving the next

morning, going south to try to find her brother. Peeping told him, in
the same moment, that she did not want to go any farther into the
wilderness. Billy gaped at both of them, back and forth between his
mother and his grandmother, two women who had been in his vision
for all of his life. He boiled up, tried to argue with his mother, and
then subsided when he saw that she would not be swayed. Then he
turned to his grandmother. His efforts there at persuasion were weaker
still, for he knew that of the two women, she was the stronger. Finally
he said stubbornly, "I'm going south, too."

Ochola said calmly, "You will not. You will stay with your mother."

Peeping smiled sadly. "Perhaps we will go north again, and live
among the whites. Would that suit you better?"

"None of this suits me," he said angrily, standing up and slapping
at his muddy shins. "But when has that ever mattered?" He stalked
away into the darkness.

"He will forgive us," Ochola said gently.

Peeping said nothing. She did not want her mother to hear the tears
in her voice.

The next morning Ochola left them, and, for a long while, Peeping
and Billy tried to make a home with the small band of refugees they
had found in the swamp. But finally, they heard that the white soldiers
were scourging the region, keeping to the river and moving down with
the water, finding what peoples they could find to send to the territory.
It was said that the slave owners to the north were angry and insisting
that the White Father in Washington rid the Floridas of the Indians
and bring back their escaped slaves.

Peeping had seen four black men join their little band since she and
Billy had arrived, and as was the custom, they were welcomed so long
as they would work. She knew it was only a matter of time before the
soldiers would find them, and this time, they would take Billy as well
as the other men. He was growing taller, and she could no longer hide
him behind her skirts.

Another family had decided to travel south to the Gulf, for they had
heard that a larger village there was still unnoticed by the whites. They
believed they might find some of their clan members closer to the
ocean, and, as one of the women told her, "at least it will be easier to
feed the children by the sea."

Peeping and Billy talked it over one night by their fire. He had never
really been happy in the little village, for there were only two boys his
own age to roam with, and one of them was sickly. He still mourned

his grandmother, and Peeping knew that he hoped somehow to find her again.

"How long will it take to get there?" he asked.

"I don't know," she told him honestly. "I've never been so far south."

"Will the soldiers follow?"

"I don't know that either."

He thought quietly for a moment. "Do you think we can make it, Mother?"

She did not answer him right away. What if they could not? He was strong enough, she knew that much. Was she? She cared for so little these days, she wondered if she could make herself keep going. Still, what else was there for them? If she stayed in this village, she would likely never find another husband. And Billy might be taken in the next raid, something which was bound to come sooner or later. She bowed her head, fighting back resignation. She felt so weary of it all. But he was young and strong. He deserved a chance at his life.

"We can make it," she said finally. She hoped he took the pain in her voice for determination.

And so, in three days, when the other family began the trek to the south, to the sea, Billy and Peeping followed along behind them. They had little to carry. In the seasons they had spent on the Suwannee, they had collected little, made still less that they could call their own.

Andrew Jackson was clearing a wide swath from Fort Scott to Suwannee Old Town. From there, he took Pensacola, ending all official Spanish claim to the Floridas. It seemed that all Indian claims were ended as well, but even as Spain ceded Florida to President James Monroe in 1819, pockets of Seminoles still survived, evading the soldiers and refusing to emigrate to the new Indian territory. General Jackson, however, stood up before Congress and said, "The Seminole War may now be considered at a close."

Sometimes called Oklahoma, sometimes merely "Indian Country," the land Congress offered the tribes was a great desert in the Great Plains beyond the Mississippi, long thought to be uninhabitable by white men. Few had seen the region, but stories circulated widely through the clans that nothing would grow there, and the water was so alkali that it would poison even mother's milk.

The northern tribes were being removed slowly but surely, with little difficulty. But in the south, where the tribes were larger and stronger, the Five Civilized Tribes—the Creeks, the Choctaws, the

Chickasaws, Cherokees, and Seminoles—were far less pliable. In fact, many considered themselves Americans, since they were thrifty farmers, were living and trading among the whites, raising large herds of cattle, and sending their children to the missionary schools.

They refused to leave, at first politely and then adamantly. As skirmishes turned to war, they banded together and trickled away from the civilized areas, deep into the swamps, the thickets, the Everglades of the Florida wilderness, reasoning that to be evicted, they must first be found.

Billy and Peeping found themselves with just such a band, traveling south to the vicinity of Tampa Bay. They arrived the day Billy turned fifteen. On the sand, watching the Gulf waters roll in, they saw two fishermen who told them of a village near the bay. It was rumored, they said, that Peter McQueen had survived and was there. But even that rumor was only whispered, for the Indians knew that if the white soldiers heard of McQueen's whereabouts, they would descend on the village like wolves.

They walked several hours more, finally coming upon a settlement nestled in a hammock of palms, spreading back from the mouth of a river as it emptied into the sea. The land here was low and flat, hotter than it had been to the north, with less dense vegetation. The sand beneath Peeping's feet was warm and soft, and she felt her spirits rising as they got closer to the cluster of thatched huts. Billy ran a little ahead, so eager was he to see if the rumor were true.

A runner came forward to meet them, and the leader of their band called out, "We come for refuge!" the same greeting they had called to a half dozen villages they had passed before this one.

The runner came forward, holding a rifle at the ready. "Stop right there and speak your names!"

The leader of the troop stepped forward. "We are come from the north, where the white soldiers drove us out. I am Ockla, with my family. She is Peeping, mother to that boy—" he called, for indeed Billy was already past the sentry, dancing excitedly up and down, waiting for permission to go forward.

"You have whites among you?" the runner asked suspiciously, coming closer. Most especially did he peer at Peeping.

"She was married to one once," Ockla said, "but her mother is Ochola, sister to Mad New Town."

With that news, the runner grinned happily and lowered his weapon. "Come forward and be welcome!" he said. "Your mother is over there!"

He pointed to a *cheke* near the edge of the village. "And your uncle awaits you!"

Peeping burst into tears at that news and hurried behind Billy, who was racing ahead to the thatched hut to greet his grandmother. As she emerged from the hut, shading her eyes and peering at the newcomers, he threw himself on her joyfully, lifting her clear off the sand and whirling her about as though she were a girl. Peeping ran to them, and Billy pulled her into his embrace as well. "We made it, Grandmother!" he called again and again. "We found you!"

Ochola pulled them both as close as she could squeeze them, murmuring words of praise to the Maker of Breath. When Peeping pulled back and looked into her mother's eyes, she saw the weariness, the relief, the love there, and she laughed with joy.

"Come, come," Ochola said then, pulling them forward, "come and greet your uncle. He has been ill; it will do his heart good to see you safe at last."

"Are we safe at last?" Peeping asked, wiping her eyes. "Have the blue jackets been down this far south?"

"Not that we have heard," Ochola said, as they came to a hut with woven cane coverings over the entrance. She pulled them aside and called out, "Brother! Look who has come!"

Peeping and Billy went into the dim hut and stood awkwardly at the side of Mad New Town's cot. He opened his eyes and struggled to raise himself up on his elbow.

"You are come," he said.

"Oh, Uncle," Peeping murmured.

"He has not been well for a fortnight," Ochola said briskly. "But he is improving steadily. We'll have him up soon—"

Mad New Town waved his sister to silence. "I am dying," he said calmly. "And I am not afraid. Now that I have seen this man once more, I can rest easy on this bed." He took Billy's hand. "You must lead these people, my nephew. In my name, you must take them into the wilderness where they can prosper."

"He is only fifteen," Peeping said quickly. "Surely, there are others—"

"We have now only the young and the very old," her uncle replied softly. "The young men will start new families, they will be the ones to survive, if any do. The old ones can advise them, but it is the young men who will save us." He let go of Billy's hand. "We may never again have *tustenuggee*," his uncle added, using the Seminole word for military leader. "We may only have ordinary warriors. You must take them south."

"How much farther?" Peeping moaned. "Already, we are so far from any town, we cannot even trade for a pot to cook our corn!"

Ochola said, "We do not need their pots."

"Perhaps you do not, Mother," Peeping said impatiently, "but we are young yet. We are not ready to go into the brush and die like wounded bears."

Billy put his hand on his mother's shoulder. "I am hungry. Let us eat now and talk more later." He bent and kissed the old man's brow. "Rest easy, Great-uncle. The blue jackets aren't here yet, at any rate."

Ochola glanced at him sharply for an instant, sensing the usual mockery of the young for the old. But then she relaxed. Billy was older now. He was almost a man. She directed one of the women to bring food to her brother, and she took Peeping and Billy outside to her own hut to feed them.

Over boiled greens, she told them how she had traveled so far to find her brother, and how many warriors had been lost from his original band. "Some to wounds and illness, some to despair, I think," she said. "And some have gone to the whites."

"Perhaps that is what we must all do soon," Peeping said.

"Not so long as we have feet to carry us away," Ochola said stubbornly. "Look about you, daughter. This is the last of us, I fear. We hear there are other villages over the whole face of Florida, hidden in pockets of swamp and down in the Pahay-o-kee, the grassy waters. The white man calls them the Everglades, but he does not go there."

"The people are living with the snakes and the panthers," Peeping murmured.

"Yes, and proudly," Ochola said. "There are enough of us still to make a people, if we can find each other and go south. My brother says that the whites will give us those lands, if we will promise to stay there."

"What's the difference between going to the territory they have chosen for us and keeping to one in the wilderness?" Peeping asked. "If we must go somewhere, why not go where they want us to go? At least then, they will give us cattle and money and seed."

"The difference is that we choose for ourselves," Ochola said. "This is our land. This is where we are born and where we die."

"The other difference is many thousands of miles," Billy said quietly.

"Our old and our young cannot make it so far. If we go south, it is not much different or so far."

Peeping fell silent. She could see that her son had taken Mad New Town's words to heart. He was speaking as though his opinions mattered.

"How many black faces do you have among you here?" Billy asked.

"Only three," Ochola said. "And they have been with us so long, they are as family. One has four children by Fights In A Line, the woman who came from Pea Creek."

"So long as the blacks lodge among us, the blue jackets will come," Billy said.

"But they have always been with us," Peeping said. "Your own father's father was black."

Billy said shortly, "So you have told me, but I can see no part of him in me. I am Seminole."

Ochola smiled wryly. "So speaks a man of the people."

Peeping said angrily. "He is only a boy."

"He is your only fledgling, and so you are loath to see him fly," Ochola said calmly. "But he is no longer a boy. Any eyes can see that."

Billy stood then as though to see himself clearly at once. "I am not a boy," he said firmly. "Neither am I yet a man. But I will be soon, and perhaps the people can't wait much longer."

He walked then toward the river to see what sort of fishing this village provided. As he went, his mother sighed as she scraped the last bit of boiled greens from his bowl. "I should have stayed with the whites," she said. "There, he would not have to be a man before his time."

"There, he would never be one," Ochola said, patting her daughter's hand. "You have done the right thing. Now, you must let him go."

Peeping gripped her mother's hand tightly and said nothing more.

As Billy's great-uncle, Mad New Town was the only male of his mother's clan left to teach him the ways of becoming a man. In the older times, Peeping's brothers would have taken Billy in tow and taught him the way of hunting, of sacred medicine, of his responsibilities to the people as a warrior-in-training. Fathers, cordial strangers to their own seeds, never taught their sons such things. It was most properly the place of the mother's male relations to teach her son, for just as all property and houses belonged to the women, so did the children.

But Peeping's only brother had been killed at the battle of Horseshoe

Bend, when Old Mad Jackson overran their camp. Ochola's other brother had fallen in the same campaign, what the whites called the First Seminole War for the Floridas. There was only old Mad New Town left to train his grandnephew, though he was weakened from disease and an embattled spirit.

Mad New Town struggled from his hammock to take his nephew in hand. With the help of their only surviving medicine man, Arpeika, Mad New Town sat the boy down and began to tell him the old stories, sang him the old songs, and showed him his own magic bundle, the worn, soft deerskin pouch he kept at his waist which carried his *sabia*, his personal spirit medicine.

Billy was at first eager to sit with the two leaders, for there was little to do in this settlement of mostly women and children, and too few young men like himself to get up a good ball game. He joined them in the long, open-fronted shed which served as the men's gathering place, where women only came to bring food and drink twice each day. There, after bathing each morning and greeting the Maker of Breath, they assembled together, wearing their fringed shawls against the morning chill, facing east as was proper, to speak of the past, the future, and whatever else needed discussion in the workings of the people.

"War is evil but necessary," Mad New Town said to Arpeika as Billy joined them that morning. "There is no other way to train our young men in the proper art of being a warrior."

"The whites bring no honor to the art, however," Arpeika said evenly. He was a man of some fifty winters, so far as Billy could tell, but his black eyes were still bright and appraising as an otter's and his spiky nest of white-gray hair stuck up over his head like heron plumes. "They do not fight for revenge or for honor, but for greed. They want all of the earth for themselves. The white man has no respect for the earth. He has no dignity and he does not feel as we do. He is *istee futchigo*, a man of perverse natures."

"The white man forgets, if he ever knew," Mad New Town added, "the most simple truths. And yet the Maker of Breath gives him great power. Perhaps there is a reason, I do not know. But remember, my niece's son, that you are this universe and the universe is you. It is all one, all connected. Do not be a man of perverse nature."

Billy listened carefully. His people had no word for criminal. But to say a man behaved perversely was their worst condemnation.

"The problem is not only Old Mad Jackson and his soldiers," Mad New Town went on, "but the rest of the whites as well. They have no honor and seem incapable of keeping to their word, even as they swear themselves over and over with their marks on their papers and their hands on their spirit books."

Billy nodded. "Their Bibles," he said solemnly. "They carry them about like medicine bags."

Mad New Town and Arpeika turned to gaze at him slowly. It was not proper for young men to speak when the old men gathered. It was the job of the young to listen, not to voice an opinion. Billy's words were not only an indication of how far the people had fallen, but also how far he had to go before he could lead them to the old ways again.

"I am proud of my grandnephew," Mad New Town said slowly, painfully. "He has an opinion and he voices it aloud, never caring what others might think or who may be offended."

Billy flushed as he understood that though he might well be indulged in his grandmother's house, these men would not be so easily impressed. Arpeika was, after all, one of the last of the *Hobayee Tastanagee,* One Who Understands the Arts of War. He was a healer, a wise man. Billy fell silent, and he dropped his head.

"He Who Makes Men knows that many youths begin as sure of themselves as young otters, and that same spirit will become courage when they have been tested," Arpeika said calmly. He did not look at Billy. He took out his medicine pouch and handled it lovingly, carefully. "When I was a youth, we took many months to become men. Now, all things move more quickly."

"When you were a youth, Old Mad Jackson was nothing more than a wet place on his mother's nether scalp," Mad New Town said. "Times change, and we must change with them."

"So I am told." Arpeika grinned grimly. "And so, little woodpecker, you will go on a spirit quest in four days. You must be ready. Make a proper pouch for your *sabia,* your personal medicine, from the softest skin parts of an animal you kill yourself. And within that pouch, you will place your holy objects."

Billy nodded.

"Are you afraid?" Mad New Town asked suddenly.

"No, Great-uncle," Billy said respectfully.

"Be afraid," Mad New Town said. "Only a foolish man denies his fear. Use what you can of fear, however, and discard the rest. It will pass, and you will still be standing. And if you are not, it will not matter anyway."

For days they sat thus, with Billy listening and the two men talking to him, around him, over his head, as though they had all the time in the world and nothing more important to do. As though the blue jackets were not hunting them even as they spoke.

After ten days of listening and watching, Billy went out with the bow and arrow his great-uncle gave him, sharpened his arrow with fire, and killed a small opossum. Indeed, he hardly needed the weapon, the animal was so slow and vulnerable. Nevertheless, he took it back to his grandmother's hut, where his mother and Ochola dressed and prepared the meat and the skin with as much admiration and respect as if they expected it to feed them for the winter. Ochola sewed the little pouch together with fine leather stitches, and into it she put a flattened bullet which she had taken from a live oak with her own knife at the battle of Horseshoe Bend.

"This bullet spent itself on a white soldier and then tried to kill an oak as well," she said. "It is a very brave, very strong bullet and will stand between you and danger, my grandson."

He embraced her, put the bullet in his pouch, and set out on his journey deep within the swamp to discover his personal spirit guide. His head was shaved, his face was painted half-red and half-yellow, signifying the sacredness of his journey. He would eat nothing for four days but *sowatchko*, the root that would bring him visions.

In the shimmering heat of the swamp, dragonflies and butterflies swooped and dived, and mosquitoes whined round his head and arms, all bare except for the leather straps of his bow. He moved toward the west, following the sun in the sky, poling his dugout slowly and watching the landscape change as he moved from cypress grove to open, watery prairie. On his feet, he wore the hard new moccasins his great-uncle had given him.

"These were made to go always forward and never away from your life," Mad New Town said.

The *sowatchko* root made him feel light-headed and strong, all at once. Billy felt as though he could keep poling forever, all the way to the wide waters of the Gulf. He gazed down into the dark, moving waters, like the color of the Black Drink which the men consumed at the Green Corn Ceremonies. Stained by the oaks and the cypress, the water looked as if it might sicken any man who drank of it, but it was more pure than most of the lighter-colored rivers to the east.

In fact, Ochola told of the white men paying many of their silver dollars for casks of the water from the swamp's two rivers, what they called the Suwannee and the Saint Marys, for their sailing ships. They came from Saint Augustine to capture the two rivers, for their waters stayed fresh in a cask all the way across the ocean.

The water gave off a reflection like the mirrors of the white men. As the *sowatchko* made his eyes blur and his head eddy, it was almost impossible to see which clouds were real and which floated on the water, so clear were they in reflection. Above him, egret nests crowded the trees, and the stench and debris of eggs and droppings and fledglings who had fallen from the nests made large piles on the hammocks below them. Billy knew that if he looked closely, he would find tangles of rattlesnakes in the shadows of the cypress roots, waiting for more birds to drop.

Billy poled continually, ignoring the ache in his arms and the cramping in his calves. When he tired, he shifted his position and paddled instead. He could see deep into the swamp, into the morass of tangled limbs and vines of foliage which was so dense, a man would have to back up to blink his eyes. The thrushes on the grassy islands made their raspy call, and a white-beaked woodpecker flew past with his raucous cry, sounding like the king of all birds. Or at least, as though he thought himself so.

Billy had often been called "woodpecker"; in fact, it was his childhood nickname, given him by his grandmother, as was the tradition with his people, before his man-name would be earned. He would have to remember to ask the old woman if his cries were as loud, as demanding, as imperious as these.

The sun was high and Billy was thirsty, the more so since the *sowatchko* made his throat tingle and tighten. He beached the dugout on a small palmetto island and dug a hole with a pointed stick. Presently, clean water welled up in it, and he drank deeply. A huge flock of green-winged teal, more than a thousand, by Billy's guess, came hurtling overhead, and their wings made a sound like tent flaps being whipped by the wind as they split and rolled in the sky, startled by the sight of him.

Billy felt as though he were completely alone in the world. For the moment, the sun did not shine on him, but within him. The water did not flow past him but through him. He was at the center of the universe and the whole universe was inside his chest. He had never felt such peace, such contentment. This, he thought to himself, is how men must feel about women at times, he realized. Only different. This was love, not for another human but for all of life. He stretched out and closed his eyes, pulling a banana leaf over his head for shade.

Billy had often wondered about the business between men and women, and he supposed his curiosity was another signal that he was becoming a man. He frequently felt a warm tension at his groin when a maiden smiled at him or watched him go about the village. He knew, instinctively, that his mother would never be happy again until she found another man. That sometimes, her fears, her complaints, were nothing more than loneliness for someone to share her blanket. Even Ochola, aged and spicy as jerked beef, was able to make the old men grin and hobble jauntily after her in the night dances, if she put herself in the right mood.

It seemed to Billy then, as he reflected on love, that the world could be a sad and fearsome place without a woman of his own. Someday, Ochola would be gone, and then his own mother, as surely as the swamp would always be there. Someday, he would have children, and they would grow up and get on with their own lives, and the only one who might really care whether he lived or died would be, finally, his wife. She might rail at him or ignore him or love him, but at least she would likely keep him on her mind.

So far as Billy could tell, marriage had been no bargain for his mother, and he had seen plenty of unions break up as casually as they began among his people. A woman who wanted to be divorced simply built a new *cheke* away from her husband, took her pots and her children, and put his things outside. If he left his things there outside their old abode, it meant he wanted a reconciliation. If he pulled down the old hut and took his belongings away, they were henceforth parted. The only problem occurred, and it did often enough, when one partner wished the union ended and the other did not. Then, the elders would be consulted to give an opinion on behalf of the rest of the clan. Often as not, they sided with the woman, especially if there were another man she wanted who wanted her. They were wise enough to know that they could not dam up flowing water.

And yet, Billy had seen a hundred partnerships which were happy ones, where both husband and wife, sometimes two wives, seemed content with each other, making a life, beating as one heart. It seemed to him at this moment that such a thing was more important than wealth or honor in war. Such a thing was a priceless gift from the Maker of Breath.

He had been quiet long enough now that the swamp folded itself in on him and forgot he was there. He opened his eyes and gazed upward. Flying low above the water, wing tips almost touching, a water turkey came over the slowly-moving river. A big bass whirled near his boat, making a dimple on the black water, and Billy could smell the odor of bream hanging on the banks where the brush tangled into the stream. Ducks, only a hundred feet away, were drumming and splashing and chuckling among themselves, ignorant of his presence or uncaring.

Billy got back in his dugout and began to paddle once more. His belly was empty, but he felt strangely full, light of head and limb, and infinitely powerful. He went deeper into the swamp, following the turn and curve of the water.

As the sun finally went lower on the horizon, burning orange and red among the tall cypress, he sought another hammock to make his shelter for the night. The gators were bellowing and coughing, making the swamp ring with their challenges, so he pulled enough wood together to make a fire, keeping his back to the gum trees and his eyes to the water. His stomach rolled and grumbled, but he ignored his hunger, slowly chewed his *sowatchko* root, and set about to make himself comfortable.

As the sun went down slowly, Billy felt the swamp change, sensed the creatures shift places, and the animals of the daylight retreat out of sight. At the same time, the night animals began to come out of their burrows and holes to prowl the darkness. A bull gator flattened his head above the water and bellowed a greeting to the night. Farther downriver, another answered and then another, and the night frogs took up the chorus.

All of a sudden, a deer stumbled out of the thicket behind Billy, snorted in surprise, and took off away from him in the shallow water. He ran with leaden feet, burdened by mud, in grotesque, painful jumps, his alarm evident in every muscle of his body and his panicked flash of white tail.

Billy began to sing to him, in the hopes he would understand that he meant him no harm. The old hunting song he half recalled from his childhood spoke of honor and courage and the great awful beauty of death, but the words and the melody were soft, and he saw that then the buck stopped and turned to stare at him. Still snorting, with anger now at being so alarmed, the buck tossed his head like a horse, shook his small antlers at Billy in threat, and struggled to drier land. Then, without a backward glance, he stalked away.

Softly, Billy laughed at him. He bent with his flint and a sliver of pitch pine and started up his fire, wondering what it would feel like to go yet another night with no food. He murmured the prayers of a fasting warrior that Arpeika had taught him, the phrases of *Kithla*, the Knower, who whispers to every man his fate if he will only learn to listen, murmured back to him in the shimmer of the water, the creak and rustle of the palmetto leaves. His fire burned high and then burned down again, and night was settled deeply over the swamp.

Billy felt his spirit move away from his body, as tenuous and light as dew on a spiderweb. He stared at the glowing embers of his fire, feeling as though he watched himself from a great height. The eerie shrieks of the limpkin seemed to call him deeper into himself. Slowly, he moved his open palm to the coals, feeling the heat as a sort of benediction, like the sun on his body. Without hesitation, he took a small coal in his hand and cupped it in his palm, willing the pain away. Vaguely, he felt the pain, dimly he smelled the flesh scorching, but he held the coal until he sensed the fire dead in it, and then he placed it gently, reverently back into the embers with its brothers.

He stared at his palm. It was blackened, now the color of the dead coal, but no blister was rising, no red showed under the skin. Billy knew somehow that it would be healed by morning. He knew that it would be so because he would need his hands for poling. He had not felt the pain because he had willed it away, and he would heal quickly because he must. He lay down upon the tufted grass and slept.

Sometime in the night, he was awakened by a splashing, near to him and alarming. He woke and sat up in the darkness, instantly grateful that the fire was still warm enough to provide some heat and light. He could barely see, so with one hand on his knife and the other on a stick, he stirred the coals and quickly added a handful of kindling, peering into the darkness as the flame came up.

A large, sleek, dark head rose out of the shallow water, rounded like a cypress knob, and two gleaming eyes watched him without fear. He froze, as it occurred to him that perhaps the spirit of the swamp was offended by his presence and had come to chase him back to the *chekes* of the people. But then he shook off his dream state and forced himself more awake.

It was an otter, black as the night, silent and staring and not at all afraid. Billy sat up, deliberately moving to see if the creature would flee. It did not. He asked softly, "Have you come to watch over my dreams, little diver?"

Still, the otter did not move.

Billy realized with a shock that this was the vision he had been waiting for on his quest. This, at last, was his spirit animal come to bring his *sabia*, his sacred medicine. He felt a moment of keen disappointment, a brief flash of rejection. After all, the proper spirit animal for a warrior was a fierce animal, a gator, a panther, a wolf, perhaps. Even an eagle would be far better than an otter, who seemed to spend a good deal of his time in frolic.

But then Billy relaxed and sat up, determined to accept whatever gift the swamp brought him. This was his spirit animal, so be it. To his surprise, the moment he relaxed, the otter came nearer, nearer still, and finally waded out of the water and ambled toward him, long, sleek back humping in that undulating manner of a creature who seemed to swim, even on land. It was completely fearless, and, as Billy stared, the otter veered round the fire and came to within a few feet of Billy's crossed knees.

"Well then, Water Spirit, you are come." He half expected the otter to respond in the traditional way of the people, "I am." He wanted to reach out and touch the soft wet fur, rich and gleaming in the light of the fire, but he knew to do so might show disrespect. He knew, also, that even if he did reach out, the otter would not run. "Are you a vision?"

As though in answer, the otter sat up on his hind feet, webbed and leathery, balancing with his long flat tail and stared at Billy boldly. He chittered softly, and, with one paw, scratched his belly thoughtfully, exposing his male genitalia.

Billy chuckled and bowed his head in greeting. He began to murmur the prayer that Arpeika had taught him, the chant which would bring his *sabia* to him strongly, to let the otter know that he was ready to receive whatever gift of knowledge he had come to offer. His stomach was empty as a gourd, but he did not feel the pain. His eyes seemed unnaturally sharp and his vision unusually clear, as though, like the otter, he could see in the darkness.

The otter swayed in the firelight like a snake, growing larger before his eyes, until he was as tall as Billy was seated, and his gaze met Billy's evenly. He was so close now that Billy could see the droplets of water still on his whiskers, could see the dark wet nose wiggling back and forth in a curious search of the night air. Billy saw that the creature's male sack was large, larger even than his own, and he marveled at the power of such a sinuous hunter, no longer disappointed but in awe.

The otter, as though in harmony with Billy's chant, was swaying and chittering softly, chirping like a bird, chuckling like a boy. And when Billy finished his spirit song, the otter dropped down on all fours and quickly humped back to the water. Billy let out his breath in a sigh, wondering if that was all there would be to this vision. But no, after a few moments, the dark head bobbed back up again, and the otter emerged once more from the river, this time carrying something in his mouth. He waddled forward and once more took up his position by the fire, facing Billy.

The otter cracked the clam in his mouth loudly, opened it with his deft and powerful claws, and swallowed most of it with one gulp. Then, watching Billy all the while, he dropped a piece of the clam at Billy's feet and hurried back to the water. When he reached the shallows, he turned and gazed at Billy piercingly. He gave a sudden, hair-raising scream which made Billy jump and flinch. The sound awakened half the swamp, which seemed to chorus back in a cacophony of startled bird shrieks, frog yelps, and gator grunts. And then he slipped into the deep water.

Billy sat and gazed at the place where the otter had disappeared for long moments. He was not sure what exactly the message of his spirit vision had been, but he could guess that some part of it had to do with food—with the food that the river would provide him if he would partake of it. He took up the small bit of clam that the otter had left for him and chewed it. As the leathery flesh touched his tongue, his whole mouth came suddenly alive, flooding with juice, at the briny, fecund taste and odor of the swamp that the clam carried. He was instantly ravenous with hunger, and his stomach gurgled loudly as though in approbation of his choice.

His spirit quest was ended, he knew that much. The lesson of his spirit guide was too complex for him to see all of it now, but he sensed that it had to do with the nurturing that the swamp could provide him, his people, his spirit, if he would choose it. Somehow, he would make his mark in life not through war, as the wolf or the panther, but through intelligence, curiosity, and amiability. These were not, he knew, the hallmarks of a warrior, but perhaps they were those of a leader.

Suddenly, Billy was eager to return to his people, to tell of his spirit quest, to ask Arpeika and Mad New Town what it all might mean. But he settled back to rest as well as he could for the remainder of the dark hours. When the light came, he would eat heartily, he told himself, and then he would paddle for home. One more night of fasting was proper, so that his spirit guide would know that he was worthy of his *sabia*. He picked up the pieces of the clamshell that the otter had dropped, rubbed them clean, and placed them carefully in his medicine pouch as the first of his holy objects. It was a good beginning.

Mad New Town took another five seasons to die. He was mourned by the people as hard as if he had fathered each and every one of them. Ochola and Peeping dressed him in his finest war finery, his white leggings with the bells and shells sewn into every seam, and placed four pure white plumes in his scarlet turban. Then the men of the village propped him up against the men's shed as though he were holding council. For two days, the people came to sit with him and smoke, or bring offerings of shells, the white men's metal beads, and old pots and utensils. Many of the women, banned by tradition from sitting with Mad New Town in his hours with the Maker of Breath, brought instead their best pots of food for his spirit and his guests, arranged at a discreet distance from where he sat, leaning against the lowest men's bench in the shade.

Billy came to smoke with him and discuss again, as he had before his great-uncle died from the choking cough of the white man, the meaning of his spirit quest and what the sacred otter meant to tell him. When he was breathing, Mad New Town had many good ideas about what the spirits did, and he never tired of turning possibilities this way and that like a raccoon with a snail underwater, trying to find the meat of the message.

He was no longer breathing, but Billy knew his spirit hovered still. It would not depart until Mad New Town went to the place of burial, and then it would only be released by the loving rituals of those who put him in the ground.

Arpeika sat with Mad New Town for many long hours, and it was supposed by the people that, together, the two wise men were devising a plan for the survival of the clans after Mad New Town's burial. At times, Arpeika sang the old songs, pausing at the appropriate places for Mad New Town to join in the chorus. Some said they could hear the old warrior's voice in the trees above the shed, rustling the cypress boughs, shimmering through the gum leaves.

Four men carried Mad New Town's pallet to the high earthen place a distance from the village, where the dead were taken, and the women and kinfolk followed after, singing songs of purification and farewell. They were painted in their grief, and Peeping and Ochola left their hair matted and uncombed, their skirts in tatters, signifying their loss.

Billy walked behind his great-uncle's burial pallet, his eyes on the ground, his thoughts a weft of old memories. Once, when a warrior was carried to the burial place, Mad New Town had told him, "Dying is no different from sleeping, boy. Anyway, it is only more of it. We each die a little each night, when our souls fly out of our bodies in our dreams. The old ones sleep more and more as their time nears an end. And if you ask them, they will tell you that they come to prefer their dreams to their waking hours. That is how it is with death. Unless it comes to us by surprise, we are often quite ready to welcome it."

Billy hoped fervently that Mad New Town had found it so for him, that he was ready to welcome death when it came to hold him. Behind him, he could hear Ochola and Peeping wailing and sobbing, and most of the women joined them in their grief. Shared sadness was stronger, yet somehow easier for the heart to hold.

When they reached the place of death, a rectangular log box was already waiting for Mad New Town, prepared by the men for his body. It was laid east to west, which was proper. Under the spreading arms of a large live oak, whose sheets of moss hung down low and protecting, Mad New Town was carried round three times while the people chanted him to the place of spirits. As they came to the beginning of each circle, Billy called out, *"Hayah! Yo!"* and then *"Hei!"* and the mourners repeated his chants, as he led them into the song for burial of a great leader. He then began the resting song and ended with the final words, *"Ni'takintoka.* The days allowed him are finished." His voice was soft and sorrowful, but his heart was strangely light.

When he was done, Arpeika nodded at him in approval. He had told Billy that he could have the honor of singing Mad New Town into the spirit world, and Billy was so moved by his faith that his eyes had watered then, as they did now. But he was not ashamed, nor did he bother to brush the tears away. Tears, Arpeika had told him, were the mark of a good soul.

Billy helped to hold his great-uncle erect, and the men lowered him into the log box lined with cypress bark. He straightened his shirt and his turban, laid Mad New Town's rifle beside him, and the others came forward with their gifts of broken pottery, tobacco, and food. When the box was filled, it was covered with clay, lowered into a hole in the ground, logs were laid over it and more clay, and then the men fired their rifles at all four corners to send Mad New Town's spirit on its way.

Billy took his mother's and grandmother's arms and led them back slowly to the village, letting them lean on him in their grief and picking his way carefully so that they would not need to use their eyes to watch the trail. Their hair was so loose, so long and tangled, that they would have had to move it aside to see, and this would have been considered an element of vanity and so an insult to Mad New Town's memory. Women were often blinded by their emotions, his great-uncle had told him, but they could see deeper into a heart, into a life, than most men with both eyes wide and open. He knew, without being told, that already his grandmother would be thinking of the future, even as she kept her head down, wailed the loudest of all the women, and, indeed, seemed to be willing to follow her brother into death herself.

Soon after Mad New Town's burial, Arpeika had a dream where a mouse came to him with jaws bulging with peas. It was an omen, he said, and he counseled it was wise for them to move south once more, to Pea Creek, so that they might join with other clans for strength against the encroaching pale eyes who were crowding in from the north and the east.

Some of the women remembered that the berries were more plentiful farther south, and the corn grew closer to the river, so they gathered their belongings willingly and prepared to make the trek.

After ten days of walking and paddling their dugouts, the people made it to the new settlement at Pea Creek. Some of the canoes had to be carried, for they found as they went farther to the south and toward the setting sun, the land was marshier, yet sometimes not wet enough for the deeper-hulled canoes. The fleet of travelers stretched out at least two miles behind the leaders, and Billy was glad his dugout, with his mother sitting quietly toward the front, was one of the first in the long line. By the time the mosquitoes were startled into attack, he was already poled to the next meandering stream, and the ones directly behind complained more of the pestering insects than Peeping did.

Indeed, Peeping complained little and spoke less. She stared glumly out over the water, seeming to see nothing. When Billy offered her food, she ate spiritlessly, as though she did not care if she swallowed or not. Ochola murmured to Billy that his mother was tired of running from the whites, tired of having no decent pots or skirts, weary of moving her moccasins from one shelf to another. "She needs a man," Ochola said shortly, as she would speak of a man who needed the white man's bitter water, his whiskey. "We better find her one at Pea Creek, or she will become a wanton."

Billy was shocked by his grandmother's appraisal, but he said nothing to his mother. The ways of women were very complicated and thorny, it seemed to him, and he had no desire to know more of them than he must.

As they finally reached the village of Pea Creek, more and more refugees joined them, trickling down from the Gulf, from the interior, from the rivers as they made their way to the sea. In short time, the *chekes* spread out from the central square of the settlement for nearly a half mile in each direction, and the sounds of dogs, chickens, pigs, children, and boys throwing the ball once more greeted each person as they came and went to the river, the fields, and the pastures where the horses and cattle grazed.

News came that Old Mad Jackson was now territorial governor of the Floridas, and every Seminole knew that as his power grew, their own was weakened. The few chiefs who were left were old now, but they still led the people in the traditional ways, counseling that the best way to survive was to keep away from the white men when they could and compromise with them when they must.

Skirmishes broke out in many places, particularly where the white settlers tried to fence off the game trails and burn the land barren for their cornfields. Then, warriors raided cattle herds, stole pigs, and captured horses, reasoning that an equitable trade was in order. It was told round the campfires that Old Mad Jackson grew wroth when the settlers came to him with tales of missing cattle and pigs and vowed to move every Seminole out of the Floridas.

"Let him try to find us," the warriors laughed. "Let him come to this place with his cannons and his horses and his wagons. We need only stay ahead of him, and the swamp will do the rest."

The seasons passed without incident, and the people began to relax into their lives. Billy noticed the passing of the seasons more these days, and he told himself that he must try to remember the details of each one. Winter came, and the heavy dew dripped from the roof of the hut each evening; the ground fog covered the land each morning when he arose. When he spoke, he could see his life force, his breath, leave his body, as if reminding him that the days were passing. Spring followed, with the rich smell of cabbage palm blossoms in the air. The squirrels were addled, the male egrets grew long, wispy plumes, and the sandcranes danced, crazy for love. Then summer came with roasted sweet corn, orange blossom honey, vast and fierce thunderclouds, and air so damp that his skin felt wet at all hours. With the fall came the flaming leaves, the constant whisper of falling cypress needles, thousands of migrating robins, and skies filled with flying ducks. And, of course, the most important event of the year, the Green Corn Ceremony.

This sacred time of renewal was one which brought the clans from miles around, for it was at that time when relations renewed their bonds, gossip was passed from clan to clan, marriages made, new births presented to the people, and strategy devised by the elders which would affect all the tribes.

Billy anticipated the Green Corn Ceremony with particular relish this year, for at last, he would participate as an initiate. After sharing the Black Drink with every man or near-man in the ceremony, he would take his place with them as an ordinary warrior. And then, when he proved himself in war, he would be a tested man, a *tastanagee*, a true warrior. He would no longer be classed with the women and the children, as *Tchukee lai-dshi*, Those Who Stay in the House.

Every June or early July, the people brought forth their finest clothes, their best weapons, their fattest pigs. It was a time of change, of seasons shifting, of giving thanks for the harvest. The women anticipated it for weeks, readying their dance leggings and their best long, ruffled skirts and calico blouses, for whoever could travel would come together, and clans would have that one chance to see who was living prosperously and who was not. No woman wanted her man, her child, or her *cheke* shamed in comparison.

This year the sounds of the Green Corn Ceremony teased and tantalized Billy far before the actual event. The women sewed little brass hawk's bells and tortoiseshell rattles on their leggings, and it seemed to him that this season particularly, he could hear them coming far before they were actually near him. Like a scent on the wind, the sounds of women moving all round the village made him alert and prickly as a buck. It seemed to him that suddenly, women were everywhere, all round him at once, distracting, annoying, and fascinating.

He listened for the soft ringing and clicking under their skirts as they moved about the huts and readied for the dance. It was as though they were different creatures, somehow, and his ears were attuned to every rattle and jingle, his eyes curious to see beneath their long, ruffled skirts to the source of that mysterious, enticing noise.

The night of the dancing came, and all day, Billy and two other initiates had been helping Arpeika prepare the fire and the Black Drink while the women lined up, bringing their families' old clothes and pots and pans and baskets to be burned. They left baskets of corn and squash to be blessed and added to the feast, and small boys with torches ran from Arpeika's fire to the surrounding *chekes*, taking the new year's fire to the huts. By morning, each house would be cleansed, newly blessed and warmed, and the cycle would begin again.

Arpeika helped the boys to paint their faces in the colors of approaching manhood. Now, Billy had his *sabia*, his personal medicine and his spirit guide. He had proven himself in the wilderness. By tonight, he would prove himself before all of his people as a man. He prayed silently that he would not shame himself, his grandmother, and the watching spirit of Mad New Town.

The men of the village gathered as night moved over the settlement, each of them in his brightest turban, his finest ruffled shirt, wearing white egret plumes about his head. At the middle of the village square sat the large black kettle balanced on four logs which radiated outward in a star. The fire beneath the kettle had been burning for days, brewing the Black Drink made from the roasted leaves of the cassina plant, a potion which could kill a man if he drank too much, intoxicate him surely, and perhaps, if he were fortunate, empower him with vision and strength. It was a much-coveted honor among the men to have the job of pushing the logs forward as they burned in the star fire, so that the brew never stopped frothing.

Under Arpeika's direction, Billy carried a full gourd of the dark-colored, strong-smelling liquid to the men's shed, where the clan gathered, and he handed it to the leader of the Snake clan, who had brought his people the farthest from the north. As the man lifted the gourd to his mouth and drank, Billy sang out the high-pitched cry of the Black Drink Ceremony, keeping his voice as strong and unwavering as he could. It was an honor to be chosen as Black Drink Singer of the other initiates, an honor to be so singled out by Arpeika, and he kept his face immobile as he sang, so that the red and black paint which divided his face into two halves, that of the past and the future, the child and the man, would be undisturbed.

As soon as the man finished the gourd, he immediately spewed up a high, copious stream of it into the air more than ten paces long. The ceremony was officially begun. As Billy continued to sing, the other boys brought more gourds until each man had his drink, each had spewed, and many were on their second or third rounds. Then they began to drink and spew in unison, each trying to project his vomitus farther than the next, while the women watched and chanted the blessings and the children judged the lengths of the dark stains in the sand with excited glee, each one certain that his own relations were the strongest projectors.

For three hours or more into the night, they drank and chanted until Billy's voice was hoarse from singing the high, descending cry which signaled each man's quaffing and spewing, each man's refill. His hands shook from holding the heavy gourds, and he longed to get away from the noise and the clamor and the crowds watching his every move, but he knew that he must perform each task diligently and make no mistake.

Then Arpeika stepped forward and touched Billy on his shoulder. He cried out, "This man who has sixteen summers has achieved his spirit quest, honored his spirit guide, and has earned the right to become an ordinary warrior. His man-title shall be *Asi-Yaholo!*" The men chanted their blessing in unison while Arpeika shouted Billy's new name three times, and then the other boys received their names as well.

Billy stood proudly, dazzled by the singular honor Arpeika had bestowed on him. *Asi-Yaholo*, Black Drink Singer, was far more important a name than he had hoped for, certainly more than White Heron or Big Fish or Fast Runner, the names of some of the others. It was a name of leadership, of great beauty, of power. He bowed his head and prayed to his spirit guide, Otter, that he would be worthy of such faith. He looked up at the circle of women watching the ceremony, searching for his mother and his grandmother, singing along now with the men as the new men were welcomed into the tribes of the people.

He took the gourd Arpeika offered him, drank down a large draught of the Black Drink, and instantly broke out in a sweat, a wave of nausea washing over him like a salty tide. He forced himself to take another, willing his gorge not to rise. And then, he could hold it back no longer, but spewed forth powerfully, vomiting a high arc of black liquid into the air and splashing on the already-soaked earth round the men's hut.

His grandmother caught his eye and grinned at him, her eyes glistening in the firelight with pride. His mother smiled softly, dropping her head before him as she might before a grown man, a suitor. His eyes were watering with nausea and effort to keep from reeling, but he kept his face very still, betraying no emotion. His heart was swollen with gratitude and joy. He sensed Mad New Town's spirit hovering over him, and he whispered, "Thank you, Great-uncle, for your teachings and your blessings. I will bring great honor on your name."

He heard Mad New Town's reply in his soul: "Bring great honor on your own, man of my blood."

Now the drums started up, and the men scattered to the four corners of the square, the loud, deep voices leading the women into the Green Corn Ceremony dance song. The women sang in high ululations, like soaring birds, and all eyes turned to the east, where, from the darkness, they knew the dancers would come. Suddenly, in unison and with loud clamor and cries, the *estelusti,* the blacks of the tribes, danced into the square.

They were dressed in their feathers and painted leathers, some of them in headdresses and masks which they recalled from their home across the great water in Africa, before they had been stolen by the white men for their death ships. Some of them were from fierce tribes like the Mandingo or the Ashanti, others were so long taken from their homelands, they no longer remembered their old selves. Until the dances began. And then it seemed that every black face in the village recalled the songs, the pulsing beat of dances their people had performed for hundreds of years, many many hundreds of miles away.

The women circled the square with the men close behind them, so that each danced with a partner, something the Indians never did. The strangeness of men dancing so close to the women gave the black writhing bodies a beauty and power that was exotic and sexual and mysterious, and the people swayed to the beats of the drums, adding their voices to the black voices, as the women shivered and shook, as the men leaped into the air very close to them, whirling and stamping like a herd of wild horses.

When their dance was done, the women of the tribes stepped forward, starting their slow, stately, sinuous snake dance round the circle, lifting their bare arms to the dark heavens, calling for the benedictions of the Maker of Breath on this new year's harvests.

Billy, now Asi-Yaholo, stood watching the women, transfixed by their grace and beauty. They swirled by him, a moving assault on his senses, of dark gleaming skin, black whirling hair, dancing feet, jingling bells, high, lovely voices—until he felt dizzied by the beauty, the power, the drink in the near-empty gourd he still held in his hand.

And then from the fringe of the dancing women, he saw a young girl moving with her comrades, slightly taller than the others, lithe as a willow, her hair long down her back near to the middle of her legs. Her face was slender and partially hidden by the shadows and her paint, but he could see she was lovely, and his heart began to beat so quickly that he felt a faintness. He put out one hand to lean against the nearest tree, and as she whirled by, he followed her with hungry eyes.

Now, for a moment or two, the rest of the women faded away like a diminished sunset, and he could see only her. As she moved within the circle, he craned his neck to keep her in sight, setting down his gourd finally and changing position in the circle so that he might still see her. The drums beat faster and faster, the women stomped round the circle with more frenzy, and finally, finally, the drums came to an abrupt stop, and the women separated into their own clan groups, laughing and embracing each other.

Asi-Yaholo moved closer to her, suddenly unsure what he should do. She glanced at him approaching, dropped her head, and the nearest girl to her laughed and moved away. He was standing before her without even knowing how he got there. He said, "My name is Asi-Yaholo, Black Drink Singer."

"I know who you are," she said softly.

"You are so ... beautiful." He sighed then, unable to think of anything more clever to say to her.

She smiled softly up at him. Without another word, she took his hand and led him into the darker shadows, and the bewitching rattle of the hawk's bells on her leggings was the only sound as the noise and clamor of the village fell away behind them like a cloak he discarded. He was vaguely aware that the drums had started up again, that the dancers were dancing, that the feast had started, that he should likely be somewhere else, doing something else, but the moving woman before him was all he cared for in this moment, and some part of his brain noted that she could have led him to the mouth of a gator, and he would surely have followed.

Just a little ways from the firelight, she stopped and turned to him, waiting silently.

"What is your name?" he asked her.

"Quick Water," she murmured. "Of the Bear clan."

He knew instantly that she was not a woman he could marry, then, was not of his clan or a related clan. But she was very close to him in the darkness, and the scents of her oiled skin, of her fragrant hair, were all round him like a warm sea. He reached out and touched her cheek, marveling at its smoothness. She quivered under his touch, but she did not run. He drew her closer with the slightest pressure on her shoulder, and she hesitated, swaying into him slightly. He waited, knowing somehow that if she did not come to him willingly, he could not please her anyway. Finally, she swayed nearer, and came so close that the rise and fall of her breasts were visible to him in the dark, her breath beating in his ears like the waves on a beach. He reached out then and embraced her, drawing her down to the soft moss at their feet, pulling her so close that his skin melded to hers from the heat, the dampness, and their desire.

Later, as they walked back into the firelight, she shyly let go of his hand and waved to him, walking back to her clan sisters with a smile. She did not ask him to join her fire, nor did she seem to expect to stay by his side. They had been closer in flesh than he had ever experienced with another person in his life, then she was gone. He was both saddened and jubilant, all at once, and he glanced about him to see if anyone had noticed.

His grandmother was watching him from the bench nearest the men's shed, grinning at him like a baked gar. "You are come!" she called out gaily to her grandson.

He smiled sheepishly. "I am," he said.

"And was the minx worth missing the dance?" she asked archly, pretending outrage.

He nodded. "There will be other dances," he said, attempting to sound as wise as he should for his new-man status.

She snorted. "There will be more minxes than dances."

Arpeika came up then, and she subsided. "It is time for you to come to council," he said solemnly. "The men are meeting by the fires of the Panther clan when the feasting is done." He walked off then to give his message to the others.

Asi-Yaholo nodded to his grandmother as his mother approached, carrying an empty basket, one which had only moments before held the soft corn bread he so relished. "I am gone to the men," he said.

"But you have not feasted," his mother said.

"Ay, he has!" Ochola chuckled. "Leave his belly to the care of his Turtle-head, and he will soon be winnowed down to a starveling."

Asi-Yaholo grinned at them. "It was worth it."

"There speaks a man!" Ochola laughed. "Once wet, he's happy as a heron in a puddle."

The laughter of his grandmother followed him as he strode through the village now, toward the fires of the Panther clan. He was not hungry, was not thirsty, needed absolutely nothing of the body to make him any more content. He felt an electric tingling through his flesh, moving over his skin, and he knew that the power of the woman was on him still. Now, indeed, he was a man, he told himself. He walked taller, noticing that other eyes followed his progress, other hands lifted to salute him, and mouths turned up in approving smiles as he passed.

He noticed, too, that some of the smiles were directed his way by other girls, other dancers who now stood by their mothers' fires and wished, perhaps, for company. He nodded to them, knowing in that moment that he could have another, if he so chose. But he did not. He chose to be with the men, now. The women would be for later. That knowledge, he sensed, was what made the difference between a man and a new-man. He stepped into the firelight of the Panther clan, where the men were gathering, his head high, his heart strong and centered in the sureness of his right to be there.

* * *

A small drake with a distinctive crest and a slender, pointed bill was paddling on a beaver-dammed cove upriver from the Seminole village. He was a hooded merganser, *Lophodytes cucullatus*, in name, called by the Seminoles the Frog Duck because his courtship call sounded like that of a pickerel frog and could be heard a half mile away.

Mergan was making that call now, for he was two years old and ready to breed. One of the more beautiful of ducks, with a large white, fan-shaped, black-bordered crest and a white breast with two black stripes, Mergan was also one of the fewest in the swamp. It was getting harder and harder to find breeding females, and the need to find his mate was now feeling more imperative than feeding.

Mergan filled the beaver pond with the sound of his croaks, glancing about restlessly to see who might answer. After circling the pond carefully, he was about ready to give up and fly to another waterway, when he heard the faint call of a female. He flew excitedly toward the call, landing in a shallow streamlet which fed into the beaver pond. The female floated on the water, a small gray-brown duck with her head and crest like his, only warmer brown. She saw him coming and bobbed her head, pointed her bill downward to the water, and uttered a hoarse "gack!"

Mergan became more excited still, for this was the signal of a female ready to mate. He raised his crest and shook his head, gave his froglike call, and dropped his bill to the water also, imitating her movements. For an hour or more, they moved over the water, repeating their calls and their bobbings, and then he mounted her quickly, covering her with his wings, staying afloat and upon her by flapping them as best he could, and spent his seed within her.

When the breeding was finished, Mergan swam to the shallow water, caught a small crayfish, and brought it back to present to his mate. She took the creature, eyed it carefully, and swallowed it down. In the manner of mergansers, then, they were now bound to each other for the season.

A month later, Mergan's mate had selected a small hollow cavity in a cypress tree, lined it with white down from her breast, and deposited eight small white eggs, the beginning of Mergan's first family. Unsure what to do, he busied himself diving into the shallow water, bringing up caddis fly larvae and dragonfly nymphs which were plentiful in this month of March, as spring was coming fast to the swamp.

But no matter how much food he brought her, his mate was still unwilling to set the eggs constantly. Restless and brooding, she was often absent from the nest when he came back to it. He tried to pull moss and leaves over the eggs, but when she returned, she only scolded him and pulled the debris off again.

Mergan knew it was time for him to leave his mate and the nest, sensed that he should be finding new territory of his own, but he was unwilling to leave the nest until he saw that the eggs were hatched. He did not know what would happen at that time, but he could not abandon them.

The swamp was verdant by the time the eggs hatched, and the bladderwort and milfoil were thick and green in the warm, shallow waters. The moon rolled round again, full and bright, and the next morning, the eggs began to crack. Mergan watched expectantly from a fallen log near the cypress tree, listening and cocking his head with each sound of splitting and peeping coming from the nest.

His mate called to the ducklings as they began to emerge, one by one, wet and rolled in downy yellow fuzz, blinking and half-blinded by the light. They wobbled to their feet, shaking the dampness from their bodies, pecking at pieces of eggshell still attached to their brothers, until finally all eight of them were wriggling and flopping about the nest. Mergan approached cautiously, so curious to see the source of the nest noises that he was momentarily unwary. His mate flew at him in a rage as he came near, pecking him sharply about the head and crest, and he instantly backed away, hunkered down on the fallen log, and waited.

By the time the sun was high, his mate emerged from the nest at last, with the ducklings in a line behind her. Without a glance of Mergan, she led them immediately to the shallow water and plunged in, expecting them to follow. The first duckling hesitated, calling loudly to his mother, and the rest milled about on the shore, unwilling to push past him. She did not look back, nor did she slow down, but continued to paddle away from them. Finally, in desperation, the first duckling, the largest male, leaped into the water and struggled to keep afloat. Then the second jumped in behind him, the third, and finally all eight ducklings were in the water, calling anxiously and trying to reach their mother.

Mergan wanted to paddle in among them, call to them for reassurance, and somehow help them get to where she was, but he knew if he approached his brood, she would turn on him, so he stayed back, unable to muster the courage to go closer. He watched them as they managed to right themselves in the water, awkwardly begin to paddle toward where she was feeding in the shallows, and form a line in the water, moving in her direction. When the ducklings reached her, they surrounded her like the petals on a flower, clustering as close to her as they dared, peeping and bobbing up and down with every small current and wavelet on the stream.

After feeding for a while, Mergan's mate slowly paddled out farther into the river where the water was deeper, still apparently unconcerned about whether they might follow her or not. Mergan, still watching from his sheltered cove while he searched for darters and minnows, saw with alarm that the path his mate had chosen took her close to a small alligator sleeping in the shallows, his eyes and upper snout gleaming in the sun.

He moved closer, ruffling his feathers and quacking at his mate, trying to get her attention. She turned away from him, however, shook her tail, and called to the ducklings to follow her. Now they were moving steadily across the water, his mate and the eight ducklings all in a row, and the alligator submerged quietly, no longer visible from where Mergan paddled.

Mergan took to the air, calling in fear, for he knew that a submerged alligator was far more dangerous than one he could see. Like all his kin, he was one of the fastest ducks in the swamp in flight, one of the slowest on the ground or on the water, and so he was able to circle the pond twice, quacking to his mate all the while, urging her to safety. To his dismay, however, she did not regard him but only kept steadily swimming toward the shore, leading the ducklings behind her.

Mergan circled a bent and twisted oak in time to see the alligator rise swiftly to the surface behind the last duckling. The great jaws opened slightly, the alligator overtook the duckling, and Mergan beat his wings desperately, croaking loudly, swooping down toward the water, and landing as close as he dared to the ripples to one side of the moving jaws. With a great beating of wings and splashing, Mergan scattered the ducklings out of their single-file formation, and the alligator sank beneath the shallow water. Ahead, Mergan saw that his mate had reached the bank and was placidly grazing on young, spring grass, while the remaining ducklings piled out of the water and onto the sandy shore beside her.

Mergan banked over the pond, saw that the alligator was once more submerged and the ducklings out of range for the moment, and then landed in the live oak, croaking dismally. His heart was pounding with fear and anger, and he wanted nothing more than to fly away from this hammock of bent grass and twisted trees forever, never to look back. He knew instinctively that he should have been gone weeks before, knew, too, that his mate would soon leave the ducklings as soon as they could swim and dive and feed by themselves. Then they would forage together, surviving as best they could, until they could fly.

It would be the most perilous time of their lives, and his presence would not alter their fate or change his mate's behavior in any way. He bobbed his crest and shook his feathers as though he had been submerged for a good while, trying to shake the fear away. He preened himself vigorously, all the while gazing down on his mate and his ducklings, who foraged up and down the bank with never a glance in his direction.

Finally, Mergan settled himself, took a quick appraisal of the sun's position, and spread his wings. He would leave them, then, to whatever was coming. It was time. Past time. He took to the air, circled the pond once, croaking a farewell, and then turned toward the moving sun, flying a half mile or so until he came to another body of water, a wide prairie of half-submerged brush and yellow-flowered tickweed. He skidded on the water with a great splash of wings and webbed feet, and settled himself to feeding. Once, he heard a scrabble in the brush, glanced up, and then bent again to diving for minnows. When he came up again, he did not see the arrow which came from brush, only felt a piercing agony as it entered his neck, driving him down into the water, glazing his eyes, and filling his lungs.

Mergan did not see or hear the approaching man in the dugout canoe, nor did he feel the rough hands which plucked him out of the water, withdrew the arrow, and laid his body in the hunting sack.

* * *

General Andrew Jackson had often reassured his Congress and his president that the Seminole War was over. Despite his confirmations of victory, however, the settlers in Georgia and Florida saw that over the next five years the Indians still held vast tracts of land, good arable land, along both coasts and in the interior of Florida.

Furthermore, escaped slaves kept streaming into the scattered settlements, and slave owners all over the South clamored for a removal of the Indians to some other place.

The *mikalgee*, the leaders of the clans, counseled their people to outwait Old Mad Jackson. They reasoned that it would take the whites at least as long to move against them as it had taken them to agree to do so. Moreover, how could they be removed when they could scarcely be found? Their numbers included the Hitchiti who had been there first, the recently arrived Red-Stick clans, Spanish Indians on the Gulf Coast, Yuchis, Shawnees, Choctaws, Muskogee, and other Mikasuki clans who claimed none of those as authority, all of them in small villages scattered through the swamps and the river lands of the wilderness.

Jackson said no treaty was necessary. He had beaten them, he said, and they must go where ordered to go. But the United States Senate wanted a treaty. Having promised five million dollars to Spain in the Adams-Onis Treaty two years before for the acquisition of Florida, the Senate had yet to pay its bill. How better to get the money than to have the Indians give up their lands so that those lands could be sold and thereby provide the necessary cash for the United States to fulfill its treaty obligations?

But it all must be done legally. Antislavery advocates and reformers, bleeding hearts, and Methodist ladies would insist upon it. A treaty must be signed. To have a treaty, a leader of these disassociated factions of tribes must be found to sign it. So in September 1823, Governor William Duval appointed one of the Lower Creek chiefs, Neamathla, supreme chief of all the Seminoles and brought him with his delegation to Moultrie Creek outside Saint Augustine to sign a paper that would bind the entire Indian nation.

Neamathla, surprised to find himself annointed king, had little to recommend him to either side except that he could be bribed. He was an aged Hitchiti chief, a village factor, and an owner of slaves. He had long maintained that the Seminoles must stay independent of the whites, but he, himself, had retired to a life of ease outside Tallahassee.

But he had been appointed supreme head, so he painted himself white, performed the eagle-tail dance, and smoked the calumet with his delegation. Then he met with Governor Duval, James Gadsden, Bernard Segui, and the other commissioners, saw that their soldiers were many, accepted their presents of food, money, and rum, and signed away twenty-eight million acres of Florida for less than a penny an acre in exchange for four million acres of swampland in the interior, at least a day's hard march from either coast.

The treaty was to last for twenty years, the monies were to be paid out in yearly annunites, and at the end of twenty years, the Indians would relocate to lands west of the Mississippi.

When Arpeika and the other leaders heard of Neamathla's betrayal, they spoke of putting a death sentence on the old man's head. The young warriors, Asi-Yaholo among them, were ready to form an assassination party, but the elders' anger was calmed by the new-men's rage, and soon the old ones were saying to the young warriors, "You are headstrong. You are not wise in the way of men at war." And so the young men subsided in humiliation.

The elders conferred. It was finally agreed that they would protest the treaty formally and wait to see what the white men would do, while they explored the interior lands assigned to them to see if they could be acceptable. Not everyone agreed, of course, and factions immediately split away, vowing to fight the usurping pale eyes forever.

The survey crews came into the wilderness first. Men unused to the tangled cypress forests of the swamps tried to set up their tripods where little land was dry, much less firm. They had to drag their transits and chains through jungles of saw grass and hack their way into hammocks so thick with brush that they could not make fifty feet in one day. They cut their clothing and then their skin on the palmetto and saw grass, they lost their temper and patience from the mosquito and chigger bites, and they grew ill with fever, dysentery, and infected wounds. But they kept moving deeper and deeper into the swamp, sometimes not making more than a mile in one week.

The clans did not know whether to plant their crops or sell their cattle, so some did neither, some did both. When the storms of 1824 washed away the crops, they hunted more deer, but so did the settlers who came right behind and ahead of the surveyors. In 1825, the rains were replaced by a year-long drought, and once again, the corncribs were barren. Some clans sent emissaries to the white governor for food; others said they would rather starve than take the white man's rations. Many gradually began to do so.

It was at this bleak time of confusion and degradation that Asi-Yaholo was asked by Arpeika to accompany the main party of surveyors into the swamp.

Leaving the village was then the farthest thing from his mind, for Asi-Yaholo had discovered love for the first time in his twenty years. It happened on an otherwise unremarkable evening, and ever after, when he looked back on the moment, he would remember that it was the first time in his life not only for love, but also for complete agreement between his body and his heart.

Since he had become a man, he often shared the pleasures of women in his village, and he was quickly initiated into the complexities of desire. The girls of other clans watched him when he played the ball game with the other men, and they laughed winningly when he followed the ball into their midst to retrieve it, lifting their long ruffled skirts in mock alarm and smiling at him under lowered lashes. He noticed that they sometimes found occasion to be on the hunting trails as he was going and coming to the village, or they would wander out to the herds when he was tending his grandmother's cattle. And always, they smiled at him in such a way as to make him think that they found him good to look upon.

Soon, he no longer was surprised to look up and see a girl in his near vicinity, even if he had gone to the river to bathe. Some were bolder than others, and he followed them willingly, eagerly, when they took him by the hand and led him into secret glades and bowers to share pleasure with him, when he should have been hunting or fishing or rounding up his grandmother's hogs from the swamp.

But after the pleasures, the complexities began. If he enjoyed a girl once, she usually believed he should enjoy her again. And if he enjoyed her again, she began to expect that he would soon call at her mother's hut and discuss a more permanent arrangement. Then he must endure her anger or sadness when he did not, and it seemed to him that there were more and more girls of the settlement who watched him now with sideways glances when he passed by, their eyes spiteful and jealous or downcast and dispirited.

He talked often with his friends, Alligator and Mad Dog, two other new-men from different clans, and they both agreed that women were nearly as perverse as the pale eyes.

"If you pursue them, like a hunter with a deer, they run. The moment you stop pursuing, they turn and accost you like a wounded bear," Alligator said, shaking his head in bewilderment. "If you take what they wish to give you, they are only pleased for the moment, and if you say then after that your stomach is no longer hungry for that particular meat, they tell their friends that you are a miserable hound."

"Which does not stop their friends from wanting to see for themselves," Asi-Yaholo said morosely. The three were sitting on the side of the river astraddle a fallen live oak, more or less fishing for bream and more or less doing little at all save pondering their troubles.

"Ha!" snorted Mad Dog. "The more one woman says you are not worth spitting upon, the more the others' mouths water to the task!"

"That is true," sighed Alligator. "When I told Green Apple that I would no longer meet her after the evening fires as I had, she told anyone who would listen that I had a heart colder than a rattler's." He smiled wistfully. "I was never more popular."

"Why do they say they wish to share pleasure," Asi-Yaholo asked, "and then act as if it was something they were tricked into doing?"

"Like old Neamathla," Mad Dog scoffed, mimicking both an ancient man's quaver and the high treble of a girl all at once, "Oh please, pale eyes, I will be honored to sign your papers and take your silver beads"— here Mad Dog used the old-fashioned word for white man's money which had long ago fallen out of use—"but oh! I surely never thought you meant to take my lands! I thought you meant only to *share* them with me!"

The men laughed bitterly. It did not have to be said that for them to be fishing for bream was enough evidence of how far the clans had fallen. It was a task for the young boys, not warriors. But food must be had, game was scarce, and so anything at all they could catch was worth their time.

"It is enough to make a man's parts pull back into his sack and refuse to come out again, no matter the persuasion," Alligator said.

"Speak for your own parts, *Choontah*," Mad Dog laughed. "Mine find it worth the trouble, still."

"I also find it worth the trouble," Asi-Yaholo said. "But I sometimes wonder how a man gets to be as old as Arpeika without being made crazy by them."

"He *has* been made crazy by them," Alligator said. "All the old men have. So crazy that they will take several of them into their huts at once—"

"More than one wife!" Mad Dog held up his hands in mock defense and alarm. "That is like more than one alligator in the house. I think even one makes a mess of the bed."

The men talked thus as the late afternoon wore into the evening. And as they returned to the village with their meager catch, no fewer than three different women found reason to be in their path, some of them looking somehow surprised to be there and others beckoning to them gaily, tossing their long hair so that they looked like young, healthy mares.

Because the others were there, each man turned the girls away and stayed steadfastedly to the trails to their huts, but Asi-Yaholo guessed that Mad Dog would go back and find at least one of them; Alligator might try for two.

He asked his mother that evening over the roasted fish, "Are women taught to make men crazy, or do they all do it as naturally as birds fly?"

Peeping laughed softly and handed him a bowl of warm *sofkee*. "We do it naturally," she said. "And we get better at it as we get older."

Asi-Yaholo groaned.

"Are they plaguing you, my son?" she asked. "If so, take a wife, and your torment will end."

"And so will the fire in your belly," his grandmother added as she approached the fire with an armload of palmetto leaves for weaving. She laughed at Asi-Yaholo, who sat with his face in his hands, and gave him a soft kick with her bare foot. "You need some real problems to fret you, O Moaner, and then you will be grateful for these little inconveniences."

"Little inconveniences!" Asi-Yaholo replied. "I can scarcely come or go without a skirt before my feet, yet on the other hand it seems that half the girls in the village think I'm as welcome as Old Mad Jackson at their fire. Why don't they leave me alone?"

"Because they find you good to look upon," said his mother gently. "You are strong and comely, and your body is finely made as a young beech."

"And rare as snake feet," Ochola said. "There should be more than a hundred new-men this season, and there are only a dozen. When I was a girl, the young men fought over us like bees over a blossom—"

"When you were a young girl," Asi-Yaholo said morosely, "Old Mad Jackson's grandfather was an egg."

"When *I* was a girl, men did not wail and whine like starveling pups, but did what men do with relish." Her eyes gleamed. "I am old, but still, I remember well enough—"

"Peace, Mother," Peeping said quietly. "I do not think our son needs to hear of your many coups beneath the blankets."

"No, it would only make him green as spring oranges. If you are finished whimpering, pup, go over to the Snake clan fire. Sleeping Bear caught one of my hogs today in his *cheke,* and he says he will roast it up proper if it's not retrieved by the time he goes to his bed."

Asi-Yaholo rose wearily then and walked through the village to the fires of the Snake people, a distantly related clan which had only just arrived several days before from the north. It was said among the settlement that they would be moving on soon, just as quickly as they could rest their women and children and fill their storebags with enough food for their journey.

His mother had changed so much, he thought, since she had taken a new husband. Wed to one of the older warriors from the Alligator clan, she was remarkably more peaceful, more gentle, and happier at her fire. Her husband was rarely with her, it seemed, so often was he off hunting with his clan brothers. But just to know that he would come to her hammock when he returned seemed to make all the difference to Peeping. Ochola had been right. She was a woman who needed a man. Perhaps all women were like his mother in some hidden way which he did not yet understand.

As he thought of this, he came upon the fires of the Snake, set apart slightly from the rest of the huts. He came up to the largest fire, wondering which hut confined his grandmother's pig, and he saw a young woman standing near, slightly turned away from him. At the noise of his approach, she turned suddenly to face him, her lips slightly parted in surprise.

Asi-Yaholo stopped so quickly that he swayed. She was tall and slender, and her black hair fell down her shoulders to the middle of her back like the shining hide of a mink. She glanced at him and then away, and he felt his stomach arch and flip and light somewhere about his throat. She was the most lovely woman he had ever seen.

"I am come," he said in the normal greeting of his people.

"Yes, you are," she replied courteously. "You have come for your grandmother's pig?"

He hesitated. She knew who he was, then. "You are the daughter of Sleeping Bear?"

"His granddaughter," she said.

He flushed. Of course, if he had his wits about him, he would have known this. He stared at her, feeling as though he was moving through waist-deep water in a dream. He could not believe that he had never seen her before, in this crowded settlement of huts in which every person knew and was known by most every other person, but it was true. She was a stranger. And then he realized with a start that he had said nothing for such a long moment, she must think him either stupid or rude.

"I am Asi-Yaholo," he said, his throat thick with nervousness.

"I know who you are," she said.

He cursed his stupidity silently. "May I know your name?"

She glanced away, hesitating. Then she looked back again, directly at him. And she smiled softly. "I am called Morning Dew. My mother is Stamping Crane, of the Snake."

He smiled as confidently as he could. "I apologize for my grandmother's hog." He tried for wit. "He pays no more heed to boundaries than my grandmother does." And again, he was instantly furious with himself, for she did not smile.

"Your grandmother does not have your respect?" It was a mild question, but the soft rebuke was unmistakable. How could he have said such a thing to a woman, who likely loved and respected her own grandmother as much as she did her own mother?

He decided on honest contrition. "I made only a small, weak jest," he said quietly. "I am unable to think when I look at you. Please forgive my clumsiness."

She smiled then, teasingly. "Your animal awaits you, Asi-Yaholo." She led him to the rear of the hut where his grandmother's hog was tethered.

He took hold of the hog's rope and coaxed him in a way which he hoped would display great patience and gentle firmness. He cleared his throat and said, "I would like to come to your fire again, Morning Dew, granddaughter of Sleeping Bear. May I do so?"

She hesitated again, glancing away.

He dropped his head, unable to let her see his despair. She was the first woman he had ever seen who made him feel in this way, and the possibility that she might not welcome him was nearly unbearable.

"Next evening," she finally said softly, "my mother will welcome you, Asi-Yaholo." She said nothing more but turned and went into the shadows of the hut, leaving him outside, holding his pig.

He walked away slowly, pondering her words. Her mother would welcome him. But she would not? What did this mean? Was he someone she might consider? Could she already have found another? That thought plunged him into such turmoil that he scarcely saw a single fire or hut before he found himself back before his mother's fire once more. Grandmother and Peeping still sat where he had left them, and he wondered briefly how it was that the hut, the women, the night, the world, looked the same when he felt so immeasurably altered. He tied up the pig with the others at the rear of the hut and sat down gingerly before the fire, gazing into the flames.

"You saw her, then," his grandmother said with no preamble. It was not a question.

He glanced up, surprised. "You sent me for that purpose?"

She laughed, shaking her head. "You must be more aware of quicksand, boy, and ambushes. The soldiers or the swamp will get you, else, one of them for sure."

"Have you seen her, Mother?"

She smiled. "I have taken a walk in that direction, yes."

"Is she not beautiful?" He grinned then, full of the joy of his discovery.

"Passable," his grandmother said. "She is of the Snake clan, of course, but a different set of fires than ours, and the women of those fires are mean as their namesake. But since you have worn out your welcome with most of the others within walking distance, I thought perhaps—"

"Does she have a suitor?" he interrupted impatiently.

"Of course," Ochola said shortly.

"She told me that her mother would make me welcome tomorrow night," he said with some bewilderment. "What does that mean?"

"It is their custom, that clan," Ochola said. "I told you the women were difficult. You go, you meet the mother. If the mother finds you acceptable, she will perhaps call her daughter to the fire. That is, if her daughter has told her she might entertain your presence. If not, she will not call her daughter, she will merely pay you courteous compliments, and wait for you to take your leave. Then she and her daughter will make mock of you behind your back." Ochola laughed, a bark of derision.

"Her name is *Chechote*. Morning Dew," Asi-Yaholo said wonderingly, scarcely hearing his grandmother's teasing. "It suits her. She is the most lovely woman I have ever seen."

Peeping raised one eyebrow delicately. "And you have seen them all, my son."

He flushed for the second time that evening. "I shall go there tomorrow night," he said, with as strong a voice as he could muster. "And if she will have me, I will send a betrothal gift to her mother as soon as she will accept it."

"You won't take pleasure with her first?" Ochola laughed.

He shook his head. "Not this one."

Peeping shook her head gently. "Ah, my son—"

"And what if she is dry and brittle as last year's pine straw?" his grandmother grinned. "How will you console your Turtle-head then, O Lusty One?"

"She will not be," he said confidently. "I know that much, at least."

"You know nothing," Ochola scoffed. "But you will soon know more than you bargain for, if I know the Snake women."

The next night, Asi-Yaholo waited impatiently for the suppers to be finished, for the fires to grow quiet from the bustle and conversation of eating, for the children to retreat to their beds and the men to gather for their smokes. Then he walked with his head high, hoping to show far more confidence than he felt, to the fires of the Snake clan at the far side of the settlement.

He had bathed very carefully that afternoon, and then spent hours braiding fragrant balsam into his hair. He wore only his knife at his waist and his leggings were blindingly white and clean in the shadows. He had put a single white egret plume in his hair also, but then took it out, not wishing to seem too vain. But he looped his best many-colored beads round his chest, and the embroidered vest he wore had all the varied hues of the flowers.

Not a few female eyes followed him as he crossed the village, but he did not waver from his course nor glance to one side or the other. In that way, he hoped that others might mention to the mother of Morning Dew that he was thinking of no one but her daughter, before he was even within her reach. As he walked, he was filled with a sense of rightness, of inner serenity. It did not matter if her mother found him pleasing, he told himself, for he would win the woman herself, with or without her mother's approval. The smell of *coontie*, the soft pudding made from the ground-up roots of the arrowroot plant, wafted out to him from the hut as he came round the corner, and he saw that he was to be made welcome, at least.

An older woman sat by the fire, stirring the large pot of pudding. She looked up at him and smiled. He could see in her face some of the beauty of Morning Dew, a softened, looser version of the girl's angled jaw and her high cheeks. There was nothing soft about the mother's eyes, however, and Asi-Yaholo knew immediately that he would have to be at his best.

"I am come," he said courteously.

"You are," she replied, gesturing to a log beside her. "Would you take some nourishment, warrior?" She used the word for ordinary warrior, *tastanagee*, and he was pleased. "I am Stamping Crane," she said, "of the clan of Snake."

He bowed his head briefly at her introduction, nodding at the bowl of *coontie* she passed him. He balanced it carefully on his knee. "I am Asi-Yaholo," he said, "grandnephew of Mad New Town, grandson of Ocholo."

"Your granduncle was known to me," she said mildly, not meeting his gaze. "A man of wisdom and strength." And then she cocked her head and grinned. "Many women, also, if I am not mistaken."

Asi-Yaholo laughed in surprise, suddenly liking this mother very much. He shook his head ruefully. "I was too young to know of such things," he said. "But my grandmother still tells the tales . . ."

Silently, she watched him as he ate his mush. Of course, he scarcely tasted it, but he knew to leave it unenjoyed would have indicated that he was unwilling to eat at her fire, a grave slight. He smacked his lips decorously, scraped the bowl as he finished, and belched with appreciation.

She smiled teasingly. "You have met my daughter, Morning Dew?" she asked innocently.

"I have," he said. "But only briefly."

"She is the most beautiful girl in the village," she said easily. "The loveliest one in our clan."

He knew that any mother was expected to praise her daughter, and he knew, also, that such praise was designed to make her more valuable in any suitor's eyes. A clever negotiator would either mention that another girl was an excellent cook or was unusually clever at weaving or would say nothing at all. He would do neither, however. "She is the most beautiful woman I have ever seen," he admitted.

"And coming from your granduncle's nephew, I would say you have seen more than your share," she said.

He dropped his head in seemly silence. Let her think he had seen every woman in the Floridas, he thought, so long as she knew that of all of them, he had chosen her daughter.

"Do you think of going farther south?" she asked suddenly.

He glanced up, surprised. It was, of course, the custom of his people that the man left his mother's fire and went to his wife's mother's people. He had simply assumed that Stamping Crane would wish him to do so; that such a choice was the price to be paid for her daughter.

He thought quickly. This branch of the Snake clan had most recently left the white man's borders, fleeing south to this settlement. Likely this mother wanted her daughter as far away from them as possible. He decided in that moment to take a chance. "I will go south to the wilderness," he said firmly, "as far as I must to keep from the whites. If the land they have given us is good enough, I shall make my home there. If not, I shall go to the edge of the sea to keep from them." He set down the empty bowl, indicating he was finished with courtesies. "If I learned anything at all from Mad New Town, I learned this much. The whites mean to share this land with no one, not even the birds who fly above it or the ants who dig beneath it."

She smiled grimly. "Perhaps you would like to speak to my daughter a while." She glanced back into the shadows of the hut, and Asi-Yaholo realized that, of course, Morning Dew had been listening to every word. She came forward quietly, with the careful, graceful step of a doe.

He stood as she came into the firelight, dropping his gaze. She seemed even more beautiful to him now than she had on the previous night. He was suddenly breathless and very afraid. Every word, every gesture mattered now. Stamping Crane melted back into the shadows, but he knew that she would not be far away.

Morning Dew took her mother's seat on the log, turned to him, and smiled shyly.

"I am come," she said gently.

"You are," he murmured. "If I would speak freely," he added, hesitating, "I would tell you that this man is very glad."

She was silent.

"This man has thought of nothing else since he saw you last."

She lowered her eyes and took a deep breath.

"This man fears that perhaps another has spoken for you, and he must be, therefore, an empty man all the rest of his days."

After a long quiet moment, she said, "This man need not fear."

He let his breath out in a sigh of relief. Now he found the courage to turn and look at her more fully. "I come from a different set of fires," he began slowly. "You know of my grandfather and my granduncle. Both of them were leaders of my people."

"And you will likely be as they were," she said calmly.

"Do you think so?"

She nodded. "You speak and move with grace. You are good to look upon. You have—" Here she hesitated. "Passion in your heart and your words. You will be as they were."

"Your words are good to hear," he said, amazed at his good fortune.

"I was taught to speak the truth," she said simply.

She said all this calmly, but he thought he could perceive a tension in her body, though not in her voice. "Our people need strong leaders now," he said, "and I mean to take my place in that leadership." He hoped he did not sound too arrogant. "The whites would drive us off this land, if they could, altogether. They wish to pen us like pigs."

"Many believe it is the only way we can live with them at all."

"There are other ways," he said, his voice ominous with anger.

"You are of a people who know war well. Your clan has often said no to the pale eyes," she said sadly. "My people do not wish war. They wish only to go to lands where they can live in peace."

"There will be no peace with the whites," Asi-Yaholo said firmly then, and he surprised even himself with those words, for he had not realized that he felt so.

"Not if your leaders do not wish it," she said softly.

He looked across the fire to her fearfully. He would lose her, he knew, if they spoke only of the differences between them. Somehow, he must turn their words back to the traditional phrases of courtship, those words which would woo her to him, regardless of their contrasting beliefs about the best way to deal with the whites. He must speak to her as a man does to a woman—

"Tell me, then," she said, "where will you go, warrior? To rid yourself of these whites. To save your people."

He was struck by a powerful wave of longing for her. "I will stay where you wish to be, daughter of Stamping Crane. If you will have me."

She was silent again for a long moment. "You could never be happy with such a bargain. You are a man who must go where he will."

"I am a man who must have this woman," he said gently. "And so, I will do what I must."

She smiled at him, a barely perceptible smile of mingled triumph and surrender. "Send your grandmother to my mother's hut," she whispered. "We will let them decide." And with that, she rose and went back into the shadows of her hammock.

Asi-Yaholo stood up and strode quickly back through the village, his heart soaring with pride and joy. She would have him! He barely noticed the rest of the settlement around him, and reached his grandmother's fire as out of breath as though he had raced with the wind all the way. He strode into the light and said, "Grandmother, you must go right

away to the fire of Stamping Crane. Tell her that I offer four deer—
no! Six deer for Morning Dew!"

Ochola looked up at him with a sly grin. "Six deer. And you have
not even bedded the mink. You grow more stupid with every season,
grandson."

"Go now!" He pleaded frantically. "Before she changes her mind!"

Ochola called to Peeping, who sat quietly mending one of her skirts
by the light of the fire, a small smile on her lips. "Have you ever heard
such stupidity from a new-man? From a boy, perhaps, but not from a
man. Six deer! There are not six deer for a day's ride in all four directions
of the sun, and those which are left are hiding from the best hunters.
But this largemouth bass intends to kill six of them to impress some
silly Snake woman—"

"Will you go?" he asked again, this time with more dignity. "Or
must I see to the bride-price myself?" He knew that threat would
move his grandmother, for such a negotiation was never made by anyone
but the eldest woman of the family.

"You are addled as a sunstruck dog," Ochola yawned lazily. "But I
suppose I must go if only to save my own good name from the mockery
you will undoubtedly bring down upon it. Six deer! The Snake woman
will be lucky to get one—"

"Grandmother, I will not bargain with her like a white trader for
pelts. Give her mother whatever she asks."

"Oh, of course," Ochola said blithely. "I shall do exactly as you say,
grandson. Leave the task to me." And laughing merrily, she hauled
herself up from her log, gathering her skirts about her, and went in the
direction of the Snake clan's fires.

Asi-Yaholo sat down wearily beside his mother.

"You have decided, then? She is the woman for you?" His mother
did not look at him when she asked the question, only kept her needle
moving rhythmically in and out of the worn cotton cloth.

"I have decided," he said.

"It is not a good time to take a wife," she said gently. "The whites
are pushing us off the land, and many have barely enough food for
themselves, much less for others. We have been fortunate, for the
people will not see the daughter and sister of Mad New Town go
hungry."

"Also, my grandmother had more pigs than all the chiefs in the
territory."

"Yes," his mother smiled. "But once you go to the fires of the Snake, you must feed not only your new wife but also her people. It is not a good time."

"If you felt so, why did you send me to her fire?" he asked.

She shrugged. "It is not a good time to take a wife, but it is also not good for you to wait much longer. Soon, you will have angered most of the young women in the territory," she teased. "And then what will your grandmother do for pleasure?"

"Now that I have seen her, I cannot turn away," he said quietly. "Do you understand, my mother?"

She nodded silently and touched his knee. "Then it is the only time, even if it is not the best time."

Soon, they heard Ochola muttering to herself as she approached the fire again, and Asi-Yaholo forced himself to stay seated, to wait until she was ready to speak of her meeting.

"The mother is smarter than the daughter," Ochola finally said, groaning as she lowered herself down on the nearest log to the fire. "She knows that it would be a mistake to let you two make a union."

"What did she say?" Asi-Yaholo asked fearfully, his heart freezing in his chest.

"*I* said, it would be far better for you to bed the wench, tire yourselves of each other, and go your separate ways. She agreed."

He looked at his mother, hoping for help from that quarter. Her face was inscrutable in the shadows. "Never mind," he said then, angrily, standing up. "I will go and ask for her myself. I should have done so at the start."

Ochola laughed wearily. "I told her you would say such a thing. I told her you were addled." She shook her head with disgust, motioning him back down. "She says her daughter is similarly addled."

He felt his heart unfreeze as suddenly as it had died.

"Two deer," she said shortly. "Twice what the wench is worth. Likely it will take you a full moon just to find them, and perhaps in that time, you will come to your senses."

But he scarcely heard his grandmother. He heard only that he was accepted as a suitor. That he would bring two deer, only two deer, and she would be his.

It took seven suns up and down before Asi-Yaholo was ready to be grateful to his grandmother for setting the price at two instead of six deer. For seven suns, he had walked, and he had seen only one deer, and then not near enough to use his bow.

Where had the game gone? It was not only deer he could not see, but also fox, panther, and wolf. All the big mouths in the swamp had gone elsewhere, it seemed, perhaps following the disappearing deer. Of raccoon, skunk, squirrel, and bird, there were plenty, and he even saw the track of otter at the edge of water. But deer were few and too nervous to get close enough to kill.

Finally he decided that it was more important to go back with something, some large kill, rather than stay out another set of nights. He cut a strong straight sapling, hardened it with a slow fire, and then tied to it with leather thongs his iron hook, one of his most treasured hunting tools. He took off his breechcloth and covered his naked body with river mud. Then he painted his face with slanted, horizontal yellow stripes, so as to look more like an alligator hatchling.

Now, instead of searching the dry land for tracks which might lead to deer, he searched the wet land for trails which might lead to alligator dens. He found one at last, a wide swath in the mud which led to a hole in a steep embankment: the home of a large bull alligator. He could see that the muddy road was well used, and the width of it was a good indication of the size of the creature, likely twice his own height. Such a prize would be better than two deer, and if he could capture and kill such an alligator alone, Stamping Crane would surely be pleased to accept the trophy as a proper bride-price.

The den of the alligator was deep inside the mud bank, and he sat for a while on top of the mud, knowing that the animal was sleeping several feet beneath him. It was the heat of the day, and the gator would not be out until dusk. Not without some determined prodding.

He sang his *sabia*, prayed out loud to Otter for more than an hour, asking for strength and courage and, most especially, agility. He danced lightly on the top of the gator's den, to let him know that a man had come to hunt him, for he knew that to surprise the alligator would be impossible. Instead, he should show respect and proper preparation.

Every man understood that to hunt the alligator alone, most particularly a large bull alligator, was to invite death. The gator would be fast and angry and unafraid. If a man could pull him from his den, and that was a mighty large unknown in and of itself, the gator would try to eat him, would lash him with his tail, would even run him over in a mad dash to water, snapping his huge jaws as he went past. Normally, Asi-Yaholo's people left the largest alligators alone in peace, contenting themselves with the smaller females or the yearlings. Only the Alligator clan hunted the largest bulls, and then only for ritual occasions.

This was no yearling within this embankment. On the other hand, if he could manage to capture him, no one would ever be able to say his desire for Morning Dew was less than impressive. It was worth the risk. Especially since he would rather face death than return to the village with empty hands.

Asi-Yaholo took his sapling spear and began to prod with it into the soft mud underneath him. The embankment was yielding, and at last he was able to break through the roof of the alligator's den to what felt like unresisting air. He put his nose to the hole and took a deep snuffle of the foul, dank odor within, that of decay and wet mud and cold reptile flesh. He was within the creature's tunnel. He prodded around a bit more until he finally felt the spear touch something more firm than mud and also different. "I have found you, Elder," he murmured. "Please forgive my intrusion, but I need you to win my wife."

An answering grunt, muffled and angry, came from the mud beneath him.

"You, yourself, must have had wives aplenty," Asi-Yaholo entreated him. "I wish only one. And I must prove myself to her people. You must help me to do this." He withdrew his spear, made sure the hook was securely attached to the other end, reversed it, and plunged it down again into the widened hole he had made into the tunnel. Now he felt the hook prod the alligator's flesh. "Take it, Elder," he crooned. "Take it and come for me, then."

With a roar and a snap, the alligator bit onto the intruding hook, attempting to wrest it from the pole. Instead, the hook caught him in the jaw. Asi-Yaholo could feel him jerk it from side to side, trying to snap it loose. He could only pray that it would hold through the long battle ahead.

His plan was that the sapling spear and hook would hold the alligator in place while he dug him out from the entrance to his den. And so, he clambered down the mud embankment quickly, taking up the large freshwater clamshells he had gathered, and began to dig determinedly at the mud opening. He did not need to enlarge it much, he saw, for he could almost get his shoulders inside as it was. But he needed to be able to reach the alligator, and it was more than two times his arm's length.

Asi-Yaholo dug frantically for as long as he could, listening to the alligator fight the hook inside the den. The musty stench of the creature filled the hole and billowed out at him with every twist of the animal's body, smelling like decayed fish, cold mud, and old blood. As he dug, he explained to the alligator again that he had no choice. "If there were deer, Elder, I would not disturb your rest. But I cannot take another seven days in the hunt, and I cannot go back to the fire of Stamping Crane without a large kill in my hands. You are the largest kill for a day's walk, and so you must understand. It is your turn to die, Elder, not mine."

He dug for what seemed most of the afternoon, and as he nearly reached the end of his strength, suddenly the alligator erupted out of the tunnel, having snapped the sapling spear in two and nearly swallowed the hook. His jaw emerged first from the dark hole, and then right behind that, ten feet of hissing, roaring bull alligator came rumbling out like a runaway wagon, snapping at Asi-Yaholo's scrambling legs and feet with long, sharp teeth.

He dodged aside, leaped on the alligator's back, and managed to hold on to the bony ridge of the creature's spine as it twisted back and tried to snatch him off and rip him in two. He plunged his hunting knife deep into the place right behind the alligator's eyes, driving it home with a final prayer to Otter, hanging on for dear life.

Now the alligator was even more enraged, even more determined to kill him, and he roared and raced toward the water, the better to dislodge the man and knock him off with his viciously lashing tail. But as he reached the water, Asi-Yaholo felt the creature's strength begin to diminish, his steps slow, and he rolled aside out of the way of the snapping jaws. It seemed to take forever for the knife to have some effect, but finally, the huge bull gator stopped writhing and was still, his jaws still agape, even in death.

Asi-Yaholo lay beside the huge animal in the water, panting with exhaustion. It had taken most of the day to dig him out and all of his strength to hold on to him once he emerged. He had never been so close to such a large death, and he was saddened to see such a proud elder of the swamp taken down by such an insignificant thing as a man. He took hold of the gator's leg and towed him to shore.

"Elder, I am in your debt," he said, as he finally was able to get to his feet. "And when I return to the village, after I have presented you to Stamping Crane, then will I go to the old ones of the Alligator clan and apologize for your death." He bent down and examined the gaping jaw and the teeth. A large black leech was clinging to the underside of the alligator's jaw, still feeding on the creature's cooling blood. Asi-

Yaholo took his knife and slit the leech, throwing it into the water for the bream to devour. Then he put his knife tip to the place where the leech had been and began the first cut which would turn such a large kill into his bridal offering.

Stamping Crane was gracious about the substitution of an alligator for two deer, and he had ample reward when he saw the beaming smile of pride Morning Dew gave him when he staggered through the village carrying the hide of the huge bull. He had to half drag it, for it weighed nearly as much as he did, and the bundles of meat he delivered would, he knew, keep her mother amply provisioned through at least two seasons.

The connubial ceremony was brief, as was their custom. Before her mother and his own, they promised to care for one another so long as they loved. Of course, separation might come, as it often did to joined couples. She was free, at any time, to take his possessions and put them outside the hut, signifying that it belonged to her alone once more. The hut and all within it, including any children, always were the woman's.

He, also, was free at any time to depart her hut or to take another wife, if she agreed. But she could not take another husband, not and still live with him. And so, in that way, the relations between man and woman stayed in order.

For the first month they were joined, he left her hut before first light and kept from her parents, for that was custom. And after that first month, even then, he left her after the morning meal and went about his business during the day with the men; she did the tasks she must do with the women, and they came together again in the night.

Asi-Yaholo wondered if all men waited for the night as eagerly, as impatiently as he did. He thought not, as he observed the old ones, smoking and chatting in the shadows. They had either never had or had long forgotten the ecstasy he knew with Morning Dew.

It was not that she was his first woman, but that after her, he could scarcely remember any other before her. She had somehow become all women in his mind and his heart, and when he held her close to him under the soft blanket, her warm, soft skin melted into his own so that he could not say where he left off and she began. In her arms, tangled up in her legs, he knew the most profound joy and quiet peace he had ever known.

"Beloved," he murmured to her as he loved her, "beloved of my soul." And she gently stroked him into a yearning urgency which made him cry out like the limpets at dawn. Quickly, eagerly, he learned to make her cry out as well.

* * *

It was another spring, her third one, and Geni could feel her skin stretching once more, readying itself to split. This time, she knew it would be her last. She clung to the bottom of her rock in the moving river, gathering her strength for her first and only flight.

Geni was a mayfly, *Ephemeroptera heptageniidae,* and she had spent all of her life in the naiad or nymph stage, as a small creature, less than an inch long, with three tail filaments, leaf-shaped gills, and a mouth which more or less constantly fed. From the underside of her rock, she ate microscopic plants and tiny organic particles in the water debris, as the water moved by her, moulting and growing for three years. Now, she was ready.

Geni crawled to the side of her rock and waited for the sun to dry her body slightly, feeling the numbness, then the pain of the impending split of her shell. The sun felt warm, soothing, and for the first time in her life, she did not fear the light, did not wish to hide in the dark riffle under her rock. She strained suddenly, as though with a large swallow, and felt the seam behind her tail filaments fall away. She clung to her rock precariously, shaking slightly in the breeze.

The process seemed to take hours, and Geni struggled, trying to extricate herself from her old skin, moving slowly about the rough surface of her rock, sensing that hundreds of her kind were near her, doing the same thing. Finally, she felt her wings emerge, smoky silken folded things, wet and crumpled. She waited, trembling with fatigue.

Gradually, as she tried to lift and move them, her wings began to dry and spread. All around her, in the air, hundreds and hundreds of mayflies were emerging from the river and swarming into the air. Geni felt the rush of excitement of so many of them, saw the huge clouds forming in the air, moving toward the sun, and she moved her wings even more frantically, trying to get up the courage and the strength to let go of her rock and soar. She moved her mouth incessantly from side to side, feeling the lack of feeding parts as strange and light. She had no stomach, and she felt no hunger. She was only eyes and wings and a long, graceful tail. Nothing extra, nothing superfluous, as young as spring itself.

Geni could not know it, but she was one of the oldest creatures on the river. Her kind first appeared in the swamps of this region more than three hundred and fifty million years before, and had, every spring, filled the air with their millions for a brief moment in the year. There were more than two thousand different species of her kind, including more than five hundred of them on this continent. But again, Geni knew only that she was one of many. She felt very small, and she knew that only in numbers did she count for much. Indeed, without her kind, the fish, the frogs, the birds, each would have suffered for lack of prey, for the mayfly was a major source of food in every form.

But Geni knew only that the air was calling her. She suddenly took a breath, let go of the rock with her tiny fragmented legs, and flew into the air on her new wings. Instantly, she was in a swarm of males, all of them hovering near her, over her, under her, as though they had been waiting for her arrival. In the flurry, she saw many other females entering the swarm, but there was no time to flee or descend again. One male was on her in a flash, landed on her back and gripped her tightly with his feet. Before she knew what he was about, he had entered her, leaving her abdomen heavy with his fluids. She flew for a brief moment or two longer, then lowered herself over the moving water of her river.

She lowered her abdomen to the surface next to her rock and deposited a cluster of tiny eggs on the water, ridding herself of not only the weight of them but also the male's intrusive fluids. It took her only moments, and then she was aloft once more, winging into the light and the breeze, feeling more free than she had ever felt in her whole life.

For an hour or more, she swooped and dived and flew round the river, in and out of the swarms of other mayflies, now ignored by the males who frantically danced and buzzed round each new female who flew into their midst. After a bit, she felt quite exhausted by her new adventure and, dizzy with exertion, she flew back down again to her rock to rest in the sun.

The sun was warm, the air was soft, and Geni rested for long moments. When she went to try to fly again, she found that she was even more tired than she had supposed. She slowed her breathing and tucked her wings down, feeling the sun as heavy on her back as a warm stone. In an hour, she was dead. Her grip loosened on the rock, and she toppled softly into the moving water, only to be carried downstream and snapped up by a feeding minnow.

Geni had been an adult mayfly for less than seven hours. In less than a day, she had mated, reproduced her kind, and died. Her eggs, borne downstream and eddied into a small shallow pool, nestled under a large stone, where they would hatch into nymphs. And every spring, Geni's children and grandchildren would repeat the dance of May.

*   *   *

The surveying went on for more seasons, the white men going deeper and deeper into the swamps. As they pushed back the brush and marked the trees, the people seemed to become more divided, less whole, even as the wilderness felt each intrusion of the axe, the trencher, the fence post. And, of course, as life would so often have it, Asi-Yaholo was never more desirous of staying home at night when Arpeika asked him to go into the wilderness and see that the surveyors were marking the peoples' lands fairly.

"I know you are newly joined," Arpeika said solemnly to him on the evening he asked him. He used the Seminole word for "wived," which had an almost sacred meaning, and he inclined his head respectfully toward Morning Dew, who hovered in the near background. "But I ask it for the clan, Black Drink Singer. The people must know that someone they trust has seen the land we must go to with his own eyes. They must know that someone has spoken for us with words they can believe. It will take all of this season and much of the rest. Will you go?"

Asi-Yaholo knew that Arpeika could have asked any of several other men, some of them older warriors than himself. As much as he hated to leave Morning Dew, he knew that he was being given a chance to prove himself in leadership, when there were no battles to offer such an opportunity to young warriors. He glanced at Morning Dew and she drew forward to stand behind him. He guessed, without asking, that she understood what he must do. "I will go," he said to Arpeika. The steady pressure of her hand on his shoulder, light and grounding all at once, never varied.

That night, he held her especially tightly, caressed her longer than he might have, as though his whole flesh knew it might be the last time. Apart, they were vulnerable. Together, they were impervious to harm. And yet, he must go. He spent all of the next day readying himself for the journey into the world of the whites.

He sat in the sweat hut with the elders, chanting softly to himself and fingering his medicine objects from the pouch Arpeika had given him at the making-man ceremony. He prayed to Otter for strength and wisdom and fasted for all the day and the night. Then, the next morning, he said his farewells to his mother and his grandmother, embraced his wife a final time, and set off for the north in his dugout, his musket and bow and arrow across his chest, so that all who saw him leave knew him to be both a defender of the old ways and a symbol of the new.

For days, he journeyed to where the white men were working, rehearsing in his mind all the old English words he had known as a child and used so rarely in the last few years. When he finally found the pale eyes, he knew immediately that they were not going to welcome his presence, and he would not be allowed to advise them on any aspect of the forest or how to subdue it.

He set his camp close to theirs and daily, he watched as they set up their tripods, dragged their chains through the brush, and hacked at the tangled growth. They cursed the insects, the heat, the water, the mud, most anything which crawled or slid, including their own sweat down their necks. Asi-Yaholo had never known a people to be so angry at so many things all at once. Then they spread out their markings on a large paper nearly half the size of Morning Dew's hammock, bending over it and consulting it as the old women might consult the entrails of a deer for signs of coming drought.

Meanwhile, some of the men did nothing but dig; others did nothing but cut, while still others did nothing, it seemed to him, but struggle through mud carrying heavy pieces of equipment and machines. In his village, when there was a huge job to be done for the good of all, the men divided their strengths and shared the tasks, each taking his turn at a piece of it. In that way, everyone knew how to do most of the job and everyone could complain equally. These white men worked, instead, like ants, each doing the same thing over and over, and so he soon grew tired of watching them slowly make their way through the wilderness.

At night, he sat and listened to them over their fires. Rarely did they come to speak to him, and when he ventured toward their circles to extend friendship, he got the sure impression they mocked him behind his back once he left. They did not seem to like each other much more than they liked him, however, so he finally stopped taking offense at their lack of manners.

They battled the land constantly, that much he saw for certain. They fought the wet, the dry, the heat, the cold, the gators, the mosquitoes, their equipment, and themselves. They insisted on trying to walk through thigh-high mud, spiked with sharp cypress knees and rotted logs, and would not go around the widest trees. He wondered that the spirits of the forest could witness such bitter, stubborn struggle, but then he realized that the spirits had long ceased to watch these men or to care about their fate.

Tired of watching the surveyors, Asi-Yaholo then went farther south to see for himself the lands which were to belong to his people. He found many places which pleased him and so, finally unable to keep from Morning Dew another week, he turned his dugout for his village.

He had been gone four months, and the most obvious evidence of his absence greeted him slightly ahead of Morning Dew's arms. Her belly was rounded under his embrace with a firm, pleasing ripeness, and the shine of her hair, her skin, her eyes told him what his hands could already feel. "How soon?" he asked, filled with joy and pride.

"Four more passings of the moon," she smiled.

"And you are well?" He gently put his ear to her belly to listen for the life within.

She laughed, pulling him toward the hammock. "I am well enough, my heart, but *hauka'kis!* I am oh so hollow!"

As he tumbled her within, pulling down the grass mats around them for privacy, his heart was full to bursting. "I thought of you with every stroke of my oar," he said, "every step I took, every birdsong I heard."

"I thought of you with every breath," she whispered, pulling him over her, wrapping her arms and her legs round him fast. "And so, my emptiness is larger than yours—"

He laughed and caressed her belly. "Something here surely is."

"Fill me, then." She smiled up at him, already moving under him with hypnotic grace and easy strength.

And so he did.

Later when they came out of their hut, they found Arpeika waiting patiently at the fire. He had not even coughed to let them know of his presence. He gestured to the palm log beside him as Asi-Yaholo emerged, saying, "Please excuse my haste to speak with you, Black Drink Singer. I am an old man, and I have less time than some."

Asi-Yaholo sat down and prepared to give Arpeika his full attention, even though Morning Dew's coming and going with their cups and warm *sofkee* kept diverting his eyes. "The whites are nearly finished with their work on the land," he said. "And from what I can tell, they will never wish to come back to it again, so roundly do they curse everything about it."

"Good," Arpeika nodded. "Did you walk it well?"

"I did. I saw enough to know there are places within it which will please the people, I hope. But most important, I think it is not land which the whites will covet."

"Was the game ample?"

"Better than here. The birds darken the sky when they take to wing.

It is wild, even by our ways. The land will feed us, I believe. And though it is not quite so beautiful as this place, it will do."

"We must travel there as soon as we are able," Arpeika said. "The children have gone now two seasons with not enough to eat, and too many of the women are not letting new ones grow in their bellies until they know they can feed the ones they have." He nodded to Morning Dew. "You will be the man to tell them that this new land will feed their children. You will be the one to show them that the people will live on."

Asi-Yaholo glanced up at Morning Dew. He felt a sudden powerful mix of fear, heady responsibility, and dizzying pride. How could he possibly convince the people to move? Was it even in their best interest? "I am not an elder," he said. "I am not a *tustenuggee*, a war captain. I am only an ordinary warrior—"

"Many watch you," Arpeika said, with a noticeable impatience. "There are not many young men from whom to choose. The people will want to hear from one who has seen the land with his own two eyes."

Asi-Yaholo listened more carefully now. It was rare for Arpeika to show impatience. It occurred to him suddenly that the old man knew that his time was limited, that he had few years left to do what must be done for his people. He felt the old man's frustration and sadness all at once, and he said, "I will tell them, then, what I have seen. But each man must decide for himself."

"Naturally," Arpeika said. "We will call a council in two days. That will give them time to speak of it by their own fires first."

"Is there a reason for haste?"

The old man fixed him with a hard glance. "Already, the blue jackets are moving the people out of the north, herding them ahead of their horses like so many cattle. We have too few *tustenuggee* to stand against the whites at this time. We must wait and gather strength."

Asi-Yaholo saw Arpeika's plan. The people would move, but only for a time. When they were able to join together and prosper, build in numbers and power, then they could leave the lands Jackson had assigned them and take back their old territory once more. But for now, survival dictated that they seem to agree with the plan for removal.

"You will take your family and all who will go with you," Arpeika said, "and join with Micanopy to the south. He waits for you now."

"Then we must move quickly," Morning Dew murmured. "For the women say they live on sweetbrier root and bad water to the south."

Arpeika glanced up at her appraisingly. It was unusual for a woman to speak when men were in council. But she did not melt away into the shadows. Instead, she added, "Many of them are unwilling to leave this place."

"So am I," he said formally, nodding to her in recognition. "But we will go or be driven, I think. And so it is best that we go."

"Many of them say we should fight."

"If we fight now, we die. All of us," Arpeika said.

"Then let us die," Morning Dew said calmly. "The women tell, over the grinding of the corn, that the soldiers drive our northern sisters so hard, they can scarcely stop to suckle their babies. Some women have given birth too soon, and the babies have been dead as they came from their bellies. They wonder why their men do not fight."

"Because their men know they cannot win. Not now," Arpeika said, dismissing her with a wave of his hand, gently but firmly.

Morning Dew fell silent.

"Will we take our blacks to the south?" Asi-Yaholo asked.

Arpeika nodded. "The whites want them for themselves, of course, as they want all things. And in the north, I am told that the whites come into the villages and take the blacks, even if they are not slaves. Old Mad Jackson has given them permission to do so, they say. Some of them have been living among us since their mothers were children. It is yet another reason to leave here, before the whites come to drive us. In that way, we can take our cattle"—and here he grimaced wryly—"what few we have left, and our blacks with us."

"I will tell them what I have seen," Asi-Yaholo said gently. "That is all I can do."

"No," Arpeika said stubbornly. "You must tell them to follow you. They will do so, if you tell them."

He thought for a long moment. If he failed, he would look weak. If he did not try, he would look weak. If he succeeded, he would be a leader of his people, but would they prosper? If they starved in the new lands, they would look to him for responsibility. It was a large stone to carry in his belly. He glanced again at Morning Dew. She smiled softly at him.

"I will speak for the new lands," he said finally. "I will go there, and I will take my family. I will help anyone who wishes to join me."

"That is enough, then," Arpeika said. "Begin tomorrow."

Peeping was the first to tell him that she would not go to the south, no, not even to follow him there.

"I am tired of moving my fire," she said to him gently when he asked her. "My man does not wish to move once more."

"But the whites will find you here—"

She shrugged eloquently. "I have never minded living among them. If they take us, we will go without a fight." She smiled sadly at him. "I am too old to fight."

"I am not," his grandmother said testily. "She has ever been without a warrior's spirit," she added confidentially, when her daughter was out of hearing. "Do not force her to be stronger than she is, she will only disappoint you."

Asi-Yaholo tried for days to persuade his mother, but she would not be moved. And so when it came time to leave, he had to say farewell to Peeping, wondering if he would ever see her again.

Ochola and her new husband, Stands By the Horse, however, were as eager to make the journey as two young lovers. She sold her hogs at high prices, saving only her best breeding pair for the new land. "Hogs can be pesky in a canoe," she said wryly, "but no hogs in the winter months can be more pesky still."

When the talks were finished, ten families chose to follow Asi-Yaholo and Morning Dew, mostly young families headed by ordinary warriors like himself. They called him *Talasee Tastanagee* and treated him like an elder, even though he was not yet twenty-five years old. Together, they paddled far to the south in their dugouts, taking with them their seed, their personal goods, and what animals they could fit into baskets and crates to be carried on poles between the canoes.

After more than a week of travel, they came to the land that Asi-Yaholo recognized, the new lands that Old Mad Jackson had given to them. They raised their *chekes*, the women brought up buckets of clean river sand for the new ball fields, and at night, they gathered in the square before the main fire to tell the old stories and sing the old songs. Soon, it began to feel safe there, and Asi-Yaholo could even imagine his son or daughter playing and hunting in this new wilderness.

Over a few months, more families trickled south to join them, and from their tales, it was clear that the soldiers were pushing farther and farther south, shoving the clans ahead of them as they came.

Asi-Yaholo took two other men and went even farther south, searching for a place to make a hunting camp, for though the game was more plentiful than in the north, still it seemed less than they would need for a permanent home. Asi-Yaholo remembered a place he had seen with the surveyors which was so densely forested, he doubted that the white men would ever be able to penetrate it again. The waters around it were too shallow for the white boats and the earth too wet for them to bring their horses or wagons. There, he set up camp in a wide marsh they called the Cove of the Withlacoochee.

He was there with Morning Dew and the rest of his hunting party when her labor began. They had carried the supplies for the hunt up the trail, climbing up over an embankment and cutting their way through a tangled thicket and wading through muddy water to the higher place where the camp would be created. They cut saplings and bound them together, building sleeping platforms high enough so the snakes and the water creatures would not disturb their provisions and supplies. Morning Dew worked alongside the men all that afternoon, carrying and lifting and binding the fronds together.

Normally, few women went with the men on hunting parties, but Asi-Yaholo had been gone for so long with the surveyors that he did not want to be away from his wife again. Morning Dew tied her long hair up under her straw hat to keep off the sun and the insects, left off her ropes of beads, gathered her skirt at two points on her waist, and came along, then, as much a part of the camp preparation as either of the two men.

But as the sun began to go down and they kindled the fires, she felt the low pains begin in her abdomen and back, and she sighed heavily, leaning back against the tree. The child was early, as many as ten days so, by her reckoning, and suddenly, she was very sorry she had climbed into the hunting canoe.

Asi-Yaholo looked at her face, and he quickly moved closer to her. "You are weary, my heart?" he asked softly.

"The child has decided to come," she winced. "I wish it had not so decided, but there it is."

"I will take you back," he said quickly, rising in alarm.

She shook her head. "It will take too long. And we would have to travel in the dark." It had taken them all of a day to reach the camp, with three men rowing. She could not ask the others to return so far and abandon their plans, and with only her husband to row, she would likely bear the child on some riverbank, with no fire and little shelter. "No," she shook her head. "It will be here."

Asi-Yaholo sat back down gingerly, taking her hand. "Then I will help you," he said. "You must tell me what to do, and we shall deliver the child together."

She smiled at him, wincing again as another pain came on her harder.

"Build me a hut, away from the camp. Build a fire outside it and tend it well. Collect clear water from the spring," she added wearily, wincing once more, "and heat it with clean stones." She eased herself into a new position. "Never mind," she added, moaning softly with another pain. "There is no time for the hut." She struggled to stand, catching hold of his arm. "Perhaps you can help me to the shelter, and ask the others to excuse me, husband. I will do this alone."

"Not alone," he said firmly. "I will be with you, as will the Maker of Breath. And I will pray to Otter to make you strong and flexible in the birthing."

She let him lead her, then, away from the fire and the eyes of the other men, to the farthest shelter, where he helped her upon the sleeping platform, tying the blankets so that she would be shielded from all eyes and some of the biting insects of the dusk. He took the water pouches and hurried down to the spring, filling them with the clearest water he could collect. Then he came back, poured them into the single cooking pot they had and went to see how she was faring.

Morning Dew was stretched out on the platform, panting like a dog in August. She had taken off her skirt and her blouse, and they were pillowed under her head. Her knees were up, and her eyes were closed. When Asi-Yaholo entered her enclosure, she modestly lowered her knees, but he could see that the effort was painful for her.

"I have gathered the water, my heart, and the stones for the heating. Is it time for the child to come?"

She shook her head, her face a grimace of pain. "Not yet. Go out, husband. Do not come in again unless I call you."

He hesitated, wondering if he should obey her. If they were back at the village, she would have had a dozen women to tend her, all of them expert in the lessening of pain, the safe delivery of a child. Now, thanks to his need of her, she was here in the wilderness, all alone with her struggle. He had been weak and selfish, and now both she and the child would suffer for it. He moved closer and touched her forehead. "I did not think of you or the child," he murmured. "Only myself and my desire to have you with me. I am ashamed."

She shook her head. "If you had not asked me, my heart would have been broken. There is no better place for me than by your side." She gasped suddenly and rolled to one side. "The child, too," she groaned. "Now go and leave me, but do not go far. When I call, bring the water and clean cloth for binding."

He backed away from her, hesitating.

"Go," she moaned. "Do not make me worry for you as well as for myself and the child."

He turned then and let the blanket fall down, so that she was once more hidden from view. He climbed down from the platform and sat cross-legged before the fire, his face solemn and his heart thudding with fear.

"She is a strong woman," his friend and hunting partner, Alligator, said to him gently. "Did you see the way she pulled the saplings down to cut them? She will bring the child forth with no harm to herself, alone, like a warrior."

"I should not have brought her," Asi-Yaholo said morosely. "With no other woman about to help—"

"There's another woman here, I think." Wild Cat smacked him on the arm. "Right here, moaning at the fire. She will be well, I tell you, old man. Women have been doing this longer than we have had private parts to impregnate them, I think."

"I doubt that," Asi-Yaholo said dryly. "I think the Maker of Breath has more sense of the proper order of things than that."

"Don't be so sure!" Alligator laughed. "I know a few women, your own grandmother, in fact, who are likely more than capable of giving birth to something without the help of a man's parts!"

Asi-Yaholo grinned wryly. But his grin slid from his face. An audible groan came from the sleeping platform behind them.

"Try not to listen," Alligator counseled him. "She will not want to know, later when she is delivered, that you heard her cry out. She is a woman of pride and strength."

Asi-Yaholo nodded, but his eyes were dark with fear and concern. He faced the fire silently, praying to Otter to give his woman the courage to bear the child alone.

After a few moments of silence, Wild Cat said, "We should make spirit medicine to help her. Who is your spirit partner, Alligator?"

Alligator looked a bit sheepish. "Squirrel," he said finally, mumbling the word.

"Squirrel!" Wild Cat laughed. "And yet you carry a name large enough for the pride of two men."

Alligator shrugged. "When I made my spirit journey, I killed a bull gator." He rolled his eyes. "A small one. And so, they gave me the name. But when I made my spirit medicine, the only vision I had was of Squirrel. It is another of the Breath Maker's grand jokes." He grinned. "But it is of some good use when I am pursuing pleasure." He stared down at his crotch. "One thing squirrels are good at is pleasure."

"Fast, perhaps," Mad Dog said laconically. "Good, I would doubt. Unless a woman is fond of being chased up a tree."

Morning Dew's groans were coming quicker now, and it was all Asi-Yaholo could do to sit and keep his voice calm, his eyes away from the platform a hundred feet away where she labored. The fire near her was still burning, the water was at the ready, and there was nothing else he could do but sit hard on his fear and keep it as small as possible.

"When the child is born, you must give him a name befitting his birth," Alligator said. "A name suitable for a great hunter, a cunning stalker of the largest bucks and bears and panthers."

"It will likely be a girl-child," Wild Cat said.

"Why do you say such a thing?" Alligator asked, appalled.

"Because its mother has such a strong spirit. Her strength will flow to the child and make it a woman."

"Whatever it is," Asi-Yaholo said quietly, as Morning Dew cried out suddenly in sharper pain, "I hope it is swift in the coming."

"We should sing it into life," Alligator said.

Asi-Yaholo nodded in agreement. He began, then, the chorus to the Black Drink song, his own personal anthem, and from that song, they sang a hunting song and then a mating song and then a war song, their voices rising and falling in benediction and hope and power, filling the tangled thicket with the strongest medicine they could muster. Over their voices, sometimes they could hear Morning Dew's cries, but in the midst of their singing, she sounded less like a woman in pain and more like the haunting farewell of a migrating crane overhead.

After many songs and a good while, they fell silent. Morning Dew was silent as well. Finally, finally, after an almost unbearable wait, he heard her call his name faintly. He rose instantly and went to where she lay.

Pulling back the curtains, he saw that she had the newborn child on her belly, still connected to her by a bloody, whitened birthcord. He gasped and knelt beside her, instinctively reaching out for her shoulders to try to cradle her. She murmured weakly, "Get the water, my husband, to wash your daughter."

"A daughter!" he said.

"Strong and fierce as a panther," she said.

He burst from the curtained platform, his arms outstretched as though to embrace all the forest. "I have a daughter!" he shouted to his comrades.

Alligator gave a loud war whoop of joy.

Asi-Yaholo brought the heated water back to his wife and helped her cut the cord and wash and bind the baby. He then held the child close to his breast and gazed into her tiny wizened face. "Such a lot of trouble you have caused, little one, by being so impetuous. You could not stay where you were a few more nights?" He smiled at Morning Dew. "I, myself, wish for many more nights in that place."

She slapped his hand softly. "Do not speak of such before your daughter, husband. You will give her ideas too old for her small heart."

"There is nothing small about this heart," he said as he stared down at his daughter, who had opened her eyes and was returning his gaze solemnly. "And no ideas too old, I think. We must give her a name which tells of her birth and her courage."

Morning Dew was silent for a moment, considering. Then she said, "Comes Alone, I will call her, for she chose her time when no one was here to help her, no grandmother, no sisters, and truly she did most of the work herself."

He thought it over. "I had thought perhaps of Small Warrior. For, indeed, she is all of that."

"No," Morning Dew said, "that is a name of war. I want nothing of war in my house."

"Comes Alone," he pondered. "Do you think it a sad name? I would not wish a loneliness on her throughout her young time."

"For her, it will not be lonely. It will be a name of power," Morning Dew said.

He nodded. Staring down at his child and washing her brow with the warmed water, he said to her, "You are come, then, Comes Alone. And you are very welcome in this world."

The settlements in the southern lands grew over the next few seasons, with more and more of the people being pushed from the north to that one place which had been promised to them forever by General Jackson. They came without their cattle, which the white men had bought at ruinously low prices, without most of their blacks, for the white men had taken them away, and without their trade goods, for much had been lost in the two years before. But they came, whole and alive, and many of them wished for nothing more than never to see a white face again in their lives.

They built their *chekes* as though they intended to stay, with twelve-foot-high ridgepoles, steep roofs of cypress bark or cabbage palm thatch to keep off the rain, and solid walls of mud at the rear. In no time, the lizards, crickets, and mice moved into the thatch, and spiders decorated the ridgepoles. The women put their tools and fishing poles in the rafters, hung their families' clothing on pegs round the walls, and put down their deer hides on the floor. As a signal that they intended to begin to make children again, they hung blankets from the rafters for privacy. In weeks, it looked as though the settlement had been there for years.

Morning Dew's fire was now the place where men came to speak to *Talasee Tastanagee*, as they called her husband, the Leader of the Talasees. Some of them had traveled more than five days to see him and counsel, and they ate from her kettle and slept in the guesthouse she had him build. Her daughter grew from a crawling infant to a noisy toddler among men who bowed to her with solemn respect and treated her with the same dignified manners they extended to her mother and her father.

The newcomers told of great confusion to the north, for it seemed that few white men knew what the law was to be, and all of them believed that the lands of the whole territory were rightfully theirs, as though the people of the Seminole had been defeated in battle.

"But we have never warred with the whites," Asi-Yaholo said, "at least not formally. So how is it that they think we are defeated?"

"They think we are defeated because we do *not* fight," Wild Cat said angrily. He was at Morning Dew's fire almost as frequently as Ochola. "We should have pushed them back into the sea when they first stepped on our land. We should have killed them all at Moultrie Creek, when they said we could have our lands for only twenty years."

"Yes, and the turtle should not lay her eggs in the nest of the alligator, either, but she does, and they are eaten, and she does it once again. So and so. In the meantime, we are here and they are there, and so long as they stay there and not here, we can do without war," one of the new men said impatiently. He had come a long way, and he had no stomach for the thought of going back again, even if it were to gain glory in battle.

"What does Old Mad Jackson do now?" Asi-Yaholo asked.

The newcomer shrugged. "The whites say that he will be the next Great White Father of them all. And if he is, they say he will be a Father to all of us at once."

"Ha!" Wild Cat snorted. "Like the bull gator fathers the hatchlings he finds in his mate's den! We will be eaten up like so many min-nows—"

"Perhaps Old Mad Jackson will be too busy then to bother with our people," Asi-Yaholo calmed him. "He will be only a grandmother's tale to frighten children who will not behave. If he believes he has vanquished us, then we are the better for it. He has demanded tribute, as he believes his right, and now we will be left alone on our own lands to live our lives as we choose."

The rest fell silent, hoping that Asi-Yaholo's words were true. There was little they could do if they were not.

The lands they owned now were not, they found, as fertile as those they had left behind. The soil was alternately wet and sandy, and though the women worked the hammocks diligently, their squash vines and corn rows did not prosper so easily. They had to plant a small fish with each mound of corn, had to build small fences for the squash and pumpkin to grow up and away from the water, else the crops would fail. But still, they managed to bring the land to fruition.

Soon, the dense tangled undergrowth was a network of trails and footpaths between the settlements, and the lowest branches of the trees had been claimed by the youngest children in their games. The ball fields were cleared and always filled with running boys and girls, and some of the newcomers spoke to Asi-Yaholo about bringing their neph-ews to him for proper training.

A few pigs had been brought from the north, some ponies, and enough chickens to start a village flock. A trading party was sent to the east to bring back cattle, but so far they had not returned. In the meantime, the deer passed so close to the settlement that their scat was often seen in the morning, out on the ball field, and wolves howled from the swamp shadows nearby.

In 1828, Andrew Jackson was elected president of the United States, as the Seminole leaders feared. His new Indian agent, John Phagan, announced that it was the will of the citizens of the country that all Indians be resettled to the west of the Mississippi, on special lands that had been allotted to them. All tribes which went peacefully would be given the choice parcels, ample provisions and supplies to begin their new lives, stock, and a reward of money for their abandoned lands. All tribes which refused the order of the president of the United States would be forcibly removed, and would receive nothing but the scorn of their captors.

At first, outrage flamed through the settlements, but then the elders explained. Arpeika himself made the long trek to the north and back again, calling council with Asi-Yaholo and the other men of his clan, to tell of the newest decision by the pale eyes.

"I am come," he said to them, "from the coast." They had all gathered before Morning Dew's fire. He took a long draught of the hot tea she had offered him and an equally long pull on his pipe. His hands shook noticeably, but Asi-Yaholo did not lean forward to help the old man, knowing that his dignity would be wounded. If it had not been for Arpeika's two young wives and three sons, he would not have been able to make the journey. They waited for him at their fire now, and Asi-Yaholo marveled once more that they had given up the peace of their own lives, essentially, to see that the old man could fulfill his responsibility to the people.

"The Americans held a council with the *mikalgee* of the villages, all they could call together, at least," Arpeika continued. "Old Mad Jackson wants us now to move west, across the great muddy water."

The muddy water, everyone knew, was the Mississippi, the largest river in the southern lands. Few had seen it, but all had heard of its power. Several of the men frowned fiercely and murmured among themselves. Two of them hawked and spit angrily into the fire. But they did not interrupt Arpeika.

"Did Old Mad Jackson tell you this himself?" Asi-Yaholo asked.

"No, only his word-worker, a man called John Fay-kan," Arpeika said.

"Did you make your mark on their leaves?" another man asked. All knew that the white man did nothing without pages of paper to sign and seal, large and flimsy like leaves of a magnolia, marked with a splash of red wax like a blood oath.

"We did," Arpeika nodded, holding up his hand for silence as the murmurs now erupted round the circle with new anger. "But we did not agree to move. We agreed only to send a few leaders to look at the western lands, as Old Mad Jackson has asked. When they come back, we will all hold council."

"I will not go!" a man said now, "I do not care how many leaders say to do so. This land is ours, and I have moved my fire for the last time."

"Nor I," said another. "When that time comes, I will take my woman's advice, rather than that of the elders, and I will make war on every white man I see."

Arpeika looked at Asi-Yaholo.

He sighed deeply and glanced round the circle at his comrades. He had hunted with them, played ball with them, helped to train some of their nephews. They were his people. And yet he knew that if war came, they would be destroyed. "I cannot," he said quietly, "imagine telling my family that we must go west to new lands. To live among our old enemies, the northern Creeks. That seems impossible to me this day. But perhaps," he shrugged, "if all of the elders together counsel such a thing—"

"They will not," Arpeika said softly. "No matter if the lands to the west are finer than these we have, we will not go. No matter if the Creeks offer us their wives and their best ponies, we will not go. It is already decided. But we will go and see them, if only to show Old Mad Jackson that we are a fair people who will consider the wishes of our neighbors, the whites."

One of the men, a black who had married a cousin of Wild Cat, said sadly, "They will make you go. But we black ones will have to stay. They want to take us back as slaves. They will drive you forth from these lands, and then they will pen us like cattle."

"Then we will send messengers of war to every settlement," Arpeika said solemnly. "And we will fight until there is not a single white fort standing unburned."

The men looked morose and unconvinced. Asi-Yaholo glanced into the shadows at Morning Dew who, as usual, had not retreated into the hut but stayed close enough to listen and catch his eye. He saw that she, too, looked alarmed and fiercely resolute. "It is difficult," he said slowly, "to make such gestures of fairness to men who seem so often to be perverse. I worry that perhaps, once the elders have been to see these lands, the Americans will believe that these sojourners can sign their names for all of the people." He looked up at Arpeika. "You know, the Americans have always believed so. They think that if the *mikalgee* agree, then so do we all. They have never understood that each man must finally choose for his own fire and his own family, no matter if they say the lands to the west are so fertile that the corn grows in the dust between the rocks."

"I think it is unimportant what the white men believe or do not believe now," Arpeika said. "They cannot break their own treaty. We have their papers giving us this land—"

"For twenty years only!" a man interrupted him. "What will we do when that time is finished?" It was highly unusual for an ordinary warrior to stop the speech of such a respected elder as Arpeika, but all knew it was only an indication of how much rage and frustration simmered now around their circle. He was collectively forgiven without a comment.

"In twenty years, we will be so strong," Arpeika said calmly, "they will not be able to drive us forth. But for now, we must bide our time and appear to agree with them, to be their allies, until we can be strong enough to be their enemies. Therefore, Jumper, Chaolo Emathla, Mad Wolf, and Blue King, Mole Leader, and Black Dirt have gone to the west." He smiled grimly. "I did not inflict myself on their party, though John Fay-kan was fool enough to ask."

The men grinned now, the tension eased somewhat. Everyone knew that Arpeika was the strongest leader of the Seminoles, though he was perhaps weaker in body than those who had agreed to make the journey across the Mississippi. In fact, those who had gone would most likely follow Arpeika's judgment, no matter what they eventually saw for themselves. So in that way, indeed, the decision had already been made, no matter what this agent of Old Mad Jackson might think.

"But will the whites expect us then to go, once they have returned?" Asi-Yaholo asked. "That seems to be their habit, to believe that once they have said a thing, it is so."

"I do not care what they believe," a man said angrily. "I say I will not go. They can believe that the water flows uphill, but it will not do so."

"Ay." Asi-Yaholo smiled. "I saw that much, at least, in their measuring party. They believed that the strangler fig should stop where their tapes said so, but it did not."

"Nor shall we," Arpeika reassured them. "The sojourners will return to our lands within three moons, I think," Arpeika added, relighting his pipe. It was a signal that he was almost finished speaking. "When they return, we will call council and tell the white men that unfortunately, though we were very impressed with their kind and generous offer, we did not find the new lands to our liking." He rose then, unsteadily, and strolled slowly off to other fires to see old comrades and sons of comrades, leaving the men to talk quietly among themselves. He was a wise enough leader, Asi-Yaholo saw, to know that the men must chew this meat again and again before they could finally swallow it, to be brought up once more and fed to their mates.

He wondered if he would ever know as much in his years as Arpeika seemed to understand with no effort. When the men finally dispersed to their own fires, he took Morning Dew to their hammock and held her tightly, while she murmured into his chest. Still angry at Arpeika's news, she needed to tell him so before she could love him.

"We should never have let the white men unroll their blankets on a single handful of our land," she said bitterly. "The first one who tried, we should have cut the tendons in his knees and given him to the women. Then they would not plague us like a million mosquitoes, always sucking us dry."

He knew enough at least to be silent, stroking her while she spoke. He might not be as wise as Arpeika about the ways of the people, he smiled to himself in the shadows, but he did know his woman.

"The Americans are like the honeysuckle, with their trade goods and their courteous words. Pretty flowers and a sweet smell. But they take root next to the strongest trees, grow up through its branches, steal its light and its power, and finally cover it so completely that it dies. And then nothing is left but the honeysuckle, supported by the bones of what grew there before."

He felt tears of anger and fear fall on his bare chest, and he held her more tightly. "I will not let them move us again," he said to her gently. "I promise you, my heart."

She pulled back and stared into his eyes, pulling out his heart with her gaze. "Thank you, my husband," she finally whispered. "I believe you will not." And then she was able to sleep.

His daughter was nearly walking when Morning Dew came to Asi-Yaholo with her next request. She waited, he noticed, until he was well fed, with a belly full of her good carp stew, and the embers were low, the child asleep. The night was hot, but a breeze moved through the higher branches. She sighed as she sat beside him, a heavy breath of fatigue. He reached out and patted her leg softly. "Weary?" he murmured.

"Every night," she said. "There is so much more to do, these days, with the people coming and going."

He gazed into the embers. It was true enough, he knew. Visitors from other settlements came often now, and they all wished to speak with him before his fire. It required them to be refreshed and fed, often sheltered in their guesthouse, and their women usually needed to wash clothes, do necessary mending, gather provisions, and clean out water baskets, all of which his wife helped them accomplish before it was time for them to move on once more. "These times are difficult," he said finally, taking her hand. "They will get more so, I fear."

"So do I." Morning Dew took his hand in both of hers.

"You have had to do the work of two women," he said, squeezing her hand gently.

She smiled suddenly, lifting her slender shoulders with new energy. "You are right, my husband," she said. "And so, I think you should have two women, so that I do not work myself into the arms of the Maker of Breath before my time."

He glanced at her skeptically. "What are you saying?"

She moved so that her head was nestled under his chin. "I think it's time for the Black Drink Singer, leader of men, to have a second wife."

He laughed, pulling back and looking at her with amazement. "And I suppose you have her already chosen?"

"I do," she nodded.

Now he frowned, pulling slightly away from her. Of course, many warriors had more than one wife, some of the strongest leaders had as many as four round their fires. He had always wondered how such men found peace, but the system seemed to work well enough. However, he had not visioned himself so—so burdened. Or enhanced. He did not quite know what to think. And then, to hear that Morning Dew had gone so far as to select a wife for him! Surely, other husbands did not have wives so bold.

She was watching his face carefully. "Have you never considered such a thing for yourself?" she asked gently, patting his face.

He knew her well enough to say the right thing. "Of course not," he muttered. "I am well pleased with you, beloved, and need no other woman in my bed."

"And that is well enough," she said evenly, "but it is a mark of a great man that his family is large and thriving—"

"In these times, it is a mark of a great man if he can keep one woman and one child."

"The more hands to work, the better fed the bellies, my love," she said. "There is too much for one woman alone to do for you. And for your child."

He thought silently for a moment. Many men, he knew, would be eager to take another new and willing woman to their beds. And part of him, of course, rejoiced at the prospect. He grimaced ruefully. He full well knew which part. In fact, at the thought of another woman to lie with, he could feel his maleness stirring and stiffening slightly against his leg. He shifted uncomfortably as though she could see his response through the covering of his long shirt.

But she was saying calmly, "It will be good for Comes Alone, as well. She is walking, soon she will be running, and I must be more vigilant then. I will be even more tired, and she will see less and less of me when she should see more. Also," she smiled, "it will be good for her to have a sister to keep her from becoming so full of herself."

"She is already that," he nodded. His daughter was the tightfisted owner of a large piece of his heart. And she knew it well enough, for she played with him as she might play with her stick bundle, whacking him about the arms and legs and head, chortling with glee as he tossed and tumbled her, and not the least afraid to raise his temper, so that she could clamber in his lap and soothe it again. She was every inch her mother's daughter.

But could he handle two of her? Perhaps a son, as well? "Who do you have on your mind, wife?" he asked, already weary in the contemplation of the upheaval ahead. But also, he had to admit, intensely curious and not just a little intrigued.

"The black woman of my clan, Otter," she said slyly, snuggling closer to him once more. "You have seen her, have you not?"

He had, indeed. Otter was younger than Morning Dew, with large full breasts and the high rounded bottom of her people. She coiled her long black hair on her head in intricate ropes, like beads, and she was quick and agile at the ball games. His unrepentant member stirred and throbbed again, nudging at his leg like a persistent memory. He felt compelled to be stern now with his wife. "She is a child," he said, scoffing. "Of what use could she possibly be to you?"

"She works well; I have watched her often enough," Morning Dew said. "At the river with her mother's linens, in the corn rows with her digger, she is tireless and uncomplaining. Her mother says her sisters are very fertile, and she does not chew the air with useless gossip as do so many of her clan."

"Where would she sleep?" he asked baldly, thinking that this would either stop the conversation altogether or move it to its conclusion quick enough.

"In her own hut," Morning Dew said calmly. "She will only join us if she is promised a house of her own."

He pulled back, again amazed. "You have already spoken to this girl?"

"To her mother, only," Morning Dew nodded. "She understands that the final decision must be yours, my husband."

"And you understand this as well?"

"Of course," she said demurely. She waited a long moment. "Otter. It is a fateful name, is it not?"

"Perhaps," he said carefully. "And you are certain this is what you wish?"

She hugged him quickly. "It will be best, I think. Will you speak to her mother?"

He laughed, shaking his head. "Don't you think I should speak to her first?"

"There is hardly any need," she smiled. "She will be proud to be your wife, dear one. Any woman would be."

"Still," he grinned, "it might be fun to see if the girl is as . . . strong as you claim. Perhaps just a short visit to see—"

She cuffed him smartly on the arm, drawing herself up in a mock huff. "Better save your strength, my husband, for the building of her hut. And your wit for when I ask you questions of her later." She hugged him once more. "You will see, she will be a fine addition to our fire."

That night, as he held her and loved her, he wondered if he really knew his wife as well as he had imagined. What was the real reason she was pushing him into the arms of another? Was it truly that she wanted another pair of able arms to help—or that she wished to move slightly away from his own? He felt somehow slighted, as though she had shown an interest in another man, herself. But then he quieted his doubt. It was fitting and proper that he take another wife, he knew as much. As he moved his hands over her familiar belly, breasts, and flanks, he thought how pleasing it might be to have those same parts be those of an unfamiliar woman instead. The idea of her as at once strange and at once well-known excited him, and he entered her swiftly, with little of his usual preamble. She murmured under him in surprise and surrender, and he was excited all the more.

Morning Dew was right. The woman's mother welcomed him cordially, as though the arrangements were already completed for the wiving of her daughter. She asked only a single deer as a bride-price, a mere formality, and that Otter have always a house of her own.

"A large one," she said, grinning, "to accommodate her many children."

He embraced the woman and held his cheek to both of hers in turn, as was the custom, and the bargain was sealed, conditional only on his approval of her daughter as a suitable mate. She called Otter forth for his inspection in a high, singsong voice, as one might call a favorite pet, and he sat waiting, holding himself as tall as possible and attempting to seem slightly aloof from the proceedings.

A tall black woman came into the firelight with her head high as his own, her long legs and arms dark and oiled and gleaming in the shadows. She wore her black, braided hair coiled about her head and hanging down in single ribbons bound with beads which clicked together when she moved. Her bodice was blindingly white, embroidered all about with green leaves and red berries of the smallest stitches, and her high, full breasts strained at the light fabric. From under her long, full skirt, a pleasing soft ringing of bells accentuated every step. Only the huge gold hoops in her ears and her black skin said she was not of the people but from some place wild, mysterious, and exotic.

She stood before him silently, but there was nothing shy or maidenlike about her posture. Instead, she struck him in that moment as a female warrior, someone anticipating battle with a rare and quiet exultation. Only the quick pace of her breathing gave away her agitation. He stood before her and inclined his head in a formal recognition. Only after he bowed, did she drop her head as well.

"The night is fine," her mother called out as she left them alone, "show Asi-Yaholo your garden by the moonlight, my daughter."

To his surprise, Otter laughed lightly, almost mockingly, and took his hand, leading him away into the shadows, down the path toward the gardens the women had made to the rear of the village by the river.

They reached the gardens, and she showed him proudly where her own squash, pumpkin, melons, and corn rows stood, moving gracefully over the ground, interweaving herself among the tall stalks and the twining vines. Playfully, she touched him several times on the shoulder or the arm, but she said little.

Finally, he said, "My wife wishes you to join our family, and your mother is agreeable enough. What do you think of this, I wonder?"

"I am agreeable also, Black Drink Singer," she said, her voice teasing him from the depths of a corn row.

He struggled with his next words for a moment. He did not wish to hurt her, but neither did he wish to give her false illusions. "You understand," he murmured, "that Morning Dew will always be first wife. She is—"

"She is first in your heart," Otter finished for him calmly. She came now out into the open moonlight, her head high and proud. "That is how it should be. I will be second wife to a *tustenuggee*, and that is well, for such as me."

He took her two hands in his, feeling a wave of tenderness for her youth and her beauty. "You are lovely," he said. "You could be first wife to another man."

"A black man, perhaps," she nodded. "But that is not what I want."

"Not necessarily," he said. "You are young and strong. There are other men of the clan, other warriors who might—"

"I do not want another man," she said. She took a deep breath and said firmly, "Morning Dew and I will give you sons and daughters, and you will not let the white men take me away and sell me for a slave."

He was surprised, as he saw now that this promise, too, was a part of Morning Dew's plan. "No," he said slowly. "I would not allow them to take my wife."

"Then I will be your wife," she said. She took his hand and led him back out of the garden. As she reached the edge of the village, she stopped and turned to face him. Dropping his hand, she put her arms round his neck and came closer, just letting the soft fabric of her bodice, the rustle of her skirt graze him. He pulled her slightly closer, understanding that so far, she had bested him and that could not continue.

"I will deliver your bride-price in three nights," he said.

"And my house?"

"It will be completed within the moon."

"Then I will come to you," she murmured, swaying closer and kissing him lightly.

"No," he said gently. "I will come to your mother's fire for you, as is proper."

She kissed him again, this time more probing. Her lips were musky with a flavor of plums and scented oil and darkness. Very different from the taste of Morning Dew. He felt a surge of desire flood him, and he pulled her against him, almost roughly. Again, she laughed, that light, dark mix of delight and self-mockery that he had heard before. She pulled away slightly and said, "In one month, Asi-Yaholo. I will prepare myself."

"As will I," he whispered.

And then she let go of him and walked alone back to the village, her head high, her step sure and smooth. As the sounds of her beads and her bells drifted away from him, he felt bereft and emptied of youth, somehow, as if she took that with her as well. He hurried back to Morning Dew's fire to reassure himself that he was still the man he had been the night before.

A month later, with her house complete and the bride-price paid, Asi-Yaholo went to her mother's fire and took Otter away back to his own, and he saw with some pride how the eyes of other men followed them as he walked with her through the village that night. She walked in front of him, as was the custom, and he watched the sway of her hips and the smooth movements of her shoulders in the firelight they passed. When they reached Morning Dew, waiting by her fire, she stood and bowed to them both formally, taking Otter to her house to make her welcome.

He waited the decent interval, waited while Morning Dew made her preparation for bed, and waited a while more until the village quieted for the night. Then he rose slowly and walked as though he were in no particular hurry, to the skin which covered the open doorway of Otter's house. He scratched politely on the doorpost and waited. After what seemed to be a very long moment, she called out softly only the word, "Yes."

He entered, ducking his head under the low, thatched roof of her hut, into the shadows. A single glimmering oil lamp in one corner illuminated the darkness. He could not help but recall that Morning Dew always liked to welcome him with several candles strategically placed about the bed, so that they might take pleasure from seeing each other in flickering half-light.

But this woman would have her own ways. He must remember that. "I am come," he said, clearing his throat past the roughness there.

"You are," she said formally. She was lying upon her hammock, with a light linen thrown over her body. Her breasts were bare and dark as the black water out beyond the open walls of her hut.

He went to her side and watched her intently, kept her eyes pinned with his own as he slipped off his long shirt and unwrapped his beads from around his neck. When he stood finally naked before her, he saw that she did not drop her eyes to his maleness, even though it jutted out before him like a spear ready for battle. The ache of it made him want to take himself in his hand, but he did not. Instead, he put his hand on her hammock, and she slid over to give him room. Still, her eyes never left his face.

With less of the slow tenderness than he remembered with Morning Dew, he climbed into the bed with her and embraced her fully, pulling her nakedness next to his own. It seemed to him that he must be, somehow, different with Otter than he was with his first wife. She accepted his caresses willingly, and it was only as he was poised to enter her for the first time, that she drew in her breath sharply and put her hands on his chest, signaling him to stop.

"Have I hurt you?" he murmured.

She closed her eyes. "No, my husband," she said. "But you are the first to take me."

He pulled back, surprised. It was startling enough to hear the word, "husband," from her lips and realize in that instant what he was doing. She had been so confident in her manner, so womanly and teasing. He could scarcely believe he was the first to love her. There were few women past sixteen summers in the village who were still maidens. She was well past that age, perhaps five summers past, of robust health and some beauty, and surely she should have had lovers aplenty by now—

"I have not wished such . . . such nearness," she whispered, for the first time, nervous in her speech.

He thought for a moment. Such a thing might mean that she was somehow misshapen as a woman, perhaps missing some essential part which kept her from feeling natural desire. Perhaps, even worse, she was built normally within and without, but her heart was closed to men. If that were the case, he had made a sorry bargain, indeed. And yet, both her sisters were fertile enough, according to her mother and Morning Dew—

Morning Dew. Could it be that she had selected a woman deliberately who could not return his desires? Someone who, truly, would be more wife to her than to him, when all was said and done? He dropped his head to her neck and began to slowly nuzzle her, softly moving his lips up to hers and down again, tracing the lines of her cheeks with his kisses. "It does not matter," he said softly. "We need be in no hurry."

She almost whimpered in relief.

After long moments more of stroking her into relaxation once more, he asked, "You have never wanted a man before?"

"Yes," she murmured, "but I have not allowed myself that pleasure."

"Why not?"

She hesitated.

"We are husband and wife now," he said to her evenly, "and I wish to know who you are. Can you tell me your heart?"

"It is difficult to explain," she began, dropping her eyes.

He waited, still stroking her softly.

"I felt," she said finally, "as though something waited for me. Something important. And that I must be purified and strong to receive it."

He smiled at her as one would a child. "And I am that something?"
She opened her eyes wider, surprised. "Oh no, husband!"
He frowned, a little crestfallen.

"Not you, but what you will do," she smiled at him. "What you will
do with your life, with the lives of the people. It will take all of our
strength and courage, I believe. And we must be worthy."

"Ah," he said, a little sorry he had asked. He put his lips to her face
once more, seeking her own lips to silence her. "Well, and perhaps
you have waited long enough?"

"Perhaps," she moaned with some heat, and drew him down once
more upon her.

This time, she did not stop him but guided him into her with both
capable hands as though she were pulling in a fish. He tucked all this
away to think on at a later time, when he was not otherwise so distracted.

*   *   *

At the edge of Otter's new hut, where the digging for the frame
posts had disturbed the soft earth of a rising bank pocked with vermin
holes, the largest North American snake also made his home. He was
Riser, a blue-black indigo snake of almost seven feet in length, *Drymar-
chon corais*, and a well-known neighbor to the clan. Children called him
by name, *"Pucha Chobee,"* Large Grandfather, and greeted him with
respect and curiosity when their feet crossed his path. Nonvenomous
but extremely strong, the indigo lived at peace with his neighbors,
when allowed to do so.

Indeed, Riser did his best to tolerate the people near him, for their
corn brought the rats, and the rats brought him satiety. He was a heavy-
bodied snake, slow-moving and slow to anger. His chin and throat and
the sides of his head were suffused with red, and he frequented the
turtle burrows, alligator nests, heron rookeries, and rabbit holes of the
swamp for ten miles in all directions. More than twenty winters old,
he could well recall when no men stomped his earth and vibrated his
sensitive temporals and upper labials with the poundings of their heavy
feet upon the ground above his burrows. But then, he was a tolerant
creature, and he had learned to take the best of what came.

Now it was the time of the falling leaf, when the oak trees in the
swamp turned the color of his throat, and the hatchlings from his last
mate's nest were well gone. Mating would begin soon in another moon,
but for now, Riser felt a calm quietude with his kind and his world.

Except for one intruder. In a palmetto stand near the river, a large
canebrake rattlesnake had taken up residence, and Riser could not
extend his patience to that particular neighbor. Besides, one rattler

meant more, in time, and Riser could tell by his sign that he was a male, would mate soon, and then all peace would cease in this space on the river.

And yet, he was hesitant to go to war with this most ancient enemy. Since long before Riser could remember, indigos and rattlers had battled each other for supremacy, for each sought the same game, each needed the same shelter, and each feared the other's weapons. Riser was not a constrictor, but he was strong as an alligator and immune to the rattler's poison. The rattler was quicker, more aggressive, and more effective in the hunt, but his temper betrayed him. He could not turn away from a fight.

Riser knew as much, in his cells, and yet he hesitated to do battle. His opponent was every inch of five feet, perhaps more, and nearly as wide round as a man's calf. Riser had fought and killed rattlers before, but this one was the largest.

On the other hand, he had no intention of abandoning such rich hunting territory to an intruder. Since man had come to his territory, the vermin fed well, bred prolifically, and made easy hunting with little travel. Females were easy to attract to such a well-stocked larder, and he did not wish to have to go so long and so far as he might have when he was of fewer summers.

And so, the rattler and his get must go. Riser knew that as the season went by and the heat diminished, the rattler would become more difficult to find above ground. During the long hot hours, he was usually beneath the surface or resting half-in, half-out of shallow water to keep his blood cool. As the time of the falling leaf passed, he would go underground more often, and then his mate, if he had one, would be even more vigilant of her nest. And he would he harder to ambush. If Riser wanted to overcome him with the best chance of victory, he must do so soon.

Riser was hunting several of his favorite burrows one late afternoon when the decision was made for him. He rounded a corner of the hill, readying himself to descend into the earth to find prey, when he came face-to-face with the rattler, coiled by his favorite feeding place. The rattler was waiting for prey, partially hidden by a palmetto frond, silent as stone, his eyes mere cat-slits against the dappled sun.

Riser instantly froze. The rattler did not move. Riser tested the air with his tongue and saw that the rattler did the same. He showed no fear, and he did not flinch. Riser lifted his head and flattened it, vibrating his tail rapidly on the sandy ground. He opened his mouth and hissed loudly, to repel the intruder.

The rattler, coiled wide and high, rattled viciously in return, shifting his head slightly in readiness to strike. Riser moved forward, slightly to the side of the rattler, daring him to attack. The snake did not follow Riser's lead, however, and stayed coiled, tightened his coils down, and buzzed loudly.

Now, of course, any chance of ambushing prey was gone, and Riser grew more angry when he realized that nearly half the day was over, and his belly was empty. He moved aggressively toward the rattler, and the rattler swiveled on his coils, keeping his head up, focused, and ready to strike.

Riser suddenly lunged forward, aiming for the length of coil directly behind the rattler's head, but quick as a blink, the rattler turned and struck him in the neck, sinking his fangs deeply into Riser's muscles. The venom was useless against Riser, but the pain was intense, and the burning sensation of the rattler's digestive juices made him wince away and writhe for a moment as he collected himself.

Then he came back again, this time faster and even more angry. In a flash, he snatched the rattler by the neck and pulled him off his coil, avoiding the gaping jaws, as the rattler tried again and again to bite him. Twisting, feeling for purchase with his powerful tail, Riser pulled the rattler closer to the palmetto and tried to anchor his body around its base. The rattler saw what he was trying to do, and he fought more savagely, striking again and again, hitting Riser twice in the middle of his body. Riser finally managed to wrest the huge snake to the palmetto, rolling with him in fury, and wedged his tail around the tree as tightly as he could. With all his strength, he gripped the rattler by the neck and held him to the ground, using the unmoving tree as an anchor.

The rattler twisted, gaped, and rattled furiously, but he could not dislodge himself from Riser's jaws. He struck again and again, mostly missing, for Riser kept his head down into the dirt, moving over him relentlessly, using the weight and muscle of his big body to pin the rattler into position.

Then when Riser had the intruder almost motionless, he swiveled his head, opened his jaws, and clamped hard onto the rattler's head. He held him down, feeling the snake strain against him, feeling the rattler fighting the strength of his body, the smothering hold he had him under. Riser did not use his body for constricting, as other snakes did, but for holding and overpowering his adversary. He was incredibly strong, had fought many battles, and sensed when, finally, the rattler began to tire.

Even as he tired, however, Riser did not loosen his grip. He let the rattler do most of the fighting; he simply held him flat into the ground. And then, when he finally knew that the rattler was nearing exhaustion, he released his hold on his head just long enough to shift and take the rattler by the nose, clamping his mouth shut with his own powerful jaws. Now, he used the muscles of his neck and body to hold the rattler where he wanted him, used his tail as a lever to keep the rattler pressed into the ground, and began to stretch his jaw wide. He forced the rattler's head into his mouth, gaped his jaws, and began to wrestle the rattler down his throat.

Swallowing slowly, convulsively, Riser unhinged his jaws and kept walking his teeth up the rattler's neck, inch by inch. When he finally had the rattler's head down his throat, he stopped, feeling almost sick with the stretching of his head and jaws. He rested for a moment, feeling the convulsions of the rattler still struggling for release. Then he began swallowing again, relentlessly, slowly, until he had another foot of the rattler down his belly. Now, the movements of the rest of the rattler had slowed, had diminished to little more than rhythmic shivers and slidings, as his tail still twitched slightly in the sand. Riser continued to swallow. When he had more of the rattler down him, he unhooked his tail from the palmetto and slowly stretched out to his entire length.

Now, he was at his most vulnerable. If he should be discovered by a fox or a hunting hawk, he could be taken easily enough, for he was nearly paralyzed with the girth of the rattler filling him so completely. He slid back into the shelter of the thicket, as deep within the brush as he could push himself and still keep his whole length under shade. He convulsively swallowed the rest of the rattler and lay, stupefied, swollen almost beyond capacity with his meal and the fatigue of the battle.

Riser dozed now, waiting for the discomfort in his belly to pass. His neck and body were scored in a dozen places by the rattler's strikes and near-strikes. He knew that he must get to cool mud soon, to draw out the poison and help heal the wounds. If he lay long enough, immobile enough, the ants might think him helpless and attack him.

It was nearly dusk when Riser felt he could move enough to seek the safety of his burrow underground. He crawled slowly toward his hidden entrance, an excavated hole partially covered by an overhanging rock. Distended as he was, he could barely get within, could hardly make the first turn underground which took him to a wide burrow where he might lie up.

Finally, Riser was alone and safe within his burrow. He slowed his breathing, and when he had his breathing steady and deep, he allowed himself to move into a state of near-hibernation, something he only did after a very heavy meal or if the weather was unusually cold. The rattler would keep his belly full for at least a month. The vermin near him would be safe for that amount of time, at least.

Filled and satisfied, he understood that in that time, the rats would have bred again, their litters would be weaned, and the hunting would be excellent once more. All was as it should be. He slept, knowing that his territory was once more his alone.

*   *   *

The news came by runner: a council was called to the west in Tampa. The runner told Asi-Yaholo, "It is said that we are betrayed. The leaders came back from the western lands and told the whites that we will move there to live with the Creeks." He spit into the fire. "I must go to the Bear and the Panther clans by nightfall, so do not hold me. Arpeika asks that you come for your people."

"Is there talk of war?" Asi-Yaholo asked. He asked it as much for Morning Dew and Otter who stood behind him listening as he did for himself.

"More than talk of it," the runner said hurriedly. "The young warriors are already preparing. Arpeika himself says now it will come. He will hold council in ten days." He dropped the bundle of sticks showing the number of suns which would pass before council, gripped Asi-Yaholo's arm in the traditional gesture of brotherhood, and went to the next clan fire.

There was, of course, no question that they must go immediately. Morning Dew and Otter took a day to provision the canoe, packed up Comes Alone and their necessities, and they left with the dawn and a dozen supplications from their clan members ringing in their ears.

"Tell them we are sick of waiting," one man had said. "I want to kill a white man. Tell them that."

Another told Asi-Yaholo, "It is time for the young men to earn their war honors. We have waited too long already. We must drive the whites from our land and take back our souls."

A woman came to him and said softly, "They will not let us live in peace, even here. And we will perish among our enemy, the Creeks across the Great Water." She put her arms around her rounded belly protectively, for she was huge with child. "I would have my son born to freedom, or I will kill him before the Maker of Breath can blow into his mouth."

Not a single voice spoke for peace, Asi-Yaholo noted sadly. The decision was already made, at least around these fires. War with the whites was coming as surely as the rains.

They made their way to Tampa, following the Withlacoochee River, through tangled swamps and slow-moving water. As they neared the sea, Comes Alone sat up in the dugout and asked, "What is that smell?"

Asi-Yaholo realized then, with a pang, that the child had not smelled the salt ocean since she was too young to recall. That a child of his should have been so separated from her heritage seemed to him in that moment almost enough for war alone.

They arrived at Arpeika's camp and went to the clan shed prepared for them. While Otter and Morning Dew set up their belongings, Asi-Yaholo went to the men's council shed to see who had arrived so far. To his surprise, most of the leaders were already present, sitting in their circles and smoking. The mood, he could see at once, was solemn, and most of the voices were low.

Men rose and greeted him cordially, and after all were settled once more, Arpeika spoke up, his voice soft but piercing in the grim silence. "We have still to wait for two others, but it is good to speak of all of this many times. Those of you here know Black Drink Singer, as you knew his Great-uncle Mad New Town. He is a leader of his clan, and we welcome him to our council as a man of sense and good words." He turned to Asi-Yaholo and nodded.

"I thank you for your welcome," Asi-Yaholo said. "My people of Talasee are few in number, and I am a minor warrior. But I am bound to bring their voices to you, as best I can."

"No doubt, they speak for war," another warrior said.

Asi-Yaholo nodded. "They do. But they have few illusions that it will be easily won. They know the soldiers are many and their weapons superior to ours." He sighed. "Nonetheless, they speak for war."

Arpeika said, "The whites have claimed that the leaders who went to the land of the Creeks beyond the Great Water agreed that if they found the land to their liking, *all* the people would move there."

"But did they make their marks?" Asi-Yaholo asked, unbelieving.

"They did," Arpeika said. And he looked to the side of the room where the seven men sat who had made the journey west. "They will defend their actions when all have arrived."

"I am certain they will have good reasons for their actions," Asi-Yaholo said politely, "for they are men of good heart. It is not an easy thing to do, to travel so far for the will of the people." He rose and nodded cordially to the group. "I will take my leave now and return after I have settled my family." He smiled. "I have taken a new second wife," he said confidentially to those men nearest him. "And so things are now a little less ordered in my life."

Those close enough to hear this last smiled knowingly, nodding their heads. Asi-Yaholo knew that by admitting this personal detail, he would give them an opportunity to know him and to feel amusement at his expense, for each man knew or could well imagine what challenges two women at the same fire might present. If any of the old ones here were wont to envy his youth, this statement alone might soften their resentment. Arpeika caught his eye as he rose and nodded in approval. He had spoken well.

That night, he had word that the awaited leaders had arrived and council was to begin. He wore his whitest tunic, the golden and red beads coiled large round his shoulders, and an egret plume in his head coverings. He took his seat at an outer circle of men, not wishing to seem overbold. He was young, after all, and not tested in either council or war.

Arpeika had already greeted the council, and now it was time for each leader who had signed the white man's treaty to stand and defend his position. After several hours of statements and questions from the listening leaders, only two positions were clear: they all maintained they had been tricked by the white agent, John Phagan. Some said they had never touched the pen; others said they had signed, but had been told if they did not, they would be left in Oklahoma to die among the Creeks, this from an old man of almost sixty. Another said that he had signed, but had been told that *all* of the clans must agree, and so he only signed out of courtesy, to keep this Fay-gan man believing that they were reasonable people. He thought, he added, that this was what Arpeika wanted to accomplish.

By the end of two hours of speaking, tempers were shorter and confusion was still boiling among the leaders. But one thing was clear: no one wanted to move to the lands west of the Great Water. One of the black translators, Abraham, rose and said that some had accused him of taking a bribe of two hundred dollars from the white men to misread the treaty and thus convince the leaders to sign.

Abraham said, "Every man here knows that the white men want the tribes to move west. We who are black know also that the white men want to keep us here to sell us as slaves. I have lived among the clans all of my life. My children were born free among you. Why would I sell myself, my wife, and my children for two hundred dollars? Would any of you do such a thing?"

Asi-Yaholo looked round the council. The faces that were angry when Abraham rose to speak now looked less so.

Arpeika said, "If betrayal has occurred, there is no reason to believe it has come from one of our own."

"It has not!" shouted one of the older leaders. "It has come from the same place it has always come. From the hearts of the whites!"

"This agent Fay-gan told me the words on the treaty," Abraham said, "for of course, I could not read them. I told the leaders what they said, then, in our tongue. But Fay-gan told me the words he said they said, not the words on the treaty. He said, 'If this delegation be satisfied,' we would move west, but what was then signed and told to the leaders later were the words, 'If they be satisfied,' which means the whole nation of peoples. I was tricked. We were all tricked." He sat down with great dignity.

The leaders spoke then, one after another, and as they did so, Asi-Yaholo grew more and more subdued. It seemed to him that the consensus was obvious: war was coming, and soon. The whites were determined to drive them from the region, no matter how many concessions they made, no matter how far south into the wilderness of the Everglades they were willing to move. Even if they offered to occupy only the lands underwater, still the whites would have them gone from their midst. There was no way to appease them, nor could they be trusted to keep their own agreements.

In a momentary lull of conversation, Asi-Yaholo spoke up quietly. "Can we win such a war, do you think?" he asked Arpeika. He did not dare address such a question to others, for they were far more angry than the oldest leader. Arpeika seemed, more than anything, sorrowfully weary.

"We cannot," the old man said evenly. "Even if we succeed in driving the white man back for a few years, even if we go deep into the places where they think they do not wish to be for now, they will eventually decide that those lands, too, must be theirs. Whatever gains we make in terms of time and lands, we will pay for dearly with the lives of our warriors, the peace of our families, the ruination of our lives."

"And yet, you still counsel defiance," an elderly leader said. This man was responsible for the clans of the Bear and the Alligator, and he spoke for more than a hundred people.

"I counsel refusal to move west to live among our Creek enemies in lands which cannot support us," Arpeika replied. "That seems to me a worse choice than living here among our enemies on lands which we know and which know us." He shrugged. "But the next step is up to the whites. If they will have war, then we will have no choice in that next step."

"I say, we cannot wait for them to decide our fate," one of the younger, angrier leaders said. "If a man sees a cottonmouth is about to drop into his canoe, he does not wait to fight with it once it is about his feet. He knocks it off its branch before it can make the decision to attack."

"Ay," Arpeika said, "but if that branch has a score of cottonmouths, perhaps the man would be more wise to paddle elsewhere. Until he can come back with more men and more sticks."

There was silence once more, as the men digested this parable.

Asi-Yaholo said, "Arpeika's words seem to counsel patience, until patience is impossible. This is wisdom, for with each passing moon, the people grow stronger. Every season we can forestall this war, we give ourselves a better chance of victory."

"Asi-Yaholo speaks my words well," Arpeika said. "I appoint him my sense-maker to the southern peoples. And I ask that others consider appointing him sense-maker to the whites, as well."

Asi-Yaholo looked up in surprise, and he saw the same surprise on the faces of many round the council shed. He raised his hand, beginning to protest, when Arpeika added, "It is important that the whites see that we have young, strong warriors who have positions of leadership with the people. Let them not assume that only the old ones stand against them. Perhaps this will cause them to think before they strike."

"The cottonmouth does not think before he strikes," the young, angry leader said morosely. "The longer we wait, the more of them will come to these lands. And if they see that we have strong warriors, they will only send more blue jackets and stronger guns."

Arpeika nodded. "Perhaps. But I believe we have seen their strongest warriors and their strongest guns. Let them see ours, in talks of peace.

If we are not able to dissuade them, then we, at least, will know our enemy better than before."

The elders nodded in agreement. Without preamble, then, or even preparation, Asi-Yaholo found himself appointed sense-maker to Arpeika. After the council ended, he sat long by the old man, listening as he advised him what he must do and say when he took their answer to the white agent, Phagan.

As he left the council fire, he said to Arpeika, "You honor me. I do not feel ready for such honor."

"No one ever does," Arpeika said tiredly. "But good men rise to the occasion when it is thrust upon them. You speak well, and your presence is one of strength and honor. Our hearts have always understood each other, and you are able to persuade men with your words, that much I have seen since you were a boy. Now, go to your women and begin to practice with their ears."

Asi-Yaholo walked back to his hut where Morning Dew and Otter and Comes Alone waited, almost dazed by what he had become during the hours he had been away from them.

That night, he spoke with Morning Dew long into the night, telling her all his impressions of the council and their decision. "We must keep them at bay," he said to her. "Somehow, we must become less visible to the white men, even as we stay among them. We must tell them we will not move, but we must also not let them begin to war against us." He sighed. "I do not expect us to be successful. But it is our only plan."

"Why do you think the whites will beat us in battle?" Morning Dew asked him, almost impatiently. "They must find us to beat us, and we can go so deep into the swamp that their horses will never even smell our firesmoke."

"How long can we run?" he asked. "How many times can we move our fires? You made me promise never to move you again. Now do you wish me to break that promise?"

"It is a part of war to evade the enemy," she brushed away his argument. "How will you ever persuade the people if you cannot persuade yourself?" she countered. "The whites are a perverse tribe with no soul. The Maker of Breath does not favor them, neither does the land. These things you must remember and believe, my husband, for the people will look to your heart for courage." She gazed into his eyes and held him tightly. "Will they find it there?"

He bowed his head, overwhelmed by her bravery and her belief in him. "They will," he said finally. "If you will stand behind me—"

"I will stand by your side," she smiled, "where I belong. And so will all people with courage and love for the land. Let the whites do their worst; they will not drive us forth."

He laughed lightly. "My grandmother was right about you. You should have been born a man."

"She said that about me?" Morning Dew huffed, drawing away in indignation.

"And she likely meant it as highest praise," he mollified her.

"She did not," she smiled grimly. "But I hope that you do."

In answer, he kissed her. And through the night, as he woke and felt her against him, he took comfort from knowing that whatever mistakes he might make, whatever the whites might do, and whatever disaster might fall upon them, she would be the one unalterable reality of his life.

In the months to come, the white agent, Phagan, made repeated demands to the clans that they assemble for council, but it seemed impossible for all of them to come together at one time. Arpeika sent his regrets that he would not be able to make the journey to the west because of his age, and then he had no more communication with the agent. Meanwhile, Asi-Yaholo and the other warriors began to train the young men for war.

Arpeika sent out messages to all the clans saying that he supported a nonremoval faction, and that any leader who sold his lands or marked a white man's paper would answer to that faction with his life. It was the first time in anyone's memory that a single leader, however respected, had announced such a decision, but it caused few murmurs around the fires. The clans knew that they could only now be betrayed by outsiders.

Meanwhile, the young men flocked to those villages where training for war went on, and Asi-Yaholo, together with the other warriors, tried to teach them something few of them had actually experienced themselves: how to kill the white man.

The young, untested warriors ranged in age from ten to twenty summers; many of them were so young they still wore their hair in the topknots of youth, and few of them had their own personal medicine yet. Asi-Yaholo and the other warriors who could be spared from the business of hunting and the crops trained them in the handling of the smoothbore rifles, the making of lead balls, the priming of powder, the cleaning of the touchholes, and of course, target practice. Many boys brought old guns which had belonged to their fathers or grandfathers, old fusils, Spanish fowling pieces, and ancient muskets.

In another clearing, where the sheds hid the stores of ammunition, the women boiled cow hooves to keep the guns oiled, dried meat in large quantities for the time when the men would be too busy to hunt, and pounded corn into meal for storage. In pots which were kept always boiling, they prepared the roots and herbs that would be needed to salve wounds and keep insects off when the men would not be able to kindle fires.

And so the seasons passed. After many months of training and drilling, news came to the villages that the white agent, Phagan, had been sent away by Old Mad Jackson. "He was too perverse," Arpeika said, "even for the whites. And that is perverse, indeed. He is replaced by a man named Tom-son. He is older, the chiefs say, and may be a wiser adversary."

"The young men grow restless," Asi-Yaholo told him. "They ask when the war will begin."

Arpeika shrugged. "Every month we wait, we are that much stronger. Perhaps Old Mad Jackson has forgotten us."

"It has been more than two years since they said we had to go, and still, we are here."

"The white men move very slowly. They must talk among their leaders for so long, they likely cannot recall the thing that made them sit down to talk in the first place. The people still take their baskets of fruit and fish to the steps of the fort to trade for tobacco and flints, as if the whites had never ordered them out. They trade for powder, too, and the white men sell it to them as though they had no memory of any disagreement between us."

"Meanwhile, I must keep a passel of young warriors at the ready," Asi-Yaholo sighed. "They have sung their battle songs and carried their rifles now until they are ready to fight each other, simply to have adversaries to face. They have gone on their spirit quests and made their battle medicine, and still no enemy comes to fight them."

"They must learn patience," Arpeika said. "And you are a good one to teach them that."

Asi-Yaholo smiled grimly.

"I understand you have a new daughter?" the old man asked cordially.

He nodded. "Her mother calls her Mink, for she is slender and brown and swift." He laughed ruefully. "I am a man beset by women now, so I suppose that I am well acquainted with patience, as you say."

"You are well acquainted with good fortune," Arpeika said softly. "The Maker of Breath has favored you ever since you took your first step."

"That is true," Asi-Yaholo nodded. He thought of Otter and how he had been reluctant to disturb the peace of his life with another wife. But she was a fine woman, had given him a healthy, beautiful daughter, and she and Morning Dew were as two sisters in their affection for one another. Comes Alone was growing tall and strong, and she carried her baby sister about on her hip as she went about in busy joy. His fires were hot, his meals well prepared, his beds clean, and his women inviting. What man could ask for more?

On Arpeika's next visit, he asked Asi-Yaholo to take his family and visit the fort, so as to take the measure of this new man, Tom-son. "He has called a council, and I will not go. But I need a pair of good ears there and a mouth of reason. The other chiefs think he is a man of measure," Arpeika said. "Some are saying he will not make war on us, even if ordered to do so. I think they are wrong. I would value your thoughts."

And so, he traveled with his two daughters and wives to Fort King in late summer, 1834, to see what measure of man this Wiley Thompson might be. When a handful of chiefs had gathered, Wiley Thompson told them that the meeting had been called not to see if they would go west: they must go west. It was only to decide what form of transport they wished, whether they wanted their annuities paid in goods or currency, and what they would do with their cattle.

When several of the leaders said that their people were not agreed, Thompson lost his temper and spoke too loudly, considering that the circle of chiefs only sat a few feet from him. "Your laws will be set aside," he said wrathfully, "and your chiefs will no longer be chiefs. Your condition will be one of hopelessness and starvation. I tell you for the last time: you will go. If you do not go willingly, you will be forced to go at point of gun."

Asi-Yaholo leaned over and spoke quietly to one of the elder chiefs, conscious of the fact that he was young and inexperienced in such councils.

Thompson pointed his finger at him and shouted, "What does that man say?"

Asi-Yaholo stood up and faced Thompson.

"What is your name?"

"Asi-Yaholo," he said quietly.

"Osceola," the man repeated. "What does that mean?"

Asi-Yaholo noted the man's mispronunciation of his name and also another thing he had noticed before: the white man was ever curious about what Indian names meant, as if by knowing, they might somehow discover the man . . . or his weakness. "It means Black Drink Singer," he said in his own tongue, waiting for the black man to interpret.

Thompson made a rudely dismissive gesture, for the name meant nothing to him, of course. "And what is that you said to the chief?"

Asi-Yaholo listened as the black interpreter told him what Thompson wanted. He took a deep breath and faced the white man. "I say, the people will not go. Our chiefs have considered the question and made their decision. The people have discussed your plan, and they have decided to stay on their lands. They have charged their leaders with telling you so. Nothing more remains to be said." He sat back down as the black interpreter finished telling Thompson his words.

Thompson pointed to the chief who had heard Asi-Yaholo's whisper. "And what do you say to that?"

The old man said quietly in near-perfect English, "I do not intend to move."

Thompson's face grew red round the collar. He was a large man, of military bearing and dignity. He stomped out of the council shed then, and the guards glared at the chiefs around the circle. One by one, they rose and filed out. Asi-Yaholo was the last to leave, for he thought that if one of the guards decided to punish a leader, let it be himself who took the blow. None came.

He went out to his family and drew them aside into the temporary huts built for them near the fort. "The agent, Tom-son, is a man of wrath and spirit," he told them calmly. "He bears himself like a soldier, but he cannot keep his temper."

"Then he will be easy to beat," Morning Dew said.

Comes Alone piped up, "Can we go back home now?" Ever restless, the fort was not a place she could roam, so it held little allure for her.

"We will," Asi-Yaholo said. "I have seen all of this Tom-son that I need to, I think."

Otter and Morning Dew began packing again with a will, as if they could not escape the view of the fort walls fast enough. On the long journey back again to their village, Morning Dew asked him many questions about the white men and their faces, their postures, their words. As though she felt she might somehow sense the future in what he was able to tell her.

"I can only tell you," Asi-Yaholo said finally, "that I do believe we will war against them. And I think it will come soon rather than late, now that Tom-son is in charge. He is a man of anger, but also very strong will. I cannot think he will allow much moss to grow under his boots before he brings his guns against us."

"We will fight them all!" Comes Alone said angrily. "They cannot run us off our lands."

Asi-Yaholo looked at her gravely, his heart filled with pride and also great sorrow. "Where have you heard such words, such wrath?" he asked her softly.

She looked up at him defiantly. "All the young men speak so, and many of the old ones, too."

"And few of them have killed men before," he said wryly. "I fear it will not be nearly such a pleasure as they anticipate."

Otter was holding Mink in her lap, and the child was squirming, anxious to reach her sister, as though she sensed tension in her heart and wanted to be near her for solace. Comes Alone reached out and patted the child's head, and she instantly quieted, but her eyes never left her sister.

"If the white men come," Otter said, "my people say that all those who are black will be stolen away, and their children also. They say we will be sold as slaves to the white men in the north."

Asi-Yaholo said calmly, "They will have to kill me first," he said.

"That will be small comfort," Otter said bitterly, "when I am hoeing some pale eyes' cotton."

He looked up at her, surprised. For the first time, he realized how frightened his women must be, whether or not they spoke of it. "It will not come to that," he said, trying to soothe her. "I promised you, remember?"

"I do remember," she said. "And it will also be small comfort to me if you are killed keeping that promise. But I will not be taken, for I will cut my throat and drown Mink in a shallow pond before I let them take us."

Comes Alone shouted, "I will protect you! I will not let them take my sister!"

Morning Dew, who had been very quiet all afternoon, spoke up then softly and shook her head at her daughter. "*Shta, Tastaukucheed.* Hush,

Little Warrior. It is not for young girls to speak of killing. Your father will not let anything happen to his family."

Comes Alone looked at Asi-Yaholo appraisingly, and he could feel some doubt in her gaze. With more conviction than he felt, he said, "Your mother is right. Let us hear no more talk of war and killing. We are getting stronger every day the white men wait. Like fools, they talk and talk and rage and threaten, but they never do anything to back up their threats. By the time they finally come for us, we will be too strong, and we will drive them back to hoe their own cotton fields."

The children settled down then, and Otter turned her attention to nursing little Mink. He gazed over her head at Morning Dew, and in her smile, he saw that she did not believe his brave words, but it did not matter. She still put her faith in him, as she had for so many years. He sent a swift, silent prayer to the Maker of Breath that he would be always able to keep that faith whole.

Ironically, Asi-Yaholo's words turned out to be truth, for it was almost a year before the leaders were once more summoned to Fort King to a new meeting of treaty commissioners. Many of them questioned why they should make the journey at all, since few doubted what would be said there. But some of the old ones who still remembered how terrible war could be prevailed upon the younger ones to meet with Thompson one last time.

"There are white men who are less perverse than others," Alligator said. "There are some who believe that we should be left undisturbed on our lands. They are not many, but their voices clamor on our behalf. If we do not come to listen when Old Mad Jackson sends his sense-makers, then they will no longer speak for us. I say, we can afford to take one last trip to hear what they might say."

"And I say," Mad Dog replied as they sat round Asi-Yaholo's fire, "that I do not need to travel to the white man's camp to be insulted. I can stay at my own fires for that." Mad Dog had recently taken on a new, young wife, and his old wife was making war on him with the vigilance that only a woman of the Panther clan could muster.

"One thing is certain," Asi-Yaholo said. "If we do not go, we will not be reckoned in the tally. Whether for war or peace, our names will not be counted."

Alligator glanced up at him, amused. "And that, of course, is important, I suppose."

Asi-Yaholo dropped his head. "I have grown used to people listening when I speak," he murmured. "It is a weakness in me now, that I enjoy such recognition."

Alligator slapped the younger man on the back. "Not a weakness, 'Osceola,'" he grinned, deliberately mispronouncing his name as the white man did. "Something you will tire of when you are decrepit as we. Just be sure they say it correctly, so that all the generations may remember."

"If there are any left," Wild Cat said gloomily. "I hear that Old Mad Jackson is sending no less than five new treaty men to tell us what is in the new pages. What odds do you give that any of them will tell the truth?"

"Why bother to wager? You will make the journey regardless," Alligator said, "if nothing else, to give your ears a rest from your women."

They laughed ruefully together, and Asi-Yaholo glanced up to see Morning Dew standing in the shadows. She had heard most of their conversation, no doubt. He nodded to her. She came forward into the light. "There is talk that the white men to the north are attacking the villages there and taking the blacks away from those who have owned them for generations. Have you heard such news?"

"These things have happened before," Alligator said calmly. "Those who live close to the edge of the white man's territory know the risk of such a choice. It is not reason enough for war."

"It would be, at this fire," she said softly.

Wild Cat rose then and clasped Asi-Yaholo's arm in farewell. "I congratulate you," he said jocularly. "You have a woman who will be of great use when the battle begins."

Five days later, Asi-Yaholo and his family left the village once more for Fort King. When they arrived, they quickly saw that few of the leaders intended to stay long for this treaty gathering. The women were clustered in the shade of an oak grove, within sight and hearing of the open tents set up for the meeting. They sprawled with their children, nursing their babies and gossiping softly with each other, but they did not attempt to set up even temporary shelters for their families.

Asi-Yaholo took his position next to Arpeika in the circle of leaders, and he quickly appraised the new white faces ringed before them. Five new men from Old Mad Jackson's Congress had been sent to them this time, five men who wore the fancy dress and high black hats of treaty commissioners. They spoke among themselves, taking little notice of the leaders arrayed before them in their plumes, their best tunics, and their clean white leggings.

One man stood and made grand gestures with his arms, speaking boldly and attempting to pin each individual chief with his pale, blue eyes. He talked for long moments, and the leaders waited respectfully for him to finish, for of course few of them could understand much of what he was saying. Then Abraham, the black translator for the tribes, stood and spoke the white man's words. He told them that the men had come all the way from the Great White Father's place in Washington, that Old Mad Jackson had sent them to get final agreement on the term of their departure for the lands to the west. "Each chief must come and sign the removal paper," Abraham said solemnly, "or the government of the United States will make war on the Seminole beginning now and lasting until every man, woman, and child is buried in the ground they refuse to leave."

There was no sound around the circle of leaders, more than twenty of them sitting quietly, their eyes on the black man before them. But a ripple of breath moved through them which sounded almost like a wind sighing in from the nearby river.

It was come at last, Asi-Yaholo thought. And he felt a flood of almost-relief. At least, he would attend no more of these meaningless councils.

Wiley Thompson stood then, and he also spoke at great length. Asi-Yaholo heard his own name mentioned once, the strange sound of "Osceola," which he caught in a stream of other words. He could only assume the man was naming those leaders present, though he did not look at each man as he spoke. He talked longer than the other man had spoken, and his gestures were more emphatic, less controlled, with an undercurrent of frustration.

Clearly, he had been found wanting, Asi-Yaholo guessed, as a leader of his own people. If Old Mad Jackson found it necessary to send five more men down to help him, this Tom-son must be shamed, indeed.

Abraham stood again and told them Thompson's words. There was nothing new in his speech, only still one more threat of war, of total extermination, if they did not come forward, one by one, and sign the new set of papers which said they would move to the lands of the west.

Now, Thompson and the other chief of the treaty men came forward together, with their papers spread out on their platform of wood, and one by one, followed by Abraham's translation, they called up each individual chief by name. As each leader's name was called, he did not move. When he was called again, he shook his head, refusing to come forward to sign. After Thompson and the other man called more than ten names, Thompson stopped the proceedings with a raised, shaking hand.

He shouted the words, "As of this day, I strike the names of these chiefs from the rolls of leaders of the Seminoles. As of this moment, these men are no longer representatives of their people." Abraham translated as Thompson took his pen and marked through the paper the names of ten leaders, one by one, blackening them out against the whiteness of the leaves.

Now, the men rose in anger, and what was silence became filled with murmurings and angry shouts. It was unthinkable that a white man could have such perversity, even in a race known for that quality. To tell a leader that he was no longer the voice of his people, without consulting the people themselves, was a final insult that Asi-Yaholo could scarcely believe. It occurred to him that, perhaps, the whole tribe of white men were mad and many times mad, as some of the elders claimed.

Suddenly, Thompson called out, "William Powell! Osceola!" and Abraham translated the call for Asi-Yaholo to come forward. He stood slowly, glancing at the two leaders on either side of him. Arpeika looked up in some surprise, but his face was calm. Not a sound came from the chiefs.

"Will you sign the treaty for removal or be stricken from the roles as leader of your people?" Thompson asked, his voice loud and strident in the silence.

Asi-Yaholo walked to the table where the papers were strewn about and withdrew his knife swiftly from its sheath. As the man in the tall black hat leaped in panic from his seat, overturning his chair, Asi-Yaholo plunged the knife into the wood of the table, impaling the papers there.

The chiefs instantly jumped to their feet, roaring their approval, shouting war cries, and Morning Dew and Otter, hearing the clamor and seeing Asi-Yaholo standing before the white men, quickly unsheathed their own knives and set down the children with commands to stay and be silent. If their man was to be threatened, they were ready to leap to his defense.

Wiley Thompson cursed Asi-Yaholo roundly, but his words were only understood by the other whites and the soldiers who stood guard. Asi-Yaholo silently walked out of the tent, away from the still-shouting warriors and chiefs, and down to the oak grove where the women waited.

"Come," he said softly to his family. In seconds, Otter and Morning

Dew gathered their belongings, tied up their skirts for quick movement, and took each child by the hand. Together, the little band left the parade ground, walked through the gates of Fort King, and paddled away in their dugout back to the village in the tangled swamps.

After Asi-Yaholo's dramatic rejection of Thompson's last treaty offer, the white men to the north began to believe that, indeed, the Seminoles might take longer to remove from their land than they first thought. They grew impatient for the possessions of the tribes, most particularly their blacks, and news soon came to the clans to the south that outlying villages were being attacked by lawless whites, bent on stealing slaves.

Asi-Yaholo was now recognized by most of the leaders as the strongest voice of them all. The people sought him out for advice and followed him with their eyes as he traveled from village to village, gathering information, helping train the young ones for war, and making sure that the stores of meat, grain, and powder were growing and safely hidden.

One night, as they sojourned in a village of the Panther clan, Otter came to him, weeping quietly. He took her in his arms and to his bed, though it was not her turn for his company. "What is it, dear heart?" he asked, stroking her softly.

"My mother has been taken," she said, fighting to keep her tears under control. "They tell it at the Panther fires. A man saw her taken by the whites with the other blacks." She choked on her words. "They tied her to a mule and made her walk behind."

"She is an old woman," he murmured, amazed at the white man's foolishness.

"They took every black in the village," she said. "Even the children and ancient ones. No one knows where they have gone."

"Someone does," he said, angrily. "And I will find out who that someone is."

"Will you get her back?" Otter asked him, tearfully.

Asi-Yaholo pulled her close, soothing her with his embrace. "That is one thing you counted on, was it not? When you became my wife. That I would never let the white man take you away."

"Yes. But, you made no promises about my mother."

"That is so, but even as I would not let them take you or our child, I will not let them take the grandmother of my child."

She buried her head in his neck, sobbing now in relief. "Thank you, my husband. I could not bear to think of her ending her life under some white man's lash."

The thought of it, the complete degradation and lack of respect which the whites showed to the people inflamed him all over again, but he kept his temper and concentrated instead on comforting Otter until she slept. Long after she did, he lay awake, making his plans for rescue and revenge.

The next day, he spoke with other warriors, who counseled him not to go to the north to find his wife's mother. "Tom-son has made laws which say that we cannot travel freely across those lands which are not ours, according to treaty," one elder said worriedly. "Not without a paper with his mark."

"To think that we need a white man's permission to travel these lands—" Asi-Yaholo shook his head in sorrow.

"But if we do not follow these laws, they will say we started the war."

"The war will start, whatever they say," another, younger warrior said defiantly.

"Perhaps," Asi-Yaholo said then, reluctantly. "But I will not be the one to bring it on my people. Not if I can avoid it by going to meet with Tom-son."

"It is a perilous thing to do."

"I have no choice," Asi-Yaholo said. "Neither would you, were it a member of your family."

And so, despite the anxious protestations of Morning Dew and Otter, Asi-Yaholo went again to Fort King, this time to get permission to track the white men who had taken his wife's mother without legal claim.

He went to Thompson's office, where he knew the man would be handling his papers at his desk. Bowing respectfully, he waited for Thompson to bring his translator, and then he told him of his promise to his wife and vow to bring her mother back to her unharmed. "She is very old," he said calmly, "and the whites who took her likely have no use for her anyway. But she will be lost and confused away from her people, and her daughter and granddaughter cry for her at night."

Thompson listened to the interpreter's words, his eyes never leaving Asi-Yaholo's face. He said, "You have caused me a good deal of trouble, Powell. You have mocked the United States government, the president's treaty, and the representatives sworn to bring peace to this land. I will not give you permission to track white men." He called his guards quickly, while Asi-Yaholo was listening to the translator. "Lock this man up," he said to the soldiers who approached with eager roughness, "and tell him he will be freed when he signs the treaty for removal. Not before."

To Asi-Yaholo's amazement, before he could react, his hands were yanked behind him and bound, and he was hurried out the door. He shouted back to Thompson, "I come in peace! According to your laws!" But, of course, the man did not understand him.

He writhed under the soldiers' shackles, tearing himself almost out of their grasp, enraged and shrieking. "I will not forget this day! The agent has his day, and I shall have mine!"

Thompson came to the porch of his office and watched as Osceola was dragged away. He called out, "Put that man in irons!"

The soldiers pulled him to the parade ground and threw him inside a small cell. As he struggled, they forced chains on his ankles and his wrists, pinioning him on his belly to the floor. As they slammed out the door, they took most of the light and air with them, for only two small slits windowed the heavy wooden cell, and Osceola was left alone to heave and fight the chains and scream out his rage and betrayal until he exhausted his strength.

After two solid days of screaming and raging, Osceola finally fell silent. The darkness was his only comfort, for then the sweltering heat of the cell was slightly diminished. In the darkness, his prayers to his spirit guide, Otter, were constant and crooning, as he sang his medicine as best he could, facedown in the dirt. He could just barely reach the bowl of sour water and meat the guard had left, if he lapped and snapped at it like a dog. On the second night, he had a vision of Mad New Town, who came to him and sat cross-legged in the dirt of his cell.

"You will not kill many of them from here," the old man told him in his old voice.

"What should I do, Great-uncle?" Asi-Yaholo sighed.

"Get out so that you can kill them."

"And how do I do that?"

"Give them what they want."

"Sign their papers?"

"And then kill them."

"Promise to do one thing, then do another?"

Mad New Town's spirit laughed grimly. "Do you worry they will mistake you for white?"

Mad New Town went away then, but Osceola knew what he must do. When the guard brought fresh water the next morning, he made the sign of writing with his manacled wrist and murmured, "Tell Tomson, I mark his paper."

Thompson came then with a translator and stood in the door of the open cell, the sun blazing about him like fire. "You will sign?"

Osceola nodded. "I will sign."

"I do not trust you," Thompson said impatiently. "You have affronted me and this government too often. I will release you only when the rest of your renegades come in to sign as well."

"Send for a runner," Osceola said tiredly. "It will be done."

Two days later, Arpeika led a band of more than seventy men, women, and children into the parade grounds, dressed in their best shirts, skirts, and leggings. Morning Dew rode behind Arpeika on a borrowed horse. Few horses were left now in the villages. They waited while Arpeika consulted with Thompson and the interpreter, and then the men filed by slowly, touching the pen as Thompson signed their names to the paper agreeing to removal to the Oklahoma territory.

After all had touched the pen, they listened to Thompson's speech impassively. Then the soldiers brought Osceola down the hill from his cell. He was ragged and filthy, and his ankles were darkly mottled where the shackles had cut him. Osceola mounted Morning Dew's horse behind her, as Otter and the children walked behind. As they departed, with their band behind them, Osceola turned and gave a long, quavering wolf's cry which rang up the hill and over the parade ground for long moments.

After they were out of sight of the fort and the soldiers, Osceola slid down from the horse and put his children up behind Morning Dew. He walked alongside Otter, holding her hand. "I am grieved, dear heart, that I cannot keep my vow."

"I know," she said. She dropped her head and squeezed his hand. "These are hard times," she murmured. "But I cannot lose my husband to save my mother."

"I will seek revenge for her. And for all of us."

"Kill that fat, white, bewhiskered carp," she said calmly. "And that will be my comfort."

He stopped and embraced her briefly, and they walked on.

The council gave Osceola the rank of *Tustenuggee Thloko*, Great Warrior, although some murmured that so long as the man who had chained him still lived, his magic was still not powerful enough to vanquish the enemy. But there were no others who could lead the young men into battle any better, and so in 1835, Osceola became the war leader, with Wild Cat as his captain. Soon after he was named *Thloko*, Osceola led a raid on a wagon train bound for Fort King, capturing arms and provisions and taking scalps. The whites would come to call this the Battle of Black Point, the start of the Second Seminole War.

Indeed, the war had begun, and Osceola had struck the first blow. News blew through the scattered camps like a hurricane, and other men, determined to be part of Osceola's defiance, hurried to his hidden settlement in the Cove of the Withlacoochee to ready for battle. A moon later, organized bands of warriors set out under Wild Cat's direction and burned five plantations along the Suwannee and other rivers. From Saint Augustine to the Keys, white men now knew that the war for Florida had commenced.

Osceola still had not evened the score with Wiley Thompson, and he knew, also, that his people expected him to do so. He waited until the weather turned colder, for he hoped the white soldiers would be inside their barracks, with only scant guards posted around the fort. He took Wild Cat and two other warriors, and he set out for revenge.

On the trail, they met Trout Leader, one of the old men who still maintained that war with the whites was futile. He had succumbed to pressure from Thompson, and he had signed away his meager lands, promising to lead his small band to the western territory. When Osceola found him, he was riding a dismal-looking mount at the head of a straggling line of women and children, on his way to surrender to the soldiers.

Trout Leader said, "You are come, nephew," when Osceola blocked his path.

"I am," he said, sadly. He did not relish this role, but he had no choice. "In the name of the National Council, Uncle, I ask you to turn back. You betray your people."

The old man shook his head wearily. "I betray those who would take them into war," he said. "I cannot see them massacred by the white man."

Osceola raised his rifle, his eyes suddenly blurred with tears. He could remember when Trout Leader was a younger, stronger man. He could recall, quite clearly, the affection Mad New Town had for the man Trout Leader used to be. The women behind him began a frantic cry when they saw Osceola take aim. With dignity, Trout Leader faced the rifle and unhooked his feet from the stirrups so that he might fall cleanly from his horse. Osceola took a deep breath and fired. Trout Leader fell, dead before he hit the ground.

While his wives and daughters wept, Osceola went to the old man and cut off his purse from his belt, tossing the silver coins on the ground. Thompson had put those into Trout Leader's hand, he knew, when the old man signed his papers.

Leaving the women and children to their fate, Osceola turned and led his band up the trail to Fort King. Filled with wrath and bitter sorrow, he only regretted that he had not saved two silver coins for the eyes of Wiley Thompson.

They reached the fort, slipped inside, and hid themselves in the brush near Wiley Thompson's house. The rain came on, as chill and relentless as Osceola felt his spirit to be. He watched as Thompson moved through his house, could see the man light his cigar, move a lamp from desk to table, walk from room to room. He waited patiently. He had waited seven months to kill his enemy. He could wait a few hours more for the right moment. Wild Cat and the others were hidden in the brush so well that even Osceola could not tell exactly where they were. But he knew that the moment he gave the signal, they would leap up, their weapons at ready.

The rain stopped finally, and Thompson stepped out on the porch to glance up at the sky. Osceola was so close, he could see the lit end of his Havana. He stood and fired swiftly; as he did so, Wild Cat and the other two warriors stood, firing directly into Thompson's chest. The man's hands shot up in the air as he was knocked back by the bullets against the porch, and he fell behind his rocker.

Osceola gave his war cry and raced from the brush, seeing that, already, the sentries were hurrying toward the house. He raised his knife and plunged it into Thompson's heart. "You took my spirit when you chained me. Now I take it back again and yours in the bargain. I have my revenge!" He heard shots from the approaching soldiers, and he grabbed the agent's hair and cut it away from his scalp raggedly, ripping it off with a jerk of his wrist. Wild Cat and the others were pillaging Thompson's rooms for ammunition and weapons. They grabbed his pistol and his rifle, Osceola shouted at them to come at once, and they vanished into the palmetto brush before the sentries could see where they had gone.

As they left, he shouted his war cry back at the soldiers, keeping trees between his body and the shots from their rifles as they struggled through the brush to reach him. He tied Thompson's scalp to his shoulder strap, shouldered the agent's rifle, and turned toward the south and the hidden settlement.

* * *

A female fox was hunting one cool March evening not far from her den. Cina was a gray fox, *Urocyon cinereoargenteus*, only a year old, but fully mature. Indeed, Cina had a new litter of four pups waiting for her back at her den, and if she were ever able to catch the rabbit she had been chasing for what seemed like half the night, she would be reunited with them.

She rounded the palmetto hammock again, her nose to the ground like a tracking dog. The rabbit had flushed once, and she almost caught it then, but it escaped into its burrow, and now Cina was trying to find its alternate exit. She knew, though she was young, that the rabbit had to have a back door, but the earth was crisscrossed with so many scents, it was hard for her to unjumble them all to find the trail to the place where the rabbit might emerge next.

Cina sat down on her haunches, her tongue lolling out, and rested for a moment. She was about twelve pounds, covered with coarse salt-and-pepper fur, with a red neck and legs. Her tail was long and bushy, black-tipped, with a white streak on the top.

Cina was hungry. Because her prey was so small—frogs and nestling birds, lizards, and little rodents—she had to hunt every night. Now that she was nursing her young, her belly rumbled at her more fiercely than ever before.

She opened her eyes wider in the darkness and listened carefully, her ears pricked toward the rabbit's burrow. Cina's eyes were, like most foxes, particularly well adapted to night hunting. During the heat of the day, she tended to lie up in the den and conserve her energy, only going out if she must. In the sun, her eyes contracted into slits, but at night, they were wide and black and eager.

The rabbit was scratching at dirt under the ground. This told Cina that, likely, his exit was somehow blocked. She listened intently, poised to leap. The rabbit was small, barely grown, but an excellent catch for a young fox. She did not intend to go back to the den without it. She moved silently closer to the burrow and behind the hole, so that she was partially shielded by the low palmetto scrub.

The scratching went on, moving slightly away from her. It seemed to Cina that the rabbit was digging closer to the surface. She froze. Sure enough, the scratching increased and suddenly, a movement of frond showed the rabbit's claws breaking through the soil. She stayed very still, scarcely breathing. The rabbit quickly enlarged the hole, stuck out its head, and sniffed the air, popping back inside again so quickly that Cina could not have caught him even if she had been right there. She was so close, she could see the small droplets of saliva on the rabbit's wriggling nose.

She waited, motionless. Again, more digging, and the rabbit emerged more fully now, widening the hole, squirming out of it, and just as the rabbit turned to pull a branch over his new exit to hide it, Cina struck, leaping high over the brush and pouncing like a huge cat with both paws and teeth, pinning the squealing rabbit to the ground.

She swiftly snapped the rabbit's spine with her jaws and one foreleg, shook it until it hung limp, and snatched it up by the back of the neck to carry it home. Though a small rabbit, its length dragged on the ground as Cina hurried to get to safety. At any moment, her prize could be stolen by another hunter, and she had no more energy to hunt again this night.

Soon, she was at the base of her tree, a tall oak with a twisted spiral trunk and few leaves at the top. Holding her rabbit securely, she ran up the tree, mewing in greeting to her mate and her den-sister as she climbed. Cina was as agile in a tree as any cat. Answering mews from the den told her that the other female she shared her den with was nursing the pups, a chore they frequently shared. She was proud she had such a large prize to bring back. Most often, she ate her prey when she caught it, gobbling it swiftly, leaving only a hunk of skin or a pile of feathers. But this night, she had a rabbit, and she growled happily around her jaws full of rabbit flesh, as she dropped the meat within the den.

Her mate emerged first, a larger fox of more mature years. Cina was his first breeding of the season; the other female that shared his den was his second. Both of them had healthy litters, and he did what he must to keep them safe and thriving. He nuzzled Cina happily on her flanks, keeping well away from her rabbit, for she growled at him with mock ferocity to warn him off.

She tumbled into the den, a large hole thirty feet high in the old, hollow oak, and dropped her rabbit at the entrance, mewing to her pups. They were half-tangled with the other pups, some of them just finishing nursing, but her den-sister rose unceremoniously, letting them drop from her teats, and claimed the rabbit eagerly, yipping at Cina in greeting. The two females tore it open, letting the warm flesh and blood scatter on the pups, who yelped and licked each other and their mothers in a frenzy of excitement.

The two females finished off the rabbit handily, and the scraps were left for the pups to growl and tussle over with their tiny milk teeth. As Cina stuck her head out of the den to offer the carcass to her mate, she heard a snarl of anger and fear. Her mate was out on a lower limb and looking down at the ground. All of his fur was on end, making him appear twice as large as his size, and his eyes were slitted in fear. She could see that he trembled, though he did not move.

She stared below into the dark brush, and she saw the huge form of a panther, tawny in the shadows, crouched and ready to spring. She pulled her head back inside the den and whimpered in fear, quieting the pups with a quick snarl of command. Her den-sister stuck her nose out of the hole silently, sniffing the air with desperate urgency. Cina pushed her nose out as well, and they saw that the panther had leaped up the oak tree within striking distance of their mate. He still had not fled his limb.

With a low growl, the panther jumped the male fox, yanking him off the limb easily and plunging down again to the ground in one fluid movement. They heard the yelp of pain and snarl of panic that meant he was taken; they heard the savage ripping of flesh and bone that meant he was dead. The panther then took him up in its jaws and hurried away with his body, leaving the tree in silence.

Cina and her den-sister sat in the dark hollow with the pups nestled against them, nosing each other and whimpering softly in loss. For hours, they stayed quiet, fearing the panther's return. Of course, they must move the pups, for they would all be endangered now. But they could not move them in darkness, when all of the forest was alive with hunters.

Near dawn, they heard a snarling and felt the tree shake once more with the panther's jump into its lower limbs. Without hesitation, Cina's den-sister emerged from the hollow and moved out onto the branch where she could be seen and snarled viciously down at the ascending cat. Cina pushed her way out of the tangle of pups and shouldered out of the den next to her sister on the limb. Together, they looked down into the yellow, gleaming eyes of the hunting panther, who snarled and swiped at the air with one clawed paw upward at them.

They stood their ground, the two vixens, snarling fiercely, their long canines exposed, and every hair extended on their bodies. The panther glared at them and growled once more in frustration. Two sets of teeth, two snarling jaws of desperate defense, proved to be more than it was worth. The panther turned tail, descending the old oak and disappearing into the shadows.

Panting, Cina and her sister went back inside the den, where the pups mauled them joyously. Cina knew that she must rest. It would take all of their strength and courage to move the pups at first light, but together, they would do what they could to defend them.

* * *

For sixty miles from Fort Brooke to Fort King, the trail was dense with forest growth and tangled brush, so close to the path that a man could hide within six feet of it and not be seen. Tall cypresses shadowed it densely, and moss hung from the trees and waved to and fro like gray curtains. About halfway between the two forts, the trail descended into the Wahoo swamplands, where the water was black and stinking, and the snakes hung from the low tree branches like dark globular fruit. Alligators moved easily across this trail, since it was partially submerged, and clouds of biting insects plagued anything that moved.

It was along this trail that the army crawled in late December, 1835, under Major Francis Dade's command: one hundred men with cannons and horses and wagons. Waiting for them in the brush were just under two hundred Seminole warriors, led by Alligator and Jumper, two of Osceola's lieutenants.

Seventy of the blue jackets were slaughtered by the first Seminole attack, many of them falling before they could even get their muskets unfastened from within their coats, where they had put them because of the rain. Thirty men left of one hundred, some of them injured, managed to build a barricade of trees. When they had it almost two feet high, the Indians came on again, and the massacre was over.

The Seminoles had lost three warriors. Obeying Arpeika's and Osceola's orders, the warriors did not scalp or loot the bodies. They took the weapons, left the soldiers where they lay, and went back to their villages.

Three soldiers survived the attack. One of them dragged himself nearly sixty miles to Fort Brooke, and it was his account of the Dade massacre which convinced the United States Army, at last, to take the war seriously.

Word came soon to the camps of the Seminole that General Clinch was marching toward the Cove of the Withlacoochee with 750 soldiers, bent on the final eradication of Osceola and his people. By Arpeika's count, Osceola had one thousand warriors. He was expected to be victorious.

The women worked almost as hard as the men did, preparing for battle. The older ones stayed in camp with the children, but the women of fighting age, like Morning Dew and Otter, carried the extra water and the rifles, the cloth for bandages, the hatchets, the pots and ladles, and tinder, flints, and powder. Together, in teams, they carried fifty-pound kegs of powder strapped to litters, and they dragged them through the woods as their men walked alongside.

Otter and Morning Dew carried parched corn, *coontee* cakes, and dried venison for Osceola's hunger. Between their breasts, they strapped powder flasks, medicine bags, and small sacks of tobacco. When they reached the place where Osceola said the battle would begin, they made camp. They erected lean-tos to keep the sun off the wounded, laid out the weapons and the cleaning rods, patches, and balls, and brought up fresh water to keep the rifles cool.

The men, meanwhile, sang their medicine chants and prepared to defend their lands with their lives.

When the sentries came running with the news that the soldiers were close, the men formed a long line in the tangled forest for ambush. At Osceola's signal, they opened fire, killing many of the soldiers with their first blasts. For the next five hours, under constant fire, the soldiers attempted to build a wall between themselves and the deadly barrage of the Indians, but by the time the first night of battle came upon the woods, several hundred were dead on the ground.

At dusk, Osceola formed ragged ranks of six hundred warriors and let Alligator lead them in straggling parade, just out of rifle range. They were naked, painted, and strutted to the tuneless blare of a bugle someone blew. Alligator waved a banner and wore only a blue soldier's coat. When they tired of the fun, they went back to their camp, where their wives cooked them fresh meat, and they could bathe in the cool water of the river.

Meanwhile, the soldiers in the barricade sweated, drank stale water, and endured the stench of nearly a thousand men, horses, mules, and dogs crowded into a chest-high fort less than fifty feet on each side.

Osceola kept his warriors waiting five days. It took all his leadership to do so. The whites might think them hesitant, but in fact, it was harder for the warriors to wait than to fight. They amused themselves by setting fire to the brush close to the soldier's barricade so that there was no cover close by. Now the whites must relieve themselves within their fort, rather than outside it.

Major General Gaines, leader of the troop, had deliberately planned his position for one single factor: there was a small spring which trickled from the earth right in the center of the barricade. It barely provided enough water for the stock and the men, if it was rationed carefully. They could see the bend of the Withlacoochee not more than three hundred feet away, but to attempt its cool depths was suicide. His best hope lay in the arrival of General Clinch and reinforcements.

The horses had eaten every last kernel of corn and any fodder which could be gleaned from the trodden ground. They nibbled at the mules' manes and neighed constantly in hunger. The mules, meanwhile, had eaten all the canvas off the wagons and much of their own harnesses. The men were playing dice for the dogs.

Eight long and tedious days passed relentlessly. The soldiers became desperate and with desperation came carelessness. Gaines no longer had the patience or will to keep shouting, "Get down!" and each time he did not, a shot took out a man, often only wounding him enough to put him in agony and make his neighbors wish him dead. They had eaten all the dogs days before, all the horses except Gaines's own gaunt mount, and there was no more wood for fires. The last wood detail came back with two men dead, four wounded, and no wood collected. No other would be risked.

Osceola discussed the situation with his lieutenants and decided that the whites had had enough. Surely, they would now give up and go home and leave them in peace. They fashioned a white flag of leggings and walked to the barricade, three abreast.

General Gaines met them with his own envoy and his black interpreter. He would not speak of peace, but he would consider a truce, he said. As he was explaining his position to Osceola, gunfire opened from behind them. General Clinch had arrived with reinforcements. Not realizing he fired on a peace envoy, he moved his men into position rapidly, but not rapidly enough. Before he could give the order for a full attack, Osceola and his seven hundred warriors melted into the swamp.

General Gaines had lost four hundred men, all of the stock, and had to carry back more than two hundred wounded and sick. When they arrived back at Fort Drane, they found a haggard mob of settlers waiting for them in anger. Wild Cat was making life outside the forts impossible. More settlements had been attacked and burned, and the civilians demanded an end to it.

General Gaines told the settlers that the enemy had been met, beaten, and forced to sue for peace. In fact, he added, Osceola was in the process of surrender when General Clinch arrived and fired upon them. The war would be over before it was time to put in crops, he promised, and the Indians would be packed up for the western lands within the year. He went to see that his men were fed, then retired to his tent, where he penned a letter to his wife saying that Florida was, in his opinion, the sorriest piece of land any two peoples had ever fought over, and he did not expect to wrest it from those who now held it. Frankly, he added, he hoped for a transfer soon.

Osceola, at council more than fifty miles away, told his lieutenants that the struggle would continue and that they would be victorious, even if it took the rest of his life.

"We should have killed them when we had them," Alligator said morosely.

"We were so close," another warrior nodded.

"We were almost out of lead," Osceola sighed, "and more soldiers were coming. I was surprised it took them as long as it did to get there."

"No matter how many we kill," Alligator said in Osceola's defense, "they have more to send after us."

"I truly thought our best hope was to demand that they go and leave us in peace. We had beaten them, after all. Men of honor would have done so."

The warriors shook their heads.

"The day the whites become men of honor is the day the mosquitoes decide to make honey," Alligator said. "We are going to have to kill them all."

General Gaines was soon sent home by General Scott, a man celebrated for brilliant offensives. His plan was to surround the Seminole camps hidden deep in the swamp, surprise them, capture them, and ship them to the western territories. He led two thousand soldiers, supply wagons, and stock in three separate wings. The eastern wing made only seven miles in two days, the men slogging through dense undergrowth and bogs, hacking at the tough green wall of palmettos until they were exhausted. The moment they stopped hacking, the mosquitoes settled on them like black capes from head to foot.

The western wing of General Scott's offensive, led by Colonel Lindsay, was lost in the morass somewhere to the south. In an attempt to locate the others, Lindsay fired off cannons every hour or so.

Scott's own division, together with two six-mule teams, cannon carriages, and teams of oxen dragging two flatboats on trucks, had selected the driest route and still took three days to go twenty-five miles, for the warriors plagued them round every turn in what passed for a trail. Now they were in the lowlands, and men walked alongside each cannon and flatboat and wagon to push when they were mired, which happened every quarter hour. Osceola and his men watched from the brush and the low branches of trees, so close that they could hear the men swear at the chiggers and the mud. They had known the soldiers were there long before they heard the cannons, of course, and they watched them flail through the swamps from comfortable berths in trees.

"They must be insane," Osceola said to Alligator. "This is more than perverse, this is stupid."

"Almost do I feel sorry for these fools," Alligator said, watching as men only fifty yards away tried to wrest a wagon from the mud. It was bogged to its axles, and the mules were near dead with exhaustion. "White men are as stubborn children."

"Why do they wear their heavy jackets?" another warrior wondered aloud.

"Wild Cat sank the supply boats on the Oklawaha," Osceola said. "They have nothing else."

Alligator looked down at himself, naked except for his rifle strap, powder pouch, and knife. He laughed softly. The fine coat of mud and grease he wore kept off the mosquitoes, and his brown skin blended in perfect camouflage with the brown, curled ferns in the heat of March.

"Have the women moved?" another warrior asked Osceola. His family had come from the north most recently so that he could fight with Osceola's army. He had a new daughter, and he still thought as much of his wife as he did his rifle.

"The camps have dispersed and gone to the Everglades," Osceola nodded. "The white men will find nothing but old fires, if they even make it as far as the Withlacoochee."

"We need not waste powder and lead on these," Alligator said, as the men nearest him dropped to their knees and cursed weakly, whipping the oxen in a futile effort to budge the wagons. A horse suddenly reared and fought the reins, his legs bleeding from hock to hoof. Like all of the stock, he was cut from the sharp saw grass until his patience was gone. His soldier struggled to calm him, and he neighed furiously in anger.

"You are right, old friend," Osceola said.

They moved from cover, tracked quietly to their hidden dugouts, and poled away.

A month later, General Scott marched his exhausted men back to Fort Brooke, most of them sick and broken. He was called before a court of inquiry, where he blamed the very land he was attempting to take. And General Gaines for not having killed Osceola when he had the chance. He was acquitted.

July of 1836 was one of the hottest summers Morning Dew could remember. To her relief, the war seemed to have abated for the season, and the men lolled in the shade as they should, telling stories of battles, recounting coups and failures, bragging and commiserating, and letting their pipe smoke drift up into the hot, humid air. Mink was now five summers, old enough to explore the camp and its surroundings without constant supervision, so long as her big sister Comes Alone was nearby. It was a special joy to hear children in camp laugh again and run unfettered, without fear of rifle shots from a pale eyes' ambush.

Otter was over her mourning for her mother, their man was not so preoccupied with thoughts of revenge and death, and she felt that she could breathe again for the first time in many months.

It was well that the men were not at war, for they were sorely needed for hunting these days. Because of the constant movement, few crops were planted. Harvest would be lean in the months ahead, and the stores of grain were very low. Morning Dew felt the pangs of hunger more often now than she had remembered anytime in her life. She knew her daughters felt the same, but they were their father's children. They did not complain.

The blue jackets had failed to capture the camps, but the people were so scattered into small bands, hidden deep in the swamps, that the women missed each other and their clan sisters. Even Ochola and her new man had left the camp, for he said that he was too old to fight, and she was too loud to hide if the soldiers came. No one spoke it, but all knew that anywhere Osceola slept, the soldiers were more likely to come. The dances would be few this year; she sighed as she swept the *cheke* with a palmetto broom. But at least they still had their lands.

It was told among the spies who stayed close to the forts that nearly a third of the soldiers within were sick. Bad stools, what the white man called the flux, chills, fever, the spotted sickness, and a dozen other maladies which the white man got in the swamps had brought the workings of the fort to a slow crawl. Morning Dew and most of the women agreed: they cordially asked the Maker of Breath each evening in their meditations to relieve the white men of their suffering by taking their spirits to the sky.

Indeed, her only real worry was her man's health and the strength of his spirit. On one of the last raids, when they went out to take the supply wagons along the roads to Fort Drane, he had come back with the shaking sickness. It was a sickness which the white men got often, but the Seminoles did not.

No one spoke of it, but Morning Dew wondered if it were, perhaps, his white father's blood which had so weakened him. The news he brought with him likely made his heart susceptible to disease, as well. Peeping and her man had been taken in one of the raids and sent to the western territory with almost a hundred others. He had wept when he told her, wept for the first time since she had known him. "I can do nothing," he said over and over, until she thought she would despair.

He spent more than ten days in his bed upon his return, something she had never seen him do before in her life. Arpeika came with his infusions of catfoot and everlasting for strength. He blew into the medicine tube, chanted through the night, and conferred with Asi-Yaholo's spirit as it roamed outside his body.

"He has bad dreams," Arpeika told Morning Dew and Otter. "He must be kept warm when he shivers with the fever, no matter if he fights the blankets. His soul is traveling too far from his body."

He had slept most of those ten days, rousing only to drink the good broth she made him and the tisanes of roots and herbs. She could do nothing more but bathe his body with cool water. His hands trembled like those of an ancient one when he held the ladle to his lips.

And then he was well again, or seemingly. But a moon later, the fever returned, no less fierce than before. So it had gone on, for much of the hot months, and she feared he might never be strong again. His head pounded, he said, when he made the slightest exertion. His excrement was watered and bloody, and his skin felt prickled and stretched, as though it no longer fit his body.

Morning Dew cried once, briefly, in worry and heartache, wept as she hugged Otter, and they dried each other's tears. They did not want the children to see their fear. Only with each other could they say quietly what they could scarcely admit to themselves: their man might never be himself again.

One thing only she did not share with her sister. The last time she had bathed her man, had helped him stand to stagger to the bushes to relieve himself, he had wrapped his arms around her and hugged her intensely, long and tenderly. Drawing away, he looked deeply into her eyes. She knew what he was saying to her without words. Life was more precious to him than ever, now that he could see its end. Hearts he loved were sacred, and every touch was to be savored. It was a lesson many men learned as they drew near death, either in battle or in years. She almost wept then, at his sad smile. For he was too young to learn this lesson yet, as much as she loved the urgency in his embrace. He must be a *tustenuggee* yet a while more, else the people would perish. He could not be reckless with his love or his strength.

She told Otter only, "Do not be wounded if he does not wish to share your bed, sister, and take his usual pleasure there. He must save his powers now for other things."

Otter nodded in understanding. Nothing else needed to be said.

In December of 1836, General Thomas Jesup took over command of the forces in Florida and brought with him a new and more effective strategy: instead of sending out hundreds of men to kill, he sent out small bands of raiders to destroy. In countless hidden camps across the swamp, the people would return from hunting parties to discover their huts burned, their crops destroyed, their stores ruined. Any blacks or part-blacks they ambushed were taken prisoners and marched back to the forts to be penned up like cattle until they could be sold. Women and children had been abducted, families were sundered, and those who were still free were facing a winter of starvation. Hundreds had been boarded on ships bound for New Orleans to make the trip up the Mississippi and, from there, to the Oklahoma lands.

In May of 1837, Alligator, Jumper, Mikanopee, Wild Cat, Arpeika, and Osceola sent a message to General Jesup that they would come in and talk, if he would let the women and children go free.

"My husband, you have done this once before," Morning Dew said worriedly when she learned of the plan. It had been decided mutually by the elders and the war leaders. "Last time, they put you in a hole in the ground."

"I recall it well, beloved," he said quietly. "But the women are weary, and those children we have left are hungry. Too many have been taken from us. Too much lost. We need rest."

She wanted to weep, but she forced back her tears. It was her man who needed rest, she knew, more than anyone.

"We have shown that we will fight for our lands," he said tiredly. "We will ask the new white leader, Chess-up, to mark the leaves that say it is ours forever."

"And if he will not?"

Asi-Yaholo shrugged, a ghost of his former self. "Then we will fight until we die."

Her tears came to the surface then, no matter how she tried to suppress them. "I am going with you," she said.

To her surprise, he nodded his head. "Yes. My family will go with me, as will the other women and children. They cannot put us all in jail, I think. And if they see that we are serious, perhaps we can put an end to this war after all."

Otter and Morning Dew then began to prepare for yet another journey to the fort. Comes Alone helped to collect his clothing and beads, to clean his rifle, to restitch his moccasins.

"You are my sun and my moon," he said to Morning Dew and Otter as he rested, watching them work. The malaria had returned, and he was weak and fevered. "And you," he said to Comes Alone and Mink, "are my stars." He embraced them each as though he might never see them again, as he did several times now every day and evening.

By the time all was readied and the leaders of both sides could assemble, it was October. Osceola and the others came into the fort, followed by their people, under white flags of truce.

Ironically, the meeting was set for Moultrie Creek, the same spot where fourteen years before the leaders had signed a treaty that promised them their land for twenty years. Osceola could remember hearing the stories of that council as though it were only last season. Then, there had been dancing and feasting and white men from far away came to watch them and marvel at their beauty. Now, Osceola thought grimly, the women and children were weary and ragged, less than half the number they had been fourteen years before, and most of their blacks were gone.

He glanced over at Morning Dew, who waited with the rest of the people in a shaded grove. She was no longer young, of course; neither was he. But he could still recall as though it were only a few seasons ago, the way her flesh cleaved to his, the way her dark, silken hair fell over his face as she rode astride him, her head thrown back in passion and the loveliness of surrender. And Otter. She told him, so long ago, that she had saved herself for something important. For something of which she must be worthy. He bowed his head in pain. It had been many moons since he had the strength to love his wives as a husband should. Yet one more thing this war had taken from them.

More than three hundred soldiers stood at attention at the outside ring of the council circle. The leaders assembled and took their places, sitting in the places they had sat so many times before, though the treaty conventions had moved from fort to fort. By now, the customs and arrangements were set in their minds. The white flags of truce snapped in the wind over their heads, and Osceola realized as he took his place that this was a trap. There were far too many soldiers for a peace talk.

General Jesup sat next to General Hernandez from the far coast, the city of Saint Augustine, which Wild Cat had terrorized with particular relish. Both men sat at the treaty table with their assorted translators, sense-makers, and assistants. Osceola tried to see into their hearts as he watched them speak among themselves, glancing often at the soldiers closest to the leaders in the back rows. He saw nothing but treachery there.

For a swift moment, he thought of leaping to his feet, lunging for the closest rifle, and laying about him, killing as many as he could before they cut him down. But a great weariness settled over him. He could not make himself move. And he knew that if he did, the women and children and blacks who had been taken would be deported or sold as surely as rain would come again in the autumn.

General Jesup stood and addressed the leaders cordially, and his translator carried his words to them with no betrayal of emotion. After many words of welcome and a statement of regret that the war had cost each side so many, Jesup said, "We are glad that you have come, at last, to surrender yourselves, that this war can finally end."

A wave of alarm rippled through the leaders then, and they cast their eyes about to each other and most particularly, to Osceola. He stood up and faced the general. "We came to make peace. We come to arrange the release of our black people and our families. Not to surrender," he said firmly.

"There will be no peace so long as you and the other renegades are free," General Jesup said. "We have been deceived by you before, Powell. Now, we need more than your word. The war will end only when you are out of the battlefield. We will exchange our prisoners, the ones who are not black, for the leaders. The blacks will be given back to their owners. Will you come with me peacefully, or must we restrain you?"

Osceola hesitated, looking at the armed soldiers surrounding the men like a bristling corral.

"You will be treated with honor," Jesup said softly. "Your family will be cared for, and you will be given every comfort. The United States recognizes you as a great leader of your people and a warrior."

"I cannot surrender," Osceola said.

"I understand this," Jesup said mildly. He nodded to his closest aides, and they came forward to flank Osceola.

"You and the other leaders will be taken to Fort Marion," Jesup said, "where you will stay until arrangements can be made for transport of the people to the Indian territory. They will be given food and supplies and annuities for their land, just as promised before." He lowered his voice. "You must come with me, now, Powell. There is no other way."

"And my family?"

"They will accompany you or stay, as you wish." Jesup sensed Wild Cat and Alligator starting to rise in the back of the group, and he signaled to the nearest soldiers. They went instantly to the two men and flanked them, and again, all eyes went to Osceola.

He saw that he had no choice. There were too many of the soldiers and his people were too few and too tired to make a defense. There were still hundreds of them hidden in the swamps, and he knew that no matter what he did, no matter what Jesup decided, those hundreds would be extremely difficult to find, much less remove to the western territories. For now, however, he must think of himself and his family. He suddenly, terribly, did not wish to die.

He turned to the outside of the circle and said to his brethren, "I shall go with them now."

"But what of the prisoners?" Wild Cat called out angrily.

"Those who are not black will be released," Jesup said again.

The soldiers moved in, closing ranks.

"Bring up a mule for Powell to ride," Jesup said kindly. "I will not have the Black Drink Singer walk all the way to Fort Marion."

When Osceola walked outside the council area, away from the tent and the white flapping banners, the people waiting under the grove of the trees saw immediately that he was flanked by soldiers. Behind him came Wild Cat, Alligator, Jumper, and Arpeika. The people surged forward, Morning Dew and Otter at the front of the anxious crowd, but Osceola lifted his hand and said, "We have agreed to peace. We will exchange ourselves for the women and children who are being kept from their families."

The men murmured in anger, and the women set up a wail. He could hear Morning Dew's cry, could see Otter standing resolute and fierce, the children beside her, her knife drawn and ready for battle. He almost could not bear it. "Please," he said gently. "Let us do what we must do."

Before the people could decide what action, if any, they should take, they saw their leaders led away, Osceola and Arpeika mounted, the others walking behind.

"It is fifteen miles to Fort Marion," General Jesup told them then. "We will arrange for transport for any who wish to join their men. The others will stay here, under our protection."

While the soldiers assembled and readied for the trek to the fort, most of the people slipped away into the brush. Morning Dew, Otter, and some of the other women and children, however, prepared to make what camp they could right where they were.

As Osceola rode off between two columns of marching soldiers, he did not look back at them or wave a farewell. He did not know if it would be more comfort or more pain to them to see his face or his signal, so he did nothing at all.

By the end of November, the winds were chill around the high gray walls of Fort Marion, and the cells Osceola shared with Wild Cat, Arpeika, and Alligator were dank and cold. They were free to roam the inner courtyard where the bleak sun might warm them slightly, but if they did so, Wild Cat thought the soldiers would hear them plotting.

For the hundredth time, Wild Cat said to Osceola, "You must come with us. You will die if you do not."

Osceola only shook his head. They all knew the reason he could not scale the walls of this place with the others, for his family was there. If he left, they would be held hostage, likely shipped to the west without him, and he could not hope to get them all out. "No," he said softly. "For me, there is only one way."

"Chess-up will never agree to your terms," Alligator said.

"He might," Osceola said. "Once you are gone, he will see that I could have escaped with you and did not. He will then see that I can be trusted to keep my word."

Wild Cat snorted angrily. "That is one of you, at least."

Arpeika sighed. "These winds have edges like none we knew in our own lands."

"You must go inside," Osceola said to him gently.

Arpeika shook his head, ignoring the suggestion. He would not miss even a council of four, no not if he froze. "Even if he agrees to let you go with your family to Pahay-o-kee, to the sea of grass," Arpeika said slowly, "how will you live there with no others?" He shook his head doubtfully. "A woman without her clan about her is like a woman with no hands. Your wives will perish out there without their sisters."

Arpeika was an old man, Osceola thought, and he had always lived for the people and with the people. He could not imagine that it might be possible for a warrior to live with his family alone. Indeed, he noted wryly, he might be right. They may well starve in the Everglades, with no clan members to share the work of provisioning. But he had few other choices. His brain was sore with thinking, and the malaria kept him too weak to see the future clearly. His mother was gone, perhaps his grandmother as well, no one knew. His family was camped outside these walls, living for the brief time each day when they could be together. His mouth twisted grimly. It was perverse of the white men to cage such an old man as Arpeika. It was an action of dishonor, more to his captors than to himself.

The cold walls of the fort smelled like decay and old ocean water. He felt that he was buried alive beneath the sea. He ached for the soft voice of Morning Dew, the touch of Otter's skin, the laughter of his daughters. He would have given ten seasons just to hear his grandmother's laugh once more, to see his mother's smile. Mad New Town came and spoke with him more and more these long, dark nights, but he had no advice.

There was nothing for them to do but escape. The warriors had spent many days fasting to make themselves as lean as possible, and in the night, they had carved the single, high window ledge in their cell as deep as they dared, replacing the stones each morning. They had twisted ropes of their bedding and hidden them under their bunks, and sharpened one leg of each bunk into makeshift weapons. One night, by agreement, they all squeezed out of their cell windows, lowered themselves to the ground, and took off through the palmetto brush.

The next morning, the soldiers found eighteen men missing. The fact that Osceola and Arpeika still remained did not keep General Jesup from flying into a rage. He ordered the remaining prisoners put into irons. When the fort doctor objected, citing Osceola's weak state of health and Arpeika's advanced age, Jesup said, "The sooner they die, the sooner this war will be over. Alive or free, they are something to fight for. Leg and wrist irons, no exceptions!"

And so, Osceola found himself alone in the cell, chained to the walls by iron bands attached to an iron ring. He was allowed to come outside the cell each morning to see his family, but his leg chains were kept in place at that time, so that he could only shuffle slowly. It was more trouble than it was worth to try to move, so they came to him, sitting as near him as they could, speaking softly of the old days, watching Comes Alone and Mink play with colored stones in the dust.

"What do you miss most in this place?" Comes Alone asked her father wistfully.

"Besides your sweet face?" he asked her, smiling. "I miss most the sun. And the smell of green earth. Small things, I always thought them. But they are the pulse of life."

Morning Dew took his hand and pressed it to her face. "There is a strong pulse here yet, old man."

He stroked her face tenderly, reaching for Otter as well. "It is too quick," he said softly. "This sickness has me fast, I think."

Otter took his other hand, and both of them ignored the way it trembled. "You will see many summers yet, my heart. The sun will warm those bones and you will bury Chess-up's, if the Maker of Breath hears our prayers."

"How many warriors have we?" Osceola asked then, a topic he turned to again and again.

"More than a thousand still," Morning Dew assured him. "They are going to the south, to the Pahay-o-kee. When you are well enough, we will follow them."

"The pale eyes try to capture them, but they cannot," Otter said scornfully. "In the last battle, our warriors killed 130 white soldiers."

Osceola raised his brows in surprise. "So many? How many warriors did we lose?"

"Five, we heard," Otter said. "Can you imagine that the pale eyes would still be allowed to lead men after such a defeat? If a *tustenuggee* lost so many, no warrior would follow him again, not even into the bushes to clear his bowels."

They laughed together then, and Osceola saw how his daughters' eyes brightened, watching first their mothers and then him for signals that they might laugh as well. He pulled them to his arms and smelled their fresh girl odors, and his eyes watered with mingled joy and pain.

As the afternoon dwindled, the cold grew stronger. They went back to his cell. Now that he was alone there, Morning Dew and Otter had done their best to make it comfortable for him, spreading mats on the floor and building a small fire in the corner of the room. Each time the soldiers came in, they put out the fire. Each time they left, Otter rekindled it.

A month later, the news came that all the prisoners and their families would be moved to Fort Moultrie, South Carolina, where they could not escape, for there was no way off the island except by boat. Osceola told his family, "There is always a way to escape, that is one thing the white man still has not learned."

"Will they take those off?" Mink asked her father, gesturing to the irons on his legs. She had wept when she first saw them and still could not be reconciled to their presence on her father's body.

"I believe they will," he told her. "And so, we will be able to greet the Breath Maker each morning again together, as we did before."

Mink smiled shyly and hugged him hard. It had been one of her favorite times, when she and her father and Comes Alone went to the edge of the river each morning, faced to the east, and greeted the morning sun.

When they reached Fort Moultrie, they discovered that the white people found the captured warriors of more interest the farther away from their own lands they traveled. Most particularly did the pale eyes who came over on the excursion boats want to see this Osceola, the brave Seminole chief. So every day, soldiers escorted him outside the walls of the confinement yard, so that tourists could come and speak to him or sketch him, talking among themselves often in a way that suggested they did not think him capable of understanding what they said.

He was reminded of something Arpeika told him once. That it was a terrible fate to live among *Tsilokagalgee*, People of a Different Speech. He could not understand many of their words, and so he learned to ignore them. He remembered the way his grandmother sang to the panther so long ago, when they were on the trail down the Suwannee. She sang in the face of danger, even death. He could do the same. And so, when the whites circled him, speaking about him and laughing among themselves as though he were a penned prize hog, he closed his eyes and crooned his war songs, his songs of *sabia*, and those praises to the forest he recalled from so many years before. In this way, he often did not hear the white voices at all.

Comes Alone understood enough of what they said, however, to take offense. "When I am a warrior," she said to her father, "I shall kill as many white men as my father has hairs on his head."

"I shall kill more," Mink said resolutely.

"You shall not be warriors," Osceola said mildly. "You shall be women. Like your mothers and your grandmothers before you."

"I shall be a warrior," Comes Alone said firmly. "I shall make my spirit quest, and I shall ask Otter to come to me, in my father's name."

Osceola laughed kindly. "No doubt, your prayers will be answered, brave heart. I know few who can say nay to you. No doubt Otter will bend to your will, as well."

January was colder than November, and still the tourists came to see the last of the Seminole chiefs. On one particularly windy and chill afternoon, Osceola sat huddled in his blanket and came back inside to his cell shivering with the fever.

"How do you feel, Old Man?" Otter asked him anxiously when she saw his pale face and his trembling hands.

He pointed to his throat. "Pain here," he said hoarsely.

That night, they slept together, Otter on one side, and Morning Dew on the other, warming his body against the chill as best they could. By morning, however, he was no better.

Morning Dew and Otter cooked the *sofkee* for him, but he could scarcely swallow. His speech was slow and painful, and his eyes looked at distant things rather than at their faces. That evening, he sat quietly with his children at his feet, and Morning Dew watched him with growing alarm.

"Can you drink some tea?" she asked him.

"Some," he said hoarsely, "but I do not really want it. I was thinking just now of our old village on the river."

"The Suwannee," she murmured.

He nodded. He could not tell her all he pictured in his mind, for the pain in his throat. The way the schools of fish used to spread two or three miles, and the splashing they made as they passed over the shoals so loud that it kept the people awake at night; the phosphorescence of their scales was blinding in the lowering sun. The taste of mangoes and figs and papaya, the bananas his grandmother grew, and the tamarinds which filled his mouth with tart juice. He saw a large black bear near the river once, picking oysters off the mangrove roots, reaching high into the branches to swat down the long seedpods shaped like the pale eyes' cigars. Mad New Town told him to use fear and discard what he could not fashion into something for his spirit. Well, and it seemed to him that he had lived that counsel. He thought of Otter, his sleek black spirit guide who had come to him on the riverbank that night. What was the message he had brought? Something which had to do with the river. The river. It had coursed through his life, his dreams, for so long, he could close his eyes and hear it, smell it, as effortlessly as he could hear his own heartbeat. He slept then, walking back through his life and his memories.

Sometime in the night, Morning Dew sent Comes Alone to fetch the soldier doctor. Her daughter asked fearfully, "Is my father dying?"

"Perhaps," Morning Dew said gently. "Only *Kithla*, the Knower, can answer that question. Go quickly."

The doctor came and looked in Osceola's throat, poked and prodded him with his long, metal instruments, and generally brought him more pain than he had before. "His tonsils are horribly inflamed," the doctor said. "The infection is running rampant through his body. If you would let me scarify them, perhaps apply leeches—" but Osceola shook his head and refused to open his mouth for the man again.

In the early-morning hours, Morning Dew and Otter, sensing that it was time, helped their husband to sit up, to paint half of his face and his throat red, and to don his finest shirt, beads, and leggings. When he was ready, he motioned for his *sabia* pouch and took out his holy objects, arranging them in a half circle before him where he sat. He fingered the clamshells that his spirit guide had given him, his gaze opaque and far away. He put his knife in his waist sheath and hummed his old song to Otter, crooning the chant when he could not force his throat to make the words.

Comes Alone and Mink came to him, weeping, and he hugged them tightly, smiling and stroking their cheeks, murmuring small sounds of comfort.

Otter bent to him and embraced him. "Do not worry for us, Old Man," she said. "The pale eyes will never take me."

The two white soldiers and the doctor who were in the cell stood against the wall quietly, giving the family as much space as possible, but Comes Alone turned to them and shouted at the soldiers, "Get out! Leave us now!" They obeyed her commands as though she were a warrior, going outside the door and closing it gently behind them.

Osceola put out his hand to Morning Dew, and she came into his embrace. "Beloved," he whispered, his eyes closed with the pain.

"My heart goes with you on your journey," she said, fighting to keep her voice steady and her eyes clear.

"Do not haste to join me," he murmured hoarsely. He laid himself down then on his back, his hands together over his knife which rested on his breast.

He was comforted by Mad New Town, who sat alongside him. "You are come, grandnephew. It is good," the old man told him confidentially, "to know that you are not the last of our people. It is a bad fate to wander the earth alone, after all the fires of your clan are out."

Osceola smiled slightly, feeling lighter. "I did not surrender."

"You did not surrender," repeated the ancient voice. "But it is time to do so now."

"Yes," he murmured. And that was the last thing he heard, as the darkness swirled around him like the waters of a river, deep, cool, and welcoming.

Two days later, the papers carried the announcement that Osceola, the last of the Seminole chiefs, had died at Fort Moultrie on January 30, 1838, at the age of thirty-four. He was buried under a marble headstone donated by a Charleston writer who had been inspired by Osceola's courage and spirit. His head, however, was cut off by Dr. Frederick Weedon, who had tried to treat him. The doctor carried it back to Saint Augustine, where he displayed it proudly for years, hanging it on his sons' bedsteads when they misbehaved.

A week after Osceola's death, another piece of news was reported in the Saint Augustine paper, to less attention. A shipload of passengers, among them Indians bound for New Orleans and hence on conveyances to the western territories, had docked, and her captain reported that some of the Indians had escaped over the side as they neared port. He did not know their identity or their number, but it is supposed that Osceola's wives were among their number.

Arpeika escaped Fort Moultrie and, then in his nineties, fled with several hundred of his people into the Everglades. After many years of chasing them, the United States government declared the Seminole War over. No treaty was ever signed by those in hiding, and their descendants consider themselves victorious to this day.

Meanwhile, the settlers moved south, pushing aside what swamp-lands they could, living in small shacks on what dry land they could find. Some built fine homes; most soon forgot their dreams of wealth and high cotton. The swamp and the river would not cooperate with such dreams.

Part Two

1860—1865

"It is a land of swamps, of quagmires, of frogs and alligators and mosquitoes! A man, sir, would not immigrate into Florida. No, sir! No man would immigrate into Florida—not from hell, itself!"

(John Randolph of Roanoke, 1830)

*F*or years following Osceola's death, the United States Army hounded the Seminoles, from one secluded hammock to another. Sometimes the soldiers came upon the bodies of young children who had not been able to keep up with the fleeing clans, their nostrils and mouths stuffed with mud grass by their mothers.

The Seminoles fought when they could—at a sugar plantation on the Saint Johns River, at a cotton plantation near Tallahassee, on roads used by the army, at the lighthouse at Cape Florida on Key Biscayne, and exposed settlements west of the Apalachicola in the panhandle. In retaliation, soldiers, sailors, other Creeks, black spies, and double agents roamed Florida to discover and destroy Seminole camps. Bloodhounds, prairie fires, and poison in the springs were used to keep them moving deeper into the Everglades or into the recesses of the Okefenokee Swamp.

If they were captured, parties of exiles, including blacks or part-blacks among them, were sold to white plantation owners to the north, mothers sobbing as they were sent in one direction, their children and husbands in another. Some Seminoles who were misfortunate enough to have darker skin than their kin were enslaved along with their black clan members.

Often, however, scattered Seminoles were able to survive right under the noses of their pursuers, blending into the brush as expertly as the copperhead, burying dugouts in the sand and digging them back up after soldiers passed, hiding their huts under dense thatch and their corn rows under high, thick canopies of palmetto.

By 1850, the Suwannee River belonged to the white settlers, farmers, and government who claimed it. But the wilderness was still dense, the hold of human hands on it was tenuous, and would remain so for at least another fifty years.

1860

Not Black crept slowly to her usual hiding place, the copse of thick honeysuckle which bordered the cabin's yard, and settled down silently to watch. She had come to the white man's cabin three times before, a place she knew was forbidden by her mother and her own good sense, but she could not obey her best instincts.

The chickens clucked and bickered among themselves in the open space of the yard, blind to her presence not twenty feet away, watching. The mule dozed, still in harness at the grinding stone, and he did not flick an ear in her direction.

Not Black smiled to herself. The white man's animals were as oblivious to what was around them as the white man was, her mother would say. She stretched out her limbs carefully, readying for a long vigil.

She was fourteen, comely enough her mother and grandmother told her, and of pure blood. That was why her mother named her Not Black, so that she might not be mistaken for what the whites called maroon, anyone with black blood.

"There was a time," her mother had told her, "when daughters had names of beauty. Summer Wind or Laughing Duck or Morning Dew, like your grandmother's. But now, we must name our children by what they are not, rather than what they are. You are not black, my heart, and must never be mistaken for one."

"I am not dark of skin," Not Black had said with a sulky tone, "and *your* name is none too beautiful." She was of an age when much that her mother said caused her irritation.

"My father thought it was," Comes Alone said firmly. "It is a name of courage."

"And you could not give me such a name?" she had asked indignantly. "I hate my name. I'm brave. I should have a name of courage, as well."

"Your father said when you were born—"

"I know," she said shortly. "That I was the future. You have told me before."

"That you were the future of our people and that he could not bear to lose you," Comes Alone continued patiently. "And so he gave you a name which might protect you. Now stop being so stubborn, my daughter, or we can change your name right now. Would Snapping Turtle please you?"

Not Black had laughed then, in spite of her determination to be angry. Her mother was often able to make her laugh, to make her father laugh as well. Likely, that was one reason he loved her so.

The cabin door opened suddenly, and Not Black held her breath. The old man came out and went around the porch to the rear, heading for the mule. "Soon," she whispered. "Soon, he will come out as well."

Long moments passed, and she felt the hot sun above her head through the honeysuckle, smelled the dust in the yard, the scent of the foliage, the pigs in their pen at the corner of the stable, and the distant cattle and horses in the farther field. The white man was rich. Rich with stock, rich with wonderful objects, rich with the odors of things which belonged to him. But that alone was not what drew her to spy on his house, what pulled her almost against her will to come to this place of great danger and sit, when she had corn rows to weed and melons to turn and pigs of her mother's to move from one forage to another.

The door creaked again and she froze. He came onto the porch.

Tom Craven let the cabin door slam and looked around for his father as he pulled the straps to his overalls over his shoulders. He ran his hand through his lank, blond hair, whistled a snatch of a tune, and walked down the steps, scuffing his bare feet on the wood planks in time to his whistle.

Not Black knew the boy's name just as she knew how many cattle his father owned, how many roosters, how many pigs, how many skins dried on the cabin wall, and how many lamps the two men lit inside the cabin at night. She knew no woman lived in the cabin, that the man often left Tom alone when he drove the cattle to market, and that Tom's dog was buried near the scuppernog vines by the stable. For the days and the nights she had watched him, she knew him as well as she knew someone in her clan.

And yet, she knew him not at all. For he was white. She let out her breath in a careful sigh as he walked around the porch toward the tethered mule, where his father was rehitching the animal. She waited for his voice. She would not leave until she could hear him.

"Pa, I don' see ol' Gus. You think a hawk crombed 'im?"

"Biggity fool's flinderin' the settin' hens agin, I 'spect. Go shoo him out."

Tom came back around the corner with a stick, opened the henhouse, and stepped inside. In a moment Gus, a large, red rooster, came squawking and flapping out in front of Tom's feet, and Not Black grinned in pleasure to see the bird fly. The boy was good at most anything he tried, and it pleased her.

Not Black crept quietly through the small tunnel she had made with frequent passage into a place within the honeysuckle where she could see what Tom Craven did. She brushed against some poison ivy, tendriled through the honeysuckle, and grimaced. Poison ivy often grew right next to honeysuckle, but she thought she had found all of it within her hiding place. Well, and she would have to go immediately and find some jewelweed to crush and hold against it, to stop the rash. The Maker of Breath often grew the antidote to the poisonous plant right next to it, in low and damp places. She knew just where she could find some.

"How long you fixin' to be gone, Pa?" Tom was asking his father.

Not Black listened carefully, holding her breath.

" 'Bout four days," his father said, slapping the mule on the hindquarters to start him round the circle again. Round and round the poor brute went, Not Black had seen it often enough, grinding the man's corn. It was a wonder the animal did not bite or kick; her people's horses would never have put up with such tedious work. But the white man's mule obeyed.

Not Black watched as Tom went in and out of the stable, working on harness and fetching tools for his father while he fixed the wagon wheel, and then she slipped away, backing out of the honeysuckle as quietly as a rabbit. Once she was away from the yard, she ran to the hidden trail which led to her people's camp.

Less than eight miles away, hidden in the swamp, twenty families lived in their *chekes*, kept their cattle and pigs, and tended their corn rows, melons, squash, and orchards. For ten years, since they had finally believed that the soldiers would no longer hound them, they had lived there. Over time, the bitter memories of their exile were beginning to soften, but many of the old ones still spoke of the last flight to this land as though it had happened only a season before.

Not Black hurried around the corner of the village, picked up her hoe and rake from the corn patch where she had left them, and came back into view of her mother's fire, wiping her brow as though she had been working hard for hours. Her mother sat by the fire, mending a pair of her father's leggings. The white cloth splayed about the varied colors of her long skirt, and her hair shone radiantly in the slanting afternoon sun. Comes Alone looked up at her daughter and smiled.

"Are any melons ripe yet?" she asked.

Not Black flushed slightly, busying herself putting away the tools over the rafters of the *cheke.* "Not yet," she called overloudly. "In a few days, I think."

"Well, and I hope the raccoons do not take them the day you are watching the white man's house instead," her mother said evenly.

Not Black stopped still as a mouse when the hawk goes over. Her heart thudded mightily in her chest. She took a deep breath to calm herself and went out to the fire. She sat down on the cypress log across from her mother. "How did you know?"

Her mother laughed softly. "Did you think you could go creeping off every day—"

"Not every day!" Not Black said indignantly.

"—leaving your hoe leaning against a corn stalk and not have someone notice you were gone? Your moccasin prints always went in the same direction."

Not Black hung her head.

"Why, my daughter?"

Not Black could say nothing.

"Is there something at that place you want?"

Not Black looked up at her mother dolefully.

"Ah," Comes Alone said. "Now I am very much afraid."

"Why?" Not Black brought her head up sharply. Her mother was afraid of nothing.

"Because I think I understand what you are looking for at the white man's cabin."

Not Black flushed more deeply this time. Her mother had always had the knack of reading her mind. It had been bothersome enough when she was a child, but now that she was a grown woman, it was downright alarming.

"Your grandmother told me that Osceola's mother had a similar problem."

Osceola again, Not Black thought. It seemed that her grandfather's name came up in two out of every three conversations that anyone had in the village, and three out of three around her mother's fire. It was good to have a grandfather so loved and respected but impossible to live up to his example.

"Osceola's own mother had a yearning for things of the white man," her mother was saying, "a desire for his pots and pans and colored cotton—"

Not Black giggled suddenly with nervous relief. Her mother thought she wanted the things which hung on the white man's walls or stood in his cabin!

Comes Alone glanced up sharply. She regarded her daughter carefully. "Well. I see that I must be even more afraid than I supposed."

"Why do you say that?" Not Black asked.

Comes Alone kept her mending needle moving smoothly, her head lowered.

In the long silence, Not Black felt her heart pounding just as hard as ever again. When her mother was silent and did not regard her, it made her feel somehow as though she did not exist at all and might never again. Finally she blurted out, "I will not go there again, I promise. I am sorry for having disobeyed you, Mother."

Comes Alone looked up, her brow serene. "I have never told you to keep from the white man's places. I never thought such a thing would be necessary to say. So you have not disobeyed me. You have disappointed me, daughter."

That was even worse, Not Black knew. She hung her head once more.

"I wish to hear your own words. Tell me what you do there and why."

"I go to see the white man's son," Not Black murmured sadly.

"And why do you do this?"

Not Black caught her breath in her throat. "I do not know," she whispered.

Comes Alone was silent for another long moment. Finally she said, "I remember well enough when I saw your father. It seemed to me that I had never looked upon a man so full of grace and power. That

I would never look on another like him again in all my days." She kept
her fingers moving deftly. "Perhaps, you have such feelings in your
heart?"

Not Black nodded. Her mother did not look up. Comes Alone did
not need to see the nod to feel the agreement any more than she had
to see an ear of corn to know if it was ripe.

"Then indeed," Comes Alone said, "I am afraid for you, my heart."

"Why?"

"Because love is hard enough without choosing to find it among
rattlesnakes. How many times have you heard it said round this fire
and all the others you have known? The whites are not to be trusted.
They have no hearts. They have no souls. Even the Maker of Breath
turns away from them."

Not Black was silent.

"How is it that you can have known such things all of your days,
and still you go among them?" her mother asked quietly.

"I saw him, Mother," Not Black said. "And I wished only to see
him again. And then I saw him again, and I wished to go back."

"You will not go again," her mother said firmly.

Not Black was silent. She said, after a long moment, "I do not see
the danger." She looked up at her mother with urgency. "The man
and his son have such wondrous things, Mother, you should come and
see for yourself. They have a chair on the front of their cabin which
moves back and forth when they sit in it, and they have fire inside
glass boxes. They have a mule which goes round and round in a circle
all the day to grind their corn and—"

"I know the wonders of a white man's world," Comes Alone said
dryly.

Not Black heard her mother's tone and stopped speaking. She knew
she would not be convinced.

"I will have your promise," her mother said. "You will not go there
again."

"I still do not see the danger!" Not Black said indignantly. "They
do not even know I watch them."

"The danger is not to you from them," her mother said. "The danger
is to you from yourself. There is no need for you to understand. You
have only to obey."

Not Black knew that her mother did not extract such promises lightly.
In fact, as she thought of it, she could not recall a single other time in
her life when her mother had seemed so adamant. She knew that if

her mother told her father—which likely she would anyway, they had no secrets from each other so far as she could tell—he would probably be more angry than her mother was now. If she told him that his daughter had refused to obey, the punishment would be far more severe. She really had no choice. "I promise," she said stiffly. "But I still do not understand."

"I will hold you to that promise," her mother said, "and I shall hope that someday you *will* understand."

"Not that it will matter then," Not Black murmured as she rose to go from the fire.

Her mother looked up sharply at her, but she did not ask her to repeat herself.

It was days later, and Not Black had kept her promise, though it was harder than she had thought it would be. Several times a day, she thought of the white man's cabin and the boy who lived there. Many times, she stood in the corn rows or by the river, gazing in the direction she knew he was, and she grew more and more resentful that there was now someplace in the world where she could not go. Never had she been hobbled, she thought, like a pony. There was not a stream, a tree, a swamp, a hammock she could not explore. Until now.

She had heard her friends say that once their monthly flux began, their mothers sometimes kept them closer to home, watched them more carefully than they had before they became women. Her flux had started the year before, and Comes Alone had never inhibited Not Black's desire to roam, had never forbidden her a place, a people, or a person. Until now.

Several weeks went by, and Not Black felt as tense and tight in her skin as a moulting locust. The heat of the summer began to come on, and she thought she had never been so irritable in her life. Like a wasp, she buzzed through her days almost looking for something to offend her, and when Small Bear, her best friend from the Wind clan, refused to lend her a string of blue beads, she surprised herself by bursting into angry tears.

"What is the matter with you?" Small Bear asked her that day in exasperation. "You're sour as a green tamarind."

"I am not!" Not Black had shouted at her.

"You are, and I think I'd rather go hoe the melons than be hollered at anymore." Taking her blue beads with her, she left Not Black alone at the river.

Not Black wiped her eyes impatiently and set off walking upriver

to a place where she knew she could bathe without having to hear the
noise of the village. Her skin felt too small for her body and her heart
too squeezed in her chest. As she climbed the rocks and jumped from
one pool to another, she complained out loud about her most recent
ill treatment from Small Bear, Red Bird, and the other girls she had
known for as long as she could remember.

The day was hot, and Not Black felt that none of her usual pools
were exactly what she wanted, though she looked forward to the feel
of the cool water. She was not in the mood to settle for less than what
she pictured in her mind, and so she kept moving upriver. The farther
she got from the village, the calmer she felt.

She came then to an upper pool that she could not remember seeing
before, a wide expanse of the river with high rocks on each side and
a deep, shadowed pool. A perfect place for large fish or quiet dives,
she thought, and she began to climb down closer to the pool to see
where she might enter the water easily. Her long skirt was tucked into
her belt on her hips, so that it was high enough to walk, but as she
jumped down, she saw that she had torn it on something at the hem,
palmetto perhaps, and she was immediately jerked back into an evil
frame of mind. She steadied herself with one hand on a rock as she
examined the rip, and she suddenly whirled when she heard the scrape
of movement from a nearby rock. She turned and saw, across the pond,
Tom Craven coming down the other side of the river, his fishing pole
on his shoulder.

He saw her just about the same time she saw him, and he stopped,
hesitating.

Not Black dropped her skirt instantly and edged back against the
rock so that she was partially hidden.

Tom Craven paused, gazing at her. He looked back up at the rocks
he had just climbed down, looked down at the pool, and then stared
at her. For a long moment, neither of them moved.

"I mean to drop a line in, if that don' jower you none?" he called
across the water.

She could not find her voice, even if she had been able to think of
a thing to say. Of course, she could almost understand him, for she had
heard enough English to know his words. She could imagine herself
answering him, but she could not force herself to open her mouth.

"Don' be 'afyeard!" he called out brightly. "I don' mean you no
harm."

She came out from behind the rock then and stared at him boldly. Whatever else she might be, she told herself, she was not a coward. "This is my place," she said.

"It is?" He looked about uncertainly.

"I swim here," she added, a little louder.

"I ain' never seen you," he said. "I been here a passel o' times."

"Well, and it is my place," she repeated. "You go other place on the river, Tom Krave-in."

His mouth opened in surprise. "How you know my name?"

"I know all about you, Tom Krave-in," she said, unconcernedly as she sat down on the rock. "My people know all about you. You go other place to fish."

"Your people?" He sat down on his rock as well, setting his pole down beside him. "You from that camp downriver?"

"You know of my people?" she asked suspiciously.

"I know all 'bout your people," he grinned at her. "Ain' seen much o' them, though. You 'bout the first. Mostly, I seen tracks an' sign, but Pa, he seen y'all plenty, years back, an' he told me."

"What he say?" she asked curiously.

He shrugged. "Oh, jus' that you been here since dirt. So I reckon, if you say this is your place, I s'pose it must be."

She nodded firmly. "It is."

He thought for a moment. "How 'bout we make us a deal?"

She was silent, watching him. It seemed to her that she had heard plenty in her lifetime about making deals with white men. In fact, now that she thought of it, this was likely just the sort of deal the first white man made to the first Seminole he saw when he came to this land. And that deal led to the death of her grandfather and that deal was the reason her mother wanted her to have no truck with those men now. She saw how he flipped the long shock of hair which fell over his eyes when he moved his head, shrugged it back as easily, a movement of sun and youth and energy. She could see no harm in the boy. "What deal?" she finally asked.

"We share it? I fish here sometimes, an' you swim here sometimes."

She said nothing. It was no deal. She gave up rightful ownership and got back nothing in return.

"Or I reckon I can go fish along an' along," he said, his face dropping. He rose up off his rock and picked up his pole, slinging it over his shoulder.

There was something about his gesture which made her belly feel as though she had just missed a foothold while climbing and recovered herself barely in time. "You stay," she said quickly. "We make a deal."

He turned and grinned at her again.

She felt the corners of her own mouth turn up as though they belonged to someone else.

"What's your name?" he called across the water, turning now to climb down the rocks.

"You said you knew everything," she said, still smiling.

"I guess I'm nigh the second biggest liar this side of the Suwannee," he said amiably. "My pa's the biggest, but I'm a quick study."

"Fishing is good here?"

"Yep," he said, settling himself now on a rock near the edge of the deepest part of the pool. "Got a right smart chance o' bream last evenin'." He rummaged in a pouch he had slung over his shoulder. "But there be one ol' grandaddy bass that mocks me regular. Maybe I get lucky today. So, what you called?"

She came down from her perch then, closer to the water and sat on a rock. Slipping off her moccasins, she dangled one bare foot in the cool water. "Not Black," she said softly.

"Not Black? Well, any eye can see that, I reckon. Why they name you such as that?"

She shrugged. "My mother did not wish for me to be taken by the soldiers." She glared at him. "They steal our people and chase us into the forest."

He shook his head. "Must a' been a long time ago."

"My people do not forget."

"No," he said quietly, "I s'pose not." He dropped his line in the water and let it move over the surface lightly. "You 'afyeard o' me?"

"No," she said firmly. "I am afraid of nothing."

He smiled softly. "That's good, I guess. I'm 'afyeard o' plenty, myself."

"What you afraid of?"

" 'Afyeard I might not get a bite," he grinned. " 'Afyeard Pa might come back with his pockets blowed out—"

"He go to sell your cattle," she said. "He come back with silver."

"How you know where he go?" he asked curiously. "You really do know 'bout me, I guess."

"I know you will not catch grandfather bass," she smiled.

"Why is that?"

"Because he wants something better than a worm."

"What he want then, Miss Know-Everythin'?" He grinned at her like the sun.

"Grandfather bass want a Mud Warrior," she said, using her people's name for what she meant.

"Do how?"

"A—" and here, she hesitated, knowing that she had few words to explain. She made the gesture of pinching with both fingers, scowling ferociously, and wiggling backwards, all the while still sitting on her rock.

"A crawdaddy!" He laughed.

She nodded happily.

"You think ol' grandaddy want him a crawdaddy, eh?"

"I know it." She smiled smugly.

He kneeled and began to rummage round the smaller rocks at the edge of the pool, setting down his pole. She began to look under hers as well, lifting up first one and then another, searching for a crayfish which would scuttle away as quick as a blink if it could. She caught one first and held it up, crowing with triumph.

"Grandfather fight this one!" She laughed as he clambered over the boulders to her, slipping and sliding on the rocks and finally reached her side.

"He's a real light'ood fighter," he said. "Catch ol' grandaddy an' granmammy, too."

He held out his hand and she gingerly set the crayfish into his palm. The creature immediately rose up on its tail and extended its pincers in a fighting position.

"He great warrior," she said mock-serious. "He fight pale eyes and take many coup."

Tom Craven sat down beside her then, baited his hook with the crayfish, and dropped it down into the water. "Let him fram it with ol' grandaddy."

As the sun lowered, they sat and talked between themselves until Not Black suddenly realized that she had been gone for much longer than she intended. She rose suddenly and said, "I must go."

"Will you come back?" he asked.

She gazed down at him. "You want me to?"

He laughed. "Do I want a pretty gal to come an' help me catch ol' grandaddy? Bet your wagon, child."

She could not help but laugh at his words and his happiness, but what she heard in her heart, ringing over and over like a clarion, was "pretty, pretty, pretty." He thought she was pretty.

"Perhaps, someday," she said, and she skipped off the rock and over the top of the ravine before he could say anything else. When she reached the top, she stopped and looked back down at him. He lifted one hand and waved to her, and she lifted her hand in return.

All the way back to camp, she was throbbing with joy, filled with a light excitement which made her spirit soar like a lark to the top of the trees and beyond. She sang aloud as she ran, she laughed out loud once as she remembered a look on his face, a quizzical lift of his brow. When she neared the village, she slowed, and her guilt overtook her finally. She had not disobeyed her mother's words, but she had certainly ignored her warning.

She knew, without knowing, that if her mother or father had come upon them at the pool, they would have been afraid for her, even angry. They would tell her never to go there again.

And she knew also, as sure as she knew that the river would flow forever, that she would go back to meet Tom Craven at the secret pool again soon. She thought, what harm can come of such a meeting? He is white, that is true enough, but he is a good man. It is time, she told herself, that the fears and hatreds of the past generation are set aside. It is up to the young to do this, to teach the old ones that what once was true is true no longer.

As she thought of this more, she almost relished the prospect. She walked back into the village with her head high, her spirit confident. It was not necessary, she told herself, that her mother knew every beat of her heart. She was grown now, a young woman with a life of her own. She would do with it what she thought best.

As she walked through the camp back to her mother's fire, a young man, Teal, spoke to her and greeted her as she passed. He was a friend, and she knew that he hoped to be more than that someday soon. She smiled at him magnanimously, but she did not stop or speak. He must not hope for much, she told herself. It is better to be a little cruel now than to break his heart later.

Two evenings later, Teal came to their fire after the evening meal was over. Not Black was mending her fishing pole, while her father sat across from her, tying flies. Her father, Standing Horse, was a quiet man, not given to idle conversation or social amenities. Indeed, when she was small, Not Black often wondered how it was that her mother came to love him, for they seemed very unalike. But now that she was older, she could understand the gentle strength such a silence could mean, and she relished this private time they shared.

When Teal approached the fire, she felt a shrug of resentment grip her shoulders and tighten her mouth. But she welcomed him politely and moved over on her cypress log to make room for the boy.

Teal was the middle son of Wind Woman, of the Tree clan, and he was an excellent fisherman in his own right. When the boys went out, it was often Teal who brought home the largest catch, and no doubt, when he became a man in the Black Drink Ceremony this season, his new-man name would reflect his prowess. He was a slight person, with pleasing features and a shy manner. She had always liked and trusted Teal, but tonight, she did not wish him near her.

"I am come," he said to her father first, as was proper.

"You are," Standing Horse said amiably, waving the boy to the log with a welcoming gesture. "And what mighty water-warrior did you vanquish today, Teal?"

"A fair-sized bluegill," the boy said, smiling over at Not Black in greeting.

"Fair-sized means large enough to fill two pots, I wager," Standing Horse said.

"Mother was pleased," Teal admitted with an embarrassed shrug.

Not Black sat stiffly, rubbing down her pole with hemlock leaves, and she said not a word. The hemlock would stain the pole a distinctive dark and mottled color so that it would be less visible to the fish underwater. She wished Teal would be less visible as well.

Standing Horse and Teal spoke of this and that, fish and hunting, for longer than she would have supposed her father would have entertained such empty speech. She grew increasingly annoyed with them both. And so, when Teal finally turned to her shyly and said, "Perhaps when you are finished, you would like to walk to the river?" she felt her heart squeeze shut to the boy as though with a wince.

"I think not," she said shortly. "There's nothing at the river I have not seen plenty of times."

Standing Horse looked up at her in mild surprise, in time to catch the sudden ducking of Teal's head, the sagging of his shoulders. "It is a beautiful night," her father said evenly, his eyes now back again to his work. He picked up a gossamer bit of duck down and examined it as though he had never seen such a rare thing before.

Not Black almost snorted aloud with impatience like a tethered pony. "I have had quite enough of walking for one day," she said.

"Oh?" Standing Horse looked up at her again, this time with more penetration.

She instantly recognized her mistake. Of course her mother had spoken to him of her visits to the white man's cabin and of her promise to go there no more. She could have kicked herself for being so careless. Now her father might well ask her, and before this fool of a boy, where it was she had walked so far this day that she was too weary to walk again this night!

But to her vast relief, he did not. He smiled across to Teal as though to say that men must forgive these unreasoning lapses in women and said only, "You must tell your mother for me that when she has the time, I would like to barter for one of her saddle blankets. My wife is a wonder, but the weavings of Wind Woman far surpass her expertise."

Teal stood and brushed off his backside. "I will tell her, Standing Horse." He nodded to Not Black politely. "Perhaps we shall walk another time," he said, with nothing of disappointment now evident in his voice.

But, of course, it was too late. Not Black knew she had hurt him, knew, also, that he would not be back to her fire for many days. She felt a wrench of guilt and regret. However, she could not bring herself to speak a farewell with anything more than cool correctness in her tone.

After Teal was gone, her father said only, "I do not consider myself a wise man. But if I did, I should know better than to meddle in the business of a man and a woman."

"Teal is not a man," she scoffed lightly.

"Well, and you are not a woman," her father replied, "but both of you are fast approaching a time when you shall be, and when that time comes, he would be welcome at your mother's fire."

"Invite him then," she said, standing up and picking up her tools and her pole. "I am certain the two of you will have many pleasant discussions together." And she went to her hammock, grumbling to herself and shoving her pole up into the depths of the rafter as though it were a knife between Teal's narrow ribs.

"I must remember," she said to herself, "to thank that foolish boy for ruining what should have been a private moment with my father. What makes him think he can wander to our fire at will? People in this village take altogether too much for granted and meddle overmuch in each other's affairs."

She readied for bed and put herself under her mosquito net, and only after she was settled down did she remember that she had not said good night to either parent. It was a lapse she could not recall ever making before, but somehow it seemed far too much trouble to get up again, seek them out, and then resettle herself. She moved fitfully on the cot, finally found her accustomed position of comfort, and forced herself to calm and sleep.

The next morning, she was up and away from the village before her father came back from his morning bathing and smoke with the men. She walked upriver without being aware of any particular destination, but as she walked it seemed to her more and more of a good idea that she go to her pool. She had not been swimming there, after all, and it was a day so warm that even with small exertion, she was damp. As she stretched out her legs and moved with purpose, she felt better than she had for days.

It took less time to reach the place where the river and rocks made her refuge than she had remembered before, perhaps because she had so much to think about as she walked. She came upon the tall rocks which sheltered the water, climbed them quickly, and as she came over the top, stopped and stared down at the water in wonder. Tom Craven was there before her, fishing on the same stone he had chosen before, his blond hair glinting in the sun as bright as the reflection on the slowly moving waters.

Without thinking, she called out to him, "Tom Craven!" and he looked up in surprise.

"You came!" he called back, waving at her. "I was jus' thinkin' on you."

She grinned and hurried down the rocks, throwing her long braid back behind her, glad she had worn her clean bodice, conscious suddenly that her face was likely less clean than she wished. She stopped at the edge of the pool, suddenly shy now that they were separated only by water. "I told you, this is my place."

"Yep, you told me, I reckon. Ain' we made a deal?"

"We did not!" she said indignantly. "I did not agree."

He dropped his head in mock retreat. "I will leave it to you, then, ma'am. Sure am sorry to trespass . . ."

She laughed delightedly. "We make a deal, mister," she said, struggling to remember every English word she ever heard. Small Bear spoke the ugly tongue better than she did, for her father had done much trading with the whites, and she had often teased Not Black by speaking to her in the strange-sounding speech, pretending to insult her in a language she could not comprehend. She had learned it quickly enough then. "You stay. But you must pay tribute."

"Gladly," he said. He leaned down and plucked a handful of swamp candles and offered the delicate yellow flowers to her with a courtly bow.

She took them from his hand shyly, watching him, her hand trembling slightly. He saw her shyness and took her hand, gently folding it in his own. "I was frettin' you might not come," he said.

She stared at her hand encased in his. "I should not have," she said.

"Why not?"

"My mother—" she stopped, for of course she could not tell him of her mother's command without revealing how she had watched him.

"She don' like whites?" he asked.

Not Black shook her head. "My grandfather was Osceola," she said, half-regretfully, half-proudly.

"Truly?" He thought for a moment, still holding her hand. "Then I be honored to meet you, ma'am. A real princess."

She flushed and dropped her hand from his. "No," she said. "I am only Not Black. Not a big person."

"No," he said, "you not big, I reckon. But you important enough, to me, leastways."

She looked up at him wonderingly. "Why?"

He shrugged, now shy himself. "You the first gal friend I ever had. That makes you important." He smiled and took her hand again, pulling her down next to him on the rock. "An' you pretty an' smart, besides."

She laughed. "Smart? Why?"

" 'Cause you smart enough not to hate whites, jus' 'cause your mama do. We ain' all scrapers, after all. I ain' thrashed nobody lately, leastwhys."

Her smile faded at the mention of her mother, and he saw it. He still had not let go of her hand, and he folded it inside his two. "You got the most scrimptious lil' ol' hand. No bigger than a lily an' jus' as soft."

"You have a honey tongue, Tom Craven," she said with mock scorn.

"Nope," he said. "I ain' no hobbiedehoy rascal. I speak the truth."

They sat and gazed at the moving water in silence for a moment. "There be jus' one thing I don' fancy," he said then, quietly. "That name don' suit you at all. Ain' near soft nor pretty enough, to my mind."

"What you think it must be?"

He looked at her intently then, and she felt her eyes unable to move from his. Her heart was suddenly pounding, and she did not know whether to flee or stay rooted to this rock for the rest of her days. "I would call you Lily," he said. "It fits you like a glove."

She did not know what a glove was, but she knew the word lily from some faraway memory. It was surely more beautiful than her own name.

"Can I call you that, instead?" he asked.

She nodded.

He looked at her again, his face closer to hers now. "I ain' never kissed a girl before, Lily. Can I kiss you?"

Without scarcely being aware she did so, she nodded again. Slowly, softly, he touched his lips to hers, and she felt her stomach lurch again, as it had before. She moved her lips to follow his as he pulled away, for she did not want that sensation to cease.

"You ever been with a man?" he murmured.

"No," she whispered.

"I never been with a gal, neither," he said. And he leaned in to kiss her again, this time taking her into his arms. She went into them willingly, dropping her clutch of swamp candles on the rock.

The sun moved over them slowly, the water murmured at their feet, and her skin felt more alive under his hands than it had ever felt in her lifetime. When he kissed her, repeatedly and with more intensity, she returned his kisses eagerly, for she felt no shame, only shyness as he uncovered her breasts, as he softly explored her body. But his joy at her beauty, his pleasure at her touch took away her shyness, and soon she thought of nothing but his touch, the taste of him, the feel of his weight on her, and the intense pleasure of his closeness.

* * *

Her name was Uma, and she had been coiled around her clutch of two hundred eggs for more than four months without moving. She was even more irritable than usual and would have bitten something badly if it got too close. But those denizens of her swamp bottom knew not to stray within her reach, and so she was undisturbed.

She was *Amphiuma means*, a two-toed amphiuma. Long and eel-like, she most resembled a salamander with four tiny legs, each with two toes. She was dark gray with a light belly, and she had fifty-eight grooves on each side of her back—a back which was almost three feet long. Seen underwater, she looked like a dusky fat snake, except for her small legs and her milky blue eyes. She was nocturnal, only emerging after dusk to feed on the crayfish, frogs, and small fish which made up her diet.

Lately, of course, she had not emerged from her mud bottom den at all, and she was hungry and cross.

Uma was more than twenty years old, and she had seen many changes on the river. Twenty springs, she had laid her eggs in the same cavity and then defended those eggs. Twenty winters, she had found a mate, quickly had from him what she needed and then ran him away from her territory. Many of those matings had actually taken place in wetlands or damp places out of the water, for her legs could carry her surprisingly far from the depths, and she could breathe air as well as water.

Uma had eaten well before her eggs were laid, of course, for she knew from long experience how empty she would become in the full five months she must wait for them to hatch. Once they hatched and her offspring came forth, less than two inches long and completely defenseless against predators, she would leave them and her den in relief, to once more hunt as she needed to survive.

She closed her eyes briefly in weariness. It was harder and harder each year to summon the energy for the mating and the laying and the hatching. She sensed that she would not repeat the process many more springs. She had laid over four thousand eggs in her lifetime. Of those four thousand offspring, less than a tenth had survived, to populate the nearby rivers and swamps with their kind. But Uma had no knowledge of this, of course. Each egg was as precious as the one before; each egg represented something to live and die for, however briefly it might be in her life.

The waters of her pool were cool at the depths where she lay, and Uma was able to drift in and out of awareness unless she sensed a trespasser. Her eyesight was not keen. Like most nocturnal creatures, the sun left her feeling confused and disoriented, but in the depths of her mud den, little daylight intruded. Water currents and the smallest particles of food were her fascination, and she paid particular attention to changes in heat around her.

This evening, she felt a rippling sensation along the grooves on her side which told her that something large had come close to her hiding place. Something much warmer than the outside of her skin, than the water which was disturbed by its passage. She tensed and coiled slightly tighter around her eggs.

Uma had confronted most every predator on the river at one time or another. Alligators, large bass, snakes, and other eaters had always plagued her, but much less so as she grew older and larger. Now there was little she feared, yet she watched for every ripple. Here came another one, and she arched her back and faced the disturbance, alert for a possible struggle.

Suddenly into her view came a swirl of dark, a fast rush of water, and she was confronted with a big river otter, nearly as long as she was. She snapped at him viciously as he went by, wriggling deeper into the mud and covering her eggs with her body as best she could. The otter was a perilous enemy, she knew, for he might well damage more eggs than he ate, as careless a hunter as he was.

Careless perhaps, but fast and deadly. The otter swirled closer this time, opening his jaws in a grin which showed all of his teeth. Uma snapped at him again, and he stopped in the water, now riveted on her and her eggs. With a huge paw, he reached out and swatted at her. She arched her back and showed her teeth, curling and coiling as fast as she could, trying to look as large as possible, while keeping her head out of range.

The otter raced for the surface in a whirl of bubbles, and as he took the moment to breathe, Uma buried about a third of her eggs in deeper mud, frantically trying to make the clutch look smaller. Of course, he had seen them. They were too large to escape his notice. But perhaps he had not seen them all and would not be interested in so small a meal for so large a fight.

And fight she meant to provide him. Uma had only just nosed those eggs she could maneuver quickly under more mud when the otter returned in a surge of water and frenzy. He went for her neck, right behind her head, and she twisted to try to avoid his jaws, sinking her teeth into his flank. He squirmed loose, and she wriggled away from her eggs, trying to draw him into deeper water. He followed her, snapping at her tail, and she turned on him, gaping her jaws wide like a rattlesnake, forcing a plume of bubbles out of her lungs to obscure his vision.

The otter snatched at her again, but she ran pell-mell across the pond, as far as she could get from her eggs, fleeing for her life. He grabbed her tail with his teeth, reaching for her body with his claws, and she turned on him with all her fury, suddenly aware that if she did not survive, neither would this season's get. She bit him furiously on the shoulder, on the ear, and he let go with his teeth, wrestling her around with both paws now, trying to get her to the surface.

Uma knew that if he got her on land, she would die. She could breathe, but he would have her at such a hard disadvantage, her fate would be certain. No matter what, she could not let him drag her to the shallows. She took a desperate chance and turned right into his teeth, almost into his open jaws, dodged his canines at the last instant, and sank her teeth into his nose as deeply as she could grind them.

The otter squealed in pain, thrust his paws between her body and his nose and tried to push her off, but she held on, twisting her tail like a leaf on a limb, corkscrewing with every ounce of strength she could muster. The otter wrenched himself away in a spurt of blood and bubbles and raced for the surface.

Uma sank to the depths of the pool, coiling and curling in a state of high agitation, looking all about her for other danger. She made the mud on the bottom roil with her turnings, gaping at nothing and thrashing until finally, she could begin to calm. She stopped still at last and felt for other vibrations in the water, listened for the approach of the otter. She felt and heard nothing. The otter was gone.

She darted back to her eggs quickly, her sides heaving with exhaustion. She coiled around her eggs carefully, nosing them out of the mud so that she could see all were safe. After each had been rolled, turned, and checked, she recovered them all again to exactly the right depth for incubation. Then, her breath finally coming to her normally once more, she again coiled around them, her head out in the defensive position.

She could still taste the slight sour tang of the otter's blood in her gullet, and it made her very hungry. But she would not leave her eggs to feed. For defense, but not for food. There was much which was alterable in her world, many things which could not be depended upon, but one thing was sure. Uma would guard her nest until her offspring no longer needed her. And then, if they did not leave her pond within a single cycle of the moon, they would be prey along with everything else she could catch in her waters.

*   *   *

A season had passed since she had been forbidden to go to the white man's farm. A full season, and she had scarcely missed a week without meeting Tom Craven at their secret pool. On those days she could not be with him, she thought of him with every passing hour. She held the memory of his face as she had last seen it, picturing his mouth, his eyes, the way he spoke and moved and touched her, comforting herself with those thoughts when they were apart.

And still, her mother did not know how far she had strayed from the intention of her command. At night, Not Black lay in her hammock and thought of all she must tell her mother, of what words she would use to explain how such a thing had happened: that she, granddaughter of Osceola, was pledged to a white man.

For pledged she was and had been since the first time they had lain together. He had told her that he wanted to be with her always, that she was the most beautiful girl he had ever seen. He said, another time, that he wanted to go to her father and ask for her, but that he was afraid he might run him off. She had reassured him that her father would wish her happiness above all, but he was still hesitant. She could only hold him and tell him of her heart. He must do the rest.

But she knew that if her mother could be made to welcome him, her father would finally follow. That was how it had always been between them.

And so, she must tell her mother that she loved this Tom Craven and wanted to be his wife.

"What will your father say to this?" she had asked him once as she lay in his arms.

He had grimaced. "He be 'bout as kickified as your pa will be, I reckon."

"Because I am Seminole," she murmured.

"Because you're strange. Pa don' fancy strange, much. He aims things to stay the way they always been. But I fancy things different." He smiled. "We ain' much alike in that, I wager."

"What will you tell him?"

"That I be growed enough to pick my own wife, thank'ee. He ain' gonna nose 'bout my life much longer." His voice softened. "He be a fair man, Lily, don' you fret none. He been a little mean round the edges since Ma was took, but when it comes down to blood, he been always on my side. I just got to make him see that you is what I want."

"And am I?" she asked him, cuddling closer under his arm.

"Pretty nigh near all I want," he said, " 'cept maybe a good mule an' a cow."

She slapped him playfully on the back. "Well, and where is that honey tongue now? Now that you have had your pleasure—"

"Here it be," he said, holding her while she pretended to struggle, "right where it belongs." And he kissed her deeply, driving out all thoughts of anything but his mouth, his arms, his embrace.

But her mother must be told, she knew. And the sooner she knew, the sooner Not Black's conscience would let her sleep well again.

She chose a night when she thought her mother would be ready to hear such a thing, if ever there could be such a time. It was warm, the night was soft and lovely, and the village was quiet. She had heard her parents having their pleasure the night before, so she knew that her mother would be calm and happy. Her father was meeting with the men about the upcoming horse trade to the east with the Hitachi clans, so they had several private hours together by the fire.

She took up her mending, something she knew her mother wished her to be more diligent about, and she sat across from Comes Alone with the embers of the evening meal between them.

"Mother," she began slowly, "I want you to know that I have kept my promise to you."

"Your promise?" her mother looked up with a smile. "I never doubted it, daughter. But what promise do you mean?"

"My promise," Not Black said patiently, "to keep from the white man's lands."

"Well, and that is good," her mother said evenly.

Not Black took a deep breath, felt it tingle all the way down to her fingertips, and added, "But it has not been easy."

Comes Alone said nothing.

"And it did not matter, after all," she continued.

"Oh?"

Not Black closed her eyes and plunged in, as though she were diving into a dark, deep pool and could not see the bottom.

"Because the white man's son found me, Mother. I did not seek him out—"

Her mother held up her hand for silence. "You went to his lands and you watched him, day after day. And yet you say you did not seek him out."

"He did not know I watched him. He came to the river when I did, to the same place. It was fate. It was not my fault."

"It was his fault, then."

"No, no! He is not to blame!"

Comes Alone put down the pot she was cleaning and faced her daughter. "You defend this white man to me. You put yourself between my anger and him. You have become crazy before my eyes."

Not Black moaned to herself. This was even worse than she had feared. "I am not crazy. I love him," she said quietly, trying to keep her voice steady. "I love Tom Craven."

Her mother stared at her in horror. "How has such a thing come to us?" she wondered aloud. "My daughter's mind has been stolen by a white man."

"He did not steal me," she whispered. "I gave myself gladly."

"You gave yourself," Comes Alone repeated bitterly. "You have lain with him?"

Not Black flushed and looked away. Her voice was low and vibrant with longing. "Do not blame him, Mother. I have loved him, I think, from the first time I saw him."

"You love him! You are a perverse child!"

Not Black began to weep quietly.

"There were a fistful of fine boys in the village, sons of warriors, who yearned for you, Not Black. Or would have, if you would let them. And you take into your flesh a man of perverse nature. A man whose people have murdered your people!" Comes Alone was pacing by the fire now, her hands gesturing wildly to the sky, the darkness, the gods themselves.

Not Black had never seen her so distraught. She was cold with fear and sorrow. But she knew that she must go to the end of this road. There was no turning back now. And at the end of the road, Tom would be waiting for her. "He is not a man of perverse nature," she wept. "He is a good man. He should not be blamed for the evils his people have done."

Comes Alone's face changed in that moment. Her anger crumpled, and she went to her daughter and embraced her. "My child, my child. You have given away your heart to a man who cannot possibly revere it. But no matter. This is not a thing for tears. You have had your first experience with pleasure, and though I wish it had been with a man of our clan, still, it is not a bad thing of itself. Now, you will see him no more. Men are much alike, really. You will find another to please you. One more suitable for your heart."

"I will not," Not Black wept harder. "Tom Craven is the one I want."

"That is impossible," Comes Alone said calmly. "The white man will never honor you with wife status. And your father will kill him if he comes to this fire."

"He wants to marry me! He will come and meet with you and father to discuss my bride-price!"

"He has told you this?"

"He has!" She wiped her eyes angrily. "He loves me."

"The promises of a white man," Comes Alone said scornfully, "are like the calls of the geese. Loud and constant, and then they take flight. You cannot believe him, my heart."

"I do," she said stubbornly. "I believe him, Mother."

"Your father will kill him."

"Then I will tell him to keep from my father. And I will go where he goes."

"You will go nowhere," Comes Alone said firmly, putting her from her arms. "You will listen to your mother, who has loved you since you took your first breath—"

"I will go to him," Not Black said.

Comes Alone sat down slowly on the palmetto log, appraising her daughter with narrowed eyes. "How did you come to be so willful, daughter? I did not see this in your heart before this time."

"How did you come to be so forgetful?" Not Black countered. "Can you not remember what it was to be in love? To find such pleasure that you would die to have it again? Did you not feel this way for my father?"

Comes Alone laughed, shaking her head. "I think every daughter must believe that her mother has forgotten such things. Of course I have not. But neither will I let you give your life to a man of perverse natures. A man not of your own clan. A man who calls himself Tom Craven."

"It is my life," Not Black said soberly. "To give or not give, as I choose."

Comes Alone looked down, and her voice was low and gentle. "You are very young yet. Your words prove as much. You say it is your life. It does seem so, when you are young. But the truth is that your life is only partly your own. Your life also belongs to your mother and father, your mate, your children in the future—oh, most especially to your children!" Her mother shook her head. "And to your clan. Those who would keep their lives only for themselves have not much of a life at all, in the end." She looked down. "But you cannot know this truth. Not with only fourteen summers on your heart. Wait until you have twice that many, as I have, and you will know that your life is no more your own than the air is the birds'."

"That is your truth," Not Black said. "It is not mine."

They both turned then as Standing Horse approached the fire. "I am come," he said courteously. Then he saw their faces. "What do my women speak of so solemnly?" He asked this amiably as he drew near. "I thought to hear laughter tonight." He smiled at his daughter. "There is always laughter when Not Black fights her battles with her needles."

Not Black turned a tremulous smile on her father. He was intensely
dear to her in that moment. She did not even mind that he teased her
about her poor skills at mending. He could have teased her about
anything at all, and she could only rejoice at his presence. He had
always understood her. Now, he would surely stand between her mother
and herself with a voice of reason and compassion.

Her mother looked at her and instantly read her expression. Her
mouth turned down in anger. She turned to her husband and said, "Not
Black has something to say to you, my heart. Perhaps you should sit
down."

Standing Horse glanced at his wife curiously, but he sat down, facing
his daughter. "I listen," he said.

Not Black's courage suddenly failed her. In that moment, she hated
her mother for having trapped her in that way. "Mother will tell you."

"I listen," her father repeated calmly, "to you, daughter. Tell me
what you will."

Not Black took a deep breath. This one did not lighten her as the
last one had. "I have found the man I wish to marry," she said swiftly,
before she could lose what courage she had left. "He wishes to marry
me also, Father. He wishes to be made welcome at our fire. But Mother
has forbidden me to see this man of my choice. She tells me I must
choose another." She turned a pleading look to Standing Horse. "I
cannot choose another!" she wailed. "I ask you to understand my heart,
Father!"

Her father stiffened at her last cry, glancing to his wife. "She is
young," he said, to no one in particular. "But that alone is not cause
enough for anger. Tell me, daughter, why does your mother deny your
choice?"

"It is Tom Craven," Not Black murmured. "The white man who
lives at the edge of our forest. Mother hates all white men and wants
me to hate them, too. She forbids me to go onto the white man's land.
But I did not disobey. I did not break my promise. He came upon me
at the river one day and spoke to me. He is a gentle man!" She calmed
herself with an act of will, for she knew that her father disliked intense
emotional outbursts of any kind. "We found each other by no one's
fault, and the Maker of Breath made us love."

Her father heaved a long and sorrowful sigh. "The Maker of Breath
does not, I think, make any heart love. It is the heart which does this,
of its own will."

"And will it is, my husband," Comes Alone interjected. "This is not love. It is lust. The white boy has taken his pleasure with her and—"

"I have taken my pleasure with him!" Not Black said angrily. "Do not forget that, Mother!"

"Well, and I do not think I ever will," her mother said coolly.

"I see now," her father said slowly, "why there is no laughter at the fire this night." He sat down with a heavy sag of his shoulders. "This is not cause for joy."

"Neither is it a cause for despair," Not Black said. "I have found a man who loves me. I have given him my heart, and we wish to be man and wife. Is this such a terrible thing?"

"You do not know what you do," Comes Alone said wearily. "And it is our duty to protect you, well and even from yourself if we must. You will see this Tom Craven no more. You will not stray from the village alone. You will not go to that part of the river which he frequents—"

Not Black put her hands over her ears. "I will not listen to this! I will not obey!"

"You will obey," Standing Horse said gently. "And you will regain your good sense once you are rid of this man in your vision."

"I will run away from here," Not Black said coldly. "I will go to him and never return."

Comes Alone had been standing with her back to her daughter, her arms crossed in obdurate anger. Now she turned, and Not Black saw the tears on her face. "You do not know what you say, my daughter. And you do not know the damage your words have done to our hearts. Now go to your bed and let us decide what is best to do."

"*I* have decided what is best to do," Not Black said.

"Leave us now," Standing Horse said. "We will speak of this again in the morning."

"You may speak of this all you wish," Not Black said, "but the morning will change nothing. I have given this man my heart and my pledge. I will not change my mind." And she walked away from the fire, into the *cheke* to the rear where her sleeping alcove was apart from that of her parents.

Comes Alone sat down on the palmetto log and covered her face with her hands. She did not sob. She could not. But her heart ached for release from its pain.

Standing Horse came to her and put his arm around her shoulders. He said nothing for the longest while.

She was grateful for his silence. Many men, she knew, would have tried to soothe her with empty words, meaningless promises, but he knew the power of simple comfort in her grief. Simply to feel the weight of his arm on her shoulder kept her rooted to the ground, stopped her from soaring up to the sky and dissolving in her sorrow.

After she had calmed and taken her hands down from her face, he said quietly, "I remember when she was small and she would fall and bruise herself. It was hard to hear her cry. When she was sick, when her stomach pained her—remember? Those nights when you fed her *sofkee* from your own mouth, trying to ease her pain. I thought that was difficult to bear. When she came to you weeping because Small Bear would not be her friend. That was sorrowful, too."

She nodded sadly.

"But all of that passed, in its time. Each pain of her growing was supplanted by a pleasure. I suppose that will happen again, but it is hard to believe that it will."

She turned and put her face in his neck.

"I think this must be the hardest part of having a daughter, truly. All those other times were merely to make us strong enough to endure this final test. When she chooses someone over her parents is difficult enough, but when she chooses a man who we would not wish even to feed at our fire, that is the most painful of all."

He held her silently for another long while. "What do you think we should do?" he asked finally.

"Tie her to her bed," Comes Alone said faintly, "and hobble her each day out with the ponies."

He laughed softly, a sound she loved so close to her ear. "You are right, as always, my heart. I shall find the softest cords, so her lovely ankles will not be marred."

"Do not make them too soft," Comes Alone said then, dryly. "Mar those ankles just a little."

He hugged her hard, making her meld her breasts against him, her belly tight to his. "Let us sleep on this dilemma."

"I will never sleep again."

"Well and I will sleep for us both, then. In the morning, we will feel strong enough to wrestle with her and wiser for the rest."

"She'll be stronger, as well," Comes Alone smiled sardonically. "I do not think I can bear it if she gets any stronger, husband. Why could we not have raised a daughter who had the spine of an eel?"

"Then she would not be your daughter," Standing Horse said, pulling her to her feet. "She is an oak. Like her mother and grandmother before her."

"More like her grandfather," Comes Alone said with a wry twist of her mouth. "She never looked more like him than she did tonight."

"No doubt, he is watching well, and he and the Maker of Breath are laying wagers as to which of you will win out."

"He better have a large purse," Comes Alone said. "Because this is one war I do not intend to lose." She let him lead her then back into the *cheke* and into their bed, where she took comfort from his body and his love, just enough to let her forget Not Black and finally fall into a fitful sleep.

Hobbles were not necessary, after all. Comes Alone found the solution the next morning, just as her husband suggested she might. She simply went everywhere with her daughter for the next five days. If Not Black went to the fields, she gathered up her mending and went along. If she went to the river, her mother took her pole and accompanied her. If she went to the woods to gather greens and berries, Comes Alone found that she also needed plants for her dye work, and she picked up her basket to go, too. Curiously enough, Comes Alone even found that when her daughter needed to go to the common latrine, her own body needed the same release at the same time. And so, they were together every moment of every day.

At first, of course, Not Black ordered her away, refused to speak to her, and tried to evade her. But Comes Alone stayed close to her as a loyal hound, did not let her out of her sight, and refused to respond to her angry words. Finally Not Black resigned herself to her mother's presence, reasoning that it was better to be free to wander with her mother at her side than to be confined to the camp or the *cheke* as her father had threatened to do.

Comes Alone did not speak of the white man, Tom Craven, nor did she allow Not Black to speak of him, either. When her daughter mentioned his name or her feelings, Comes Alone simply did not answer. However, if Not Black wished to speak of any other subject, her mother was companionable, witty, and full of entertaining conversation.

After five days, Comes Alone began to know her daughter better than she had since she was a young child. She learned to recognize the rhythms of her daughter's footsteps, of her speech, of her pauses and hurryings, even of her thoughts. Like shadows of each other, they went to and fro through the village, the fields, the forest, the swamps, and in some ways, Comes Alone came to feel that those days were some of the sweetest of her time with Not Black since she had been an infant at the breast.

A second week began of shadowing, and Not Black no longer chafed against her presence. Indeed, she seemed to be resigned to all constraints, all limitations of her life, not even caring whether or not her mother came with her to bathe or to the woman's hut. Toward the end of the second seven days, Comes Alone noticed a certain weariness in her daughter, a listless loss of spirit which began to concern her.

And yet she knew she was doing the best thing for Not Black, to save her from her own passionate attachment to the son of the white man and all he represented. She had seen it before. She knew the hallmarks, she told herself, of a disintegrating soul. Her memories were still painfully clear of how such a seduction could occur and how damaging it must eventually be.

She recalled her father's words so well that he almost seemed to be speaking inside her body when she repeated them to herself. "Times are changing," he had told her. "Once, we could have annihilated the whites and driven them from our lands. But that time has passed. Now, if we are to survive as a people, we must keep from them. We must bargain, we must protect ourselves with cunning, negotiation, and guile. And when all else fails, we must hide. We are fated to be an island in a great sea of whites and to live with the knowledge that our power as a people is gone. But still, we must salvage and protect who we are— the Seminole nation. We must not surrender. We must not give in to the temptation of the white man and his ways."

"We must punish those who consort with the white man!" she had said to him, still young and passionate about such ideals.

"There can be no punishment if the people will not accept it," Osceola had said sadly. "Do we put half of our leaders to death? Put every woman with a white man's pot in a cell?"

She had subsided then, seeing the difficulty of what he described. There were no easy solutions. The whites were too many now and too powerful. Did the women wish to give up their iron hoes and shovels and axes? Would the men bury their rifles and take up the bow and arrow again?

No, she told herself. But each family can do what it must to keep the purity of the people intact. And giving up a daughter to one of them was a step farther into pollution than she was willing to go.

Some argued that the best way to defeat the white man was to live among him and take from him the best of his ways and then perfect those ways. "We should plant cotton," she heard some of the young men and women say. "It is from this that the whites get their strength." They repeated the ancient story of the fox pup who was eaten by a snake. The pup stayed alive inside the snake by feeding on what the snake swallowed, and so finally changed into a wolf and ate the snake's heart.

"But we are hunters," the old ones protested.

"We *were* hunters," the young ones replied. "It is a new world with new ways. We must have slaves, like the white men. Then we can plant cotton and become rich as they are. It is not courage and valor in battle which counts anymore, but money. We must grow cotton and sell it to the other white men across the oceans." Many thought this way, and they spoke constantly and loudly about the best way to become like the white men, taking only the best of the white ways.

But others did not wish to become like the white men. They did not wish to keep black slaves and be imitation white men, with fields of cotton and money in bags under their beds. And so the people began to divide among themselves, some going to the white ways, others staying with the old ways of the Seminole. And in this way, they lost as many young warriors as they had lost to war, and the result was the same: the people were weaker.

The whites had moved onto Seminole lands, even though they were forbidden to do so by treaty. They cut down the forest, planted their acres, built houses and slave quarters, and squeezed the game out. Some hated the nearness of the whites; others were fascinated by their wealth and tools. There was no easy answer.

Comes Alone could remember so well the days of the old sadness, when the people went on the long walks to the lands set aside for them west of the Father of Waters, the Mississippi. West to Oklahoma, that place where they said the dirt was dry as corn husks in the sun. So many were sent, her own great-grandmother among them. Her father had explained to her, however, that all was not as it seemed.

"The Cherokees are a good example of this," he had said. "It appeared that the whites were making them go, and that was not false. But in fact, their own chiefs betrayed their people. The chiefs signed a paper that said some of their people must move, in exchange for being allowed to stay themselves. The richer Cherokees got to stay in their homes, in the ancient towns along their rivers, and they were given private property besides, a custom they had learned from the whites. So you see, they sold the poorest of their people, scattered villagers who knew little of the white man and his ways, and who had no one to speak for them but their chiefs. They were told to go, herded together like ponies, for the walk of a thousand miles, or put on boats which would take them but a little way, and then forced to walk the rest of the way. Four thousand of them. And they did not ask what happened to their leaders, the richer among them who could afford to stay in the wide, rich valleys of their home."

"That is perverse!" she had said.

"It is," her father had replied. "A perversity which they learned at the white man's fires."

She had never forgotten her father's burning anger and resolve that such a thing would never happen to the Seminole. And yet, all around her, it seemed to be happening, even at her own fire.

She could not allow it. But Not Black seemed to grow smaller and smaller, quieter and quieter with every day she was kept from the white man's son. She was no longer angry, no longer ready to fight her mother's will. She simply gave in. And the sadness which Comes Alone felt coming from her was, finally, more alarming even than the thought of the white man in her daughter's heart.

She knew well enough that women sometimes died of such sadness. Some of them ate of the water hemlock plant when they no longer wished to live, and it was a well-accepted custom that women who took their own lives in that way, particularly for matters of the heart, were thought to be somehow more lovely for their sacrifice. All the young women had heard the story of Wren, the woman of the Horse clan from another village, who had found her husband in the arms of another. She had taken her own life with the poisonous plant and put the ground stems and leaves in the food of her three children. Her husband came back to her *cheke* to find their bodies cold and dead. Many said she had taken the only road to a dignified closure. Others said she was an evil fool. Comes Alone thought it dangerous indeed for such stories to be told to the young women, for they more than any were infatuated with tales of love, lost and won.

And so finally, seeing that Not Black only grew more sad and listless with each passing night, she consulted her husband about the proper steps to take. She had succeeded in separating her daughter from the lure of the white man, but at what cost?

"Perhaps if she is courted well by another, she will stop thinking of this Tom Craven," her husband said. "Is there not another young man in the village who has shown interest, one who has won her favor?"

There were several, of course, and Comes Alone made it her business to visit the fires of their mothers over the next nights, to mention that her daughter had mentioned their son's name—in passing only, naturally—and that she might favor a visit from him sometime soon. To her surprise, few of the mothers greeted her suggestion with enthusiasm.

"It is said," she was told candidly, not urgently, by one of the mothers, "that Not Black has fallen in love with a white man's son. That she has given her heart to him and will have no other." The woman was courteous enough not to add, "and her body, as well."

Over the next seven nights, two boys came to visit Not Black at her mother's fire. Fewer by half than she had hoped, and since her daughter did not welcome them with particular enthusiasm, she doubted others would make the effort.

"There are plenty of squirrels in the woods," Standing Horse said. "I will take her with me when I go to trade with the Bear clan, and she will see others who might find her as lovely as we know her to be."

The Bear clan was at a village more than ten miles farther south. Comes Alone hated the thought that her daughter might find a mate so far distant, but she saw that there might be little choice. "She is more lovely when she smiles," she said wistfully.

"And we have seen little enough of that lately." Her husband nodded. "But she will forget this white boy in time. We must be patient."

And so he took her, first to one village with him on the trade journey, and then to another closer village to breed some ponies. Both times, her daughter returned with no higher spirits than when she had left.

"Did she show no interest whatsoever in any young man?" Comes Alone asked anxiously.

"She spoke to no one unless spoken to first, and then made only small, quiet responses of courtesy," Standing Horse said. "Several men came to greet her, a few even sent their mothers to our fire to ask if she were accepting visitors—"

"Ah! Well, and that is a good sign!"

"Yes, it was," he said evenly, "and I welcomed every young man who wished to come and sit next to a silent, sorrowful girl who had nothing to say for herself and no smile to give away. Frankly, I felt sorry for them. Of course, they did not return, and after two nights, most men in the village knew that she was not truly open to their visits. No matter what her father might say."

"There is too much gossip in our people," Comes Alone said shortly.

"No doubt some of the mothers had already heard of her before she even arrived. I would not doubt that tales of Not Black and her long mouth have run before her."

"The fault is not in those who speak of her," Standing Horse said quietly. "The fault is in us, I fear. We have made of our lovely daughter an old and tired heart."

Comes Alone bowed her head, feeling suddenly very weary and defeated. "What shall we do?"

"We must be patient," he repeated again, something he had told her many times in the last five months.

"It will be difficult," she said. "But we must stand firm against her choice of a white man. I cannot allow her to go against all my father stood for, all my mother endured—"

"And yet," he said, "there are some of our people who might not think ill of her for such a choice."

"There are many of our people who are fools," Comes Alone snapped. "And more who will scorn her than will praise her."

"And this is to be the best test, then, of the wisdom of her decision?"

She frowned at Standing Horse. "Do you wish her to go to the white man? Is that what you are saying? Do you wish your grandchildren to be lost to our ways forever?"

"Of course not," he said. "But neither do I wish to have my daughter lost to herself forever." He ignored Comes Alone's stiff back and unyielding posture and embraced her.

Gradually, she softened in his arms. "I do not know the best path to take," she said sadly. "I cannot see the future clearly."

"None of us can," he said. "We must wait and see what it brings."

And so they did wait, for many more months. But finally, as it became more and more clear that Not Black would not come back to her former happy self, they made a second, painful decision.

"You may invite this white man's son to our fire," Comes Alone told her. "If he is your choice, we will be willing to meet with him."

"It is too late," Not Black said, lifting up her head slowly and gazing at her parents with distant eyes. "Too many moons have passed, and I have not seen him. He likely believes that I have no feelings for him and has found another."

"Well and if he has done so, you are better to know that now," her mother said briskly.

Not Black said nothing.

"Do you wish to go to him and find out for yourself what his feelings might be?" Standing Horse asked gently. "I will take you there, myself."

Not Black thought silently for long moments. Finally she said, "Yes, I will go there. But I will go alone."

Her father nodded.

She turned to her mother. "I have your permission, then, to go where I was forbidden?"

Comes Alone sighed and sat down next to her daughter. "I wish only for your happiness," she said.

"Actually," Not Black said gently, "that is not true. You wish for my happiness, but you wish me to be happy only in the ways you believe best for me to be happy."

Comes Alone lifted her head proudly. "I make no apology for my hopes for you, child. I think that this Tom Craven will be a bitter choice for the granddaughter of Osceola, and I have not changed my view. But I also cannot see you eat up your heart many more moons over this man, and so I tell you to bring him here. We will see for ourselves what sort of husband he may be."

"He may not wish to love a woman who promises herself to him and then disappears from his sight." Not Black stood up to put distance between herself and her mother.

"Perhaps he will not," Comes Alone nodded. "But you will never know if you do not go to him."

Not Black left the fire. She turned at the edge of the *cheke*, and her eyes gleamed in the darkness. "Perhaps you have killed my heart, Mother. And it will never love again."

"I doubt that," Comes Alone said firmly, keeping her voice light and confident.

Only when Not Black had gone to the back of the hut did she gaze at her husband and let her fear show full in her face. "Do you think it is too late for her?" she murmured.

Standing Horse shook his head. "She will forgive us," he said softly.

She was silent. "I remember when I first saw you," she said finally. "I told myself that no one else would ever make me feel in that way again. If my mother had tried to keep me from your side, I think I would have battled her to get to you."

"And I to get to you," he said. "But we are of the same people."

She passed a hand over her eyes. "I am weary of worry. Let her go to him, if that is what she must do."

"I think nothing else will show her their differences faster," he said.

She glanced up. "You do not think the white man's son will accept her?"

He shook his head. "I think she is going to find more heartache at his fire than at ours."

Not Black went to Tom Craven's house and hid in her usual place in the honeysuckle shrub close to the porch. After so long away, after so much had happened between them, she felt foolish for hiding like a child, but she felt unsure how he would respond when he saw her. And most of all, she did not wish to be seen by his father until she knew if he still loved her.

She waited until she saw him alone in the yard, and his father was well away from the cabin before she showed herself. She edged out of the honeysuckle, smoothing her hair and her skirt and then came around the house where he was sharpening tools at the iron anvil.

He looked up and saw her, and his face opened in a broad smile. "Lily!" he called out. "Where you been all this time?"

She came forward shyly, so pleased at his smile that she almost wept with relief. "My mother forbade me to see you," she said. "But my father changed her mind."

"Y'all gowered over me? They hobbled you?"

"Not hobbled," she flushed. "Forbidden. My mother went everywhere with me, to see that I kept my promise."

"You give your word to get shed of me?" He set down his sharpening tools and came to her where she stood, a little apart and in the shade of the cabin.

"I had to," she murmured.

"Why?"

"Because—" she looked down at the ground, confused. "Because they are my parents."

"You a growed woman," Tom said gently, taking her hand and pulling her to him. "You got a right to choose for yourself."

She nodded. "That is why I come," she said. "My mother has changed her heart. She says, you are welcome at our fire."

"She did? She say that?"

Not Black smiled hesitantly.

Tom laughed and hugged her. "Well, anyways, she won' be scalpin' me, if I show up. That's more likely what she said. But you're here now, an' that's what matters." He started to pull her in the direction of the barn. "I got time, Lily, I'll get my pole, an' we go get our toes wet—"

She pulled her hand away and shook her head. "I must get back. I came only to tell you to come to my mother's fire tonight."

"We can talk about it on the river," he said, taking her hand again and tugging her along. She followed him reluctantly while he grabbed up his pole and his fishing pouch. "Pa won' be back 'til evenin', an' if I get him a mess o' cats, he won' fuss much over me shimshackin'—"

"I cannot be gone long," she said anxiously.

He stopped and pulled her close to him. "I plumb missed you, Lily. It be like comin' to life again, to see your face."

She took his hand then, happily, and followed him down the path to where the forest began, into the dark green tangle that would take them finally to the river.

He loved her tenderly that afternoon, and as she lay resting in his arms, she said, "My father will come to like you, I think. And perhaps, then, my mother will follow him."

"It don' matter," he said lightly, caressing her with his fingers so gently that she could scarcely tell where his touch left off and her own skin began.

"Why do you say that?" she asked, sitting up. "They are my parents. It matters much."

He laughed ruefully. "You might as well get used to it, Lily, they gonna put up a calaberment, an' my pa'll do the same. If they be cordial, we is lucky, an' let it go at that."

"Your father will not accept me?" she asked, alarmed.

" 'Course not," he said, pulling her back down again.

She thought that over for a few long moments and then pushed it out of her mind. "Perhaps it will not matter," she said then, stubbornly. "The old people never wish change to come. It is why they are old." She laughed. "But you will come to my fire and ask for me, and they will see that you are a good man."

He said lazily, "They gonna have to take my balance some other way, sweetheart, 'cause I ain' goin' to no Indian camp."

"What?" She sat up and stared down at him. "What do you mean, Tom Craven?"

He shaded his eyes from the sun and looked up at her. "Ah now, Lily, don' go gettin' all biggity. I love you better'n butter, but I ain' gonna go stand at some fire an' be gowered at by a passel of Indians—"

"My parents must meet you."

"Why? What do it matter, anyhow? We can jus' hie ourselves to a preacher an' let him say the words over us, an' let your mama an' daddy an' my pa find something else to fram over."

"No, I cannot," she said. "You must come to my mother's fire. That is our way—"

"Well, it ain' my way," he said. "Tom Craven don' need a say-so from nobody to take hisself a woman."

He had not said "wife," she noticed immediately. But perhaps it was merely his manner of speaking. She understood most of what he said, but there were still words he used, gestures and tones of voice, that she had to learn. She said, "It will not be hard," trying to soothe him. "You need only come to eat what my mother will prepare and make small conversation with my father. I will be there. You will not be alone—"

"I ain' 'afyeard," he said. "I jus' don' see no sense to it."

"The sense is that I ask it," she said.

He kissed her quickly and began to rise. "Ask somethin' else, sweetheart. I ain' gonna hie myself to no palmetto shack to beg leave of no squaw."

She may not have understood all his words, but there was no mistaking his tone. She instantly stood and pushed away his hands. "Then you will not have me, Tom Craven," she said angrily. Before he could stop her, she took off running away, heedless of his calls. Fleet as a bird, she ran through the woods, glancing back to see if he were following. He was not.

She slowed finally and turned back toward the village. She began to weep as she walked. She had been such a fool to think that he would fall easily into line like the mule that turned round and round in a circle. She could not believe he had refused her. When she thought of it, she was certain that she would be willing to give her life for him. And he was not even willing to give up some small piece of pride, to come and ask for her properly. She had not expected him to like the ways of her people, but she had thought he would honor them.

Men were different from women, she thought as her pain began to ebb and her tears ceased. This was something she had heard all of her life, but only in the past year had she come to know it under her skin. He was somehow able to separate his pride from his love for her, and though he would love her, he would not give up some essential part of himself. She had no pride when it came to loving him, she realized. And there was no part of herself she would not give up, for by giving up herself, she gained herself back again. She began to feel more peaceful as she came nearer the camp.

This man loved her, that much was certain. And she loved him more than she had ever believed she could love. If she loved him more than he did her, well then, she would simply teach him, through example, how wonderful this love could be. She would make up whatever difference there might be between them with her own strength, and she would make him love her and need her as her own father loved and needed her mother. She held her head high as she walked through the village, knowing that many looked upon her with curiosity. Let them look, she told herself. Let them see how a beloved woman walks.

When she came to her mother's fire, she saw her mother sitting near the pot of *sofkee*, stirring it and watching her daughter approach. She lifted her head even higher and called out, "I am come!"

"So you are," her mother replied, smiling at her. "I see you have met with him, then."

"I have, and he has missed me sorely," Not Black said with calculated triumph in her voice.

"And he will come to meet with your father?" her mother asked, glancing down at the pot as though it held the most interesting brew in the camp.

"He will come," Not Black said firmly. "He has promised me."

Not Black was not really surprised when her grandmother arrived several days later. Whenever her mother was worried, somehow Morning Dew seemed to sense it on the wind and she mounted her old mare and made the three-day journey from her village on the western bank of the Suwannee to Comes Alone's fire.

Her father joked, whenever he had a serious disagreement with Comes Alone, "Well and I had better prepare the second hammock for your mother." He knew by experience that sooner rather than later, Morning Dew would ride into camp.

And so when she saw her grandmother's mare hitched behind the *cheke* upon her return from the fields, she only shook her head in rueful appreciation for the strange and powerful heart cord that connected the two women. She embraced her grandmother, who rose unsteadily from the palmetto log to hug her fiercely. Morning Dew had not grown stout like so many grandmothers, but her legs wobbled as though she weighed twice herself. Since the long journeys she had made when Osceola was still alive, miles she had walked to be with him in the prison and miles more she had traveled to leave that place behind her, she was not as strong in her knees as others her age. But her eyes were still bright and the strength of her embrace as young as any granddaughter could wish.

"You are come," Not Black said to her, gazing into her eyes. Last year, she had been her grandmother's height; now she had to look down to meet her eyes.

"And how could I not?" Morning Dew said teasingly. "My granddaughter has discovered the pleasures of a man, and I am to stay by my own fire and miss the choicest gossip?"

"My mother has a mouth like a magpie," Not Black flushed. "And have you shared your views on this subject with many along the trail?"

"Only those who had daughters." Morning Dew grinned. She drew her granddaughter down next to her, glanced around conspiratorially, and whispered, "Tell me, then. Is he worth all this moaning and groaning your mother indulges in?"

"I think so," Not Black said shyly. She could not help returning her grandmother's smile. "But perhaps she simply enjoys wallowing in worry, like a pig in a pool."

"Speaking of pool, I wonder that you can say the word without blushing," Morning Dew said. "I understand that the fishing in a certain deep and secret place will never be the same again."

Not Black laughed, despite her embarrassment. She knew full well that it was the custom with her people to tease new lovers nigh to death, just to let them know that not only had they not invented the act of love but also they need not take it too seriously. She also knew well enough that her grandmother's teasing was only a preamble for what would surely follow next.

"You have talked to my mother, then?" she asked.

"Of course. Not that I needed to. They speak of Osceola's granddaughter's foolishness as far as the Suwannee," Morning Dew said lightly, "and so I came to see for myself if all they say is true. He is a white man's son." It was not a question.

Not Black nodded, dropping her head in confusion, despite her intention to keep it high and proud.

"Well and that is not a disaster by itself," Morning Dew said confidentially. "Many women wish to try something different before they wed themselves to a man for their life. After all"—she smiled—"it takes as many years as I have to learn that they are all the same, under the skin. So you have tried him, and he is fine enough, I am sure, or you would not be flushing so prettily. When you tire of him, then you will find someone to marry who is of your clan, and all the gossip will cease."

"I wish to marry him," Not Black said quickly. "I love him, Grand-mother."

She shook her head impatiently, "I understand, child. I felt the same way a hundred times, believe me."

"I do *not* believe you," Not Black said, smiling. "I have heard the stories of you and my grandfather too many times to believe such atrocious lies. To hear you tell it, he was the only man to ever pleasure you in your entire life—"

"Yes, and that is fine talk for when your mother is within hearing or even when you yourself were young and full of dreams. But now I tell you the truth. You will fall in love many times in your life. This is the first. But it will not be the last, nor, likely, even the best."

"You are not listening to me, Grandmother. I wish no other man. I will marry Tom Craven."

Morning Dew leaned back and gazed at her granddaughter with narrowed eyes. "Then your mother is not worried for nothing."

"There is nothing to worry about," Not Black said soothingly. "He loves me. He has promised to come and ask for me, according to the ways of our people. We will live close to the village in a house he will build for us himself. We will be happy, and I will give you a dozen great-grandchildren—"

"None of which will be Seminole."

Not Black glared at her. "All of which will be your grandchildren, nonetheless."

"No," Morning Dew said evenly, "they will not." She took Not Black's hands in hers and said gently, "You are grown now and you will make the decisions about your life which you must make. But I am too old to change my mind about something so important. I have spent a lifetime keeping as far from the whites as I can. Indeed"—she laughed softly—"if I were a man, I would have killed as many as I could put between my rifle sights. But I am not a man. I am a woman. I can only do what I can do to keep our people safe. I have a duty to my people and to the memory of my husband and my children. I will do that duty, child, even if it means breaking both of our hearts. I will not acknowledge any grandchildren who are not born of Seminole fathers. I tell you this now, while you still have a choice to make."

Not Black stared at the woman, appalled. She had not considered that this might well be one result she might face. The gentleness of her grandmother's voice never faltered, but neither did the soft pressure she felt on her hands. She knew that Morning Dew's decision was final. She would not be wooed, and she would not change her mind.

Her eyes filled with tears. "How can you say such a thing to me?" she murmured. "My own children? You would not accept them at your fire?"

"I cannot," Morning Dew said. "To do so would be to go against everything I have believed all of my life, everything I have taught my own children. Everything your grandfather fought and died for— I cannot. If you came to me and told me that your belly was ripe with a white man's seed, I would beg you to rid yourself of that burden. If you did so, I would mourn your pain, but I would not mourn the child. And if you would not cleanse yourself . . ." She bowed her head as though in prayer. "I would never see the child again."

"And me?"

"You would always be welcome, so long as you came alone."

Not Black stood up, suddenly furious. "Did you and my mother plan this betrayal? Did she tell you what to say to best break my heart?"

"Your mother's own heart is too damaged to be wishing still more ill fortune upon her only child," Morning Dew said sharply. "Now sit down and tell me what are we to do about this?"

"There is nothing to be done," Not Black said stiffly, not taking her seat. "You have made your decision, I have made mine. Now we have only to live our lives."

"And lonely ones they will be indeed, child." Morning Dew reached up, took Not Black's hand, and gently drew her down. "There is no man worth this, you know that? Not a one of them. Even your own grandfather was not worth giving up a whole family for, though he was a warrior among ordinary men."

"I will not be giving up a family," Not Black said. "My family will be giving *me* up. And all because I fell in love with a white man." She looked at her grandmother, tears coming to her eyes. "Do you think, any of you, that I did such a thing on purpose? Do you think I planned to choose a man who would so alienate all others who love me?"

"I think you were weak," her grandmother said softly, relentlessly, "and perhaps very foolish. Each time you went to watch him, you knew what you did and why. And even when your mother warned you away—"

"I did not disobey her! He happened upon me by accident."

"And was it accident when he found himself between your legs?"

Morning Dew's voice never changed, even as her words were so coarse as to lacerate.

Not Black could find no answer. She hung her head, her shoulders slumped.

Morning Dew put her arm around her shoulder and drew her head close. "What shall we do about this problem?" she asked again.

"I do not know," Not Black moaned.

"Can you find the courage to refuse him?"

Not Black closed her eyes and tried to picture herself telling Tom Craven that she would never see him again. She could not. Even if he refused, finally, to come to her mother's fire, even if she had to leave this place forever and never see her loved ones again, she could not. "No," she whispered.

"Your mother tells me that your sorrow was eating you up, child. And that is why she reconciled herself to this white man's visit. I believe you are stronger than that."

"I am not," Not Black murmured. She thought of a moment. "Let him come, Grandmother. Let him come to the fire of my mother one time. Meet with him and extend him your courtesy. And then, if you cannot abide him, we will think of something." She did not truly hope that this would bridge the awful gap between Tom Craven and her people, but she could think of no other plan which would not destroy her. At least, this would give her more time.

"We will think of something?"

She nodded.

"And you will send him away if he is not acceptable to your people?"

"I did not say that."

"But you will consider it?"

"If you will meet with him one time."

Morning Dew was silent for long moments. "You may tell this white man's son to come. But you must tell him the truth. He must know that it is very possible that he will never come again. We are not at war with the whites, after all, and so it is not unseemly that a man such as this may visit our fires. But it is not to be considered approval for marriage. Do you understand?"

She nodded.

"Will you make him understand as well?"

"I will tell him your words," Not Black said. "He is a proud man. He may refuse to come at all."

"And then what will you do, little jay?" Morning Dew used Not

Black's childhood name, given her because her complaints were loud, frequent, and contentious as a baby.

"I do not know," Not Black said morosely. "I will think of that another time. Will you tell my mother?"

A voice behind them made them both turn. "I think your mother knows enough to last her lifetime."

"No more whining," Morning Dew said firmly. "We have made a treaty, and the terms are clear. We will welcome this white man's son to our fire, and we shall try to keep open minds. But if, after all, we cannot accept him, then your daughter will consider sending him away."

"Then, I suppose your father will consider not killing him on sight," Comes Alone said wryly.

"Are you going to welcome him or not?" Not Black asked archly. "Because I will not ask him here to be shamed by you, Mother. After all, he did not murder your father, nor did his people."

"His people did, indeed, murder my father. His people took our land and drove us here," Comes Alone said.

"The whites do not think in that way. They do not take responsibility for everything a single member of their race does, as we do. They do not accept the guilt of their ancestors. They do not feel that they are all of one clan or all of one people—"

"Perhaps that is part of their problem," her mother replied.

"Stop this," Morning Dew said, holding up her hand. "Bring the white man's son to your mother's fire. I will answer for the terms of our treaty."

Not Black frowned at her mother and stalked off toward the river. She knew that Tom Craven would be there, sooner or later.

Not Black waited for him for hours, it seemed, before he finally came slipping and clambering down the rocks. She had known he would come. Likely he had looked for her every day since she had run away from him. She knew he loved her, knew it in every part of her being, and she knew it once more, strongly, when she saw the look of relief on his face.

"You are come!" he called, in the greeting she had taught him.

His choice of words told her everything she needed to know. She sat, unmoving on her rock, her fishing pole still in the water. Let him wonder if she came only to catch the evening meal. She watched him, without seeming to watch him, as he struggled across the river on rocks they had placed there for their crossings.

She looked up at him with a cool smile.

"You still riled at me, Lily?" He sat down gingerly beside her, peering into her face.

"You are a fool, Tom Craven," she said lightly.

"Do how?" He was indignant, but he was afraid to let her see it.

"Because you throw away the best woman you ever find," she said. "All for pride."

He shook his head. "No, I ain' throwin' you away, Lily. I jus' don' reckon to come to no Indian camp an' beg your papa to give you up to me, that's all. It ain' my way."

"If I were white woman, you would come to my father's house?"

He thought of this for a moment. "Likely, I would."

"You are bigger fool than I thought."

"Why!"

"Because I am better than white woman. Stronger and smarter. I can shoot straighter than you and am better fisher, also." She held up a string of good-sized perch she had cooling in the shade of a rock. "You will eat good, no matter what."

He laughed and reached for her hand.

"And more important thing. I can pleasure you as a man should be pleasured, all the days of your life." She said it staunchly, boldly, as though she were telling him how many miles she could run. But her hand moved up his arm and to his shoulder when she said it, a light hand which made him shiver under her touch.

"You a conjure gal, Lily," he murmured, already aroused. "An' I be a fool."

"I already tell my mother you will come. She waits for you tomorrow night."

"Why'd you tell her such?"

"Because I believe you love me. I believe you are fool, but you are smart fool. I believe you will do what you must do to have me."

"I gotta do this thing to win you?"

She nodded. "This is the last time I come to this place. I will not come again, if you will not come to my mother's fire." She turned to him with a soft smile. "I have pride, also, after all."

He put his chin in his hands and stared at the river for long, quiet moments. "An' I only got to do it once?"

"One time."

She was silent also. She took her hand and rested it lightly on his leg, halfway between his groin and his knee. She knew that he was increasingly aware of her body, her scent, and the light pressure of her hand. But she said nothing. She did not look at his face.

Finally he said, "All right, Lily, you got me overed. One time, I can do this, I reckon. I don' like it much, but I'll do it. Tomorrow evenin'."

"You swear it?"

"I don' need to forswear myself, Lily, if Tom Craven says he will do a thing, you can grow corn by it." He let his impatience show now.

She smiled. She felt a warm tide of victory flood her heart. "At sunset," she said.

He turned to her and gathered her into his arms. "Now, we got that fixed, let's talk 'bout more important things." He kissed her deeply, his hands already beginning to roam under her skirt and over her breasts. She moaned softly in her throat, welcoming the heat of his hands, his body, and she lay back against the soft moss on the rocks, opening herself up to the joy he gave her.

* * *

At the edge of a large pond, near to where the river slowed and became little more than a swamp, a feisty little turtle with two light stripes on her head kept vigil over her piece of the water. She was a stinkpot, *Sternotherus odoratus*, named for the foul-smelling, yellowish fluid she secreted from two pairs of musk glands under the border of her carapace.

Sterna did not know she was called stinkpot, Stinking Jim, or the Skunk Turtle by the humans in her region, she only knew that the center of her carapace needed sunlight, and thanks to the beavers in a pond nearby, that was becoming more and more difficult to find.

The beavers had moved in after she had her first nest, more than ten winters before. Sterna had not minded their presence, at first, for she knew that the deeper the pond, the better the hunting. And her instincts told her that beavers meant deeper water, in time.

But one thing she hadn't anticipated was what the beavers would do to the trees nearest their pond. The first trees to go were the willows, closest to the water and favorite building materials for the two beavers, which were busily erecting their nest in the middle of the water. Next to go were the maples, and then Sterna began to be annoyed. When the beavers began to take down the birches as well, she found herself in a constant state of irritation. Because although the sunlight, her most favorite thing, was at first increased by the lessening of trees, that was only a temporary condition. What she soon noticed was that smaller trees quickly grew into the spaces left by the larger trees, and the smaller trees had thicker, lower canopies of leaves. Where she might have been able to sun under an overhanging birch, for its tall canopy and spreading branches were high above her, she was unable to find sun under the shorter, denser newcomers which took its place.

And without sunshine, Sterna was a cranky turtle, indeed. In the winter, she required at least five hours of direct sunlight on her shell to stay comfortable. She could get it floating amid the water lilies and hyacinth, with only her back exposed, but the beavers had cleared out so much vegetation that she felt exposed out in the open water. Also, as the pond deepened, the lilies died off. Now, open water was her only choice, and a poor one.

Other good basking places, overhanging stumps and logs, were also being consumed and reordered by the beavers. Too industrious for her taste and far too tidy, they had cleared off more than a dozen of her best basking places in the past season, dragging every bit of wood to the middle of the pond for their nest. She would have liked to bite one of them and would have, but their slapping tails startled her and the size of their incisors kept her wary.

Nonetheless, she wished them ill, and she had decided that if she ever caught one of their kits near enough to her jaws, she would administer a nasty bite in one of its webbed feet.

Now Sterna was forced more and more to crawl slowly and laboriously up a low branch to reach sun-basking spots, and although she was a fair climber, she did not relish the process. Today, she decided that there must be a better branch for her to climb than the last one she had tried, which bounced her like a squirrel until she was forced to hold on with her jaws.

Sterna crawled up to the base of a likely-looking sweet bay, one of the few on that edge of the pond which the beavers had not yet ravaged. She gazed upward, lifting her head slowly. There was a branch, wide enough to hold her, she thought, which reached out near to the water and was open to the sun. A fork in the tree branch would make a perfect place for her afternoon doze. She snapped up a dragonfly which came too close to her head, munched it down methodically, and put her front claws on the base of the sweet bay. Then she began the long, precarious trip up the tree, clawing her way slowly, clinging to the bark with her jaws when she had to, pushing her way upward until she reached the place where her branch forked away from the tree.

Actually, it was surprising that Sterna could climb as well as she could. Few other creatures were as ill suited to arboreal adventures as the turtle, but somehow, she managed, as did most of her kind, to get up far higher than an observer would have guessed she could accomplish.

At last, weary and not a little peeved at the necessity for the effort, Sterna reached the place on her branch which she had spied from the ground, and settled into the fork of the tree. The sun was, as she had hoped, hot and bright on her carapace. She braced her rear claws and closed her eyes, sighing with some contentment.

Sterna was barely into the best part of the sun and her nap, when a sudden disturbance under her tree caused her to open her eyes and look down. A flock of coots were causing a commotion, moving quickly across the water toward her tree, gabbling and crying in panic. She looked across the water and saw that two men were walking around the pond, coming in her direction.

Sterna froze and flattened herself to the branch. Men were becoming more and more frequent in the swamp. In her first seasons, she saw only one or two each winter. Now, it seemed to her that the men walked the hammocks with impunity, and at least once a moon, she had to evade a fisherman with a pole or some man in a boat. These two were walking, their poles on their back. White men with heavy shoes. They were, she had discovered, the more dangerous of the two species of men in her territory.

Sterna watched them as they approached. The coots took wing, flapping and cackling in a raucous and unmannered crowd, and the men came nearer still. Now they were close enough that she could hear their voices, and she kept herself as still as possible, crouching low onto the branch, knowing that the slightest movement could draw their eyes.

To her surprise, an opossum came out of the brush at the base of the tree and walked in full view of the men, her babies hanging from her long, naked tail. She carried her tail over her head like an umbrella and nine of them hung upside down, bobbing as she waddled along. Sterna knew that the opossum was stupid, but she could not believe that any animal was so careless as to venture deliberately onto the trail when men were about.

The men opened their mouths when they saw the opossum, making the cawing sound they made and gabbling between themselves. Sure enough, one of them took out his stick and ran to the opossum, which did nothing but look up stupidly at him and hiss. The man raised his stick and brought it down on the opossum's head, cracking it with the audible sound of an egg breaking. He picked up the creature by the neck, stripped the babies off her tail, and threw them way out into the water. The possum kits hit the water with soft plops, and Sterna heard the second pop, pop, pop, as the snapping turtles which lived out in the center of the pond snatched them under, one by one. The man tied the dead mother to his belt and they walked on into the swamp.

Sterna waited until she could no longer see the men, waited a good while more until she was certain they were gone. The ringnecks and the ruddies finally calmed down and began to feed, and so she knew they sensed no more danger. She turned very cautiously on her branch, taking forever to balance herself properly before she moved an inch. Then slowly, carefully, Sterna climbed down her sweet bay, holding on when she had to with her jaws, inching along and digging her claws into the bark for leverage. When she made it to the ground, she moved into the brush and from there, into the water. She went down to her den below the waterline and stayed inside for a long while, sending musing bubbles up to the surface.

It had been an exciting afternoon. More excitement than Sterna wanted, that was certain. This was one more thing to lay at the beavers' den, she believed. The coming of the beavers meant the coming of the white man—it must be so, for the one had followed hard on the other.

That decided her. She would move before the next nesting season to another pond. One without beavers. She brooded over her fate, deep in her mud den, and bubbled her exasperation. Beavers and men, men and beavers. They deserved each other.

* * *

The day of the night she expected Tom Craven, Not Black was unable to eat a bite of food or keep her mind on any task. The moment she put herself to do a thing, it ceased to matter. All she could think of was how her mother would greet him, how her father would frown or smile or stand or not stand, how her grandmother would tease him or remain stony and silent.

The day dragged on, and since she had readied her best bodice, her most colorful skirt, inspected the beads her grandmother had given her for any flaws, and bathed her hair and skin many hours before, there was little to distract her from her worry. Finally, she picked up her pole and went fishing, knowing that only the sight and sound of moving water would calm her.

But even fishing did not soothe her as it usually did. She sat with her pole in the water, not caring if she had a bite, not realizing that the worm was long gone from her hook, snatched by a wily bream moments after it had settled near the bottom. She watched an otter at play far up the river, saw him arching and diving and surfacing, all sheen and splash and spangled light, and then when he was gone, she watched nothing at all but the slow pictures which jumbled her head.

She could remember every touch between them, every time he had held her, each one as unique and shiveringly exciting as when it had happened. She had only to picture his hands on her, and her stomach lurched and fell into that empty place that felt as though she had not eaten for a day. It was a queer blend of pain and pleasure, and she purposely called up that memory again and again, just to feel the sensation.

She sat for hours, simply feeling him next to her, near her, inside her. The day grew cooler, and the shadows grew long, and then she realized that she had dreamed away hours which might have been better spent somehow, perhaps in arranging flowers around the *cheke* or finding some special berries he might enjoy or cajoling her grandmother into a jovial mood. She was suddenly in a panic, not at all ready for him to arrive, and she yanked up her pole, and hurried back to the village.

When she arrived, her mother and grandmother were readying the evening meal. Morning Dew looked up and said, "He already came, little jay, and went back home again. We begged him to stay, but he said he simply could not wait another moment—"

"My grandmother's mouth gets more witty with every year," Not Black said lightly. "Soon, we will be sending you to the white man's forts to entertain their visiting chiefs. Is my father back from the men's council yet?"

"He will be here in time, do not worry," Comes Alone said.

"I am not worried," Not Black said, and she went into her area of the *cheke* to ready herself. When she was dressed, her hair long and shining, and her necklace looped in intricate folds around her neck, she came out by the fire.

"You should wait within," Morning Dew said. "We will call for you when it is proper."

"He will be more comfortable if he sees me as soon as he arrives," Not Black said. "It is enough that he comes. He does not have to conform to every old way, I think—"

"Already, you give him license to pull you from our traditions," Comes Alone grumbled.

"If you cannot keep your bargain, Mother, then I shall not be bound to keep mine!" Not Black said warningly.

"Peace," Morning Dew said, holding up her hand. "Your husband comes." She nodded to Comes Alone.

Standing Horse came then into the clearing, his face furrowed with concern. He took his seat heavily, and Comes Alone shot a warning glance to Not Black not to disturb him further. She took him a cup of the hot black tea he preferred and waited until he had supped it down. "Is there news?" she asked quietly.

He nodded, glancing at Not Black. "You are beautiful, daughter," he said gently. "I hope that this white man's son cherishes you in the way you deserve."

She smiled at him gratefully. "He does."

"And the news?" Morning Dew asked shortly.

"The white men are going to war. This time, against each other."

"The Maker of Breath has answered our prayers," Comes Alone said.

"Perhaps. Perhaps not," Standing Horse said. "The runners bring messages from the coast, and they are confusing to our elders. It seems that the white men cannot agree about their black people. Those from the north wish them to be free; those from the south wish them to remain as slaves."

"Will the battles come to these lands?"

"No one knows. The elders agree that if they do, none of our people are to take sides."

"That will be difficult to do," Morning Dew said. "It is my experience that when the white men fight, they often force others to fight with them, one way or the other. And so long as we have blacks in our villages—"

"We have few left," Standing Horse said. "We can only wait and see."

Not Black was watching her father's face, and so she did not see Tom Craven when he walked up, glancing about to see if he had the right place. Suddenly, she looked up, and there he was.

She jumped to her feet, her face suddenly flushed and her heart beating hard. "You are come!" she said, overly loud. She felt as though she spoke down a tunnel.

"Evenin'," he said nervously, glancing at her mother, father, and grandmother.

Standing Horse stood then and did his best to smile cordially to the young man before him. "Welcome to our fire," he said in broken English. He gestured to the palmetto log across from him. "Please sit."

Comes Alone was suddenly very busy at the back of the cook area, but Morning Dew took her seat close to Tom Craven and peered at him unashamedly. "Well, and you are the son of the man who has the cattle?" she asked politely.

"My name is Tom Craven," he said, speaking loudly as people often do when they are not sure of being understood. He started to put out his hand to take hers, but then hesitated.

She looked at his hand and then at his face curiously. "You are younger than I supposed," she said suddenly. "How many winters have you?"

"My grandmother wishes to know your years," Not Black said nervously, sitting across from him by her father.

"Eighteen years old, ma'am," Tom said easily.

"And how much cattle do you have?" she asked in better English.

He thought for a moment. "I 'spect my pa will give me half the herd. I ain' never asked him."

"You come seeking a wife?" Comes Alone asked suddenly from the back. She came forward into the light. "You who have no cattle?"

He glanced at Not Black, who glared fiercely at her mother. "I came 'cause Lily asked me." He smiled at her. "Meanin' no disrespect, ma'am."

"Lily? What is this 'lily'?" Morning Dew asked indignantly.

"That is what he calls me," Not Black said. She lifted her chin in defiance. "I think it is beautiful."

"Perhaps your friend can tell us news," her father broke in soothingly in her own tongue. "While your mother prepares him some food." He looked meaningfully at Comes Alone, who murmured low in her throat and went back to the cooking area. "We hear news of fighting about the slaves," he said carefully in English. "Is there to be war among the whites?"

"Don' rightly know," Tom Craven said. "Pa says sure enough, 'cause the Yankees want to take our niggers, an' Southerners won' stand for it."

"Do you have slaves?" Standing Horse asked quietly.

"Wish we did," Tom said amiably. "I'd a heap sight somebody else hoe those taters than me."

Comes Alone brought over a bowl of warm *sofkee* and offered it to the man with her head slightly averted.

"You mus' be Lily's mama," he said. "Pleased to make your 'quaintance, ma'am."

Comes Alone flushed angrily and took her seat by her husband.

"Please understand," Standing Horse said. "This is not easy."

"I reckon not," Tom smiled. "Lily had to nigh rassle me to the ground 'fore I'd come, myself."

Morning Dew looked pointedly at Not Black, who smiled ruefully and looked away.

"You wish to marry," Standing Horse said.

"I'm studyin' it, sir."

"And what do you offer for my daughter?"

Tom Craven looked to Not Black for an answer, but she kept her eyes to the ground. "Well, I don' know what your ways is, sir, but I mean to build a house near my pa, likely on the bottomland up from the river. I figure, come spring, I'll take a share of the calves, an' start my own herd. The land is fair, an' if we work it smart, we shouldn't have no trouble making a good crop, maybe two—"

"You wish to take her from the village," Standing Horse said.

"Well, I don' reckon I can make a go of it here, sir," Tom Craven said quietly. "Do you?"

"No," Comes Alone said firmly. "If she goes with you, she leaves her village forever." Her voice was surprisingly strong, her English clear.

"An' that would be a jerk up for y'all." Tom nodded. "I see that well enough, but she still would be close enough to meet regular," he added, nodding to Not Black confidently.

"And the children?" Morning Dew asked. "They will be taught the white man ways."

"I don' know no other," Tom said.

In the long silence that followed, Not Black looked at her mother, at her grandmother, and then to her father. Tom kept his face down, supping slightly at the bowl of *sofkee* to be polite. He knew enough to be still at this moment, she saw, and she loved him all the more for that wisdom. She said softly, "Well, and you have met him, then. If you have no more questions, I will accompany him to the edge of the village."

Her father looked at her with a rare and wistful sadness, as though he were already waving her farewell to a far place.

Standing Horse stood up and offered the man his hand. "You are an honest man, Tom Craven. A brave man to come to our fire alone. We will speak of this. Not Black will speak to you another time soon."

Tom got up, set down the bowl gingerly, and looked unsure what to do with his hands. Not Black rose and touched him on the shoulder. "Come," she said. "I will walk you back."

The two women did not stand, nor did they speak. They gazed after Not Black and Tom Craven with sadness, and she did not smile at them. She could not bring herself to reassure them falsely. For she knew she would go with him, no matter what. And she knew that they knew this as well.

Within one moon, Not Black married Tom Craven, according to her people's customs and traditions, before the fire of her mother with her father and her grandmother looking on. The ceremony was brief and without the usual noisy joy of many onlookers, for only two others from the village attended, Small Bear and her mother, two who had been as family to Not Black since she was very small.

But the absence of many to congratulate her did not diminish her joy. Nor did her mother's tears and her grandmother's set face. She embraced them each in turn, gathered the bundle of her belongings, and handed it to Tom to carry. As they left the village, her heart sang with triumph.

He had been quiet during the marriage ceremony, saying little and only taking her hand at the end of it, as though he were suddenly shy of his desire. Now that they were alone, she could hardly wait to hold him again and as they reached the river, she said happily, "We should make a wedding bower right here, by the water, where our love began." She glanced at him teasingly, to let him know that she wanted him.

He said, "We got a far sight to go yet, Lily. Best keep walkin' if we want to make it before dark."

She nodded. He was right. He was wise to forgo the moment's pleasure for their later comfort. They were on their way to his father's cabin, where they would spend a few nights. His father was away again on another trading trip, and when he returned home, Tom said, was time enough to tell him of his new bride.

Tom said he would put up a quick shelter for them, just a little shed off the stable until he could build a proper house on their land. "Jus' to keep off the vermin an' the freshets," he said. "An' once Pa is set on us being together, we can keep house with him until I get the roof on."

She was nervous about facing his father, but she trusted that she would have to say and do little. Tom would do all the explaining.

"We are husband and wife, wife and husband," she told herself silently, over and over. She had never felt more at peace with herself in her life. The pain in her mother's eyes would soon go away, she knew. Her grandmother would change her mind once she saw their firstborn child. And her father—her dear, loyal father—she would name her first son after his clan, against the tradition of her people which said that children belonged to the mother's clan. He deserved that much, she felt, for standing up against the two women for what she wanted.

"Well and we have seen him," her grandmother had said calmly. "We have kept our part of the treaty. Now you must keep yours. Tell him that you will not marry him."

"What?" Not Black had shouted. "What are you saying? He was mannerly and correct in all he did and said!"

"Yes, he was mannerly enough. But he does not wish to treat you with the proper respect due a bride. He offered no bride-price—" her grandmother replied stoutly.

"I do not need a bride-price to know my husband," Not Black said angrily. "I am not a pony to be bought and sold. It is time for these old ways to give way to better sense!"

"He is not a man of worth," Comes Alone said quietly. "He has no lands of his own; he has no cattle. He depends on his father for every-thing—"

"That is not unusual in a boy his age," Standing Horse said sooth-ingly. "He is young, and so is she," he continued, trying to calm the three women. "Perhaps when they are older, the match might be made successfully, but for now, I think it is wise to wait."

Not Black had listened to them talk over and around her for moments as though she were a child, and she finally said, "I have brought him to you for your inspection, like a pig to be bartered. I should have known better. Your minds were closed to him before he even arrived. Now I tell you this truth: I will marry Tom Craven before the moon changes, with or without your approval. If I must do so, I will go to him and beg him to take me to his own people. And I will never come to my mother's fire again!" Her voice was hard, and she saw the shock and pain in her mother's mouth, her father's eyes. But she saw some-thing else as well.

They knew that she would do as she promised.

It had been a fearsome battle, but she never doubted that she would fulfill her wishes, once she said them aloud. She had all the power, she realized finally, and did not need them to approve her choice. If she wished to wed Tom Craven, she simply would do so. And if they tried to stop her, tried to forbid her, she would leave and never see them again. Once she knew what her course would be, like a river, she would not admit to anything in her path. And once her grandmother saw that conviction in her eyes, she stopped speaking of alternatives. A stony silence had settled between them then, which saddened Not Black. But each time she thought of putting Tom aside for her mother or her grandmother, she knew she could not make that choice.

She walked behind him steadily, pacing herself as he did through the forest. He knew the trails almost as well as she did, and she was proud of the strong way he led them in the direction of his land.

Twice, he turned to her and asked, "You all in, Lily? We can rest, if need be."

But she smiled and shook her head. "I can walk all the day behind you, husband," she said.

"It ain' much farther," he said.

She laughed lightly. "I think I know the way," and then she left him to his thoughts. He spoke little on this journey, but perhaps he had much on his mind. Certainly, he must have as much trepidation about showing her to his father as she had had, when she took him to her mother's fire. She must be patient, she knew. When he turns to me at last, I will embrace him and drive away his doubts.

Finally, they reached the white man's cabin, and Not Black saw with some surprise that it looked somehow smaller than it had before, when she had viewed it from a distance. On the porch, she stood and felt the smooth boards with her moccasins, heard them creak as she moved over them as though in surprise. "I am come," she told the house as they entered it, and it seemed to her that the walls murmured back, "You are."

The cabin was dim and musty, but Tom moved about surely, lighting a lantern, setting down her bundle, and opening the fire flue. She sat down on a rocking chair gingerly, feeling the weight of the chair shift under her and move her slowly back and forth. It was a delicious luxury and the chair seemed to mold to her back with welcome. With the lantern bright, she looked around the room slowly, while he went outside to see to the stock.

In one corner stood a tall wooden cupboard, like some she had seen

at the trading stores in Tampa. It was filled with plate and glass and
metal cookware, more than she would have seen in three *chekes* com-
bined. Dust had settled on the plate and in the corners of the cupboard,
and she relished the prospect of handling these beautiful things in the
process of cleaning them. In another corner, a man's boots rested against
the wall, dusty with sand. His father's boots. She noted that they were
smaller than Tom Craven's boots, a good sign.

A worn braided rug lay flat on the planked floor, and she marveled
at the colors. It must have been made by the hands of Tom's mother,
she thought, getting down on one knee to touch it gently. There was
a window in one corner of the cabin with something in it which looked
like thick, rippling water. She touched it in wonder. It was cool and
smooth, like stone, but she could see the images of the barnyard through
it. Such magic these white people had, it was not surprising that they
had been able to take whatever they wanted from whoever had it
before.

A large black stove stood like a soldier at the wall, and she marveled
at what sort of things might be possible to cook on such a great machine.
Surely it would burn an armful of firewood in moments.

There were strange things and wonderful objects all around the
cabin, and she could not wait to handle them, to explore them, to have
Tom tell her how each one worked and what it did. But there would
be ample time for those discoveries. When he came back in the cabin
door, he found her where he had left her, in the rocking chair.

Tom said, "You can put your trumpery here," pointing to a place
in a wooden cupboard. "Once we get settled in, you can put it where
you like."

She stood up and went to him, nestling her head in his neck. "Tell
me that you are happy I am your woman," she murmured.

"I be happy," he said, holding her. His embrace tightened, and she
could feel the desire rise in him quickly, spontaneously, as though a
sun turned on inside him suddenly.

His heat ignited her, and she let him lead her to the small bed at
the rear of the cabin. On it was a soft sack filled with corn husks, and
when he leaned her back upon it, it rustled strangely under her. She
was not used to sleeping so close to the ground, not accustomed to a
bed which did not sway. But his body on her felt at once familiar and
safe, and she moved out of her clothing with fluid ease, pulling him
inside her with a low sound in her throat like a cooing dove. She was
a wife now. Everything they did together was sacred.

* * *

For four days, Not Black and Tom Craven loved each other, explored each other's pleasures, and did little else but sleep and eat and laugh at her attempts to understand his house, his goods, and his ways. And then his father came home, announced by the whinny of his horse calling to a mare in the nearby pasture.

Tom went out on the porch to greet his father nervously, saying, "Stay inside 'til I call for you. It be best if I talk to him alone, first."

She felt a thrill of fear go through her belly as she tried to picture what this man might say to his son. It was enough to come home and discover his son had married. But to find the woman in his house— she suddenly wanted to be anywhere but in that small cabin. But she sat down, trying to make herself as small and unassuming as possible.

She heard Tom call to his father, heard the man return the greeting, and then she could not hear their voices clearly as the man rode his horse to the stable. She sat for a long time with her eyes closed, willing herself to calm. He would take some time to get used to the idea, no doubt. But after that time was passed, she would please the old man. She was certain that she could do so. Of course, it would have been better if Tom had told his father before he married. She wished now that she had insisted he do so. But he said this was best, and he surely knew his own kin. Besides, his father was gone when they made the marriage. Did the order of such things really matter, when all was said and done?

She heard then their voices raised in anger, and she froze, her heart beating hard. She rose out of the chair to peer out the small window, but she could see nothing. The rise and fall of their voices, the two men arguing now, were too rapid and distant for her to make out the words, but the tone was unmistakably one of attack and defense. She half rose again from her chair, thinking she should simply run now, go back to her village, and wait until he came for her. After his father had a chance to think, he would likely welcome her properly.

But she sat down again. She could not go back to her village. Could not face her mother and father with the news that she was not wanted. They would never let her return to Tom Craven again.

Suddenly the voices stopped, and she rose and looked out the window again. The two men were coming up the yard toward the house. Tom was stalking stiff-legged behind his father, like a balky colt. His father's head was down, his face grim. She sat down again, holding her hands to keep them from trembling.

Tom's father came in the door and stood there, gazing at her, his mouth in a thin, angry line. "You speak American?" he asked shortly.

"Yes," she murmured.

"Well then, let me say this plain. I ain' studied on no squaw for my boy, here."

Tom was behind his father then, pushing his way past him to go closer to Not Black. "Pay him no mind, Lily. He's addled now, but he—"

"You got to go," he said firmly, ignoring his son. He glanced around and saw her bundle and picked it up, handing it to her. "Get your things an' go."

"She ain' goin' no place," Tom said, moving to take the bundle from her hand. "She's my woman, an' she stays right here."

"Not under my roof, she don't," the man said.

"Then we'll sleep out in the cow house, 'til I can get a roof up," Tom said. "The land's big enough for two plows."

"Not if one of them is a squawman's," the father said. "You think I raised you for this? Godalmighty, your ma would thrash in her grave, did I let you throw yourself away on this baggage. You plumb flumed out, boy? I been gone less than a week, an' I come home to find you got her sittin' in your ma's rocker!"

Not Black stood up instantly, her head high, her eyes bright with unshed tears. "I go back to my people," she said, her voice low and vibrating with anger.

"Damn right, you will—"

"Pa, if she goes, I go," Tom Craven said, moving to take her by the arm. "I'm gonna wed her proper an' Christian, soon's I can get us to a preacher man."

Tom Craven's father laughed then, an ugly crack of anger. "No Christian preacher's gonna hitch you to this heathen, boy! You addled as a ruttin' gobbler." He glared at Not Black. "Ruttin' jus' what it be."

Not Black yanked her bundle then from Tom's hand and strode out of the cabin, pushing past his father without looking back. She heard Tom call, "Lily!" in exasperation, but she did not stop. She got to the fence by the side pasture, almost panting with anger, her heart beating so hard that she put her hand on her chest to slow it. She stopped then and leaned against the fence so that her back was to the cabin, fighting down her sobs of fear and rage. She would not give the white fool the pleasure of seeing her weep!

Tom came out of the cabin then, and as he came toward her, she could not keep her tears inside any longer. She went into his arms, and he bent his head to her cheek. "That ol' fool. Don' pay him no mind, Lily. He come around after he gets used to the idea, I 'spect."

"He is a man of perverse nature!" she sobbed.

"No, he jus' wrongheaded. Lots of white folks are, 'bout savages."

"I am not savage!" she said, appalled, pulling back and staring at him.

" 'Course you ain', it's jus' a word. Injuns, savages, heathen, it all means the same never-mind."

"Yes," she said coldly, pulling away. "It means all the same thing to men of perverse natures. White men. White men who hate Seminole."

"He don' hate your kind, he jus' ain' studyin' on me marryin' one, that's all. Now don' take it so to heart."

"What will we do?" she said, her eyes welling up again.

"Jus' what we planned. Only we stay out o' his way while we doin' it. We can stay in the cow house 'til I get a roof up—"

"He says he will not give you land."

"Well, he have to run me off with a beatin' stick, then, 'cause I worked this land since I been tall enough to walk a mule, an' I ain' givin' it over now. Won' take me long to get a shanty up, an' we can add to it as we need."

"I can build *cheke* in a day." She smiled tremulously. "If you help me, it will be easy."

"We don' need to live in no chickee, we can do better than that," he said easily. "Don't you fret, Lily. When he sees you big with his first gran'baby, he'll come around."

At the thought of a child, she felt a ribbon of steel thread itself through her spine. She stopped weeping and gazed out over the fields with calm. "Well and I was foolish to think that this would not happen," she said. "But since it has, we are free of them all, my heart. We have each other, and we will be one."

He took her hand and they started down the path which led to an old barn at the rear of the pasture. It was near falling down with rot, and the honeysuckle grew so heavy around its foundation that it was more a bower than a building. But it was there that they spent the night together. In the morning, Not Black set about building them a proper *cheke*, while Tom began to dig a new foundation close by on higher land for their cabin. It was hard work to build the hut alone, without her mother or any friends to help. It was not large, and it would barely keep the rain from them, but it was her first home, and she thought it was beautiful. When she was finished, she went to the river and came back with enough fish to feed them, and he went boldly to the chicken yard and brought back eggs, saying, "Let him come and take them back, if he's a mind to."

For three days and nights, they stayed out in the *cheke*, and Tom Craven's father paid them no mind. The daylight hours were filled with hard work, cutting trees and dragging them into position for the walls, mixing mud and hay for the chinking, carrying water from the river, and hoisting the logs higher and higher. They could not, together, handle the larger trees, and so the walls grew slowly. At the end of three days, they had only a small room, scarcely half as large as his father's cabin, with the walls no higher than her head.

And then Tom Craven's father visited their fire that night, calling out to them as he approached as though he were a stranger unsure of his welcome. She disappeared quietly into the *cheke*, standing close enough to listen to the men speak.

For the longest moments, they did not. Finally, the old man said, "War's comin'. Heard it up to the post."

War. She shivered and held her arms across her breast. Tom Craven's father went often enough to the trading post; he must have news before most in the swamp.

Tom said, "I heard tell of it. But I ain' fixin' to go fight so's some rich man can keep his niggers."

"Ain' jus' about the niggers, boy. It's about a man's say-so on his own land. The Northern tail-waggers want to fix it so a man cain' do on his land what he sees fit. They's callin' for volunteers in Saint Augustine. They's havin' torchlight parades, an' such, an' callin' for secession."

"They been doin' that for a year," Tom said.

"They doin' it louder and more of them now. Jeff Davis been named president of the Confederate States."

"Better than that scummer, Lincoln."

"They fired on Charleston."

"Do how!"

"That's right. More'n a month past."

"Goddamn," Tom said angrily. "They ain' got no right—"

"That's what I'm sayin', boy. They's callin' for volunteers. I'm fixin' to go."

Tom looked at his father in openmouthed amazement. "When did you study this out?"

"Two nights past. I mean to sell the stock an' ride the mule to Saint Augustine, get a better price for her there, I reckon. So I come to tell you."

Not Black's heart was thudding in her chest, and she leaned against the pole of the *cheke,* closing her eyes in fear. She did not understand everything that the old man said, but she knew enough of the words to recognize stark peril in them.

"You can bide, or you can go," the old man said. "I'd be proud to have you fight 'longside me. Or you can shim-shack here with your squaw."

She saw Tom drop his head and stare into the fire. "You figure it to last long?"

"I ain' studyin' on keeping off my land more'n a year. Give that bottom pasture a chance to lay fallow, an' we can plant cotton maybe when I get back. Maybe get us a nigger," he grinned, "once we beat the tail-waggers back to their hidey-holes."

Tom laughed. "I'll go long with you, Pa. To Saint Augustine, anyways. See what all the ruckus is."

"Good," the old man said, rising and slapping his legs. "I mean to leave in three days."

"I be ready," Tom said. He stood and put out his hand for his father to shake. Then he sat back down and watched his father walk again across the dark fields.

When he was gone, Not Black came out of the *cheke* and stood behind her husband, one hand on his shoulder.

"You heard?" he asked.

She said nothing. She could not speak. Her heart was frozen in her chest.

He turned and looked up at her. "I got to go with him, Lily. I cain' let him go alone."

"You will fight?" she finally asked, her voice vibrating with pain.

"Likely not. Bunch o' hotheads on both sides, it won't come to much. An' if they do, our boys can flummox those tail-waggers faster than you can spit. But I cain' let him go alone, you see that, don' you?"

"I will come with you," she said.

He shook his head. "No, Lily. That ain' proper."

"What do you mean?" she cried, sitting down beside him and looking into his face. "When the men go to war, the women come to clean the weapons and cook the food—"

"That ain' how white folks do things," he said patiently. "The women stay home an' tend the babies—"

"I have no babies to tend," she said. "I go with you."

He stood up now and said firmly, "No, Lily. You got to go back to your mama. I'm fixin' to go to war, an' I cain' be flumed out that you ain' cared for proper. I want you to go home. Jus' for a time, an' then I come back an' fetch you."

"I will not!" she cried.

"What you reckon to do, then?"

"I will stay here," she said. "I will keep your father's house."

He shook his head. "By yourself? It ain' right, Lily. I cain' go off to battle, thinkin' of you here, without nobody to do for you. Go back to your folks, jus' for a while, an' then I come—"

"You must not go!" she wailed.

He stiffened slightly. "This is somethin' a woman cain' understand, honey. It ain' somethin' I want to do—"

"Yes, you wish to do this," she said. "You wish to go to battle. It is easier to do this than to stay with me."

He smiled ruefully and shook his head. "I tol' you, this ain' for you to understand. Now, I'll take you back to your kin tomorrow mornin'. An' I be back jus' as soon as we whip the Yankees or they think better of their damn-fool ideas."

She stood up and faced him defiantly. "You do not need to take me back. I know the way."

He reached out and took her hand. "Don' take on, Lily. I got three more days 'fore I got to go. We can enjoy that time, anyways."

She let him lead her into the *cheke*, onto the bed she had built with her own hands from palmetto thatch and moss and corn husks, a blend of his ways and her own. He gently pulled her alongside him, cupping her belly with his hands, drawing his knees up behind hers. He softly kissed her neck and the space between her jaw and her ears. "Lily, you got to understand," he murmured. "I got to go. But I swear, I be back, an' then I build us a place. But for now, I cain' stand thinkin' on you alone here. If I got to think on that an' fight Yankees, too, I don' think I can do it. Please, honey. I need you to help me. Go back to your ma and keep yourself safe whilst I'm gone."

She gave herself up to his hands then, his mouth, and the pressure of his body on hers.

* * *

Not Black said good-bye to her husband at the fire of her mother. She was doing something she thought she'd never have to do at a place she never thought she'd return to so soon. And the presence of her mother and father did little to assuage the pain she felt at waving him farewell. He promised he would return as soon as he could; he promised he would build her a fine cabin so that they could start their life together. And then, he walked off with a jaunty wave, wearing around his neck the blue beads which she had lovingly draped upon him.

For a day, she did little but sit by the fire or lie in her hammock, hearing only his voice in her head and responding to little that was said to her, nothing which was offered. Her mother quietly brought her warm *sofkee*, but it lay untouched. Her father came and sat by her hammock to silently sharpen his tools, but she did not speak to him. The first night she slept without Tom beside her, she felt she had died, so alien did she feel from her own skin.

The next morning was a little better. The next evening, she was able to eat and make small conversation. Within a few days, she was able to smile again. But at least a dozen times a day, she looked up the path where he had gone, hoping to see his face, to see his back, to keep fresh the last view of his head and his farewell wave.

And then the anger came over her in waves, once the depression lifted. He had loved her, wooed her, and wed her, and now he was gone. What sort of man did such a thing? What sort of people made war on each other so regularly? And what sort of gods allowed such betrayal? If her mother had welcomed him, perhaps he would have stayed in the village, and he would never have known of the war, would not have gone away. If his father had not been of such perverseness, they would already have their cabin up, their own fields in crop, and they would be safe and happy. She raged thus, at everyone, at the gods, at fate, for a week or more, barely able to be civil to anyone who spoke until she finally exhausted herself and her anger.

When the anger left, she was too weary to put one foot before the other. She cared for nothing. She could not weep. It seemed to her that she was suddenly very old and very empty. Even her skin looked different, shrunken and dry like an old sunflower. No one would ever love her again.

Finally, her father came to her while she sat at the river one afternoon. Her mother had sent her fishing for the tenth time in as many days, trying to interest her in some of her old habits. She sat gazing at the moving water, scarcely feeling the pole in her hand.

Her father came and sat beside her, announcing his presence as he always did with a polite cough.

She turned and glanced at him and then away.

He put his hand on her knee and said, "You must stop this, my daughter."

She did not answer.

"You are breaking your own heart. And for what? He will return, and these days will be forgotten."

"He should not have left me," she said, her voice low and dispirited.

"Perhaps. But that is the way of his people in war. The women do not follow. Besides, he likely is going a long way. You would not have been happy."

"And I am here?" She let all of the anger and scorn ring in her voice.

"You could be," her father said gently. "If you let yourself."

She turned away again. "You cannot understand. You have never been abandoned."

"You have not been abandoned. Your husband has gone to war. Your mother and grandmother have known such departures and managed to keep their wits about them. Why can you not be content with his decision?"

"Because he did not have to go!"

"That is not the reason," her father said softly. "It is because he is white. Because you do not trust him to return."

She knew the truth of his words the moment he spoke them. She leaned her head on his shoulder, her voice rough with unshed tears. "His father is a perverse man. He insulted me. He spoke to me as though I were his mule. Less than his mule."

"That does not surprise me," her father said. "Did it surprise you?"

"Yes! He shows no respect for his son—"

"You have not been near the whites for so long, my daughter. You forget how much they hate all things different from themselves."

"His son does not."

"Well and that is one of them. But it is not enough to make a clan. Much less a people."

"You are wrong," she murmured. "I do trust Tom Craven. I do believe he will return for me, as he has promised. And when he does, I shall be happy again."

To her surprise, her father laughed kindly. "You will wait all that while to laugh once more? By then, your throat will have forgotten how."

"Do you think he will be gone a long time?"

"The elders say this war will be a hard one. The whites to the north are many and powerful, they tell us. And the whites to the south are rich and arrogant. There are many slaves and many men make money from their labor. It will not be a short war, they say."

"Tom said that they will beat their enemy in quick time."

"Perhaps," her father shrugged. "Perhaps he knows more than the elders."

She frowned doubtfully.

"If it is for a long time"—her father stroked her cheek—"that is not impossible to bear."

"It will be harder to bear when the child comes," she murmured.

He pulled back and gazed at her with surprise and alarm. "You are with child? How long have you known this?"

"Not long."

"Did he know this when he left?"

"No," she murmured. "Even I did not know this."

"Well and this explains your sorrow, my daughter," he said soothingly. "Any woman would be saddened to know her husband was at war when she was carrying his child. But in many ways, this is for the best. You will be with your own people, your mother and your grandmother, when your time comes."

"Perhaps he will be home by then."

"Do not depend on it," her father said. "It will take him many days only to reach the sea. From there, it is uncertain what will happen. And so you must set your heart to making him a fine, healthy child for his return. Your heart must be strong and happy. Can you do this?"

She turned and went into her father's arms. "I am afraid," she whispered.

"It is not a shameful thing to be afraid," her father said. "It is only a shameful thing to let your fear keep you from doing what you must. You will not shame yourself in that way, daughter, I am sure of it."

"If he had known of the child, he would not have gone to war," she said.

"Likely, he would have gone, regardless."

"How far is the place where he is?"

"Seven days' journey. Perhaps more. But he may not be there for long. The elders say the war is to the north. If he is to fight, they will send him where the battle is, no doubt."

"Who is his enemy?"

"His own people," Standing Horse said thoughtfully. "Is that not an amazing thing? He fights his own countrymen."

"That is not so amazing," Not Black said staunchly. "We have been fighting the Creeks for years. And the elders say that once, we were one people."

He nodded. "That is true, I suppose. But that was a long time ago."

"I think, sometimes our people forget. We believe that our understanding of the whites is a true understanding. We believe that we are better than they are, that we do not make war upon our own people, that we do not betray our own. But there has been a great forgetting, I think. Some have forgotten the truth on purpose, so they can say that the white man is far worse than we are. In fact, there are fewer differences between us than we like to suppose."

He looked at her with a bemused smile. "Now you sound like your mother's mother," he said. "She is a wise woman, and she spoke her mind like a man, after Osceola died. She did not care for pleasing others with words which they wished to hear." He chuckled. "She still does not. The people came to know her as a woman of wisdom and to depend upon her opinion. Perhaps you will come to be as she was, when you are her age."

"I feel I am already her age." Not Black groaned. "I feel so empty, my father."

"Well and you are hardly that," he chuckled. "Pull up your pole."

She glanced at him questioningly.

"We shall go and tell your mother your news. There is nothing like a child brewing to bring women joy."

"I am not ready to tell my mother yet," she said stubbornly.

"Why not?"

"Because it was my mother who told me that she would never accept the father of this child. And her own mother said she would never see the child of such a mating. I am not ready to watch their faces struggle between shame and pleasure. I fear, if I see such a struggle, I will hie myself to my husband's house and wait out this child all alone, rather than see my mother's frown and endure my grandmother's mouth."

He nodded. "I understand, daughter. When will you tell them?"

"When I am ready. Can you keep this secret, my father?"

"Of course," he said. "It is yours to tell. When you are ready." He patted her softly. "I will leave you to your thoughts. But only remember this, Not Black. Whatever strength you would have your child share must come from you. If he is born in sorrow, he will live in sorrow."

Small Bear became her close companion again, almost as though they had never drifted apart. She was in love with Teal, to Not Black's surprise, but he did not seem to glance in her direction. And so the two of them shared a similar bereavement. Often, they sat and talked of the emptiness of their hearts. Sometimes Not Black felt they almost enjoyed their shared misery, and then she became angry at herself and goaded Small Bear into playing the ball game or seeing who could collect the most turtle eggs.

In fact, she knew herself to be more fortunate than Small Bear. At least, she had her love, even if he were absent. At least, she had his child growing within her. No matter how fearful or lonely she became, she knew that he loved her and would return. So long as he was alive, he was hers. She knew that, could understand that, like a beating heart. This was her faith. And so often, when Small Bear would be discouraged and full of sorrow, Not Black would hold her hand over her pain and lean forward to embrace her friend, full of yearning and forgiveness. Her hope kept her heart alive.

Finally, she knew she must tell her mother that a child was coming. She was a little surprised her grandmother had not already somehow intuited that fact from the air around her and arrived at the village, but the last words she said on the subject still rang in Not Black's ears. Perhaps they stopped up her grandmother's as well.

She waited until her father was relaxed, with his stomach full, and the three of them were by the fire for the evening. The sky was as dark as the inside of an alligator hole, and the clouds kept the stars from shining through. She had heard that there was to be another meeting of the elders in a nearby village within seven days. No doubt her father would attend. He had become a more important voice in the village lately. She knew that the husband she had chosen did little to raise his respect in the eyes of others, but it was time, she told herself, that the elders—indeed, all of her people—came to realize that the past was past. The whites had much to show them about the future. She curved her arms round her belly and sighed deeply before she spoke.

Her mother glanced up at her sigh. "You ate more corn than your father, even," she smiled. "It is good to see you enjoy your food again."

Her father glanced at her curiously. She knew that he wondered when she would choose her time. She smiled at him. "Well, someone is enjoying it, even if I am not."

Her mother raised her eyebrows in confusion. "What do you mean?"

"I am with child," she said softly.

Her father chuckled. "This is joyful news, eh?" He glanced to Comes Alone and nodded as though to encourage her to join him in his pleasure.

Her mother frowned. "You are with child. You are certain of this, my daughter? Perhaps it is the sorrow. Perhaps the upset of the marriage—"

Not Black said coolly, "I am with child. You cannot wish this away, my mother."

Standing Horse looked worriedly from mother to daughter. "This is not something to wish away! A child is never something to wish away, no matter who the father may be. Our daughter is bearing our grandchild, wife. Can you not be happy for that?"

Comes Alone stared at her daughter fixedly. Finally she said, "I need time to think of this."

"Did you think I would be married in name alone, Mother? He is a white man, but he is still a man, after all."

"I cannot help it," Comes Alone said softly, miserably. "I cannot help my hate, any more than you can help your love."

Not Black pulled in her breath in a gasp of understanding. In that moment, she loved her mother again as she had when she was a girl. When her mother was all things powerful, soft, and protecting and perfect. All things at once. She looked up into the night and wished she could see the stars. She had always loved the stars more than the moon. They were so constant. So unaware of their beauty.

"Well and Grandmother will come," she said then. "And when she does, there will be both of you to tell me how terrible this child must be for everyone. At least you will not be alone in your hate."

Standing Horse rose then from his seat by the fire, looking at first one of his women and then the other, with some disbelief. "I will have no more talk of this. Not in my hearing. She is with child. It is a time of joy." He said it stubbornly, with rare anger. "Tell me you understand, wife."

Comes Alone stared at him for a long moment, with that certain defiant set of jaw which Not Black recognized well enough: it usually meant she was ready to fight hard for her position. But then she dropped her head under her husband's gaze. "I will try," she said wearily. "I will try to understand how the granddaughter of Osceola could have married a white man. Could be bearing a child of that blood—"

"Osceola is dead," Standing Horse said evenly. "Our daughter stands before you now, alive and quickening."

Comes Alone put out her hand toward Not Black, in a gesture of reconciliation. Not Black went to her mother then and took her hand, holding it close to her heart. "I am so lonely," she murmured as her mother took her into her arms.

"Well and you are not alone," Comes Alone said, kissing her cheeks softly, one after the other. "Your grandmother is likely on her way even as we speak."

"What will she say?" Not Black asked.

Comes Alone shrugged. "Whatever she says, we will answer her together."

Not Black began to weep then softly, in relief and weariness. "I am afraid," she murmured.

"Of your grandmother?" Comes Alone asked.

"Of the child."

Comes Alone held her and rocked her then, from side to side, much as she had when she was a young girl. "I will not tell you there is nothing to fear," she said quietly. "But I will tell you there is no reason to face it alone."

Florida seceded from the Union of the United States in January 1861, but that act of defiance meant little to the tribes hidden in the thickets and everglades of the state. What did trickle down to them, however, was the news that three months later, Union forces seized the towns of Fernandina, Jacksonville, and Saint Augustine, occupying the entire west bank of the Saint Johns River with very little fighting. Only small ranks of Florida state militia were there to defend the towns, and they quickly retreated to the western region near the Suwannee. The elders said that the warriors who fought were green and frightened, and that the men who led them had no courage. Therefore, they lost their lands and their women. The North men, what the tribes called the invaders, had taken the cotton, timber, and turpentine from the stores in the occupied towns, and whatever slaves they were able to find, they recruited into the Negro regiments.

When Standing Horse told the news at the fire, Comes Alone said, "Will they be satisfied with the towns at the sea? Or will they chase the warriors all the way to the Suwannee?"

Not Black put her hand to her mouth in horror. "Was Tom Craven with them, do you think, Father?"

"It is hard to say," Standing Horse said slowly. "He may have been. If he got there in time to be added to their numbers. Or perhaps, he did not arrive in time, and they left for the west without finding a place for him."

"I am certain that if he was there, he fought bravely," she said.

Her father and mother said nothing.

"Either way, he may be home soon," Not Black added. "The North men have been victorious, and it will be over."

Morning Dew snorted from the corner of the *cheke*. She had gone to bed early, but of course, she listened to every word exchanged until her eyes closed. From her hammock, she called, "The war will not be over anytime soon, child, so do not get hopeful over every stray gossip from the elders. Once the whites begin to fight each other, they will be at it like breeding alligators until one side is destroyed. They are killers at heart. They enjoy it."

"I hear an unpleasant rustling from the *cheke*, Father," Not Black said coolly. "A rat in the corn, perhaps." When her grandmother fell silent, she added, "No, it was only the wind." She kept her face stolid, her voice calm. She had decided not to allow her grandmother to make her more unhappy than she already was. Since she had arrived, with tales of dire predictions and insults about all things white, Not Black had been steadfast in her determination to ignore her. It did not silence her grandmother; only the Maker of Breath could do that. But Not Black's stubborn refusal to acknowledge her hate gave her sufficient power in the confrontations between the women to make her think she might actually survive them.

Comes Alone frowned at Not Black and shook her head silently. She did not approve of her mother being so ignored, but she could not insist that her daughter take part in an argument she could not countenance. And so, since the arrival of Morning Dew, there had been uneasy silences, bursts of anger, and glances of tense disapproval across the fire of Comes Alone.

Not Black learned to avoid her mother's glance, her grandmother's voice, until she became almost a nonperson in her own mind, nothing but a vessel for this burgeoning life within her. Slowly and relentlessly, the growing infant stole from her the anger, the will to defy her parents and their expectations, and left behind a soft acquiescence to all they wished to do for her.

In a few months, her belly began to swell noticeably, and then another change came to her life. Where before, she had walked among her people, in and out of the trails and through the village with respect and smiling glances, now as she walked, she felt as though she had disappeared. Few glanced her way, and when they did, they looked away again without a smile. She knew that it was because of the child she carried in her belly, and she was sometimes enraged, sometimes sorrowed by the changes in the faces around her. After a time, she began to feel that she could come and go like smoke, like a creeping panther in the night, and even her feet would leave no marks on the ground. She had disappeared to most who had known her. Only Small Bear remained her friend.

*   *   *

In May of a year in which the rains had been heavier than normal, a pair of beavers came into the river valley close to the village of Seminoles. One was a male, large and dark brown, with a black scaly tail. He weighed more than eighty pounds. One was a smaller female, not quite sixty pounds. Both of them were young and healthy specimens of *Castor canadensis,* and though they did not know this, they were relatively rare in this part of the Florida swampland.

The male beaver had found his mate farther north, where beavers were more plentiful. Like the rest of his kind, he mated for life. Because the territory and the waters of the northern lands were crowded with other beavers, nutria, and muskrat, he set out with his mate on a dangerous journey to the south, into the swamps where his kind rarely traveled. Together, they had avoided bobcat, panther, and their most dangerous enemy, the river otter. Now, they came to the river and saw at once that it could become their home.

The male took most of the day investigating a narrow place in the river where the water ran swift. It would be a good place for a dam, but the dam would have to be bowed upstream to slow the current. His mate followed him, carefully exploring both sides of the river and the life within it, squeaking to herself and to him for reassurance. She was heavy with her unborn kits, and their family would perish.

And so the male was determined to make this river their home. Dam repair on this river would be constant, and a spillway would need to be added to the edge, but it could be done in less than a season. They would travel no more. He inspected the trees up both banks for a mile in each direction. Some were gnawed by deer or muskrat, but none had been chewed by beavers.

He and his mate were alone in these waters, and he was much

relieved. In his more northern territory competition for food in winter became vigorous, and sometimes kits were not born to those lodges which had not been able to secure enough stored branches underwater before the heavier snows came.

Here, he sensed, there would be no snows. Neither would there be much competition. The male beaver dived into the deepest part of the river, where his mate was taking small branches of willow and stockpiling them for later meals. He watched her swim for a moment, satisfied with his choice of mate. Like him, she was perfectly adapted to the water, with webbed hind feet, a tail which was a fine rudder, valves over her ears and nostrils which closed off the water, and a clear membrane over her eyes to protect them from floating debris. She swam with her forepaws tucked in close to her body, unless she was carrying a branch as she was now. She could swim nearly five miles per hour. He was faster, but less agile.

It was growing darker, and with each passing hour of diminished sunlight, the beavers became more active. The lodge must be built, the dam started, and no time could be wasted in either endeavor.

The female had finished stowing willow branches in deep water, complete with bark and leaves in place. This would be their cache near the lodge for when they were unable or unwilling to venture forth on land. Nimble and confident in the water, both of them were far less comfortable on land. They were ungainly and slow, with few defenses other than a loud slap of the tail on water for warning. Even their teeth were made for gnawing, not biting. Now she was sitting on her back legs on a log in the shallows, holding a willow branch like an ear of corn and gnawing the good bark from it hungrily. She kept one eye on him; one eye on the shore. If a threat came, she would be underwater again in a flash and could stay down more than fifteen minutes if necessary.

Together that night, they dragged large trees and branches from both shores and piled them carefully on the site of their lodge. Shelter had to be paramount. They knew they would have to move the lodge or rebuild it substantially as the waters rose, but for now, it must go up.

They found that their favorite building trees—poplar, aspen, and birch—were in short supply in this more southern range. But willow and oak were available, and they were determined to find others which might be suitable as well.

The male felled trees all night, gnawing around them until they toppled. He selected small trees, no more than six inches in diameter, though he could take down a tree as much as thirty inches around if he needed. It took him only five minutes to take down a six-inch willow tree, and the crash of the falling timber went on into the night.

As he felled the trees, his mate trimmed off the branches and carried them in convenient sizes to the lodge site. There, she poked the ends into the muddy bottom of the pond site, then braced others in place. By dawn of the next morning, they had a rudimentary lodge finished, with two underwater entrances and living quarters in a hollow near the top. The female left plenty of fresh wood chips on the floor to absorb moisture and a vent at the top to let in the fresh air. The lodge was only four feet high and ten feet wide. In time, she knew she would almost double its height and triple its width, but it would do for the moment. It would protect them from many threats. Most, in fact, except the otter.

When the sun came up, the two beavers met in the lodge and combed their fur carefully with the split nails on their hind feet, waterproofing themselves again by applying castoreum, the oily secretion they carried in scent glands near their anuses. They had no thick layers of fat built up yet, and they sensed that they would not need them so much in this climate. And so they finally slept in more peace, twined together in a warm bundle, their noses out for scents of trouble.

They worked hard for more than two months, building their dam from woven sticks, reeds, branches, saplings, all of it caulked with mud. Often, they had to rebuild, for the river was reluctant to be slowed. As they built, the river slid higher and wider, and what had been shoreline was now under shallow water. In time, the nearby grasslands would be inundated and farther trees would be submerged, but they did not notice these details, nor would they have cared. All that mattered was that the river rose high enough to provide deep water.

This was their custom, for in northern climates, it was essential that the river be deep enough to prevent freezing all the way to the bottom. They could not know that this would never happen in Florida, and so their efforts were unnecessary. In fact, had they known this, it was unlikely they could have stopped from building. They could not stop because they were beavers, and a day without building was like a day without food. Without reason, therefore, but certainly not without plan, they gradually began to alter the river and the land around it more than any dozen human settlements had since the beginning of man in the region.

In late June, the beaver kits were born. Five small and well-furred babies to her third litter, born with their eyes open and able to swim within a half hour of birth. The female nursed them prodigiously through their first month of life, pushing them into the water every chance she could. If they tired, she carried them on her back or her tail, even sometimes picking one up in her forepaws and walking erect. They would be with her two winters, she knew. After that, she would chase them off. She had done so with two previous litters, and this one would be no different. This piece of the river could not support more than a few beavers at one time.

She sensed she was safe with her family. As she nursed the kits, she closed her eyes and crooned with satisfaction. The lodge was built, the dam was growing in height, and her cache of willow branches was large enough to let her tend her litter with ease. There was nothing else she needed but a good day's sleep.

One night, however, she discovered that the lodge was not nearly so secure as she had thought. Her mate was out cutting more trees for the dam, and she was tending the kits in the shallows, teaching them to dive and surface with a minimum of splash, something which one day might be vital for their escape from a predator. She heard him squeal in anger and fear and then heard an answering grunt from a far larger animal. She reared up on her hind legs as tall as she could get to see where he was and saw a sight which froze her in terror.

Her mate was hurrying to the water and behind him, swatting at him hungrily, was a large black bear. The beast swiped a huge paw across his back; her mate rolled slightly, and recovered in time to escape the bear's jaws, recovered his feet, and was waddling as fast as he could, dodging the next blow or bite.

She slapped her tail on the water loudly and dived underwater, hurrying her kits ahead of her. She heard above her the splash of her mate diving into the water, and she could tell by his movements that he was injured. But at least he was alive. She huddled in the dry chamber of the lodge, listening to the bear on the bank growl and snort his anger at losing the prey. She shrieked to her mate as he appeared, his head popping up into the lodge, bloodied and shaken but otherwise moving well.

Now above them, the bear began to climb on top of the lodge, pushing aside the logs and the branches, snarling at what he knew lay hidden within. He could smell the prey, of course, and the squeals and yips of the five kits drove him mad with urgency. She shoved her kits down into the hole in the lodge floor, forcing them to dive again once more into the water, as the top came off the lodge, ripped open by the paws of the bar. Her mate followed her, and then pushed ahead of his family, leading them to safety on a far bank.

By the time the bear reached the inner chamber of the lodge, all of the beavers were hidden in the brush on the other side of the river, watching him silently from safety.

In a fury, the bear tore apart the lodge, scattering all of the branches and logs and brush and mud in all directions, knocking down the walls, and venting his anger on everything he could reach. All of their hard work was destroyed in moments, but at least the kits were safe. He stood and snuffed the wind, moaning to himself and rocking back and forth on his huge haunches.

For a moment, the female feared he might plunge across the river after them, for he could surely smell them on the night wind. He took a step into the water, and she instantly threw herself on her kits, smothering them into the brush and quieting their cries with the sheer weight of her body.

The bear whined and snarled, a singsong complaint of frustration and hunger. But, finally, he backed out of the river, discouraged by the new deepness of the waters. He looked toward the dam curiously, and now the male chittered softly in apprehension. In moments, the bear could destroy the dam as easily as he had ruined the lodge.

As the huge bear approached the dam, however, he heard something behind him in the brush. Perhaps a deer or a rabbit. He turned, instantly diverted, and stalked away from the river. In a few moments, they could no longer see him.

The beavers stayed huddled in the darkness, comforting each other silently as best they could. In the dawn, the work would begin again.

* * *

The months droned by, and Not Black finally stopped looking up at every footstep, half-expecting to see Tom Craven at her mother's fire. The larger she grew with child, the more invisible she seemed to become. The only thing which was large about her was her belly; all the rest of her shrank like a pond in the summer.

Her mother and grandmother seemed to take more and more pleasure in her company, the larger the child became and the smaller she shrank. They scarcely mentioned Tom Craven at all anymore, nor did they speak of the war or the future. Curiously, neither did they speak much of the child. Not Black actually understood this, in some strange way. It was as though by not speaking of him, by not mentioning anything except those day-to-day things which had always been and would always be of interest—the crops, the elders, other families and their problems—they could ignore what was growing under her tunic.

As she became so large that it seemed she might never see her own feet again, they finally began to joke about the coming child as one might joke about the upcoming visit of a well-loved but annoying relation. Clearly, they did not expect the child to be a permanent part of their lives.

But to Not Black, her condition, if not the child, seemed to be the most permanent thing in her entire existence. Indeed, it was her only reason for existence.

Finally, finally, one night after they had all gone to their hammocks, she felt the gush of water over her legs, and she knew that the child was coming at last. She called quietly to her mother, who then called to her grandmother. Together, the two of them helped get Not Black up out of her hammock and supported her on the long walk to the women's hut. There, she would be attended by her mother and her grandmother, she knew, as well as several of the more knowledgeable women in the village on the subject of birthing a child. In this way, when the child came forth, it was almost as though it belonged to the village already. And if, by chance, the birth did not go well, no single woman would have to take that regret into her heart alone.

Her harder cramps began as soon as she reached the hut, and she was grateful that she had awakened her mother and grandmother when she did. In short time, pain squeezed her eyes closed and made her pant like a dog in the hottest months. Her mother had her sitting upright and she massaged her belly with a warm liquid made of herbs and palmetto berries. Her grandmother gave her a cool drink which was bitter and biting to her throat.

"What is that?" she gasped.

"Willow bark for the pain," Morning Dew said.

"How soon will it take to work?" she asked, moaning with the agony which wrenched her mind from everything except her belly.

"Soon, child," Morning Dew said, laying a cool cloth on her brow. "But you must get up and walk."

"I can barely sit," Not Black said, pushing her hand away.

"Walking will bring the child faster," Comes Alone said, pulling her to her feet. "Your grandmother is right."

As Not Black stood and began to walk, she could feel the child dropping lower in her belly. The pain was intense, but somehow more bearable so long as she was moving. Two other women came then, women who were wise in the way of birth, and they brought with them more herbs, warm gruel, and bags of magic talismans. The fire was soon smoking with their herbs, and the scent of orange filled the hut. It was soothing to Not Black, and she felt the pain begin to be something she could hold on to, could get her heart around and keep in a space which she could manage. For hours they walked, it seemed to her, leaning first on her mother and then on her grandmother. She was surprised that Morning Dew was as strong as she was, and when she said so, the old woman laughed. "Birthing a child is not the hard part, granddaughter. It is the raising of it. Pray to the Maker of Breath that you do not have a girl. They are the ones who will break your heart fastest."

Then the time came that she could walk no more, no matter how much she was prodded and teased by the women. Her mother got on one side of her, her grandmother on the other, and they supported her arms as she squatted over a shallow depression in the earth. The women had prepared it by lining it with soft moss and scented blossoms, and as the child pushed out of her, she gritted her teeth and kept her spirit still, as they had told her to do. The only noise in the hut was the sudden squall of the infant as it slid forth, bloodied and protesting, onto the cradling earth.

Panting, Not Black leaned back against her mother, sitting between her legs as though she herself had been born as well. Her stomach was still rhythmically moving, as if it had yet another burden to release. After the child came the afterbirth, and the birthing woman who was not tending to the infant came and examined it carefully. She said nothing, but when she glanced at Morning Dew, she did not meet her eyes.

"What does she see there?" Not Black asked anxiously.

"If it is not sure, she says nothing," Comes Alone said soothingly. "Few have certain evidence of a special fate so young. It means little."

Then they put the baby in her arms. "You were wrong," she said to her grandmother, laughing weakly. "It is a boy."

"I was right about everything else though," Morning Dew said sadly. "He is white, like his father." The old woman rose wearily and shook her head. "I had hoped that perhaps, the Maker of Breath might see fit to make the child look more like his mother. But fate is fate. He is all of his father's seed."

"And he is all of his great-grandfather's spirit," Not Black said tiredly, stroking the small light-colored cheek in resignation.

"No, he is not," Morning Dew said firmly. She bent and kissed the top of Not Black's head. "And yet, because he is of you, my granddaughter, I cannot wish him anything but contentment in his life." She laid a hand on her daughter's shoulder and made as if to leave the hut.

"Where are you going?" Not Black called after her.

"Home. I have seen what I came to see."

Comes Alone began to weep softly, but she did not try to stop her mother.

Not Black could say nothing. She was too exhausted, too overwhelmed by the birth, the child in her arms, to think that perhaps she would never see her grandmother again. She watched as the old woman left the hut, feeling that as one soul came into her life, another was departing. The baby began to cry then, a wrenching, demanding scream for attention, and as the women clustered around her, she put her son to her breast in a daze of mingled joy and despair. I cannot think on this now, she told herself. Later, when I am stronger, I will do what I must to heal these wounds. But now, I can do nothing but tend to this wailing, demanding heart which pounds so fiercely in my hands.

She named the baby boy Small Warrior, for his earliest battle cry. He was pale and round-faced like the moon, and it was not hard to notice that few came to Comes Alone's fire to welcome the infant to the village, as would have been the custom with any other child. Small Bear came, of course, and Comes Alone's favorite woman-friends, but none of the men and few others came with ritual gifts and blessings for the baby.

And Morning Dew, true to her words, left the village and did not return to see to the growing of her grandchild. She sent word that she would welcome a visit from her daughter, but she did not include her granddaughter and new great-grandson in that invitation. Not Black said angrily to her father that she did not care if she ever saw the old woman again, but in her heart, she was sorrowful. To think that her child would never know the joy and annoyance of Morning Dew seemed somehow impossible. She did not believe that her grandmother would keep her word. She thought, when my child is older, I will take him to the old woman's fire. And then she will not be able to turn us away. That thought comforted her when she fell into despair.

And despair was ever at the edge of her mind, despite the wonder of holding her son, of feeling the small hands clutch at her, of watching the small pale eyes follow her wherever she went. Standing Horse had made a ceremony to welcome the child into the family, but of course, no answering ceremony was made by the village. The usual ritual of bringing the boy to the monthly center fire, where the elders gave the news and marriages and deaths were announced, was not to be for Small Warrior.

But Not Black told herself that it was for the best. In a short time, she was sure, Tom Craven would return to claim them both, and then they would no longer be living among these people. There was little use in being made a part of something she would soon leave. And so, she told herself she was content simply to wait for him and keep his son safe.

When Small Warrior was nearly a year old and beginning to speak, her contentment at the fire of her mother dimmed. She was safe, and so was her son, but she was lonely. Worse, she could only see a similar future for him. When he began to toddle after the other children, crying to play their games, they ran from him with shrieking laughter and none of the small girls came to dandle him or braid his hair, as they did with the other babies.

She went to her father and said, "I am going to take my son away from here. I do not want him to grow to believe what others believe about him."

Her father's face had become more etched with sorrow in the past year. Many of his goals and dreams had not come to fruition, and these regrets showed in the lines on his brow and beside his nose. He shook his head slowly in disbelief. "You are not speaking with wisdom, my daughter. Where would you go?"

"I will go to my husband's house," she said. "We can stay there, Small Warrior and I, until he returns."

"Your place is here," he said. "With your mother and myself."

"My place is no place now," she said. "Since I have made my choice. I do not want my son to feel as lonely as I have, since my return."

"But how will you care for him all alone on the white man's land?"

"It is far easier there than here," she said. "And you can come and see for yourself anytime you wish. You and Mother will always be welcome. But I will not stay in the village, no, and neither will my son."

To her great surprise and alarm, her father's eyes watered, spilled over, and she saw the first tears from him she had ever witnessed. Her own throat closed instantly, as though his tears were in her own eyes. "Don't," she said, touching him urgently, unable to speak anymore.

He shook his head. "I never thought such a thing would come to our family."

She felt his pain keenly, but she could say little to assuage it. It was true, everything which had come to them was strange and not in keeping with the ways of the people. Usually when a woman married, her husband came to her mother's fire for a time. Often the first children were born in their grandmother's *cheke* and the married couple only built their own house when the family grew too large to share the same fire. And then, they rarely moved farther away than could be toddled by the youngest child. But she must take her son away, to her husband's fire, and when she did so, she knew that it was likely he would see little of his grandparents.

"I cannot stay here," she murmured sadly. "I have no home 'here anymore."

"You do have a home," her father said bitterly. "But it no longer suits you, now that you have seen the ways of the whites."

"My husband will be home soon. He cannot come to my mother's fire; you know that, Father. No one will welcome him in the village. No one welcomes *me*, and I have been among them since my birth. They see Small Warrior, and they look right through him, as though he were not there. I cannot let them break his heart as they have broken mine." She embraced him fiercely. "Please, Father. Please understand. You must let us go."

"This will split your mother's spirit," he whispered.

"No," she smiled grimly. "I have already told her."

"What did she say?"

"That I must do what I think best for myself. As I always have."

He shook his head in despair. "She does not mean that. She will never be whole, once you have gone."

"You are the one I will miss," Not Black said. "Will you come and see your grandson?"

"Not to the white man's cabin," he said. "I must still sleep in your mother's hammock, after all. But I will meet you halfway at the river. And I will bring your mother, as well."

She shrugged. "If she will come."

"She will come," he said firmly, gathering Not Black once more into his arms. "How will you care for yourself and the boy?"

"We do not need much," she said. "We will be well."

"And how will you get through the long nights alone?"

"There will not be many of them," she said. "Tom Craven will come home soon."

And so the day came when she set out with Small Warrior on her back, carrying her bundle of belongings and some seed and a pot which her mother had given her, for the lands of Tom Craven's father. Her mother embraced her long and hard on that morning, but she did not weep. "I will ask the Maker of Breath to make your path easy, my daughter," she said sadly. "Remember that it is you who have made this choice."

"I know," Not Black said, unable to meet her eyes at the last.

Her father walked with her as far as the river. He said then, "I will come back again in seven days. I will wait for you here. Bring my grandson, and I will teach him to swim the deepest pools."

"I will," Not Black said, turning her back then and shouldering the bundle her father had carried. She walked away with a single, brave gesture of farewell, and she told herself not to look back. To look back would be to doom herself to walking the rest of the way in sadness.

She walked half of the day, discovering that what had been an easy journey on young, unencumbered legs was now many hours of hard travel, carrying her burdens. She had to stop to rest often and let Small Warrior out of his bundle, and she knew now that her promise to meet her father often at the river would be difficult to keep.

Finally, she reached the lands of Tom Craven's father. As she came up the road that she had gone down nearly two years before, it seemed that it had been ten years since she had last walked that path. The trees looked larger, the land wider, and the cabin in the distant falling light looked smaller and less handsome than she had remembered.

By the time she reached the porch, she was exhausted. Small Warrior had more restless energy than usual, for he was quite tired of being bound and carried. The moment she set him on his feet, he crowed loudly and toddled off to inspect every nook and cranny of the porch, never realizing that the door led to an even more remarkable discovery, the cabin itself. She slid the pack off her shoulders and sat down wearily in the rocking chair, sighing with relief as it seemed to fit itself to the curve of her back and comfort her instantly.

She had been right to come, she knew that now. Without even going inside, she knew she had done the good thing for herself and her son. Now when Tom Craven came home, she would be waiting for him. Waiting with his son, in his father's cabin, surrounded by the things he would have missed and would find most comfort in seeing. Herself and the result of their love: his own Small Warrior.

From around the cabin, she heard the sound of a rooster crow. She went to see, taking Small Warrior up on her hip. To her delight, the hens were still there, most of them, and two of the roosters. They had not strayed far from their pen, even though Tom and his father had set them free when they departed. Creatures of habit, they had managed to eke out an existence in the yard, in the fields beyond. The pump stood silent and untouched. She went to it, shifted Small Warrior to her other hip, and touched it gingerly. The chickens must have taken their water from the pond, for it had not been moved since Tom Craven left it.

She set down Small Warrior and moved the handle up and down as she had seen her husband do. Nothing happened. She went to the well, an oaken-covered hole in the ground to the side of the cabin, shaded by a single live oak. She dragged off the cover and looked within. The well was deep and dark and cool. She could not see water. She picked up a pebble and dropped it within. After four beats of her heart, she heard a distant splash. Water was there.

She went back to the pump and moved it up and down vigorously, to the intense amusement of Small Warrior, who had already tired of the chickens, for they would not let him get close enough to grab them. Finally, the water came from the ground, she heard it gurgle and moan up the pipe, and then it gushed over her hand, cool and refreshing. She grabbed up Small Warrior and put his hands under the pump. "Water," she said in English. "This is your father's water."

He looked up at her and laughed, squirming to get down and play in the mud. She let him down slowly, thinking that she had so much to teach him before Tom Craven came home. It was only fitting that his son greet him in his own tongue. She went back to the well and pulled the cover over it, glancing around. Then she saw a large rock a few feet away. She went over and picked up the rock and hauled it over to the cover, dropping it on it and moving it to center. Small Warrior was a curious boy. She must be certain that she kept him safe. It was her duty until his father came home.

"Small Warrior!" she called.

He came running obediently around the house, scattering chickens before him.

She waited until he came right to her feet and then she bent down and faced him, her nose very close to his own. "Listen to me, my son.

This is our home now. We must help each other take care of ourselves. Do you understand?"

He nodded, smiling and wide-eyed.

"This is a deep hole, under this rock, do you see it?"

He looked at the rock on the oaken cover and nodded again.

She took his hands and slapped them together hard, so that he would remember. "You are never, never to touch this rock. Do you understand?"

He nodded, frightened now. She had never struck him before. "When will Oma come?" he asked. "Oma" was his word for his grandmother.

"Soon," Not Black said absently, standing now and looking around. There was much to be done. She must get started.

The first seven days were full of discovery and excitement. They had fresh water, they had chickens and eggs, they had bananas, oranges, and papayas from the orchard, and Not Black found some melons and squash in the fields, volunteers from the last crops which had reseeded and come up to straggle untended through the dry cornstalks. Of course, she knew that such bounty would not be there in the colder months, but for now, they were well fed. She expected that Tom Craven would be home before they needed to make other plans.

When seven days had passed, she took Small Warrior on her back once more and set out for the river to meet her father. She started out at first light, since she knew it would take half of the day. Even starting at dawn, she knew she would be coming back late, and she was already dreading the path back to the cabin in the darkness. "Next time," she told Small Warrior as she trod the path, "your grandfather will have to come to your father's cabin. He can spend one night on a white man's porch; it will not kill him to do so."

Small Warrior thumped on her back rhythmically as she walked, chanting his half-English, half-Seminole words. She knew it was going to be longer for him to talk, since he was trying to learn two languages at once. But it was important for him to be a bridge between his people, she told herself. Even if it took him longer, it was worth it.

By the time she reached the river, she was too weary to do anything but sit with her feet in the cool water, watching as Small Warrior climbed over the rocks and played with whatever he could catch. Standing Horse came upon her and pulled her upright to embrace her. "You are no thinner." He grinned at her. "That is a relief, at least. You are eating?"

"Better than you would guess," she said proudly. "I have chickens and eggs, Father. Anytime I wish them. And there are oranges and bananas and even some squash left on the vines."

"That is good," he nodded. "But what about the cold months?"

She shrugged. "Tom Craven will surely be home by then. And if he is not, I will hunt for our meat and take what we need from the river. I will put seed in the fields soon—"

"So you are content, then," her father said.

She smiled at him. "I will not be content until my husband returns. But our bellies are fed, at least."

He called to Small Warrior then, lifting him up in his arms and holding him high over his head. "This little man grows like the corn!"

The boy squealed in pleasure, gripping his grandfather's topknot and settling himself on his shoulders. "Go, Opa!" he cried out, drumming his heels in his grandfather's back. And the two of them set off at a canter alongside the riverbank.

Not Black watched them play for a while, resting in the shade. If she did not let her thoughts wander, she could almost believe that all was well in her life, that her mother waited supper for them at home, that Small Warrior had a dozen happy friends to run with before dark, and that she was happy. But all she had to do was look closely at her son, notice the difference between the skin of his grandfather and his own, and she could not forget why they were here.

She sighed as they came looping back to her, finally having wearied each other enough to sit in the shade and rest. Standing Horse set Small Warrior the task of collecting ten of the best river stones he could find for trading, and then he said, "The elders say that the Northerners are getting ready to move into the lands farther to the west."

"Has there been fighting?" she asked, immediately anxious.

"Not yet," he said. "But they say it will begin soon. It will be the first time they have brought the war to these lands."

She fell silent, gazing at the moving water.

"Perhaps he is elsewhere," her father said gently. "He is likely with his father someplace to the north."

"That is small comfort," she said. "Since they are fighting there as well."

He said nothing. She knew that there was nothing to be said. "And my mother is well?" she asked, forcing a brightness into her voice which she did not feel.

"She looks up at every approaching step, hoping it is yours," he said. "But yes, she is well."

"She could have come with you." Not Black picked up a stick and made errant designs in the damp sand.

He nodded. "Perhaps she will the next time. Small Bear sends her friendship and says for me to tell you that Teal brought her mother an alligator two days ago."

"An alligator!" Not Black said with amazement. "He must be in love."

"So it appears." Standing Horse grinned. "It was a small alligator, though."

"For Teal, any alligator is a monster. He is no bigger than I am."

"Small Bear finds him big enough, I wager."

She cuffed her father playfully. "Next time bring my mother with you. She will not let you speak such coarseness before your grandson."

Her father chuckled. "Ah, it is coarseness now. And when you were courting, it was the passion of the gods."

"And so it was," she smiled. "I yearn to have it back again."

He leaned back against the tree and plucked a long grass stem, biting off the sweet white root. "Well and did I ever tell you the story of the war between the animals and the birds?"

She grinned. "No. But I expect you are about to do so." Her father had been in charge of stories when she was young. It had been a good while since he had told her one, and she called to Small Warrior to listen. The boy came trundling over and set himself between his grandfather's knees, wet and muddy and completely happy.

"The birds challenged the animals to a great ball play to decide once and for all which should be masters over the other. It was decided that all creatures who had teeth should be on one side and all those which had feathers should be on the other."

"Why, Opa?" asked Small Warrior. It was his favorite question.

"Listen and you shall hear," replied his grandfather. "So the day of the game was fixed and the ground was prepared and the poles put up and the balls conjured by the medicine men, and both sides gathered. All the animals went on one side and all the birds on the other. At last the bat came. He tried to join the birds first, but they told him, 'No, you have teeth. You must go to the other side.' So he did. And the animals told him, 'No, you have wings. You must go to the other side.' He was very sad. Most particularly when they all said to him, 'You are so little, you will be of no good anyway.'"

"I fight them!" Small Warrior said fiercely.

"That is what the bat said," Standing Horse assured him. "And so, the animals decided to let him play on their side, because at least he did have teeth. Finally they began the game. The horse was the best player—"

"We knew that, of course," Not Black said wryly.

"And it soon appeared that the birds were winning, for they could keep the ball in the air where the animals could not reach it. But the little bat flew into the air and caught the ball with his teeth, and brought it down to where the four-footed animals could play. Finally, the game was won."

"Who winned it?" asked Small Warrior.

"The animals. Because of the little bat," Standing Horse said gently. "And they all agreed that forever after, he should battle always on the side of the animals having teeth."

"That is a good story!" Small Warrior crowed, clambering now out of his grandfather's knees and running off down to see what else he could find in the river.

"You have told my little bat his fate?" She smiled up at her father.

"I have told him a story. His fate is his own."

"Yes." She thought for a moment. "But which is the side with teeth? The white men or the Seminole?"

"I suppose that depends upon who is asked the question," her father said, suddenly grave. "I expect he will discover that in his lifetime. Sooner than perhaps we would have him do so."

She sighed hugely and nestled back against her father's shoulder. "Next time we meet, bring my mother," she said softly. "Will you do that for me?"

"I will try," he said softly. "That is all I can do, my daughter."

A year passed so slowly for Not Black that each day, she was surprised to see that she was still alive, that her son was growing, that the crops came up, the chickens still laid, and the day ended with a sunset. No one ever came to the little cabin. Her mother and father met her at the river every moon, but they never made the trek to where she slept and ate and lived. And so, in a way, she felt that she actually did none of those things, but only waited until it was time to see them again. She wondered if she would ever get used to not having people around who were living as she was, ever become accustomed to the strangeness of not having the noise and bustle of the village. And then she told herself that she would not need to accommodate herself to that strangeness much longer. Tom Craven would surely be home any day.

Each time her parents came, they brought food. As though they thought she lived from visit to visit, they carried bundles of jerked meat, dried fish, ground meal, and seed. Her mother brought her beads she had strung herself, and her father brought a soft pair of moccasins for Small Warrior. They never came empty-handed. With each visit, they asked her if she were hoarding her provisions for the colder months. "Remember," her mother told her as though she had never held a hoe, "the fields will be empty by the month of the deer rut."

"We will be well," she told them evenly. "Look, see how tall Small Warrior is growing."

And in fact, he was thriving. She spent every hour with the boy, talking to him in both the English tongue and the tongue of her people. She showed him the birds and named them; she wandered far with him in the fields and the forest, helping him to discover the complex creatures and plants which lived there. At night, he slept alongside her, and even as she slept, she was aware of every breath he took.

She often gazed at his light skin, his delicate cheeks, his fine, light-colored hair so different from her own, and she thought he was the most beautiful child she had ever seen. She marveled that he had come from her, and her eyes sometimes watered with joy and pride when he ran before her, perfect and innocent, his sturdy legs pumping like a lovely animal of the woods.

She tried to make up to him for the lack of other children to play with, but she knew there were times when he was lonely. She told herself that he was less lonely with her, in his father's cabin, than he would have been in the village where he would have been surrounded by other children and still alone.

She knew he would remember little of these seasons with her. But she believed that if she could just keep him well and safe and strong for a few more years, he could weather any sorrow or fear or loss that the world would hand him.

On one of her visits to the river, Small Bear surprised her by coming along with her father. She ran to Not Black and hugged her hard, nearly lifting her off the ground with her embrace. "Your mother did not feel well enough to come today," she said, "so I came instead."

Not Black laughed and held her face in her two hands, gazing into her eyes. "My heart is so full to see you! But what is wrong with my mother?"

"Oh nothing much. It is her woman's time, and she did not feel strong enough to make the trip. But she sent along her love and this bundle of herbs for Small Warrior, to ward off the fevers this cold season—"

Her father came and embraced her, already carrying Small Warrior on his shoulders. The boy had thrown himself at his grandfather the moment he spied him, as usual, crowing and screeching in excitement. Not Black realized with a pang just how much he must need the smiles and voices of other people, just how much he was missing when he spent so much time with her alone.

"You are well?" Small Bear was asking. "You look no different, my friend. I had expected to find you wan and thin with longing, but you look plump and hale as a pigeon."

"And you!" laughed Not Black. "Your belly looks as though you are already married and with child!"

Small Bear blushed becomingly. "Well, you are half-right, at any rate."

"You are with child!"

She nodded happily. "We hope for a son. When the moon comes round again, we will be married at his mother's fire."

Not Black embraced her friend again, fighting back the lump in her throat. Now Small Bear would know the pain and glory and wonder of birth, as well as the joy and terror of having a child. But she would never know the aching loneliness that ate at Not Black's heart. She would have a husband with her, and she would be with her people until the day they put her into the earth to sleep forever.

"Fierce Bass sends his best wishes," Small Bear was saying, and for a moment, Not Black did not understand her words. And then she remembered that Teal's manhood name was given him for his fishing skills. She could scarcely recognize the boy she had known in that grand and brave set of words: there was nothing of ferocity in the boy she remembered.

However, she said, "And you must send him mine." And she drew her friend down to the shady knoll to begin the gossip which would bind them, one heart to the other, as they had been bound since they were children.

After Small Bear told her everything she could think of, about every family they knew, she asked, "Are you well, then, truly, my friend? Do you find the nights to be too long to bear without your man?"

"I can stand it," Not Black said gently. "I have scarcely known anything else, after all. He left so soon after we were wed."

"And he has not even seen his son," Small Bear said wistfully. "Does he know you bore him?"

She shook her head. "I have dreamed so often of his homecoming. I have planned it in my mind's eye over and over. When he comes, no doubt, it will all be different, but it will be wonderful." She smiled. "Do you love him, then?"

Small Bear's eyes shone with pleasure. "With all that is in me."

"Then you will be happy," Not Black said, hugging her. "And you deserve to be."

They spoke into the afternoon until finally it was time for Standing Horse and Small Bear to depart. The two women hugged each other for a long while silently. Small Bear then knelt and took Small Warrior into her arms. "You must watch over your mother," she said seriously to him. "She is my very best friend in all the world. If anything happens to her, I shall come to you and ask why."

"I am very strong," he said soberly, "and also very brave. Ask my mother."

"He is very strong and brave." Not Black nodded. "He is the best boy in the world."

"Good," Small Bear said, rising again and kissing her friend's cheeks, one after the other. "Then I will rest easier, knowing this warrior is guarding you."

After they took their leave and Not Black began the long journey back to the cabin, she thought over every nuance and gesture of the visit, not wanting to forget a single detail. Small Warrior ran on ahead, but he came back frequently to call to her, to see that she was bringing up the rear safely. It was only when they had been walking for a good while that she realized that Small Bear had not pressed her to come to the village to witness her marriage. In fact, she had not mentioned it at all.

Well and that is to be expected, she told herself, pushing away the hurt. Teal's mother never did approve of me, even before I was married to Tom Craven. When the child is born, then will I visit Small Bear. Then, she will ask for me, and I will go to her in pride. Then, when my own husband will be home once more.

One day, as Not Black was out hoeing a small patch of melons she had put in near the cabin, she heard a halloo from a man's voice. She dropped her hoe in startled excitement. Tom was home! She raced around the cabin to see a stranger standing near the porch, calling up to the house. She shrank back, instantly aware that she was all alone. Where was Small Warrior? She glanced around in fear.

From the other corner of the house, her son came running, waving a large stick and shouting to the man. "Go away! I fight you!"

The man smiled, opened his hands to show himself unarmed, and backed away from the house. "Whoa, boy. I don' mean no harm. Where's your pa?"

Small Warrior stopped shouting when he saw Not Black coming from around the cabin, and he ran to her, clinging to her legs. "My husband is not here now," she said as calmly as she could manage. "He will be back from the hunt soon. Is there something you need?"

The man looked her over carefully but respectfully. "Where's ol' Craven?" he asked. "This here is his place."

"Yes, it is," she said. "I am wife to Tom Craven." She touched her boy's head. "This is his son."

"Well, I s'wannee." The man shook his head. "Nobody said Tom done took hisself a squaw."

She stiffened and faced the man, ready to take umbrage.

"No 'ffense meant, ma'am," he said evenly, backing up another step. "We don' get word much at the post. But hey!" He brightened. "I got a letter here for Tom, hisself. When he comin' back?"

She dropped her head. Now that she knew the man was not a threat, she felt shy before him. "He has gone to war with his father. I do not know when he will return." Her English felt clumsy and heavy on her tongue, and she felt the old sense of invisibility slipping down once more on her shoulders. Small Warrior seemed to sense her discomfort and for every degree she grew smaller, he puffed himself up to be bigger than he was.

"My father is a white man," he said loudly in the best English he could manage.

She stared at him, amazed. She had never taught him that sentence.

"I thought as much," the man said amiably. "I got no axe to grind, ma'am, jus' fetchin' the mail to ol' Tom." He rummaged in his pouch, took out a begrimed letter, and held it out to her.

She hesitated a moment and then stepped forward, taking it. On the front were scrawled letters in dark ink.

"Well, I best be goin', ma'am. If I could trouble you for some cool water, 'fore I leave."

"Run and get the man a dipper, son," she said quietly to Small

Warrior. "Come and take your ease," she added to the man, gesturing to the porch.

"Thankee," he said, stepping up onto the porch and sitting down with a sigh on the rickety wooden steps.

"Where do you go from here?"

"Over to Crosshatch," he said. " 'Bout a day's walk, I wager."

She looked at the letter in her hand while Small Warrior gave the man his water. Finally she asked, "Can you tell what this means?" She held it out to him.

He took it from her again and examined it. "Made out to Tom, that's all I know. Look like a eddicated man writ it."

She took it back from him and opened it carefully, marveling at the strength of the paper and the florid dark lines which swooped and swirled over the sheet like birds' wings over water.

"Do ye wish me to read it, ma'am?" the man asked her gently.

She smiled shyly at him. "Please."

He took it from her and studied it for long moments. Then he looked up at her, and her heart stopped at the look on his face. "It ain' good news, ma'am. Says here ol' Craven is dead. Killed in battle."

She gasped, her hand to her mouth in horror. "It says this with these marks?"

He nodded. "I shore am sorry, ma'am. It's signed by some captain of the army name o' Johnson. Says Tom Craven's father was killed in battle outside Charleston. Says he died bravely."

"My husband!" she cried. "Where is he?"

He shook his head. "Don' mention Tom. I 'spect he weren't there, elsewhys this captain wouldn'a writ it an' send it here."

"But they were together."

"Guess not when ol' Craven died, they weren't."

She thought for a moment, holding the papers to her breast. "When did this captain make these marks, please?"

He took back the papers and examined the date. "Says here, October, ma'am. Three months ago."

She took the letter back as in a daze. Three months. Three moons past. Now the land belonged to Tom Craven. Now the cabin, the stable, the fields, all of it—it was his. She never would have to endure the glares and insults of the father of Tom Craven again. Then her face fell. But her poor husband. He was now bereft of his father, as her son was bereft of a grandfather. She smoothed the papers carefully with her hand while she pulled her son to her. He instinctively buried his head in her neck, to give and take comfort from her touch.

"Sorry, ma'am," the man said again. "You ain' had no word from Tom, then?"

"No. But he will be home soon." She sat up straight. "I know he will."

The man rose then and touched his cap politely. "I thankee for the water. Good luck to you, ma'am."

"Thank you," she said quietly. She watched him go down the steps and across the yard. When he was at the well, she said, "Please, man!"

He turned and looked at her.

"Where did you come from?"

"Saint Augustine, ma'am."

"How long did you walk?"

He laughed. "I ain' never quit. They give me what to take, an' I traipse. But I guess, nigh 'bout ten days or so, on this leg."

"Good-bye," she called, lifting her hand.

"Good-bye!" shouted Small Warrior.

The man lifted his hand in a salute and grinned. Then he was gone.

She sat for a long while on the porch, thinking of what she now knew. Tom Craven was without family, except for them. What must that be like, to know that there was not another living soul on the earth who shared your blood? But of course, he had Small Warrior. Even as he would be bereft at the loss of his father, at least he would have his son for comfort. She said a phrase to herself which she had known from childhood. In Seminole, it translated to "Every fruit ripens at the right time." What this meant in English, she thought, was that somehow, no matter how dire the times seemed, no matter how much pain one had to endure, somehow everything was happening as it was supposed to and everything would be all right.

It was something she wanted to teach Small Warrior. Something she must remember to tell Tom when he came home. Even with grief, everything was happening as planned. She had faith that even with pain came yearning and forgiveness for the hurt that life brought. That hope was what made the soul heal.

Old Craven was dead. But with every death came a life, she realized. And theirs was just beginning.

When they next went to the river to meet her mother and father, Standing Horse brought distressing news. The elders said that fighting was beginning not far to the north, just outside Saint Augustine. It was said that the Northerners meant to take all of the land to the Suwannee and drive their enemies out forever.

"Tom must be there," she said when she heard. "If he was not with his father, he must be there in that fighting."

"You cannot know that." Her father tried to calm her. "He could be anywhere to the north."

"No, he said he was going to join with the Florida troop," she said. "I do not know why his father did not, but I am certain he is not that far to the north. And if the fighting is to begin there, he will be in the battle."

"Perhaps he will be home soon, then," her mother said. "When this fighting is over."

Not Black nodded. She thought for a long while in silence. Then she said, "I must go to him. I must help him in the battle. And then when the battle is over, I will bring him home."

Her mother shook her head in amazement. "What are you saying? It is a journey of many days. You have never been so far in your life. And what of Small Warrior? He would never survive such a hardship."

Her father sat and listened, his head down. "Your mother is right," he said then. "You must have patience. If he is in the battle, perhaps he will be home to you soon."

She watched her son play among the rocks, sturdily jumping from one boulder to the bank and back again. He was almost two and tall for his age, but he was too young to make such a journey.

"I will leave Small Warrior with you, Mother," she said. "If you will care for him in my absence. I am going to find Tom Craven and bring him home."

Her mother grew angry in an instant. "You are being foolish! What has happened to your head, daughter? First you marry this white man, then you leave our fire to stay in his empty house. And the one good thing you have from this miserable bargain—your son—you abandon him to chase after this man who left you to go and fight his own people. Think of what you are saying!"

Not Black turned away, her chin stubborn and her mouth stiff. "You do not understand. You have never understood."

"I understand all I need to," her mother said. "You have become as perverse as any white man—"

"Enough," Standing Horse said quietly. "These words will be

remembered long after the problem has disappeared. My daughter, do you have any other reason to believe that your husband is in this battle than your own best guess? Have you had any news at all?"

"No," she said, "but I am certain he is there."

"And what will you do if you find him?"

"I will cook for him and clean his weapon." Her eyes grew full of tears. "I will bandage his wounds. If he is killed, I will bring him home to his own land, so that he will not be buried on strange soil among strangers." She stopped and recovered her calm. "And if he is not killed, I will bring him home to his family."

Standing Horse looked at his wife. "Do you understand her words?"

Comes Alone nodded. "But what of her son? He needs his mother more than Tom Craven needs her."

"I am not certain of that," Not Black said. "But even if that is so, I think he will be able to understand that I must do this. I should be able to be home in two moons. No more than three. Even if he does not understand, he will likely not remember this when he is older. But if I do not find his father and bring him home safely, he will know that all of his life."

Standing Horse asked, "What do you say to this, wife?"

"What is there to say?" Comes Alone said bitterly. "I have said what I feel, and it makes no difference. I think you go on a fool's journey. But you have been on that journey for years, and my words did not stop you. I do not expect they will stop you now."

"Will you care for my son?" Not Black asked her mother boldly.

"Yes."

"With love, as you would for the son of a different father?"

"Yes," Comes Alone said impatiently. "I do not have a choice, do I, daughter? He is my blood, even if he is not of my people. And you will do what you will do, despite my words. It is left to me to do what I can for him." She stood abruptly and walked over to where Small Warrior foraged in the water for whatever he was hunting. She sat down close to him with the air of a watchdog who had been put on duty.

Not Black watched her, thinking that this was not something a mother bargained for, the day she had a daughter. It was not something she planned, that she would one day need to care for that daughter's child. It seemed unfair, yet it happened all the time. Still, if there was one lesson life taught, it was that there was no fairness. She knew her mother would care for him as well as she could. She would wear clothes which would comfort him, she could make her *sofkee* and feed him on her lap, she would take him to sleep in her hammock, between her body and that of her husband, if need be. Women do not leave other women. Mothers, most especially, do not leave other mothers. They put wood on their fires and sit close and say, "What do you need? Tell me and I will do it."

In that moment, it seemed to her that the souls of women were like flat stones in the sun, to be laid, one on the other, to build walls against the pains of life. Like mussels on a riverbank, they anchored themselves and held on all together, each on top of the other sometimes, in times of flood. Like bees which, when attacked, do not fly away from the hive but toward each other to form a tight cluster of defense, for they are ruled by a queen, and they know that nothing matters more than their progeny. She was glad she was a mother, a daughter, a woman in that moment.

Not Black, watching her mother's back, said to her father, "She will never forgive me my choices. All of my life, they will stand between us."

"It is a long life," her father said evenly. "Many things change, not the least of which is our hearts."

"Ours will never be the same again."

He watched her son for a moment. "When will you do this?"

"Now," she said. "I might as well leave him with you today. I will go back to the cabin and collect what I need for my journey. I will leave at first light."

Her father gazed at her. "You have courage, my daughter. Whatever you may lack in wisdom, you do not lack for will."

She smiled softly at him. "You must be father to him now. Can you do that for me?"

"I will try."

"And perhaps mother, as well. I do not know how my mother will do this, even if she tries—"

"She will be mother and grandmother to him, both," he said staunchly. "That is one thing you can depend upon. Your mother will give him all she can."

"I hope that is enough," she murmured.

"Well and it will have to be, will it not? Because you will not be there."

She stood and called Small Warrior to her. He came running with joy and abandon, nearly toppling her when he hit her knees. "I have found a monster under that rock!" he cried in delight. "I will hunt him and kill him. We will eat him for supper!"

"That is fine, son," she said, pulling him to her. "Now I want you to listen to me closely."

He instantly quieted, as she had taught him to do, and gave her his full attention, his eyes wide and clear and focused on her like twin pools of sky.

She took a deep breath and kept her voice light. "I must go on a journey, my son, to find your father. The elders say there is fighting among the white men to the north of here, and I believe your father is there. I am going to go there, find him, and bring him home to us."

He whooped with glee. "We will fight his enemy with him!" he crowed.

She shook her head. "You must stay here, Small Warrior, at the fire of your grandmother and grandfather. I will return with your father."

His glee turned to anger as quickly as the flip of a fish. "I need go with you!" he cried.

"You cannot," she said calmly. "It is a far way, and I cannot carry you."

"I can run fast!" he said, now beginning to weep. "I am very brave!"

"You are, my son," she said, taking him in her arms. "You are very brave and very strong. And that is why you must stay here and take care of Oma and Opa. You must prepare the fire for your father. And when I return, he will be very proud to see that you cared for the old ones in his absence." She spoke to him in her parents' tongue, that they might understand her clearly. Also because she knew that so long as she was absent, her son would hear not a single word of English. She might as well get him thinking in that voice immediately.

But Small Warrior was not thinking. He was feeling, and he was wailing his frustration and disappointment to the world. "I go with you!" he screamed as she held him. "I go with you, Mama!"

"No, Small Warrior. I cannot take you on this journey. But I will be back soon, I promise."

He wailed louder as she picked him up and hugged him hard to her breasts. "I am sorry, my son," she said, her voice breaking at his anguish. It would be the first time they had been separated since his birth. "I promise I will come back to you as fast as I can. I will bring your father—"

"No, no, no!" he cried. "I hate my father! I do not want him!"

"You do not hate your father," she said firmly. "You do not wish me to leave, but you do not hate your father. Never say that to me again."

He dissolved in helpless tears now, unable to speak at all for his weeping. She looked over her small son's head as she hugged him and tried to comfort him in soft murmurs. Her mother's face was sorrowful and closed. She could not read her heart. Her father looked dejected. His shoulders slumped as though he carried a larger burden than he could bear. She walked to her mother and said, "Take him now," and tried to put her son in his grandmother's arms.

Small Warrior fought with every inch of his strength to stay in her arms, screaming, "No! No! I go with you, Mama!"

She had to wrench herself away, pulling her hair out of his grasp, as he wailed wordlessly, his mouth wide and hopeless with despair. Weeping now herself, she turned and walked away as fast as she could, not daring to look back. She felt as though her heart was dissolving in her chest, it ached so badly.

She kept walking until she could no longer hear the distant cries of her son. And then she sat down and wailed, rocking back and forth as though mourning a death. She had never felt such pain and loss, no not even when her husband had left. It was as though she had a large snake in her belly which was biting her, eating her up inside. The screams of her child echoed in her mind over and over, and she could only hear him cry, "I need go with you, Mama!"

It took her long moments to be calm enough to walk again. She could only keep herself going away from him with every will she had. Finally, she stood with shaking breaths and began the long journey.

* * *

Canid stopped in her tracks, sniffing the air eagerly. The scent of ripe apples came to her clearly and she completely forgot the older trail of the raccoon she was following. She whined softly, lifting up on her hind feet to catch the breeze more completely. Apples were new to her territory. She had tasted them when she was very young, for her mother had taken herself and her littermates to fallen fruit near an old farmhouse.

Frightened by the nearness of man, they had eaten ravenously and hurriedly, gorging on the sweet, soft pulp until they could eat no more. Then racing to the shadows on the edges of the field, they had vomited up some of the pulp, too full to retain it all in their bellies. She had never forgotten the intoxicating fragrance and sweet juice of that evening. Now the scent reminded her once more, and it was near.

Since man had come more and more into the swamp, there were more things to eat and also more danger. Apples on trees where once only palmetto grew, and grapes where honeysuckle once crowded the path. But with man came dogs and guns. She was still unfamiliar with the threat of both, but she knew that both must be avoided at all costs. Still, the promise of ripe apples was more than she could resist.

Canid was a young red fox, *Vulpes vulpes*, only fifteen months old, eight pounds, and just released from her first litter. She was mated by a larger dog fox in the coldest month of the year. He had found her as soon as she came in season, and together they had scratched out a den in a hollow log. She bore four pups in April. Now they were scattered, and she would never see them again, and if she did, she might not recognize them as her own. But she knew that her mate would find her again in the cold months, and then the cycle would begin again.

For now, however, she was free to wander and eat whatever she found, with no thought of pups waiting for her to nurse them, no mate with which she must share her kill. She trotted in the direction of the tantalizing smell of apples, her mouth already eager for the sweet fruit.

Canid was small, even for her kind, and she wore a red coat tinted with white on her neck and legs. Her tail was long, red, and bushy, with a white tip. Highly visible in the spring, she was more comfortable in the autumn, when she knew her coloration kept her from being seen as well against the falling leaves. She ranged over ten miles in a day, searching always for food. Mostly noctural, her eyes were mere slits in the hot sunlight, giving her an almost-Oriental appearance.

She hurried now, the scent of the apples getting stronger on the breeze. She came to an open field, and she stopped, frozen and crouched to the ground, every sense alert for danger. Canid could get very small when she needed to, for she was only a foot at the shoulder to start. Now she crept along like a cat on her belly until she reached the edge of the meadow. There were the apples. To her dismay, few were on the ground. Most were still in the trees, with the bees and wasps busily doing their best to take their share. She sniffed the air, her eyes closed in pleasure. The fruit was ripe and ample. She had only to climb to reach it.

It was a young orchard, and the trees were still small. The fruit, however, was golden and ripe, and Canid could taste the apples in her mind's eye, in the same way she could still recall, if she tried hard, the smell of her mother and the milk she took from her body. She crept forward into the field, keeping low to the ground, her ears twitching this way and that for danger.

Now she could see in the distance the house of man. A gray cabin with two buildings on either side. Likely, the man had dogs. Man usually did.

She crawled quickly to the base of the nearest tree and looked up longingly at the fruit. The buzz of the wasps and bees told her that it must be sweet, and the hot silence of the field made her eager to fill her belly and then find a cool spot to sleep. She sat up and scanned the horizon again carefully, her ears pricked forward into their most alert position. She sniffed the air with her eyes closed, so as to pick up the slightest scent of danger. Still behind the tree, with its trunk between her body and the house of man, she knew she could duck into the safety of the woods in a second if she saw trouble coming.

In the distance, a rooster crowed. Her mouth salivated involuntarily, but she knew that apples were all she dared steal. For once, she was grateful she was small and fast. Times enough, she had wished she were larger and more powerful, but now her size was an advantage.

She mewed to herself softly, a sound distinctive to her species. It was a reflexive noise she made when she was anxious and eager, all at once. With a final glance behind her and to all sides, she scampered up the tree as quick as a cat.

Nestling into the bough of the apple tree, she inched slowly out onto a limb to reach the nearest ripe fruit. She felt safe now, up the tree, for she knew that the dogs of the men could not reach her. Like other foxes, Canid and her kin could climb as easily as they could run, and she often slept in the upper canopy of a tree if she did not feel safe on the ground.

Now, Canid reached the smaller limbs, snatched an apple, and took it into her mouth greedily. The warm juice ran over her jaws as she gobbled it down, letting the pieces drop below her carelessly. Let the wasps and the bees have those, she thought, as she shook her head to free herself of the pesky humming insects around her. She reached for another apple, now exposed on the open branch, and as she did so, she heard the swift slice of a wing on the air and felt the piercing stab of sharp talons into her neck and spine.

Snarling, Canid, turned on the branch, trying to get hold of her attacker, a large red-tailed hawk. But the hawk twisted his talons deeper, lifted her into the air, and carried her up, up over the tree. Almost paralyzed with terror and pain, Canid tried one more time to reach the raptor's feet with her teeth, but the bird screamed in anger, soared higher, and then dropped her a hundred feet from where he had snatched her off her branch.

Canid tried frantically to twist her body to a landing position as she fell through the air, howling her fear and pain, but when she fell, she knew that she was broken too badly to walk. She tried to pull herself to a defensive position, but she could not sit up. She waited, panting on the ground, her eyes closed against what she knew would come.

The hawk flapped down next to her, shrieking in triumph. Hopping onto her body, the hawk took her neck in his talons while his beak stabbed into her head. There was a sudden, sharp, gasping agony, and then she felt nothing more at all.

* * *

Not Black had been walking for five days, and still she knew she was too far south to intercept the armies of the Northerners and the whites of these lands. She had followed the river to the north, moving against the flow of the water, through dense swamplands and forests, over small meadows, and always doing her best to keep moving in a straight line, but still she had made slow time.

She was surprised to see how many signs of white settlement there were on these lands. Often, she passed clearings with small cabins, saw docks with fishing skiffs tied up, heard dogs barking in the distance, and smelled the smoke of fires.

It was a cold month, and she was grateful for that, at least, for the bugs did not torture her, and the snakes were few on the trail. She slept only when she could walk no more, even with her torch for light, and she woke with first dawn to walk more. She found she did not tire, and the voices in her head were surprisingly good companions for the first days of her journey.

But then she reached one of the iron roads of the white men, where the large black smoking conveyances traveled at great speeds, huffing and blowing their whistles. She had seen them once before when she was very young, on a trip to the town the whites called Gainesville. She remembered little of that journey, for she had slept most of the way in the wagon. But she did recall her astonishment and fear of the black, rolling monsters. Now she came upon the iron road, and she turned to the north to follow it. She knew it would be easier and faster to travel along such a path than through the swamp to either side.

The towns grew larger now, and more and more white men were clustered together on the land. She thought it curious the way they made their homes, so far from one another, with large fields around each home. Her people built their houses close together, with large fields surrounding them, the better to work them together. But the white men did not wish to live so close, she saw, and so they had to work their fields alone. She wondered that they had time to do such things as make war on one another, without their neighbors to help them with their crops.

And yet it was clear to her that the white men knew many things which her people would never understand. Their roads, their houses, their wagons, their bridges, even their horses, were larger and finer than anything she had seen in the lands of her people. She was curious about them, but she avoided their houses, their fields, and their towns. She wanted nothing to delay her journey, no man to ask her where she was going or if she had a right to be going there. Like a deer, she slipped into and out of the villages and settlements, keeping to the roads when she could and disappearing into the forest when she must. In that way, she reached the southern edge of Jacksonville on the banks of the river the whites called the Saint Mary, as the moon was changing into the last month of winter.

Now the sights and sounds of the white man's war became more apparent. The closer she got to the large town of Jacksonville, the more she saw the strangers. Where the river was wide, to the south of the town, she came upon their camp. Many hundreds of men in huts made of canvas were clustered over the lowlands to the south of the town, near the Saint Mary. Their fires dotted the fields at dusk like fireflies, and the sounds of their voices reached her ears far before she came close enough to see them.

These were the Northerners. They had to be, for the sounds of their speech were foreign to her ears. They wore dark blue jackets, and their horses looked well fed and sleek. There were so many of them, she wondered if there were any white men at all left in the towns to the north. And what of their women? She saw none among them. The men cooked for themselves, carried their own water, fed their own horses, and cleaned their own weapons. It was a wonder they had time to fight at all.

She crept close that night to one of the fires. She could tell the man within the canvas hut was a chief, for men outside his house saluted him and brought him food that he might eat within his house alone. She listened as best she could to the English words spoken quietly in the dark shadows near the camp, and she heard the men speak of the "rebels" to the west, along the railway to Lake City. They said they would beat them and go to the Suwannee. From there, they would hold Florida, they told each other in boasting voices.

Not Black had heard the voices of men preparing for battle before, and she knew, from the way the women spoke of wars in the past, that what the men believed might happen did not always happen. But it was important, the women said, to help the men believe that they were right. These men had no women with them to bolster their courage and praise them. Perhaps that would make them weaker in battle.

To her vast surprise and disdain, now that night had come to the camp, the women came as well. She saw them arriving in their wagons from the village, dressed in colorful clothing which revealed the curves of their bodies. She saw by the way the men greeted them, shouting and laughing and coarsely gesturing to one another, that these women were not their own. They were women who had come to bed with the men, to trade their bodies for whatever they might get. No wonder these warriors kept their wives away.

She wondered that their chief would allow such a thing. Everyone knew that men must be purified and strengthened in their spirit magic before a battle. How could they be strong when they wasted their seed on women such as these? She frowned to herself, wondering if such a perverseness went on in all white men's battle camps. If that was so, it was well that she came now, to help Tom Craven lead his men from such defilement. Men were weak, she knew; she had heard the women say so often enough. But they could be strong with the right support and love from their women. She was very glad she had come to help him in that way.

For a moment, she had a clear vision of how very different the whites were from her people. She had never been much around them, had never seen them with their children, never sat at their tables, never worked with them or played the ball game with them. She had never seen them birth their babies or bury their dead. She did not know how they loved each other or fought with each other or chided each other or respected each other. Neither did Tom Craven know that of her people. How could they ever hope to know each other? Was it possible to love one person and not love their kin?

But she pushed those thoughts away. Once they were together, all her doubts would dissolve, she knew.

She rested in the cool, dark shadows near the camp and before sunrise, she set her footsteps resolutely toward the west, following the iron rail which led from the camp to the place the white men called Lake City. She was certain that this village would be where she would find Tom Craven.

She walked for all of another day, skirting the edges of the Okefeno- kee Swamp, always keeping the sun before her. The white man's road was easy to walk, but it was not always the most direct, and she knew that she must get to Tom and his men before his enemy arrived. She had no doubt that Tom would likely be among the chiefs of these "rebels," and her only regret was that she must bring him sadness along with the vital news of the position of the Northerners: the news that his father was dead.

As Not Black walked she thought most of Small Warrior. Had he found small boys to run with, to shout with, despite the lightness of his hair and skin? Did he think of her often? Dream of her? Ask for her?

Sometimes she yearned for him so deeply that she felt the ache like labor in her womb. Once she was thinking of him so intently that she realized she was walking with her arms hugging herself, so badly did she wish to hold him. But she threw off that weakness and told herself that her first duty was to her husband. Her child would one day under- stand this and would expect it from his own woman. This was the way of love.

She reached a place finally, two days walk out of Jacksonville, where she saw the signs of another battle camp. She came closer, creeping now quietly and close to the ground until she could find a place to look down upon the camp from a hill covered with thick brush. She sat and gazed down at many canvas huts and campfires, and this time, she knew she had come to the right place.

The men here were men who looked like those she had seen at the trading posts and villages when she was younger, men who did not have pretty blue jackets or white cotton shirts. Many of them did not have shoes, so far as she could tell, and only a few horses whickered from where they were hobbled in the shade. These were the "rebels." These were the warriors who fought with her husband.

She was too far from the camp to see faces, so she crept closer, keeping always low to the ground and behind brush. She slowly circled the camp, watching always for the familiar tall shoulders of Tom Craven, for the shock of yellow hair, listening for his laugh or his voice. After several hours of spying on the men, she still had not seen him, but she was certain he must be here. There were men who looked much like

him, with the same lanky walk and the same narrow face, but none of
them were Tom. Still, it comforted her somehow to see them, as though
they were kin to her husband in a distant way.

By nightfall, she was beginning to doubt that he was in camp, for
she had circled the camp slowly several times, and still been unable
to see him. But perhaps he was out on a scout mission, to see the
enemy's position. She decided she would wait until morning to circle
the camp once more. Surely he would appear for the first meal of the
day, if he were in camp. If not, she would find someone to speak to
and discover where he was, also warning them about the approach of
the blue jackets.

But to her surprise, the men began to move the camp before dawn,
and she could only watch in disappointment as they took down the
tents and broke up their fires. A chief spoke with them from upon his
horse, telling them that the enemy was coming down the iron road.
She could not hear all that the chief told them, though she kept as
close as she dared. The noise of the men as they stood in their lines, the
rattle and clink of their weapons, made the words difficult to understand.

And then they began to march to the east, away from camp all in
long lines, clustered together with the horsemen following, some of
them dragging large iron guns on wheels. The wagons followed the
men, and she followed the wagons. She could do nothing else, having
come this far.

The men marched for what seemed like half the day, and she could
see that they would never be very quick to battle in this way of moving.
They made a horrendous noise as they marched; it would be impossible
to surprise their enemy. She could only hope that the enemy was as
loud and cumbersome and clumsy as these men were, for certainly they
seemed unready to fight.

But fight they did, and soon enough, too, once they reached a group
of hills half a day's march from where they had made camp. They came
to a place where their chief told them to prepare for battle, and they
dug themselves holes and made small walls behind which they could
fire at the enemy. She still looked frantically for Tom whenever she
could get close enough to see the men, but it was hard for her to spy
on them when they were so spread out.

And then the sound of shots came from the east, and the men gave
up all pretense of dignity. They shouted and whooped and waved their
weapons like men gone mad, some of them half-out of the barricades
they had made to hide behind. She could see little sense to their

strategy, for their chiefs raced up and down on horseback, exhorting them to fire, yet many of them were simply firing at the smoke and noise they perceived ahead of them, rather than at the enemy.

The enemy seemed no better at battle, it seemed to her. They could be heard long before they arrived, their horses to the front and three columns of men to the rear, strung out and marching in a way that suggested they were tired before they even got there. When they reached the swamp, they came to that place in the road where it was narrow and edged by bogs on the left and the right.

It was here that the yellow men, what Not Black had taken to calling the Florida troops in her mind for the color of their jackets, rose out of hiding and fired into them.

They fought for four hours, and Not Black was appalled at the hideous waste of life she saw before her. The yellow men had only four of the large guns on wheels, and the blue jackets had sixteen of them, but still they looked as though they were going to lose the battle from the beginning. Men stood up and shot into the palmetto thickets, only to fall with screams when they were blasted with rifle fire from the barricades. The swamp made it all the more difficult for the enemy to maneuver. The yellow men had only to stand firm and keep shooting while the blue jackets tried to move past them on spongy ground which gave way under their feet, their horses, and their wagons.

Men were dying before her eyes, hundreds of them, on both sides, but it was clear that many more of the blue jackets were dying. Finally one of them gave way and ran to the rear, breaking their line in half. Then another group of warriors, black ones this time, broke also and ran, after their chief was shot off his horse. Soon all of them were running back up the road, looking back over their shoulders in fear lest the yellow men were following.

"We thrashed their asses good!" shouted a yellow man close to Not Black's hiding place, as he stood and waved his rifle, whooping in glee. The rest of his comrades stood and pounded each other on the back, congratulating themselves on their bravery. Many were herding together some of the captured blue jackets, and the chiefs of the yellow men were shouting orders still to try to keep their men in line.

But they were as heedless as children, and they jumped over the barricades, brandished their weapons at the prisoners, and generally made such a commotion that their medicine men could scarcely get to the wounded without pushing aside a shouting warrior.

She turned away in sick disgust, unwilling to watch them at their war anymore. Tom Craven was not among them; she knew that now. He would not lead such a pack of unruly hounds into battle. She walked in the opposite direction of the men for at least an hour, then turned south toward her own lands again. Her heart was hard and heavy like a stone. She had not found her husband. That was bad enough. But even worse, she had not found any new liking for these white men and their ways. How could she praise him when he came home at last, knowing that the battles he had been in were most likely no better, no more valorous, than that which she had witnessed?

Most important, most disturbing of all? How could she love the man and not his people? Was such a thing even possible?

After a day of walking, she came to peace with what she had seen. It was a grudging peace, a bewildered space in her heart, but it allowed her to believe that somehow, the war which Tom Craven fought, the war which had taken his father's life, was larger and more significant than that which she had seen. It simply had to be so.

What Not Black could not know was that she had witnessed the last battle for Florida. Never again would the Confederate and the Union Armies clash on soil so far south. Brigadier General Truman Seymour's division of three brigades of infantry, two regiments of cavalry, and four batteries of artillery, a force of about six thousand men comprised of Regulars, New Englanders, and Negroes, had been whittled down by a third in four hours by five thousand green Confederates, militia to a man and untested by battle.

It was Seymour's Waterloo. A forty-year-old Vermont West Pointer, Seymour had served bravely in the Seminole Wars, at Sumter, Second Bull Run, South Mountain, and Antietam. And still he had missed the recognition he felt he deserved. When given orders to hold Jacksonville, he waited impatiently for four days and then set out on the offensive. He knew the Confederates waited for him just outside Lake City. But he figured to whip them and gain glory for himself in the bargain, despite the orders of his superior officer, Brigadier General Quincy Gillmore, to stay put.

Instead of administering the thrashing, Seymour received it, both by the green Confederates and the land, itself. Slogging back to Jacksonville, the survivors were footsore and bitter. They had not anticipated retreat but victory, and they had certainly not figured on leaving nearly two thousand of their number either dead on the field or in enemy hands.

One captain wrote, "Ten miles we wended or crawled along, the wounded filling the night air with lamentations, the crippled horses neighing in pain, and the full moon kissing the cold, clammy lips of the dying."

Now the question was not whether or not the Union forces could take the

Suwannee. The question was whether or not they could even hold Jacksonville and thus, any part of the state at all. Florida was the least populous of the Confederate states, had furnished the smallest number of troops for the rebel armies, but she had given a larger proportion of her eligible men than any other region. Her zeal for rebellion was unmatched by any other Southern state.

Seymour was dismissed from command, and the Battle of Oulstee or Ocean Pond taught outsiders a lesson about waging war on land which seemed as much the enemy as the troops before them.

And Not Black wended her way home under that same full moon which kissed the lips of the dying Union soldiers along the road back to Jacksonville.

When Not Black arrived back in her village, she crept around the edge of the huts until she was close to her mother's fire, unwilling to be seen before she was ready to be seen. It had been a long journey, both of the body and the heart. Suddenly it seemed to her strange and frightening to be back among people, any people, and to make the words in her head out loud in the air for them to understand.

As she came close to the *cheke*, she heard the voice of her son and her mother. They were laughing together over something, his rapid, high-pitched trill of words spilling into the air like water over rocks. He was speaking Seminole, and it seemed to her in that moment that he should never, ever speak anything else.

To her surprise and joy, her grandmother was sitting by the fire close to her son, and the two of them had their heads bent together looking at something she had in her hand. He looked up as she came near and screamed, "Mama!" throwing himself in her arms with the violent passion which only a small boy can muster.

She carried him to the palmetto log close to her grandmother and wept and rocked him, stroking his hair and murmuring endearments over his own cries. For long moments, she did her best only to hold him as close to her as she could manage, breathing in his odor, touching his face, gazing into his eyes as she pushed the long hair back from his face and dried his tears with her own braid. Then she rose and her mother and father came and embraced the two of them, her grandmother also, and together they were a clumsy entanglement of laughing mouths, weeping eyes, and grasping arms. Finally, she sat down once more and caught her breath, still holding fast to Small Warrior.

"I am come," she said at last in her own tongue.

"You are," they chorused happily.

"See how he has grown!" said her mother.

"He looks taller by a head," Not Black said, nuzzling him. "You have been feeding well at your Oma's fire, eh?"

He nodded happily. "Where is my father?" he asked then, looking behind him.

She shook her head. "I could not find him, my son. Let me tell the story, and then you will know where I have walked."

She took her time with her tale, as was the Seminole custom, half-telling, half-chanting the story of her journey, the finding of the blue jackets, then the yellow men, and the vision of the battle. She told how the men had died, bravely and not so bravely, and the horrible waste of life she felt on the land. She told of the chiefs and their horses, the sound of the rifles firing, the canvas huts, and the noise of them tramping down the iron roads. She told of searching for Tom Craven while she circled the camps, hiding in the brush, and finally she told of her heartache and her long journey home, her arms empty and waiting to hold Small Warrior.

When she was finished, there was a silence round the fire, which also was the custom as each person thought over her words in quiet respect for the teller. In the silence, Not Black reached out and took her grandmother's hand. Morning Dew squeezed it gently and took it in both of her own.

Small Warrior said, "Where is my father, then?"

"I do not know," Not Black said gently. "But I still believe he will come home to us soon. The whites cannot fight as I saw them fight forever, for they will surely destroy themselves if they do. I am happy that he was not in such a battle. It was not a battle worthy of your father. Perhaps even now, he is on the journey home. We can only be strong and brave and wait for him. This war will be over soon. It must be."

"I am strong and brave," Small Warrior said resolutely.

"I know you are," Not Black said, hugging him. She turned to Morning Dew. "My heart is filled with joy to see you here, my grandmother." She said this last formally, in the old tradition, for she knew that Morning Dew had made a large compromise in her mind to allow her to come and help care for Small Warrior.

"She came right after you left," Comes Alone said.

"And what of the hardness in your heart to all things white?" Not Black asked. "Have you then decided to find peace with them?"

"No," Morning Dew said staunchly. "I have decided only to love a small boy who is of my blood."

"What of his father?" Not Black asked. She could not help herself. She knew it was best not to pursue this line of questioning, but her quest had made her impatient for peace and for resolution in her heart.

"Did you see the villages of the whites on your journey?" Morning Dew asked, instead of answering.

"I did. I could hardly avoid them."

Morning Dew nodded. "They are many. And they are growing every moon. They will continue to spread, for that is their way. Did you find new liking for such ways on your journey?"

Not Black thought for a moment. "I cannot say that I understand their ways. Perhaps if I understood them—"

"You will never understand them," Morning Dew said firmly. "Now I will speak a small talk on this, so that you will know the truth." She said these words with the formal phrasing of the old ways. "These things I know, for I am old. Some of them I remember, others were told to me by those older than me. Here is what I know. Long ago, before I was born, the white men came first as only a few. We were not surprised when the white people came, for we had known them for many generations to the north. Our elders warned us of them time and again, and we had listened well. When we lived with the Creeks, we knew many other tribes. They were strangers and yet not strangers. When they came and asked us to pass through our lands, we let them. This was the land where we hunted and lived and buried our people. It was land which the Maker of Breath had given us. It was the land where our sacred stories were born and where the animals knew us. We were a part of it, and it was a part of us. But we did not own it any more than we can own the sky. Any more than we can own our grandparents."

She took a deep breath and closed her eyes. "And then the white people came. They were strange to us, even stranger than the other tribes, but we thought they were also part of the plans of the Maker of Breath. We believed we did not have the right to stop them from passing over our land, any more than we had the right to stop the deer or the panther. So we let them come among us and we fed them and we helped them. They came, and then they were gone.

"Then more strangers came. This time they brought wagons and horses and went on paths through our lands, frightening the animals and making their camps on our sacred places. But they also brought wonderful things we had never seen, including guns that made the hunting easier. So we let them come. These are the years I saw myself."

She opened her eyes again, but she did not look at them. She watched the pictures in her mind. "And then they became like a river, instead of a stream. They shot the animals without respect, they moved the rocks and cut the trees and changed the rivers to please themselves. They were heavy on the land and they made terrible noises. We tried to stay out of their way, but they made the hunting hard, and they angered the young men. Also, the young men wanted their rifles, and the young women wanted their pretty cloth and their iron pots.

"Then the white strangers began to ask us for our land. We did not know how to explain to them that it was not ours to sell; neither was it theirs to buy. We thought they were most perverse. Then their chiefs came to tell us that we did not belong on the land anymore. They said there was a chief in Washington, which was a white village far away, and that this land belonged to him. He said we had to get off the land so that his kin could live here. We were not his kin, though they said we were his children. We knew he was not our father, as they said he was, but it did not matter."

She stood and began to pace. "Many of the Creeks laughed at first. Then they fought. We left and came to the south, where the white people did not follow. At least for a time. Then they began to flow down from the north like a flood. And this time, we knew them for what they were.

"These people were not just perverse, they were insane. They rode across the land and put up a flag and then they said that all the land from where they started to the flag belonged to them. To us, that was like riding to the middle of a lake and planting a stick and saying all the water back to the shore belonged to a man. Or shooting an arrow into the sky and saying that all the sky up to where the arrow went belonged to one man. We thought they made no sense, but our elders told us they were dangerous. We knew they were right."

She sat down stiffly. "You see, they were talking about property. We were talking about land. Finally, we came to understand the white man's words, but we could never understand his thinking. He came from a place called Europe where he had worked for other people who had all the property and took all the food that was raised on it. They never had anything because they never had property. So the first thing they did when they came here was to try to get property of their own.

"We did not understand. We belonged to the land. They wanted to own it. Their religion came from a cup and a piece of bread, and a book they could carry wherever they went. Our religion came from sacred places, sacred animals, and sacred stories which only lived on the land, where the spirits talked to us.

"And still they came, now like a great flood. Finally, their flood washed us off the land. Many warriors fought. My husband, Osceola, fought harder than anyone. Other old chiefs said we should deal with them. But when we tried to do so, they did not listen. They made promises and broke every one. First they said we could keep our most sacred places. Then, when they wanted them, they took them. Then they said we could have enough land to hunt and fish. But when they wanted it, they made it smaller or took it away completely. They they said we must go completely off the land, and that is when we went to the woods where they could not follow. But they did follow. And this boy here is the proof of that."

To temper the hardness of her words and the dignity of her voice, she took Small Warrior's hand in her own and held it gently.

"Here is what you must know. You will never understand the ways of the white man. He does not understand them himself. To us, the land is alive. The earth is our mother, to be treated with respect and honor. For them, the land is not alive. It is something to be built upon and managed and moved and altered to bear fruit. That is what their god tells them, to make the land bear fruit. How can we ever understand each other when our gods tell us something different about the land? We cannot. We never will. Your grandfather knew this truth. I know this truth. Now you know this truth in your head. But you still must learn it in your heart."

Not Black sat, silent and stunned by her grandmother's words. She had never heard her speak so long, so eloquently. The sadness in her voice moved her to tears.

"We will never take back our land again," Morning Dew said finally. "But we can take back our children and make them see the value of the old ways. And perhaps we can take some of their children to our ways as well. If we get them when they are young. Our own children and their children may yet make a path to a new place together."

"You make my heart feel heavy, Grandmother," Not Black said. "Heavy with the past and all the pain which has come and gone before I ever drew breath."

"My heart is heavy also," Morning Dew said. "But when I see this Small Warrior, I have some hope still for the future."

"You said that you would never be near him. You said, once he was born we were both no longer your people."

Morning Dew nodded. "I said many things. Most of them were the truth. But I forgot how much love can change the firmest heart."

"Perhaps you can change enough to understand at least one white man," Not Black said softly. "Perhaps when Tom Craven comes home—"

"That is one change I will never live long enough to see," Morning Dew replied shortly. "To do so would be to dishonor the memory of my husband and your grandfather. Do not hope for that, my granddaughter, for you will be disappointed. Let it be enough that his son has a piece of me. No other white blood shall, that is certain."

Not Black went to her grandmother and embraced her. "Then perhaps that will have to be enough."

And she took her son back into her arms and began to answer his hundred questions about her journey and all she saw when she was away from his eyes.

*   *   *

The young male black bear, Ur, sat on his haunches by the river, where it was riffled into shallows, and moaned his distress. He had been wandering for three days in and out of the swamplands, searching for territory which showed no signs of larger males already in occupation. Feeding signs were common, however, and he was tired of walking. He needed to find a territory and then a mate, in that order. If he did not do so by the end of the hottest months, he would likely be without a mate this year, his first breeding season.

Ur rocked back and forth, holding his haunches for comfort. There were too many bears in the swamp, that much was certain. Too many male bears. He saw their scat, the dark brown cylindrical leavings which showed they had eaten most everything they could reach or catch. Squirrel fur, bees, fruit seeds, nutshells. And berries. Lots and lots of berries. Some of the scat was dog, he knew that much, most particularly when he roamed close to the houses of man. But too many were bear.

Also, the more subtle signs were all around him, everywhere he went. Logs and stones turned over where another bear was looking for grubs, the ground pawed up for roots, anthills broken apart, berry patches torn up, palmetto leaf buds and fruits ripped off the trees, and the trunks bent down were only some. The most frightening signs were the bear trees, tall oaks or loblollies with their trunks scarred with tooth marks and claw slashes. These males were tall, and there were too many of them.

Ur lay down on his belly and rolled in the damp sand, scratching the vermin from his spine and shanks. He was *Ursus americanus*, about three feet at the shoulder and weighing just over two hundred pounds. Two dogs could whip him, and another male, even a crochety female, could likely kill him if he could not get away.

Usually he hunted in the night hours, and in fact, he much preferred the coolness then. But those were the times when he was also much more likely to encounter another bear. And so he was left with the heat of the day, while the other bears, those whose territories he trespassed, slept away the most miserable hours of the swamp sunlight.

Ur was hot, and his fur itched all over. His testicles were swollen and insistent with his need to mate. He bit at them with some irritation, snapping at his own flesh as though to rid himself of the skin as well as the flies. But he could not ignore the urgings which welled up in him this spring and summer, like sulfur gas bubbles which burst on the surface of the mud pools.

Moaning and grumbling, he crawled the rest of the way down the riverbank and settled himself in the shallows up to his neck. At least the water was slightly cooler than the stifling air. He sighed and eased himself deeper. He had walked more than ten miles this day, and the day was not over yet. He still had to go farther from the river, hoping that soon he would find a territory less crowded.

A small bream veered too close, and Ur snapped it up with his jaws. He was, like all of his kind, a good fisher. He could scoop fish with his paws or snag them with his jaws; he could climb trees and dig up burrows for rodents. He ate just about anything, even young deer if he could catch them. His mother had shown him how to roll over a porcupine by reaching under it with a quick paw and knocking it flat on its back. Then, if he moved swift and sure, he could get at the animal's underbelly and avoid the quills.

It was dangerous, but he would try it if he found the opportunity. The problem was the opportunity.

As Ur was lazing in the river, he heard the slightest splash behind him. He looked and saw a small portion of the riverbank caving in, making ripples which rolled out toward him. He turned his back, no longer interested. Whatever it had been was not there now.

Moments later, he was rolling on his back in the water, when he felt a sharp blow to his belly which knocked the wind out of him, a roiling rush, a gaping flash of jaws, and an alligator hit him with the force of a tree toppling on him.

The creature's jaws held him at the shoulder; it had gone for his head and missed. The alligator's teeth were firmly embedded in his shoulder and chest, however, and he roared his pain and anger, struggling to wrest himself from the animal's grip. Fighting and tearing himself, he tried to stay in the shallows, but the alligator was pulling him out to deeper water. He knew that once he lost footing, he might well lose his life. He swatted at the beast with all his strength, but could only use one shoulder, and each time he tried to reach the alligator, it turned in the water, rolling and tugging and roiling up great waves, which engulfed them both.

For a few seconds, Ur felt mostly terror, as he tried to see what had him and how badly. But then his anger rose swiftly and hot in him, and he turned to his attacker with his own jaws snapping, his own teeth at the ready. Reaching with one paw and kicking with both feet, he knocked the alligator hard to the head once, then again to the belly. He snagged the creature's leg with his jaws and bit down with all his strength, ripping at his soft underside wildly.

The alligator gave a huge hiss of pain and anger, trying to wrench his leg from the bear's jaws. Ur would not let go, even when the gator pulled him completely under the water. He only closed his eyes and held on, feeling himself dragged through the water by the longer alligator. The jaws on his shoulder suddenly let go, and he was free. He shot to the surface, coughing and snarling, and he saw the alligator wheel as though he were coming for him again. Ur scrambled for the shallows and stood up on his hind legs, roaring a challenge to the beast.

The alligator stopped and eyed the bear from deeper water. He then sank under the surface, and the ripples from his tail moved away to a far bank.

Ur climbed out of the river now, shaking each leg and shivering, checking himself for damage. His shoulder was bleeding deeply, and his chest felt raw and torn. He licked himself carefully, moaning aloud his complaints and residual fear. And then he realized that he had beaten back his attacker. He had vanquished a larger foe than himself, one which had the upper hand in the territory. He roared at the water, swiping angrily at the current as though daring the alligator to try again. The silence of the river was total, for even the birds had flown away at the noise of the battle.

He ambled into the shade of the trees and sprawled out to sleep. He knew now that he could fight. When he woke, he would feed in this territory, no matter who it might belong to or which bear might come upon him. If challenged, he would answer the challenge. He would wander no more.

* * *

The weather had turned cooler, and Not Black was out in the fields harvesting the last of the squash. These final rows were large and probably would be bitter, but she knew she could soak them in milk and make a good *sofkee* with the cornmeal she had ground the week before.

Small Warrior was working alongside her, pulling up the old vines and carrying them over to the burning pile. "Tell me the one about how the fox got his tail," he called to her from under a large bundle of vines and weeds.

She chuckled ruefully. "That will make three stories this day alone. What makes you think you're worth three stories, boy?"

"I can carry more than you can!" he teased her. "I am worth tens of stories!"

She once more was grateful that her father had spent so much time when she was small, telling her the stories of her people. Grateful, too, that she was able to remember them well enough to keep Small Warrior entertained. His favorite ones usually had small boys in them, like himself, who somehow managed to save an entire village by dint of their great courage or skill. This was the third time this week for the tale of the fox—

"Someone is coming!" Small Warrior called out then, dropping his load and pointing to a moving plume of dust which was coming up the road.

Not Black stopped and stared, shading her eyes with her hand. A wagon was moving closer up the edge of the field. The sorrel horse looked like a good one, even from this distance. The wagon was covered with a canvas tarp, and barrels of goods were lashed to the side. A trader, perhaps. She wondered how far he had come and over what roads. The whites must be clearing more pathways to the north, she realized, for a wagon to come through the swamp. She called Small Warrior to her and said, "Leave that, my son. Stay behind me and do not speak unless I say so." She walked slowly toward the house, keeping her long skirts between him and the wagon.

She saw that the wagon pulled up outside the cabin, and someone got down with an air of ease. It was a tall man, she could see that much. And then she stopped, her hand to her throat.

"Who is it, Mother?" Small Warrior asked, staring up at her anxiously.

"Thank you, all of the gods," she breathed. "Come quickly!" she cried, taking his hand and pulling him along.

"Who is it!"

"It is your father!" she cried out then, dropping his hand, picking up her skirts, and running as fast as she could over the fields and toward the cabin. When she reached the fence, she flew over it like a deer, only glancing back once to make sure Small Warrior was slipping under it as usual. She rounded the porch calling, "Tom! Tom!", but she stopped when she saw him standing there on the steps, his hat in his hand, a look of amazement on his face.

Suddenly, she was paralyzed with shyness. He looked so very different! So much larger, so much older. His face was covered with a dark beard, and his eyes looked as though they belonged in the head of a man twenty years his senior. "You are come," she said then, softly.

"Lily?" he said, raking his hand through his hair. It was long, darker, and pulled back in a tail. "Well, I'll be."

Just then Small Warrior rounded the cabin as well, pushing himself forward of her skirts and standing between them with his chest out like a rooster. "I am Small Warrior," he said in clumsy English. "I am very brave and very strong."

Tom Craven smiled wonderingly. "I see that," he said.

"This is your son," she said proudly. "He was born eight moons after you go away."

Tom paled visibly, his mouth open in shock. After a long moment he said, "Come here, boy." He beckoned, kneeling on the steps and holding out a hand.

Small Warrior went to him unhesitatingly.

Her eyes watered with joy and pride to see the two at last so close together. The boy was so beautiful; the man so handsome to her eyes.

"You got blue eyes," Tom Craven said. "Like mine."

"He has your mouth and your chin," she said.

"I don' see that. But I see the eyes, sure enough."

Small Warrior frowned up at her. "You said he would have a white horse," he rattled off to her in his own tongue.

She laughed. "I was wrong. It is a good horse, though."

"What's he sayin'?" Tom Craven asked.

Small Warrior said in English, "If you are a chief, where is your weapon?"

"I ain' no chief, son. I'm just a man. Just a warrior, like you." He reached out clumsily and patted the boy on the shoulder. "Seems like you an' me got some catchin' up to do."

She ached for that hand on her own shoulder, and so she moved closer to them both, her eyes downcast and her mouth trembling. "I praise the gods you are safe," she murmured.

He stood up then and gazed down at her. "I never reckoned to see you again," he said, and he glanced back at the wagon. "Annie, come out and say hey."

To Not Black's shock, a woman's small face came out of the wagon cover then, and she smiled at Tom Craven happily. "I ain' quite ready for company yet, Tom." She patted at her hair and her bonnet self-consciously.

"This ain' company," he said to her. "This is an ol' friend." He stopped for a minute, and she realized, to her horror, that he could not recall her true name.

"I have kept the land for you," she stammered. "Small Warrior and I have worked—"

"The place looks good," he said, nodding. "You have my thanks for that . . . Lily."

She smiled hesitantly at him. "I have made a home, my husband."

He stopped and stared down at her. "Well. Seems to me the house was here, sure enough. And the fields, too, of course. I thank you for lookin' out for things, but I 'spect you took your share for your trouble."

She frowned, bewildered. "I do what a wife should do. I keep your land. I keep your son."

The woman was stepping down from the wagon now, and her smile had faltered. "What is she saying, Tom?"

"Honey, this is my friend, Lily. And this is her son."

"Your son," Not Black said, her alarm rising. She turned to the woman. "He is my husband."

The woman looked at Tom Craven with amazement. "Tom?"

"Lily, take the boy round back and set on the porch there, will you? I be there in a minute."

"No," Not Black said firmly. "I am your wife. Who this woman is?"

The woman looked at Not Black for a long moment, and her eyes were clear and full of sadness. "Child, I am his wife. Married to him legal not two months ago." She put out her hand to Not Black and touched her shoulder gently. "You poor dear."

"I am not deer, I am wife," Not Black said, shrugging off her hand. "You go away. Take wagon and go."

The woman looked up at Tom sorrowfully. "I be waitin' in the cabin, Tom. You do what you got to do."

With that, she lifted her long skirts with a delicacy and grace, ascended the steps, and went into Not Black's cabin.

"Annie, you go rest up. I won' be long," he called after her.

A burning anger came over Not Black then, not so much at the man who stood shamefaced before her but at the woman who had gone into her house without even asking her permission or leave. She turned to Tom Craven with her eyes filled with wrathful tears.

"We is married, true enough," he said, shrugging his shoulders in dismissal. "Miss Annie and me. You and me weren't never married legal, after all. I never thought you'd be waitin', Lily, not all this time. An' surely, I never knew 'bout the boy."

"We are man and wife," she said staunchly. "Tell that woman to go from my cabin."

He shook his head. "It ain' your cabin, Lily. I appreciate all you done, but it ain' yours to order her out." He sighed and looked away. "An I ain', neither."

"But you are my husband."

"Not accordin' to the law," he said. "White man's law. An' that's what I got to live by. I'm sorry, Lily. Powerful sorry to hurt you, but I just thought you'd take up with your own kind. I never figured you to stay here an' wait on me—"

"I am your wife!" she cried.

He shook his head. "No. Miss Annie is my wife, sworn and signed."

Small Warrior had stood and listened to all of this, staring at the white people back and forth. Now he came to her and yanked on her hand. "Mother, make that woman go away."

She looked down into his face. His perfect, light-colored skin, his eyes like his father's. She touched his head with a trembling hand. "Son, go to the barn and wait for me there." She said it in her own tongue.

"No," he replied in English.

"Do as I tell you!" she shouted at him, pulling her hand away.

He stood, glowering up at Tom Craven as though he were a warrior his own size. "You not my father," he said then in English.

"I reckon I am, boy," Tom said uneasily. "Mind your mama now an' get."

Small Warrior stalked round the corner of the house with great dignity, his shoulders straight, his face pale and pained.

"Look, I'm sorry," Tom said gravely, standing with his arms crossed, his face closed and grim. "I didn't know 'bout him."

"Would that matter?" she asked. She yearned to touch him, but his stance seemed not to allow it. She tried to smile, but it would not stay on her mouth. "He was born at my mother's fire. But I bring him here soon after. This is where we wait for you. I tell him you are chief. I tell him when you win your battle, you come home."

"An' so I have," he said.

"I went to the north to search for you," she said. "I saw the Northerners in their battle with the yellow jackets. I could not find you. But I knew you would come."

"You went to look for me?"

She nodded. She touched his arm. "My husband, I have news of your father. A man brought a paper. He told me the words on it. It said your father is dead."

Tom sagged as though he were struck in the middle. He dropped his arms away from his body, away from her touch. "I reckoned so," he said slowly. "When I didn't hear nothin'. How long back?"

"Many moons. The paper is in the cabin." She turned as if to go up the steps and lead him to it.

"That's all right, I'll look to it later. I figured he was dead or captured. I guess for Pa, dead was a better choice." He sighed deeply. "I was at Cold Harbor. That don' mean nothin' to you, but I won' never forget it. The war's over now. I don' know what I was fightin' for, an' I guess we got thrashed anyways. That's what they say. I know I seen such a passel of death in the last four years, I cain' hardly weep no more. Not even for my own kin."

"I am sorry, my husband," she said gently.

"Lily—" he faltered, and then steeled himself. "You got to stop callin' me that. I ain' your husband."

"We said the vows."

"It weren't legal. Maybe to you, but not to me. I married Annie legal, an' I am her husband."

She looked up at him woefully. "I wait for you for four years."

"An' I'm grateful for all you done," he said. "But I never asked you to."

"What about Small Warrior?"

"Can you and him go back to your ma?"

She stared up at him, amazed. "You wish us to go away?"

He dropped his eyes. "I cain' see no other way, Lily. I'm powerful sorry."

She could not think of what to say. She felt as though a swarm of bees had entered her head, and she needed to brush them away before she could think clearly. The humming grew louder and louder, and she looked up at him through a haze of pain and confusion. "I am not your wife?" she murmured.

He shook his head. "Not accordin' to me, you ain'."

"And Small Warrior is not your son?"

"Now, I didn't say that, Lily. He likely is, sure enough."

She sat down on a step, feeling for it with her hand as though she were suddenly blind. "Four years," she said in her own tongue. "Four winters. Four summers."

He glanced up at the cabin anxiously. She followed his glance and saw a hand release the curtain. The woman was watching them.

"I am old," she said to him in English. "I am old, in the waiting for you."

He smiled wryly. "Aw, Lily, you still a young gal. A pretty one, too, same's always. I'm the old man, truth of it is. What I seen would make any man older than his years. I ain' no prize, that's for certain."

She spread out her hands on her skirt and looked at them as though she had never seen them before. They were worn with the work she had done in his fields. "Where I should go?" she asked, half-aloud, half to herself.

"Back to your own kind," he said gently. "That's the best thing. For you an' for the boy."

Her anger kindled then. "Do not tell me what is best for me," she said. "Not for me. Not for Small Warrior. You do not know what is best for us."

He looked away. "I 'spect that's so," he said. "Well. I need to go see to Miss Annie. Please pardon me, Lily." He touched his hat and passed her on the steps, carefully avoiding her skirts which were sprawled on both sides of her. He went inside and closed the door behind him.

For a long moment, she sat there, her head whirling. Inside was her husband. Inside was a woman who was his wife, according to the laws of the white man. According to the words of her husband. She was outside the cabin. She had nothing. Nothing except Small Warrior—

She stood and went around the corner of the cabin quickly, calling to her son. He came out of the barn and looked at her with suspicion.

"Come," she said. "We are going to your grandmother's fire."

"But this is our house!" he cried out, moving away from her as though she might try to take him by force.

She shook her head. "It is the house of your father. It is not the house of your mother." She spoke in the words of her own people.

"I will stay here!" he cried.

She pulled him to her sharply, embracing him so tightly that she knew she alarmed him. "You will come with me now, Small Warrior. I am your mother, and I tell you this. Do not speak of your father again unless I give you leave."

He instantly subsided and fell in behind her footsteps. She walked quickly to the road, past the wagon which still waited by the cabin, past the shaded windows and along the fence line to the woods. She kept walking very hard and fast, not looking back to see if he were behind her, not looking back to see if that white hand moved the curtains once more.

Not Black did not slow her pace until she was well within the woods and halfway to the river. Only then did she stop and take deep breaths, leaning against a tree. Small Warrior watched her from a few feet away where he had dropped to the ground to rest. He did not meet her eyes and he did not say a word.

That first night, she thought she would die. She suddenly could go no farther than she had already traveled from the cabin, and she sat down with her head in her hands, oblivious to Small Warrior, the woods around them, or her fate. Silently, Small Warrior brought small branches and pieces of wood and put them at her feet. "It will be dark soon," he said softly in her own tongue.

She roused herself enough to make the fire and to pull some palmetto cabbage off a nearby tree. She baked it and put it on the ground next to her for him to eat, then she wrapped herself in her skirt, pulling it over her head. "I must sleep," she said to him, and she rolled herself into a curved ball. "Keep the fire going," she added. It was the last thing she said to him until sometime in the night.

Finally she roused herself and sat up, looking around. It was very dark, and the fire was low. Small Warrior lay next to her on the ground. He had pulled leaves and thatch over himself to sleep, and when she saw him, she felt a hard pang of guilt. She had not been a good mother in her despair. She wondered if his stomach were empty.

She sat up and gazed into the fire, trying to clear her head. The words of Tom Craven went round and round, over and over she heard his voice, and yet she still could not make sense of what he said. He was not her husband. He had married another woman. A white woman. She was his wife. And yet he had stood before her mother's fire and

said he was her husband. That she was his wife. She had birthed him
a fine son. She looked over again at Small Warrior. He was the only
thing which was real in her haze. Everything else was an illusion. A
lie.

Four years she had waited for him. Worked the land and kept the
stock and raised his son. Days and days she had walked alone to find
him, to stand beside him in battle. To bring him home. And now he
was home and she was not welcome inside the door.

What was now to become of her? What was now to be a life for Small
Warrior? He was not welcome in the village; he was not welcome in
his father's house. He could not stay at his grandmother's fire for the
rest of his days. She thought of the other mixed men she had seen at
the trading posts and forts of the whites. "Breeds," they were called,
and neither the whites nor the Seminoles accepted them. Often they
scratched out a meager existence at the hands of the whites, like their
mules or their dogs, dependent on the scraps which might be tossed
them. She would rather see Small Warrior dead than to endure such
shame. He had too much pride, too much courage, to be broken in that
manner.

And what if she brought him back to his grandmother's fire? Her
parents would not live forever. And even though they were respected
in the village, they could not protect him from the scorn of the other
young boys, young men who had been taught to disdain all things
white. He looked more like his father than like her, she realized, bowing
her head in despair. Poor little bat. Neither side would want him.

And nobody would want her, either. No man would take her to his
mother's fire now, even though she was still young. Not with the son
of a white man at her side.

She put her head on her arms and gazed into the darkness of the
woods. If she could only disappear. Take back the last five years and
change all that had happened. But she could not. And somehow she
could not make herself care about the future.

She wept again, tiredly. She loved him still, with what strength she
had left. He would be her husband until she died, no matter if he had
a dozen wives. She ached for his touch, even as she hated his heart.
The look in his eyes haunted her, and she realized that never again
would she see such a look from a man. Never again would she love
and be loved in that way. For the rest of her life, she would compare
every man, every love with Tom Craven.

She lay back down again, this time closer to Small Warrior, curling her body around his. He was all she had. All she might ever have. And soon enough, he would be gone from her as well.

The next morning, she rose stiff and sore and heavy with sorrow. She hated to see the sun come up. She hated to think what she would have to do now. Small Warrior woke and stretched, light on the ground and already eager to begin the day. Then he looked at her and his face fell. "We need to eat," he said quietly, unsure how to speak to her.

Her heart broke again when she saw how he was almost afraid of her. Afraid of her vast sorrow. "I know," she said.

"We have to get to grandmother's fire."

"I cannot," she murmured.

"Why not?"

She shook her head. "I cannot go there now. Not yet."

"But I'm hungry," he said softly. He did not whine.

She stood shakily, slowly, feeling separate from her body as though it belonged to a stranger. "We will go back to the cabin. We will get food for our journey. Then we will decide what to do and where we must go."

"I do not want to go back there," he said, glowering.

"Nor do I. But we must have food. We will leave there as soon as we get it."

They walked for a short while, and Not Black was surprised to see what a short distance she had come the night before. It seemed to her that she had gone many miles from Tom Craven, but in no time they were back in the dusty yard, gazing up at the porch. The wagon had been pulled round to the back. She saw the handsome horse out in the pasture. Smoke came from the cabin chimney. Now that she had come, she was unsure what to do.

But as she stood there, gazing up at the house in numb and weary confusion, the door opened and the white woman came out on the porch. She had her bonnet off now, and Not Black could see the shining nimbus of her hair, light-colored as Small Warrior's, wrapped round her head like the coils of a snail shell.

The woman raised her hand in welcome. "Hello," she called. "Will you come and sit?"

"Go and get some meal, some jerky, and four eggs," Not Black said to Small Warrior. "Wrap them in your shirt and come back to me here."

He nodded and scampered off.

Warily, Not Black approached the woman, went up the steps, and sat in the rocker chair next to her. It had been her chair for long enough that the seat had molded to her body. She wondered if she would ever sit in it again.

"Tom's out in the far field," the woman said softly. "He'll not be back for a bit. We can speak our minds, I 'spect, better with him gone."

Not Black nodded, her heart faint and beating fast. She felt such a heady mix of hatred and fascination for this woman. She was light-skinned, light-haired, blue-eyed, slender and soft, with nothing of the woods or the fields about her hands or her feet.

"You understand my talk?" she asked.

Not Black nodded.

"I won' waste time with pretty words," she said, her voice low and thick with emotion. "What Tom done was wrong, an' I say it out loud. He were wrong to wed you an' wrong to leave you. Wrong to wed me, an' not tell me 'bout you, an' wrong to send you off with that boy, but Tom is my husband, an' I mean to keep him." She looked at Not Black with a liquid eye. "He don' want you, gal."

Her voice was soft and sorrowful, and Not Black could do little but nod her head in agreement.

"But he do want that lil' woods colt," she said, a little more firmly. "An' he done enough wrong without makin' it worse. That's his boy, an' he should do right by him."

"He wants my son?" Not Black looked up, bewildered. She felt the bees begin to churn through her head once more.

"He does. It's his blood, after all, an' blood's more important than pride. He wants him, an' so do I."

"My son," Not Black repeated.

"You think on it some," the woman said. "We take the boy an' raise him proper. Give him a good home an' treat him like our own. When his pa is gone, this land an' this house will fall to him. I ain'—" She faltered here and looked at her hands. She took a deep breath and smiled at Not Black. "I ain' able to give him a chile."

"You want my son also?" Not Black could only repeat herself. Her head whirled in shock and bewilderment.

"I do. But only if you wan' to let him come to us. Tom done wrong to you. I ain' gonna do a bigger wrong to you now."

Not Black sat and stared at the ground. She could not fathom how the birds could keep making their distant noise, the breeze could keep making the sunflowers wave their huge heads. Why the earth did not stop to listen and weep, she could not comprehend. "Small Warrior is my son," she said slowly.

"Of course he is, an' if you don' wish to think on this, I'll not say another word. I jus' wanted you to know that—" The woman reached out and touched her shoulder. "I jus' wanted you to know that I would welcome him an' raise him with love, if you want him to stay here. An' I know Tom would be a good pa to him."

"How you know this?" Not Black asked bitterly. "You do not know Tom Craven."

"I do know him," the woman said firmly. "I know he's a good man, good as most. An' he wants the boy for his own. He said so."

Just then, Small Warrior came hurrying around the corner with his shirt full of eggs.

"Look at him," the woman murmured. "The image of his pa. Goin' to be a handful."

"If I do this thing," Not Black said quietly, "I come back to see him?"

"Of course," the woman nodded. "Anytime you want to."

She was so sure of herself, Not Black saw then. So sure that even if Not Black came to her fire and went away again often, her husband would never choose the squaw over her. She grimaced in pain. And she was likely right enough. She had seen the pain and detachment in Tom Craven's eyes. He did not wish her to be near him. It made him feel weak and guilty when he saw her.

"I will ask Small Warrior," she said. "He can speak for his own heart."

The woman nodded. "Want I should go inside?"

"Yes," Not Black whispered. "Leave us."

The woman rose, smiling gently at the boy, who watched her warily. Once she was inside, he said, "I have the food, Mother." He showed her his bulging pockets. "Let us go from here." He had not spoken a word of English since they set foot on his father's property.

She rose off the rocking chair and walked slowly down the steps, feeling as though she were watching herself move from a very high place. She went to him and reached to touch his face. He flinched slightly away from her, and his eyes were narrow with suspicion.

"What did the white woman say to you?" he asked.

"She said that your father wants you to stay here with them for a while." Some far, aloof part of her mind wondered how she could say it so calmly.

"Well and I will not," he said shortly. "Come, Mother. It is going to be dark before we reach the river—"

"I wish you to stay here," she said. "Only for a time. I will be back for you soon."

"No!" he said, taking her arm. "I will not stay."

"Your father has many things he can teach you, my son," she said gently. "Much that is yours by right of blood. If you leave, you will lose all those things. I am not welcome here, but you are. You can stay." She smiled at him, an achingly gentle smile. "I wish you to stay."

He listened to her words and considered them, looking now at the ground. "Where is my father, if he wants me to stay?"

"He is in the fields. He will return soon. The woman will give you whatever you want—"

"She wants me to stay as well?"

Not Black nodded. "She told me so."

"And you will come back for me soon?"

She could see that the longing to stay where he had enjoyed so many happy days was strong in him. He, too, knew that he could not go back to the village and hope to find such contentment. But his loyalty to her fought his desire to stay.

"I will come back for you soon."

He wavered, looking first at the house, then at her. "I will stay, then," he said finally, reluctantly. "If that is what you want." He frowned. "But not for the white woman. For my father and for you."

She hugged him hard, once, and then let him go. "I will see you before the moon changes again," she said. And she turned and left him there in the yard.

"Mother!" he called after her. "You forgot the eggs!"

She smiled and waved. "You eat them for me," she said. She turned away, unable to keep her mouth from twisting in pain a moment longer. "My son."

When she reached a place on the road where she could no longer be seen, she circled back to the yard and watched from the bush where she had watched Tom Craven long ago. The view had not changed, yet her eyes seemed a hundred years older, as she watched the white woman take her son into the cabin, speaking happily to him and touching him on the shoulder as though she had a claim to his flesh.

Small Warrior went into the cabin easily, as though it had belonged to him forever. As of course, it had. He had few memories of having lived any other place, except for the short time he sojourned at his grandmother's fire. To him, the cabin was his own. By right, by blood, and by choice.

She waited, without the will or strength to make herself depart, until she heard Tom Craven's horse coming down the road. She watched as he took the horse to the stable, watched and waited until he came up the steps and opened the door. The woman met him at the door, gesturing with explanations that she could not hear to Small Warrior, who came to the door to greet him. Tom Craven put out his hand to her son in the manner of white men. Her spine tingled when Small Warrior put his small hand in the large hand of his father and the three of them went inside and shut the door.

Not Black stayed hidden until the darkness came to the cabin, enshrouding it in purple shadows. She stayed hidden until the gas lamps within the cabin were lit in the windows, and she could see dim shapes moving within, one tall, one shorter, one smaller still. Then, finally, she crept away into the woods to find a place where she could curl against a warm, living piece of wood and rest her exhausted heart.

Not Black slept fitfully through the night, and when she awoke to the sounds of the forest, she felt as weary as when she had laid herself down. To the very depths of her bones, she was tired. She stretched out on the ground, faceup to the canopy of the trees, and watched the sun come through the leaves. The breeze moved the uppermost branches, and the bottom leaves moved not at all in the dim shadows of the forest below. That was how she felt. As though she lived beneath the surface of life, as though all of life's currents were moving above her, just beyond her, and she was to stay always untouched by them. It seemed to her that her future was as dark and dank and musty as the inside of an alligator hole.

She tried to remember how she had felt, the simple joy she had experienced, when she was a girl. Before she knew the touch of a man's hand and the thrill of his body on hers. She could not even recall how she had been before Tom Craven. The aching emptiness in her belly, in her heart, and the crowded turmoil of her mind made her feel that she might never rise up off the earth again.

She moaned softly aloud when she thought of the white woman's touch on Tom Craven. She closed her eyes. Slow tears slid down her cheeks when she thought of her touch on Small Warrior. Now the white woman had taken everything from her. Just like her grandmother said that they did. She felt a cringe of disgust wrench her stomach. In fact, she had given everything away, weakly, with open hands. Had given Tom Craven to her, had given her own flesh and blood over to her hands. She had never felt more helpless, never hated herself more than at this moment.

And yet she could see nothing else to do. No other choice.

I will go back to the fire of my mother, she told herself. I will tell my mother and father what has happened and my father will kill him. When she tried to imagine her father, the wise, gentle, and aged Standing Horse, as he lifted his musket to kill Tom Craven, she closed her eyes again against such a degraded image. Her mother would feel pity for her. Her father would feel anger and pity, but when it was all over, there would be nothing they could do. Nothing anyone could do. Tom Craven had never intended to marry her. Never intended to make her his wife. He wanted only to please himself in the moment, to have her when he wanted her and then discard her when he no longer found her pleasing. And he had done exactly that.

And now, he had her son as well as her pride.

She knew then, in that moment, that she could not go back to her village. There was nothing for her there. The people would look at her always with disgust and pity. She would be a constant reminder to them of what they had lost, what had been taken from them by the white men. Her mother would endure the scorn for her sake; her father would defend her as he could, but their days would evermore be ones of shame and regret, if she returned. She would live as an invisible person all the days of her life in the village. And so would her son.

Her stomach was as numb as the rest of her body. She did not feel hungry or thirsty. But she realized that she had eaten nothing for almost a day. She rose wearily to her feet, feeling almost sick with weakness. She began to walk without thought of where she might go. She knew she needed food and water, but she could not seem to make herself care about those needs. She walked away from the direction of the village, to the north, with the vague idea that she might come upon an encampment of her own people, or a road, or perhaps a tree with fruit. She had no real destination nor plan, but she knew she must go somewhere so long as she could keep moving.

She walked and wandered, occasionally picking up something from the trail to eat, some bit of green or a berry, stopping to drink at whatever water she found, not caring if it were clean or clear-running. She tired often and sat staring at the ground, with no thought of what she should do next. Finally, she sickened of walking and slept again, this time into the night. The next morning, she rose and walked again, without any idea where she was headed.

After two days, she found herself back at the boundary of Tom Craven's land. She knew the fence line well; and she was vaguely surprised that she had somehow turned her feet in this direction without knowing she had done so. She had been walking so long, it seemed she must have gone a longer distance. But no, she was right back where she had started. It was as though no matter what she wanted or planned, she always ended up back here.

She walked aimlessly along the fence, wondering what she should do, and when she heard the sound of a wagon approaching, she melted back without thought into the brush. It was Tom Craven's wagon, coming down the pathway to the road. As it drew nearer, she could see that the woman sat next to Tom and on the other side of his father, Small Warrior sat close to his shoulder.

The boy looked excited and proud, up high on the wagon seat, and as they passed, Tom Craven said, "You want to hold the reins, son?"

"Yes, Father!" Small Warrior said eagerly, taking the leather straps from his hand. "I will drive us all the way to town!"

The white woman laughed softly, looking over at the boy with affection, squeezing the man's arm with love. The three of them looked like any family off for a journey together, prosperous and content and harmonious. Small Warrior's mouth moved around the English words well, and the clothes he had on his body were ones she had never seen before. Only two days away from him, and he was already the son of a white man.

She almost stepped out behind their passing wheels and called to them to stop. But she did not. They passed and were gone before she could think what she should do. She stood out in the road and watched them disappear around the bend of the road, the dust settling back as though it had never been disturbed. The fields were silent; the air was still. She turned and walked back toward the cabin, thinking at least she should eat some of Tom Craven's food.

She stepped up to the porch and stopped, struck by how different the place felt to her now. She was no longer welcome here. She was a stranger. A house she had lived in and cared for all these seasons now belonged to another woman. As did the man who slept inside. She opened the door gingerly, half-expecting it to refuse to open to her touch. She went inside and looked around slowly.

Many things had been moved. New belongings of the woman were about: a shawl thrown over the back of a chair, a little framed picture of two old people on the table, different pans hanging over the big black stove. Tom Craven's clothes were on pegs hanging about the cabin. She went to one of his shirts and put her face into the soft cloth. It smelled of him so profoundly that she began to weep once more. She stumbled about the cabin, her eyes filling at every new discovery.

There, in the corner, was the bed where Small Warrior slept. He had a fresh blanket, a small pillow stuffed with soft husks, and a carved piece of wood in the shape of a bird lay on the little table beside him. Tom Craven had carved that for him, she guessed. She took it up in her hand and marveled at its smoothness, setting it down again in the same exact place so it would not be disturbed.

On the end of the bed was the shirt he had worn when she saw him last, a shirt she had made him herself two seasons before. It scarcely fit him anymore, but he had liked it too much to discard it. She held it to her nose and smelled the boy smell of her son, smelled his hair and his skin, the jointed places in his body where his odors were most distinctly his own, male and young and healthy.

Suddenly the cabin seemed unbearable to her, and she stumbled out the door, her eyes blind with tears. She ran across the yard and down the path, finally stopping against a tree. There, she put the shirt to her face and pushed it into her mouth, wailing aloud. She heard herself making the sounds she had made when she had labored to birth him. Some part of her mind was surprised that she had any tears left. As if they were and always would be at the ready. As though she might never stop weeping again.

She turned with the shirt in her hand and ran away from the cabin. She stopped at the well and stared at it for a long moment, picturing its dark vastness into the earth. Then she ran toward the woods. She could not say good-bye to her son, not when she recalled how bitter it had been the last time. She knew that she could not go back to the cabin again.

When she could no longer run, she walked quickly. When she was then too tired to walk quickly, she slowed, but she kept on walking with a single-minded determination which she had not known before. She kept going until she reached the river. It was dark now, and her way was harder to find. Finally discovering the place where she had met her mother and father with Small Warrior so many times before, she sat down on a rock and let the weariness seep back into her bones. Almost did that numbness feel like an old, comforting friend now, so well did she know it.

She felt herself moving to a different place in her mind. It was a deep peace which came over her now, a readiness that she had never felt before. She was short of breath, as though she had been running for days and days, but she was more sure than she had been since she could remember.

She rose off her rock and stepped into the water. Walking into the deepest current, she let the river take her off her feet until she was floating on her back, looking up at the stars in the black night. The sounds of the river and the forest were quiet around her, and she was glad she could see the stars, so vast and numerous, stretched across the places where only the gods could walk.

She thought, when a person is dying, the path they walk narrows and there is room, finally, for only them. She was not distracted by any thoughts of her family, of Tom Craven, even of her son. She felt that for the first time in her life, she could truly see her life and all that had occurred clearly, in a way that it could not be seen before. This was such a great gift from the Maker of Breath, that she shivered all over in an almost-ecstasy at the grasping of it.

She let the river take her, let the water roll over her deep and slow and gentle, let her skirts fill with it, let her head slide under, and she knew then only the black silence of the end of her pain.

Part Three

~ ~ ~ ~ ~ ~ ~ ~ ~ ~ ~ ~

1891—1913

"That ol' experience is one hard taskmaster. She always gives the test first, an' then the lesson after."

(Sam Craven)

~ ~ ~ ~ ~ ~ ~ ~ ~ ~ ~ ~

*E*ven as his mother's life was ending, Small Warrior's life was beginning
anew. His father called him Sam, for he said it sounded American enough.
For Sam, it was an easy change to make. Other changes were not so easy, but
each one mantled his shoulders for a time like an ill-fitting coat and then
gradually became something so familiar that he no longer felt the weight.

As endings often do, Not Black's death made tumultuous waves in the lives
of those who loved her yet mattered not at all in the larger currents of her
people. Close to the place where she chose to end her life, near the White Sulphur
Springs on the Suwannee, travelers soon came to sample the curative powers
of the waters. The war had left many in need of such powers, and wonderful
tales were told of crippled men arriving on stretchers and crutches at the baths
built over the springs and, after drinking this water for weeks, leaving in perfect
health. The owners of the bathhouses liked to tell the legend of the beautiful
Indian princess who had ruled over the tribe in the swamp named "Su-Wanee."

Of course by then there were few Seminoles left in the region to affirm or
deny the legend, since most had pushed south into the Everglades, to get far
from the white travelers, the settlers, and the fences which were crowding harder
and farther into their lands each year.

Most of the swampers who pushed into the central Florida region were the
last remnants of Georgia's pioneers, the Crackers. Like the hillbillies of the
Appalachians and the Tar Heels of the Carolinas, they were mostly of Scotch-
Irish, English, Welsh, or German ancestry, blessed with strong backs and
stubborn spirits. Isolated from the mainstream of America, their speech, folklore,
religion, and habits were soon accommodated to the ageless rhythms of the
swamp and its creatures.

They named the hammocks and homesteads Billy's Island, Cowhouse Island, Bugaboo Island, and Black Jack Island. They called the rivers "dark meanders," for the cypress-blackened waters were here, then there, then seemed to disappear under the bogs only to reappear someplace else a mile away. Even the Suwannee, the largest river in the region, had a way of making its own path and taking its own time. The settlers had to know these rivers, though, and cross them, and they did so, often traveling more than twenty miles in one direction to the nearest small town. Laden with furs, wild duck, turpentine, and cane syrup, they came back home with powder and shot, perhaps some yard goods for the wife, and maybe a barrel of flour. But always the powder and shot, for even at the turn of the century, bears roamed freely through the forests and along the rivers, and a man who did not respect the swamp could not expect to live there long.

1891

Sam Craven stepped out onto the porch and called for his two boys in a holler which could be heard all the way to the swamp and back. Which was a good thing, since that's where the boys were most likely rambling again. "How long since you seen 'em?" he called inside to his wife.

May Craven stepped outside, wiping her hands on her apron. "Not since they got their bellies full of biscuit this mornin'," she chuckled, patting her husband's arm. "If you want to keep them nigh, best cut back on their rations."

"Or get myself a bigger switch." He grinned ruefully. "Lem'd stay put, but Gad's got a wayward foot an' a honey tongue to match."

"Like his pa," May agreed.

Mattie Craven, their youngest, and their only daughter, came out on the porch then, letting the door slam with her usual high energy. "I done the sweepin', Ma," she said pertly. "I'll go fetch Gad for you—"

"No, ma'am," Sam said, swooping her up next to his leg. The child only came to his waist, small and slender as her mother with the high brow of the Cravens and the small nose of the Chesser clan. Mattie was likely the only beauty they'd sow, and Sam had been partial to Mattie since the first time she took hold of his thumb with her tiny fist and would not let go. "Then we got all three gone 'til the hooty-owls call." He threw back his head and barreled out his chest once more, letting loose with a holler that was half-yodel, half–boar bellow.

Not a man in the swamp had the same holler, and it was generally considered the best form of communication across miles of tangled water. Each one was unique; a measured cadence of alternating head tones and chest tones, and each man prided himself on how far his holler would carry. Whether a signal to his family that he was coming home or a sheer spontaneous expression of exuberance, the swamp holler could be heard for several miles, bouncing off the still waters in all directions.

"Guess I'm gonna have to switch them boys again—" Sam started to say, when Lem and Gad came bursting through the brush to the far side of the homestead, each one running like a bear chased them home.

"We was on our way, Pa!" Gad shouted as soon as he saw his family gathered on the porch. "We was comin' anyways!"

"We's comin', Pa!" Lem called after him, his shorter legs pumping to pass Gad if he could.

"Pa's gonna get his switch!" Mattie called gleefully to her brothers. "I done all my chores a'ready, an' Pa's mad as a treed coon!"

"That's enough, sister," May said, shooing her daughter inside. "You don' need to plague your brothers; your pa can do that jus' fine all by himself." Mattie skipped inside giggling, just ahead of her mother's mock swat.

At the mention of the word "switch" Lem stopped dead in his tracks, goggled at his brother with glaring round eyes, and hollered out, "Gad said—!" His father had only switched him once or twice in his life, but it seemed to him that the memory was powerful enough to suspend his breath in his body at the mere thought of a repetition.

"Don' you be givin' him up so easy," Sam growled at his youngest. "He's the only brother you got, even if he is a rascal."

"Pa, I ain' no rascal," Gad said now as he clambered up on the porch, deeply wounded. "I come the first time I heard you holler!"

"Yes, an' if those turp barrels could holler, they'd a tole' you don' go runnin' off in the first place." Sam gathered his two sons up and led them off in the direction of the tall pine forest where his turpentine still sat waiting.

Like many farmers in the swamps, Sam had set his house close enough to stands of piney woods to cup for turpentine, as valuable a commodity as cane syrup or pelts. The process of collection was simple enough, and once the forest was cupped, it was a steady source of income, with a minimum of labor. Sam had selected his trees a few years ago and chopped away a section of bark and sapwood about a foot in length on each he chose. Then he took his axe, the one with the curved blade and the V-shaped grooves, and drove a small, thin piece of tin into the groove. This was his turpentine spout. The liquid sap or resin ran from the tree wound into a small clay pot.

It took days for one of these pots or cups to fill with sap, but once they were full, they were emptied into barrels standing about in the woods, and the barrels were then hauled to his still on his wagon. Sam cooked the barrels of sap until they yielded turpentine and the residue or rosin which was cooked still more to thicken. He always got the dark red color rosin, a good grade, and this he sold at the trade store in Fort Brooke to be made into soap, ships' supplies, and other necessaries.

The barrels got heavy as they filled, and though the boys were of little help now, he expected them to take over the still in time.

As they hiked the trail to the still Lem asked, "You goin' to trade tomorrow, Pa?"

"Likely." Sam stopped and peered up toward the top of a tall pine, calculating the height of the next cup he'd place.

"I got near twenty pelts, Pa," Gad said proudly. "I 'spect to be a man with full pockets come Sunday."

"You do, eh?" Sam grinned. "What you gonna do with all that cash money?"

"Buy me a mouth organ!" Gad said. "Like ol' Grady had at meetin', last. Did you hear him play, Pa?"

"I did," Sam nodded. "Right pretty, if you like geese a'squawkin' in your ear."

"Weren't neither no geese squawkin'!" Gad said indignantly. "An' he ain' even no good at it. I aim to be better."

"Well, that's a good aim," Sam said mildly.

They were at the first tree now, and Lem studiously peered into the clay pot that rested under the dripping spout. "Near full up," he said solemnly. "We got here jus' in time."

"Pa, I wanna go with you tomorrow," Gad said bravely.

"We done had this discussion," Sam said. "You need to stay home an' look after your ma whilst I'm gone."

"Pa, I need to sell my pelts, an' get my mouth organ!"

"And what about your ma, then?" Sam asked him, as they walked to the next pot.

Lem had scampered on ahead. "This one's full up, too!"

"Mama an' Lem can make out for three days," Gad said.

"Did you ask your ma's leave, son?"

"Nossir," Gad mumbled.

"Seems to me she might like to have a say-so, seein' as she'll be the one left with all the work to do."

Gad thought about that while they gathered the dozen pots and poured them into the larger buckets they were carrying. Lem was now of an age where he could carry a bucket all by himself; Gad carried two, and Sam managed to carry four on a pole across his shoulders. Finally they reached the last tree, poured out the precious sap into the last bucket, and headed toward the still.

"We could all go 'long with you," he finally said quietly as his father carefully unloaded the pole and the buckets from his shoulders. "We ain' been in such a long while—"

"Pa!" Lem shouted in glee. "I wanna go to town, too!"

Sam ruffled his youngest son's hair roughly. "Well now, ain' that a surprise. An' I suppose Mattie'll clamor an' carry on if she don't get to go—"

"Let's all go, Pa," Gad said, trying to seem mature and above the tumult created by his little brother. "Seems like a good idear to me."

"Since it were yours in the first place." Sam poured the buckets into the still, directing his boys to take the cover over and scrape it clean of dead insects and their debris, lest they fall back into the rosin. When they were all finished for this week, he took his measuring stick and put it to the bottom of the still barrel. "Needs another two feet or so," he murmured to the boys. "Likely, two more weeks, an' we'll be ready to cook."

Gad knew enough to be quiet and wait for his father to speak when he was ready. Lem, on the other hand, could not be still. He kept jumping up and down and trying to peer into his father's face, though he knew from his brother's example not to talk until his father decided to open up the discussion again.

Finally Sam turned for home, and as they walked, Lem bounced up and then back again, making three steps for every one of Gad's. After a torturous silence, Sam allowed, "Well, I guess a trip to town cain' hurt none. That is, if your ma says so."

Lem whooped in glee, hopped up and down like a crane, and bumped Gad nearly off the trail in his excitement. Gad shoved him good-naturedly and said, "Oh, she'll go 'long, Pa. I'll talk her into it."

"You will, eh?" Sam grinned wryly. "Well, maybe one a' these days, you'll let me in on your secret. Jus' in case I got to talk her into somethin' myself sometime."

"Ain' no secret," Gad said seriously. "Mama's like mos' women, I guess. They like to be sweet-talked all polite-like. An' it helps if you give them hugs while you're a-doin' it."

"Thanks," Sam said dryly. "I'll keep that in mind."

"You're mos' welcome," Gad replied. "Now, Mattie, she ain' woman enough for it to work yet, you got to give her a few more years—"

Sam cocked an appraising eye at his eldest. "I swan, boy, you gonna be dangerous when you get your full growth."

Gad grinned up at him. " 'Specially when I get that mouth organ, Pa. I gonna be hell to beat!"

Sam cuffed him on the shoulder. "You gonna think hell to beat if your ma hears you blaspheme."

"Yessir," Gad said, taking off in a fast dart to catch up with Lem. He threw back over his shoulder, "Ol' Grady gonna roll over belly-up when he hears me whomp that thing!"

The old oxen pulled the wagon slowly but surely through the almost-road which led to the settlement well north of the Craven homestead, the town which was Fort Brooke, just east of Tampa. Sam rarely went to Tampa, for the trip was so many days. Three days in travel each way and six days from the stock was enough, he said, and no matter how much Gad might hint that Tampa would surely be the place for the best mouth organs, he would not budge. Fort Brooke would have to do.

Mattie was happy to go anyplace, and May was happy not to go at all. But regardless, all five of them were packed inside the wagon along with last season's rosin, several barrels of cane syrup, a pack of pelts, a brace of gator hides, and six of May's prize laying hens, on their way to the largest settlement within three days' ride.

Fort Brooke was an old army post which had been cleared of slash pines and planted to cane. It had a sawmill, a foundry, a machine shop, about ten houses, three stores, a saloon, and a boardinghouse. It was a clearing in the wilderness wrested with the same determination which made men throw a railroad clear across the continent to link the seas. Sam had only taken his family two other times to Fort Brooke, and so the excitement in the wagon, at least from the three youngest members of the Craven clan, fair simmered above the heat of the road and pushed ahead of them like the clamor of hounds.

The day was clear and cool, with much of the oppressive summer heat already diminished. The tall pines and oaks which lined the road, most of them heavily laden with gray Spanish moss, hung down and brushed close to the sides of the wagon as they rode along. A thousand birdsongs announced their coming, and squirrels scolded them from the lower branches. Wild orchids waved from sheltered steeples of heavy limbs, and insects droned over their heads.

"Good day for it," Sam said to May, leaning against her shoulder as he held the harness. Caleb, the ox which had been on the homestead since he was no taller than Sam's biggest hound, would plod down the road without any shake of the reins, but Sam was not the sort of man to simply tie them off.

May smiled at him and leaned heavily into his arm. "They should be all in; they ain' slept a wink all night."

He glanced back to the rear of the wagon. Mattie was droning some lullaby to her old patchwork doll, Gad was counting his pelts and smoothing them for the hundredth time, and Lem was leaning out with a stick and wacking at the moss as they passed. "They got time to catch up now. Be more'n six hours, I reckon, 'fore we set up for the night."

She reached back and straightened the crate where her laying hens rode, and they bickered and clucked at the sight of her hand. "Gad told Mattie that she owed him a heap of thanks. Said the only reason she got to go along was that he wooed you to the idear." She rolled her eyes at her husband. "Mattie whopped him an' told him that she was gonna ask you to leave him home to hoe the melons, said he hadn't done a lick of work for a month a' Sundays."

"Did he whop her back?" Sam asked, a little sharp.

"No, no," she soothed him. "An' I laid into Mattie good. Tole' her to keep her hands to herself—"

" 'Tis her mouth'll get her retribution." Sam grinned down at his wife, noticing with pleasure the way the dappled sunlight shone on her chestnut hair. She wore it down on her shoulders, lying loose over her one "town dress." It was a pleasure to see it long and lovely in daylight for a change. "Glad you saw fit to come along."

"Thankee for askin' me, sir." She smiled coyly up at him.

"Pa, tell Lem to stop whackin' moss all over me!" Mattie hollered to the front of the wagon. "He gots dirt all over Miss Amanda!" She held the patchwork doll up for her father to see with an injured air.

"Lem, if Mattie hollers again, I'll come back there an' see to you first," May called back mildly. "An' Mattie, you second."

The two of them muttered and hissed quietly to each other, but the shouting ceased at least. A trio of white-tailed deer bounded up from the nearby brush and raced across the road directly before them, causing old Caleb to pause in his stride and snort with surprise.

"Pa, hand me my rifle!" Gad called. "Next one we see, I'll drop him!"

"Not over the heads of your ma an' sister, boy," Sam called back. "You got plenty o' pelts. Save some for the next trip."

The road faded and fell away, then meandered back into existence again, as the ox plodded on, pulling the wagon over ruts and across swags and sways in the earth. Often, Sam had to get down and drag logs away from the trail that they might pass, with both boys making a mighty heave and huff of help. Mattie drifted in and out of slumber, and even May, feeling lazy from the heat and the unaccustomed rocking of the wagon and the ease of having nothing to do, dozed alongside him. Sam realized that he felt completely happy for hours at a time, with his children near and comfortable, his ox taking him to market with an assured profit, and his wife nestled close by his arm.

Sam gazed down at May as she dozed, noticing how pretty she looked under her bonnet, with the shadows passing slowly over her features. She had always been a slender woman, small and quick in her movements; a waterbug, he used to call her when he courted her. She spoke quickly, moved her hands in the air to emphasize her words, and her eyes sparkled as bright as a young girl's even after three children and a dozen years married.

They had met at a frolic on the Withlacoochee River, to the south of Tom Craven's land. It was late fall, when the hog-killings and cane grinding brought the folks together, and the square dances and fiddling were events families looked forward to all the rest of the year. His father and mother, Tom and Annie Craven, had decided this year to make the trip to visit and trade, and they stood to one side watching the young people dance, as they usually did, as though they had forgotten what it must have been to be young, if they ever knew. But when Sam circled the square with May on his arm, he caught his father's eye and saw him wink.

The old man rarely showed much enthusiasm in those days, for he was old at forty and would be ancient at sixty. His father's rare sparkle and wink had startled Sam enough to cause him to take a second look at the gal on his arm. Once he looked close, he never wanted to look away again, and May Chesser captured his attention for the rest of that evening.

That had been the best decision of his life. When they married a year later, moving onto forty acres which Oliver Chesser gave his daughter as a wedding present, Sam Craven counted himself the luckiest man in the state. Now he knew that what had been lighthearted gaiety and a ready smile in a fair girl had mellowed into a rare quality of spirit in May as a mature and lovely woman. She was well past thirty now, but she still had a kind of innocence about the human condition which rarely faltered and always seemed capable of regeneration. She never lost her faith in possibilities.

Gad came along when they were married only a year, and Lem two winters later. Mattie arrived a year later, and it was all the sweeter for the waiting. Sam knew that May had ached for a girl-child, instinctively understanding that boys would always be more his than her own, but she never gave a hint that she was impatient with God for the lack of a daughter. When Mattie came to them, May shone all the brighter, knowing now that she must be an example to the girl in how a woman should be. And though they never spoke of it, Sam knew that Mattie had a piece of May's heart which no one would ever claim, no not even himself.

And, of course, Mattie was just like her mother, with a shine to her that had been apparent even when she was just a sprout. Folks at meeting would bend down and speak to her, reaching out to touch her cheek or pat her head in a way they seldom did more ordinary children. It wasn't just that she was perfectly made, with round pink cheeks, bright blue eyes, and a petal mouth. Mattie shone a foot round her in all directions, sending her sparkle out to the world with an energy which was as palpable as sunlight. People just wanted to get close to that warmth, and when Sam asked May, "Did you shine like that when you were that young?" she only laughed and shook her head. "That's Mattie's own, sweetheart. She were born with it."

"No," he said then, kissing her. "She's like her mama, for truth. She jus' turned up the heat a bit on the fire you put in her."

They camped two nights on the trail, the miles slowly trundled by them, and finally, as they began to get closer to the trading settlement of Fort Brooke, they began to see more and more small cabins, farms, and fenced lands. The swamp ebbed back away from the road, as though it sensed that it had lost some power, and the road became wider. Now they sometimes passed folks walking, and each one waved and hailed the Craven wagon. May took great pleasure in acknowledging the waves and hallos, and she leaned back to Mattie often, telling her who belonged to which homestead and who was kin to whom.

There was a small country inn at the center of the trading settlement, less an inn than a simple cabin with three rooms and a central cooking area. The stable to the rear was ample for the ox and a few more horses besides, however, and so it was the central gathering place for any sojourners who had no kin at Fort Brooke who might offer a bed.

By the time they reached the inn and unhitched the ox, it was dusk. May and Mattie took their provisions from the barrels and baskets packed in the back of the wagon, and by the time Sam came back from the stable with Caleb bedded down for the night, supper was almost ready. Mattie had picked some wildflowers and arranged them in a water jug on the rickety pine table, and they blessed the food quickly, for already they heard another team and wagon arriving outside.

"There ain' enough for more folks," Gad said grumpily.

"Likely, they got their own," May said cheerfully. "But if they ain', we can spare a bit."

Sam set down his fork and rose to open the door with a welcome to the newcomers, and Lem and Mattie peered around him to see who had arrived. Two men stood there, a farmer and his son by the looks of them, and with a flurry of welcomes and introductions all round, they pulled up two more seats at the table. "We can pay, ma'am," Henry Tabbs said to May politely. "We don' hold with takin' somethin' for nothin'."

"No need, sir," May said cordially. "We can spare you supper an' welcome. If you plan to be here tomorrow, well you can add to the pot then."

"We will, an' thankee," his son, Hamp Tabbs said, grinning as he helped himself to a plate of squirrel biscuits.

Squirrel biscuits were just about Gad's favorite, and he glowered at Hamp Tabbs as much as he dared.

"Gad, if you had a-plenty," his mother said mildly, "go on out an' bring in the beddin'."

"Yessum," he said reluctantly.

Lem leaped from his chair after his brother, eager to stare at the newcomer's wagon and horse, which were still hitched up at the rail.

Once outside, Gad appraised the rig carefully, giving Lem the full benefit of his experienced eye. "They ain' come a far piece," he said solemnly. "That horse ain' gonna get them through the swamp. No doubt, they come from the north, likely Fort Dade, where it ain' so thick."

"You think so?" Lem asked, amazed.

"I reckon," Gad said. " 'Course, horse like that, not much good for nothin' but light-foot travel. A plow'd nigh kill him. Likely, bust his heart wide open if he was to try—"

Lem's eyes goggled wider at the vision Gad presented, of that beautiful roan horse splattered with his own heart's blood. The horse grazed quietly at what grass he could reach, twitching his ears back to catch Gad's words as though in approbation.

The boys rounded the inn and went to unload the wagon. As they came close to the stable, a low form swooped close to their heads, making Lem jump and cry out in alarm.

"Jus' a bat," Gad said with some disdain. "You jump like a girl."

"Well, it's bigger than those we got to home!"

"An' more evil, too, I reckon," Gad said. "I hear tell the varmints in some parts of the swamp ain' never been seen by human eyes. Wolves as big as cows, some of them, an' the gators near big as wagons. Bats like herons, that suck a man's blood while he sleeps."

"Ain' true!" Lem protested, taking a swipe at his brother's arm hopefully. Lem was not a timorous boy, but somehow he could never be quite as brave around Gad as he wished to be.

" 'Tis," Gad replied mildly. "I heard tell a man went into the swamp, lookin' for gators, an' he fell into a quicksand, an' a'fore he could even think a' freein' hisself, a bat came long an' took off his head. They found the wing tracks in the mud. Said that bat had to be more'n ten feet acrost."

Lem groaned softly and moved closer to his brother. It was dark now, and the shadows around the unfamiliar buildings loomed from all sides. When they reached the stable, Lem scuttled inside, close to the hanging lantern, and they climbed up into the wagon, throwing down the bedding into the clean straw next to one of the stalls. Their ox lowed to them softly in familial recognition, and Lem was instantly calmed.

"I'm gonna ask Pa 'bout that bat," he said staunchly.

"Aw, Pa don' know everythin'," Gad shrugged.

"Does so!" Lem stared at his brother, aghast. That sort of blasphemy unsettled the younger boy, as though he had heard his mother curse the Lord.

"Does not," Gad said. "Take up them coverlets an' don' let 'em drag on the ground." They started walking back toward the inn. "Once I was huntin' with Pa, long time ago, when you was just a pint, an' we was comin' acrost a lake, right about at the widest part, an' a tremendous big bear walked in an' stepped in the lake about a couple a' hundred yards from us. The gators was so thick, you could a' walked acrost their heads. I saw one ol' gator, must a' been fifteen feet if he was a foot, an' he rose up in the water with a trout in his mouth, about a ten-pounder, had him crossways in his mouth. An' he just smashed that trout agin another gator's head, an' jammed him in his mouth headfirst, an' swallowed him down. There was that many gators, an' they was all big an' feedin' good. Well, that ol' bear weren't studyin' on no gators, an' he just jumped right in the water an' started swimmin' to the other side. An' Pa, he said, 'That'll be one less bear in the swamp right now. He is going to get caught.' An' a couple a' gators started out after him, but that ol' bear, he jus' rared right up in the water, slammed down both paws right down on the gator's head, an' kept on swimmin'. He went through safe an' walked out on the other side. He was a great big bear, a big black feller. An' Pa was wrong. Ain' the only time, neither."

Lem snorted with disdain. "That ain' no-count. Pa's right when it matters."

"We'll see," Gad said mysteriously.

They were back at the inn then, and they went inside to the light and the warmth, handing over the bedding to their mother. Sam was engrossed in conversation with the newcomers, the men gathered in close by the fire. Mattie was being hustled off to bed by their mother, and to avoid the same fate, the two boys came up close to their father's side and hunkered down to listen.

"They got near fifty men workin'," Henry Tabbs was telling his father. "Got 'em diggin' canals through the swamp, near twenty feet wide, I hear. Payin' good money for the work, mind you, an' they still reckon to make a fortune, sellin' the water to folks in Jacksonville. They'll pay plenty, they say, our ol' Dark Meander, that good Suwannee river water—"

"Who's doing the payin'?" their father asked calmly.

"Outfit out of Jacksonville, I think. Name's Captain Harry Jackson. Got 'em workin' round the clock, to hear tell it."

"How they get the land?"

"State of Georgia sold it to them! Got a whole passel of money men together, paid 'em more'n twenty-six cents an acre, I hear tell, for almost four hundred miles of swamp. They're goin' to drain it dry an' send it to the folks who can use all this water. God knows"—he laughed—"we got plenty to share!"

"Gonna cut the timber, too." Hamp Tabbs spoke up quietly. "Float the cypress to the coast, once they get the canals dug. But the water's the big thing, they say."

Gad piped up, "Pa, you gonna go an' see this Captain fella?"

Lem was amazed at his boldness. He stared at his brother as though he had never seen him before.

His father looked down at the two boys as though he had only just noticed them. "Time for you boys to go to bed," he said, a little gruffly. "May?"

Their mother appeared with a smile and a firm hand on each son's shoulder. "Come along, boys. Ain' you all in? Such a day we had—" and she led them off to join Mattie on the cots in the open-timbered attic above the living area of the cabin. Lem and Gad put up a token protest, but they knew from the set of their father's face that in his mind, they were already absent from the room.

Gad stayed awake as long as he could, tucked into the rough shuck cot. He listened while the rise and fall of the men's voices came up to the rafters like the warmth from the fire. And then he finally fell asleep, dreaming of deep, black canals threading through the swamp and men, swarms of men like worker ants, clambering all over the dark, wet earth and moving it where they willed it to go.

Sometime in the night, the decision was made, and by breakfast the next morning, Sam and May presented a united front to their children.

"I reckon I'm gonna join that crew that's fixin' to turn the Suwannee to Jacksonville," Sam announced in a calm voice over his biscuits and coffee.

"Papa!" Mattie groaned dramatically. "How long you reckon to be gone?"

Gad listened silently, every bit of his mind alert to his father's answer.

"Maybe not so long," her father said. "Cain' truly tell 'til I get there an' see. But leastwhys, likely a month or two. Whilst I'm gone, I need to know that your mama will be looked after," he said, glancing at his eldest son. "Gad, you think you're old enough to take that on?"

"Yessir," Gad said. "But I think I should go along with you, Pa, an' earn my own cash money. I can dig good as the next feller—"

"No, son," Sam Craven said, shaking his head firmly. "I cain' go off an' leave your mama an' sister alone, without a growed man on the place. Now, I'll have your word on it."

"Yessir," Gad said, dropping his head reluctantly.

"Do that mean I got to mind *him?*" Lem asked incredulously.

"No, son," his mother said gently. "You got to mind me, as always. But if I ain' there to say so, then you best listen to your brother as you would to your pa."

"Pa!" Mattie groaned. "You cain' leave us for a month!"

"I ain' pleased 'bout it neither," Sam said, "but they is payin' good money for a man to move water from one place to another, an' I reckon it won' last long. Whilst they're hirin', it seems a good idea to get some for ourselves."

"Wish I could get some of it for *my*self." Gad sighed.

His father slapped him on the shoulder amiably. "Time enough for that, son, when you're growed. Right now, best savor your freedom. 'Tis gone 'fore you know it."

"When will you go?" Mattie asked miserably.

"Well, that's what I aim to ask you all now," Sam said. "If I come on home, it'll take me nigh two weeks or more to get to where they're diggin', 'cause I'll have to walk it. Don' want to leave you without the ox, so there's no way 'round that. But if I leave you here, an' you think you can make it home without me, then I can go with these fellers that come in last night. They got room in the wagon, they said, an' that way, I can be there in a few days." He smiled at Mattie. "Might mean I get home that much sooner."

"We can get home without you, Pa," Lem said staunchly. "You go on. Don' worry 'bout us."

Gad said nothing, but he glanced at his mother with a small worried frown.

"What do you say, son?" May asked gently. "Can you drive ol' Caleb by yourself that far?"

"I reckon," Gad said after a moment's thought. "You think it's a good idear, Ma?"

She nodded. "Anything that'll get your pa back home again quicker, 'tis a good idear by my mind."

"So you gonna go right now?" Mattie asked, her voice rising in a note of panic.

Sam chuckled softly, pulling her into his lap. "Not a'fore I had my breakfast, miss, that's for certain. 'Sides, I got to see that ol' mouth organ you studyin' so hard on, Gad. An' Lem, I reckon you need to get yourself some sort a' fancy, too, a'fore this town lets loose a' you."

Mattie threw her arms around her father, burrowing her nose into that place where his shoulder met his neck. "I ain' gonna sleep a wink 'til you come back," she promised him solemnly.

"Well, I reckon I best hurry on home then," her father said, "else my Miss Mattie's gonna be red-eyed like some ol' hooty-owl."

"When they fixin' to leave, Pa?" Gad asked.

Sam addressed him soberly, as befitting his new status as family protector. "Tomorrow mornin', son."

"Well, we best get on with our tradin', then," Gad said. "We'll want to make a early start, too."

Mattie glanced up from her father's neck, staring at Gad and then back again at her father, waiting for some signal from Sam Craven that Gad had overstepped his bounds. When her father only nodded in agreement, she sighed hugely, accepted the new shift of power, and murmured, "I want a new bonnet, then. If Gad gets to be boss, I want a new bonnet."

Sam laughed, squeezing her. "I 'spect we can manage that. With what they're payin' men to move dirt, you shall have two bonnets, if you've a mind."

The next morning, they said hard farewells, and Sam climbed up on the back of Henry Tabbs's wagon, bound for the north where men were reshaping rivers and moving mud. May and her children waved him out of sight, and then she turned to her eldest son and smiled brightly at him, determined to hide her sorrow. Except for his trips to Fort Brooke, it was the first time she had been parted from her husband since their wedding night. "You ready, Gad?"

"Yessum," he said.

It seemed to her that his voice had somehow deepened overnight. His mouth organ stuck out of his back pocket. He had played it relentlessly last night, nearly driving Mattie crazy with his wild, tuneless caterwauling. Now, he looked so serious, May could hardly believe it was the same boy before her. "Did you remember to tie down the flour barrel?" she asked.

"Yessum," he said. "An' I greased that back wheel extry. We might be glad a' that, if we hit rain 'fore we get home."

She nodded. "If you be ready, then, get your brother an' sister up to their places."

She took her time with her bonnet, letting Gad be the one to put Mattie up into the wagon, to help Lem climb into his spot, and to take one last turn round the ox to check the harness.

He came to her side and put out his hand. "We be ready, Mother."

Her eyes teared up, and she ducked her head as though she still had a bit of curls to tuck under her bonnet. It was the first time he had called her that. Indeed, the first time she had been addressed that way in her life. Everything changes, she realized, every day, it slips away and becomes something else. But usually, we are not privileged to notice the change. This was once, she told herself, she meant to remember always. The day her firstborn son became a man.

She took his arm and let him help her up, settled her skirts, and waited patiently while he unhitched, climbed up, and took the reins in his hands. "Get up," he said to Caleb, slapping the leather against the huge beast's neck. The ox obliged him, and they were on their way south for home.

They rode for a good while, mostly in silence, and finally May began to sing quietly a song which she knew was one of her children's favorites. As she began to sing, Gad glanced at her and smiled shyly.

> As I sat amusin' myself on the grass,
> Whom should I spy but a fair Indian lass,
> She sat down beside me an' takin' my hand,
> Says you are a stranger an' in a strange land.
> But if you will follow you're welcome to come,
> An' dwell in my cottage that I call my home.
> The sun was just sinkin' far over the sea,
> When I wandered along with my pretty Mohee.
> Together did wander, together did rove,
> 'Til we came to her place in the coconut grove.
> An' these kind expressions she made unto me,
> If you will consent, sir, to stay here with me,
> An' go no more rovin' upon the salt sea,
> I'll teach you the language of the Lassie Mohee.
> Oh no, my dear maiden, that never can be,
> For I have a true love in my own country.
> The last time I saw her she stood on the strand,
> An' as my boat passed her she waved me her hand.

"You got a voice prettier than any bird, Ma!" Lem called to her from the back of the wagon.

"Thankee, son," she said, glancing back at Mattie. "Now how 'bout you, sister gal?" Mattie had been quiet the long miles so far, and May knew that of all her children, her daughter would pine for her father the most. Mattie had the sort of soul that took to pining; May knew that much about her only girl. Left to her own ways, she might sink down like a stone under the water and not come up again until she saw the sunshine of her father's face. But May had no intention of allowing that sort of self-pity.

"I don' feel like singin' much, Ma," Mattie said sorrowfully.

"I know, child," May said briskly, "but we each got a job to do whilst your pa is gone away. Gad's got his, an' 'tis a big burden to carry. I know he means to shoulder it good. Lem's got plenty, jus' to take up where Gad needs help an' where I cain' tote the load myself. An' sweet Mattie, you got a job to do, likewise. I'd hate to have your pa hear that you ain' up to the task."

"What job I got, Ma?" Mattie asked curiously.

"Why, to keep me smilin', child," May said softly. "An' to keep your brothers' hearts lightsome, too. Won' do if we all jus' lie down an' sorrow ourselves into sickness an' misery. When your pa comes home, he'll want to see gladsome faces, an' I do believe a song now an' agin will keep us on that path."

Mattie thought about that for a moment in silence. Then, without hesitation, she began to sing the one she knew her father loved the best.

> Oh Lord, my dearest May, you're lovely as the day,
> Your eyes so bright, they shine at night,
> When the moon has gone away.
> Then gently down the river,
> With a heart so light an' free,
> To the cottage of my dearest May,
> What I long so much to see,
> I listen to the waters as they so sweetly flow,
> The coon 'mongst the branches play,
> Whilst the mink remains below.

Gad said gallantly, "Your voice is nigh as purty as Mother's, Mattie. When you're growed, not a man in the valley will be able to turn his ear from you."

Mattie blushed becomingly, glancing away from her brother. And Lem burst into song, happily, loudly off-key and whacking away his own rhythm on the side of the wagon.

"When we get home," May said quietly to Gad, "I want you to remember that you are his brother more'n his boss. Will you promise me that, Gad? He's not nigh so"—and here she hesitated, unwilling to say anything diminishing about any of her children—" so clever as you 'bout some things."

"Oh, he's clever enough," Gad said generously. "Lazy as a hound, but clever." He patted her hand. "Don' you worry none, Ma. Pa's gonna be proud."

She smiled at him, leaning her head on his shoulder for just an instant. "I know he will, son."

Sam Craven reached the crews of the Suwannee Canal Company five mornings after he left Fort Brooke. The ride in the wagon nearly broke his tailbone, but it was better than walking, he knew, and likely a heap better than riding ol' Caleb. It was no trouble to find the camp; they heard the noise of machines long before they came upon them, spread out over the dry hammock, looking for all the world like an army come for battle.

They pulled up the wagon and hailed the first white man they saw walking by, his shovel over his shoulder. "Where's the boss?" Henry Tabbs called out to him.

The man jerked his thumb toward one of the groups of tents and makeshift huts on a rise of ground closer to the river. "Yonder!" he shouted back. "Big ol' feller with a white beard!"

They tipped their hats to the man and set out walking up the rise. Sam looked around him in amazement, for he had never seen so many men all in one place. For as far as he could see, tents and huts and shelters covered the ground. Some were wagons with canvas draped round them; others were God-for-real little cabins, built by men who evidently intended to stay a spell. He figured quickly close to three hundred bodies were in the near vicinity, and no telling how many more were working where they could not be seen.

"I hope there's still work left to do," he said to Henry Tabbs. "Looks like they got enough men to move half the state to Georgia, if they got a mind."

"I heard tell they need more," Henry said. "Cain' hurt to ask."

"Looks like they could let go o' some of these, an' take us on," Hamp Tabbs said, his voice taking on a slight edge.

Sam looked where he gestured, and he saw that another whole crew was up over against the marsh, where the ground was lower. It was a camp full of blacks by the look of them from this distance, nearly as many as the white men and closer crowded together.

Hamp added, "Damn niggers an' breeds, they work so cheap no white man can stand 'longside them."

Sam felt instantly uncomfortable. He was so used to ignoring his heritage, it rarely rose up to bite him anymore at all. His mother was a full-blood Seminole, he knew as much. He had been told he was the great-grandson of Osceola, some Indian chief, but it meant nothing to him. He could remember his mother some if he thought long and hard, moving his mind back over the years, but he rarely did. Those recollections never seemed part of his real life, only distant dreams. He never thought of himself as anything but Tom Craven's son.

He vaguely recalled that his mother had been slight and pert, with long dark hair and a soft voice. Nothing else much remained of her in his mind. Except her death, of course. He had been told of her death, and he wept long and hard. He could recall the sorrow, but he no longer could remember much of what had happened. Many years later, he discovered that she drowned in the river. He had felt, then, a mild shock and again a surge of sorrow, but it seemed very far away from his heart now. When he thought of his mother, he could picture only Annie.

When he met and married May, he told her that his mother was Seminole, but she never blinked. His father had told him he was his son and Annie was the only mother he'd ever have, and that was all the explanation he ever knew. A man did not explain, Tom Craven said. A man held up his head and lived his life in an honorable manner. That was all a man need do.

Sam never thought of himself as anything but white, but when he heard a man lump breeds in with niggers, he felt a flinch of shame. Some folks might say he belonged over there with them. But some folks were fools.

As they walked closer to the hub of the camp, they could hear men's voices shouting to one another in the distance, and above the voices, they heard a loud bugle call, like a rally to attacking troops.

"Who is this Captain feller?" Sam wondered aloud.

"Must 'a been in the war up north," Henry said.

"So was my pa, but he didn't blow no bugle for the rest of his days." Sam frowned.

They reached a core of busy activity, Henry asked again for the boss, and they were directed to a short, well-girthed man wreathed in a white beard, mounted on a gray horse. He had a bugle in his hand and a fierce glare furrowing his brow. But Henry was not to be daunted.

"Captain, sir," Henry said, doffing his cap, "we come lookin' for work. Is there any to be had?"

"Any to be had!" the captain sputtered, gesturing to another man who was in charge of a nearby crew. "Why if the Devil himself sent his minions, I expect I could use every hand. You men see that fellow to the edge of the river with the yellow cap?" He gestured to a man who was standing above about twenty men with shovels, directing their progress. "Go see him. Tell him I want that canal another two feet wider, whilst you're at it, and tell him the Rowell Island boys are fed and ready."

"Yessir," Henry said, yanking his cap back on his head.

They hurried over to deliver the messages, were handed three shovels, and told to join the crew at the bottom of the creek bed. There, another man put them in line, moving earth from the bottom to the top, and before they had even had a chance to figure out where they might sleep that night, they were part of the Suwannee Canal Company legions.

It was near dusk before the crew stopped, and by then, they could see that there was, indeed, a plan behind all of this chaos. The crews were working as a single team, digging a canal more than twenty feet wide and nearly as many feet deep, to move the water from the Suwannee River to a channel headed to the east.

The Suwannee flowed behind them, undisturbed so far. But fifty feet from the riverbank, another channel was moving closer, created by these hundreds of men, shovel by shovel.

"How long they been at this?" Sam asked one of the men digging close to him. The man was dark as the earth they shoveled, his shoulders wide and muscled. He seemed to be in charge of the black men working behind him, but he was digging, all the same.

" 'Bout a year, I wager, mister," the man said cordially. "Leastwhys, I been here three seasons, an' they been diggin' long 'fore that."

"Who pays these men?" Sam asked. He had already learned from the foreman that Henry's estimates of the wages were close enough to make the trip worthwhile: fifty cents a day for a white man, twenty cents for a black. In a week, he'd earn more than he made from a month of trapping, and a bed and victuals thrown in for good measure.

"Cap'n, sir," the man said. "Anyways, he de boss."

"An' all these fellows come from Florida?" Sam asked, amazed that so many able-bodied men inhabited the whole state.

The man laughed amiably, a deep rumble of delight. "Some come from Georgia, I hear tell, an' others from Texas. Don' know 'bout most, but plenty don' come from herebouts."

Later, Sam met up with Henry and Hamp again, and the three of them set up a tent to the rear of one of the fields, one of a hundred or more tents which stretched out across the swamp. "I don' reckon to be here long," Sam assured himself and his comrades. "Just long enough to put a good wad in my pockets, an' then I'll be goin' home."

"You got a good family there," Henry nodded approvingly. "You be a lucky man."

"I am, that," Sam said, gazing into the fire as they sat out in the darkness. He could picture May's face so clearly, could almost smell the scent of her skin and her hair, could feel the light touch of her arm next to his in the bed if he closed his eyes and concentrated. He did so, and missed her profoundly.

His shoulders were sore with the unaccustomed shovel work, and his legs felt more weary than he could remember, even after plowing all day. It was a different sort of weariness, strictly of the body, for his mind had not been used nearly so much as if he had been at home, doing a hundred different things in the daylight hours. He sighed and stretched. It was a pleasant pain, both to miss her and to feel himself used up.

Somewhere close by, a man took up a mouth organ and began a plaintive melody. Sam thought instantly of Gad. He sent a quick prayer to the dark heavens that his eldest son would stand solid and strong and keep to his responsibilities. He was a good boy. Restless and rarin', but with a good heart. A mix of his mama and his papa, Sam thought, smiling to himself. He'd be all right.

"Wish't ol' Black was here," Hamp said morosely.

Black was Hamp's best hound, and by all evidence, he seemed to think of him at least as often as Sam thought of May.

"What'd he do if he was?" Henry yawned. "I ain' seed no bear dogs on the lines, boy." Henry grinned, pleased with his small wit.

"He good on bear?" Sam asked, more to be companionable than anything. He knew that most swamp men would rather talk about their dogs than their wives or families or even their guns.

"The best," Hamp said stolidly.

"Iffen you don' care 'bout catchin' them none," Henry added with a chuckle. "Tell him 'bout the time ol' Black nigh gave hisself heart failure, son—"

"That ain' nearly so funny as you think it is, Pa," Hamp said sourly.

"Well, we jus' let Sam be the judge o' that," Henry laughed. "Ol'

Black, see, he likes to track bear good enough, but he ain' studyin' on gettin' too close. He much prefers some other hound go to the front of the class on that one. So one day, me an' Hamp was out after bear, an' we left ol' Black to home."

"He was put out, is all, Pa. He weren't hisself that day."

"No an' for days after, neither!" Henry laughed, slapping his own sides with glee. "So that time, John Nathan Dixon—you know his people, Sam? Over to Palatka? Anyways, he brought his boat, an' we was out after bear, an' when it come evenin', we was eatin' supper in the boat with a bucket of rations betwixt us. Brother Hamp here got through first an' took up the gator lamp an' strapped it to his head, an' when he shined it around, there was a big ol' bear done slipped up near us, no further than that tent yonder. When the light hit him, he growled, an' Hamp, he shot him good an' quick." He nodded to his son. "It were a good shot."

Hamp grinned ruefully. "T'weren' no way to miss, he was so close."

"So we hauled him in the boat an' rounded him up against a seat, sittin' up like he was a-preachin', 'til he got stiff. An' we got us a mess o' gators, an' when we got home, we put the gators in this ol' keepin' ditch we got near our creek, so the sun don' shine on 'em an' spoil 'em."

Sam nodded knowingly. When he went hunting gators with Lem and Gad, he brought the beasts back and did the same thing. It wasn't only to protect the hides; gators were funny about being dead. They didn't take to it well. You could not be sure the creature was dead unless you chopped through the spine. Sam had seen too many gators "killed" and then rise up to bite. Once, he could remember, he'd shot a gator three times and had it half-skinned when it started, knocked him down, and began crawling back to the water.

May preferred him to do the skinning away from the homestead. To skin the gator, he'd turn it over, cut the belly skin down each side to the back legs, rip around the legs, and then slice down to the tail. The rest of the gator, he threw away, to be devoured by other gators or the hordes of vultures which always found the hunting camp and congregated there each evening. That's why May didn't want the gators brought home. Sometimes, if the gator was big and plump, he'd take a steak or two off the tail, but the weight of a good skin, about twenty pounds or more, plus the gun, the hatchet, and rations, all made a heavy load. Sometimes he wondered if it was worth it. At half a dollar a foot, he was never going to get rich from gator hunting.

Henry was jibing and rolling his eyes at his son. "You want to tell the rest, son?"

"Nossir," Hamp said, shaking his head.

"Well, when we come down to the creek the next day to start the skinnin', ol' Black ran ahead of Hamp, here, to see how many gators we got, as if to say, we ain' likely to have done much, with him to home. An' when he come to the ditch, he thought the gators was jus' some logs, an' he walked out on 'em. An' Lord tell, if one or two ain' quite kilt yet, an' they move under his feet. 'Bout that time, he saw they was gators an' jumped into the boat to get out of their reach. An' then he jumped clean onto that bear, kind o' sittin' up, right in his lap. Well, ol' Black lit out of there with all four legs stuck out sideways, like a flyin' squirrel, an' him a-hollerin' for all he was worth. He hit the ground thataway for fifty yards, as you could tell by his trail, an' him a-yelpin' all the way." Henry wiped tears of joy from his eyes and added soberly, "Yep, that ol' Black. He's one mean bear hound, all right."

* * *

The swamps to the north, where the Suwannee Canal Company was industriously attempting to budge a river out of its banks, were one of the most dense of the wilderness areas left unsettled in Florida, and also, not coincidentally, one of the last great refuges of large numbers of alligators.

Men had shot many thousands, but in the early years of the century, their kind still ruled the swamps. They were an actual physical presence to anyone who intruded into their realm, loglike forms sculling across the bow of a canoe, cold eyes watching from the unruffled stillness of a lake, and torpedo shapes gliding among the floating plants of the prairie. No part of the land or water was empty of them. Their drag marks wound in and out of thickets, they crossed swampy stretches of islands and dug out long tunnels under the boggy muck, they hid in a turmoil of thrashed-up mud and swamp weed, and seemed to be everywhere and anywhere at once.

The alligators sustained the mood of the swamp at its most primeval. From the same stock which produced the dinosaur, the alligator was a living remnant of that great age, two hundred million years ago, when the largest reptiles ruled the earth.

Pisis knew nothing of her ancestors' great long dominance of the earth; she only knew that her own dominance of her territory was in peril. Pisis was a female *Alligator mississippiensi*, more than six feet long, and she lived in a small lake close to where the crews of working men were intruding. Their trespass kept her on guard, but the crowding of her own waters worried her even more.

Pisis was slow-moving, like the waters of the rivers around her. Her pace was leisurely, a tribute to the fact that she had already lived about thirty years and could expect to live perhaps another thirty, with good luck and vigilance. Most of the time, she was in no hurry to do anything except perhaps flick her heavy tail in a lightning-bolt surge to snatch a snake or a frog or larger prey from the water surface. When she was not feeding, she patrolled the perimeter of her lake, keeping a wary eye out for disturbance.

And lately, there had been plenty of disturbance. The problem was that too many alligators had come into these warm, still waters, driven to her lake, she could only guess, by the trespass of men in the surrounding waters.

And some of them were larger than Pisis, by as much as half her length.

Pisis stopped her swimming and lay very still in the warm water, her back half-in, half-out in the sun. Like the swamp, she was not what she seemed. This was her strength, she knew, and like most alligators, she relished stealth and surprise. If seen at daytime, Pisis looked cold and only half-alive, a motionless half-sunken log. By night, like the swamp, she was transformed. Now, in the spring, with the flurry of winds and rain which always came this time of year, she grew more active and surfaced at night with her multitudes.

It seemed to her that the whole surface of her lake was now mostly alligator. They floated in almost every size, some no bigger than her front claws, others larger than the canoes of man. They snapped up the pig frogs, themselves just emerging from their winter rest, and raced like underwater birds in pursuit of snakes or salamanders. They rooted in the mud like pigs for crayfish, and the crash of jaws and crunch of breaking bone and shells rang through the night now, every night.

She would leave her lake, but she sensed there was no place else to go. The large male who had claimed a corner of what had been her territory was nearly twice her length, as best she could tell. She had avoided him so far. One night in the moonlight, she had seen him take a turtle, a huge turtle which she would not have attempted, took him between his massive jaws, the desperate head of the thing snaking back and forth, and cracked its shell as she might have cracked an egg. Then the giant male submerged, leaving only the captive head's floating on the water. She knew it was not a good way to die. She did not wish to follow the turtle's example.

Now even the sounds of her lake had changed. The slap of jaws and the squawking of fleeing birds told the story. The water birds, the herons, rails, gallinules, and coots, walking across swamp weeds, were never sure now that a tiny disturbance in the vegetation did not mean a small alligator lurking in ambush. She saw it often, and it angered her every time, but there was little she could do. She could not control her territory as she once did; there were too many of her kind in the water. When the warm-bloods ventured into the water owned by the cold-bloods, they were certain to be attacked now, and they sensed the increased peril. Muskrats and raccoons only appeared briefly as tense statues in the moonlight, never knowing if their foraging for food at the lake was safe. Shallowness of water was no guarantee. And so they came less often to her lake.

The new alligators were more aggressive than Pisis was, many of them younger and hungrier. In breeding seasons past, there had been few deaths. Last season, there were several. This season, she knew there would be more.

Usually when males fought for females, as they did throughout the swamp in late spring, they locked their jaws and rolled over and over in an attempt to exhaust each other. These fierce fights for the right to breed looked like death encounters, but they rarely were. Pisis had seen it again and again: the males fought hard, but then the loser would usually slide back into the water, bloodied but able to fight again the following spring. That was the way of the swamp.

But now, the deaths were rising. Now, the males killed each other as relentlessly as they did the warm-bloods, for there was less room for breeding nests, and the females would refuse to breed at all if there was no room to hatch their clutches. Pisis knew that when the spring came round again, and the males followed the scent trail she left down in the mud from her cloacal glands, fights to the death would follow.

Pisis crawled slowly out of the water toward her den, a black pool of mud and dank water which sheltered her during the spring season. She did not look to the left or the right, for she was certain that here, at least, she would not be disturbed. Even the most aggressive male would not follow a female to her nest. She pushed her way into its dark interior, down into the earth where she had dug it to her liking. There was small breathing space above the surface of the water and mud, under the surface of the harder mud on top.

Pisis had created this den many seasons past, when she was a smaller animal, and the edges of its opening were frayed and crumbled with the violence of its making. It was not a perfect nest, she knew, and she had intended to move it soon. Now there was little room left. It would have to do. She dozed heavily, and she thought of what the lake had been.

The lake had always surged with life, warm-bloods and cold-bloods alike. When spring came, breaking out bright green topknots on the cypresses and a blush of flowers on the prairies, the fish thronged the dark brown water—hundreds of them together in the shallows—some infant, some adult, a countless number that fed other fish and fueled the birds, the warm-bloods, the turtles, and her own kind. The water swarmed with small bodies then: pygmy sunfish, pickerel, gar, bass, perch, chub suckers, bowfins, and a million minnows. It was easy to eat, easy to believe that food would be ample forever.

And the frogs. As the days warmed, the hosts of frogs grew to a swarming crowd. They croaked at first, then massed their voices in a chorus that rivaled the noise made by her own kind: they whined, they clicked, they moaned. They were eaten, then, by the alligators, the cottonmouths, the herons, the ibises, the egrets, the anhingas, the cranes, the red-shouldered hawks, eaten, in fact, by anything that could catch them. And still there were plenty for all. They came out of the mud in an irresistible flow. Southern leopard frogs who laid their plinths, long columns of eggs stuck together, then the longer egg clusters of the southern toad and the bands of eggs of the eastern spadefoot, and a flood of eggs from the squirrel tree frogs, the cricket frogs, the pine-woods tree frogs, little chorus frogs, carpenter frogs, and the outflow of eggs went on ceaselessly and the early breeders were joined by new breeders—eastern gray tree frogs, narrow-mouthed frogs, toads, pig frogs, all throughout the summer. The impact of their voices was stunning.

But now the fish and the frogs were so wary, fewer, and still the alligators kept coming from the nearby waters. Was there room for more? Was there room for next season's hatchlings? Likely not.

Pisis had had too many clutches to remember them all, but the urge to breed was still strong in her. She had built her mound-shaped nest, five feet in diameter, two feet high, of mud, leaves, and other debris, and deposited her eggs, usually fifty hard-shelled beauties, each and every June since she had been alive and could remember. She waited all the long weeks for the call of the hatchlings: the high-pitched *y-*

eonk, y-eonk, y-eonk that called her to scratch them forth and help them from the nest. She kept them safe for another round of seasons, and then they left her to find their own marsh or pond or lake or meandering river or swamp or bayou to make their own. There were plenty of waterways from which to choose. What would her hatchlings do this season? Would they even survive the year in her care?

While ruminating, Pisis suddenly heard a sound from on top of her den, a noise she had never heard before. It was the thudding of footsteps above her. She was instantly angered. It was one thing to share her territory in the lake, quite another to be tormented within her own den.

She heard rumbling noises above her then, the deep voices of her most feared and hated enemy. Man stood above her. There was no mistaking his sound or his smell. Another noise then: a deep-throated growling noise that sounded somewhat like a male alligator, something like a youngster. The vibrations seemed to come down into the very muck and water, and to travel up her spine like the beat of a nearby drum. Like most reptiles, Pisis was keenly sensitive to vibrations and the rhythms of the earth. Like a snake, she could feel the approach on the earth of anything which moved, could sense its heft, its speed, its danger or possibility as food. These vibrations both annoyed and jarred her, and she growled low in her throat as answer.

The vibrations increased, and she heard the low-throated bellows from on top of her den. She wrestled herself out of the mud, pushed her way into the open air, and came face-to-face with two men, carrying a hooked pole. She saw now that they had placed the pole into the water before her den and made that noise from their throats, letting the sound travel down and trespass into her domain. She grunted and growled at them, opening her huge jaws in her characteristic threat posture, backing away and hissing loudly, inflating herself as she went to look as large and formidable as she could.

There was a cracking noise and a deafening explosion of sound and smoke, and Pisis felt a blow to her body which knocked her senseless. She was bewildered, for the men had not touched her with their stick, so far as she could tell, yet she felt suddenly afraid and weak. She struggled to turn in the mud and make it to the safety of the water. Again, the roar of the stick rang out, and she grunted hard as again, she was struck by something in her back. Now the pain began to move swiftly up her spine, and she gaped her jaw in frustration and fear. Her back legs would not move at her will, and she writhed uselessly, her tail thrashing with a sluggish drag.

The men shouted to each other, a sound which seemed to her to come as though from underwater. The pain was numbing now, and she looked up at them as they approached with a great weariness, understanding in that moment that her own death was upon her. She felt a final surge of hatred for these intruders, and she turned savagely, with the last of her strength, and clamped her jaws down fiercely on the nearest man's leg. He screamed, another roar rang out, and she knew no more.

* * *

Sam had worked in the swamp for Suwannee Canal Company for a month when he finally began to understand what it was that they were all attempting to accomplish. It was nothing less than the complete reversal of a river.

Ol' Captain Jackson had the single-mindedness of a badger in a burrow. He was going to drain that swamp or die trying. Large dredges were gouging channels forty-five feet wide and six feet deep, and the steam engines operated twenty-four hours a day under sun and searchlight. Every day of digging got them forty-four feet deeper into the swamp, but that was not fast enough for Captain Jackson. The cypresses that blanketed the whole central part of the swamp called to him like the sweetest sirens, and so he sent the largest crews to dig a drainage ditch that headed east to the Saint Marys River. This was supposed to cut through the ridge which was the swamp's eastern limit and take the logs out of the swamp and into the river. It was on this ditch that Sam labored.

As he shoveled, he thought about the supreme arrogance of such a plan, but he was also very proud to be part of men who would dare such a thing, part of an animal which was not, like the beaver, content merely to alter the river, but insisted instead on moving it to the other side of the state. The Suwannee River was to be sent to Jacksonville, rerouted through the Okefenokee Swamp and directed to flow the exact opposite way it now moved. The river would, when they were through with it, run into the Atlantic Ocean instead of the Gulf. As he sweated and labored in the humid, hot air, he told himself that there were worse ways for a man to make his money.

He thought of May constantly. And Mattie and Lem and Gad, of course, but most of all, he vibrated with the remembered scent and sound and touch of May. At night, he rolled over on his cot and clutched

his pillow to his belly, comforted somewhat by the sensation of something close to his body, but missing May all the more. During the day,
he held long conversations with her as he shoveled, sometimes moving
so far away from where he actually was and what he was doing that in
his mind, he was on the porch at home, rocking in the chair next to
her with the dusk of evening coming on, hearing the sounds of the
farm and the children in the distant growing shadows. Sometimes, he
could even dispel the heat from his skin, by thinking hard on the
smoothness, the coolness of her touch. He missed her with an ache he
had not imagined. As the days went on, he began to wonder if the
money was worth such a longing.

So far as Sam could see, more and more men kept coming, drawn
to the company by the promise of fast money and hard work. Some of
the men actually relished the work at first: it was easy, it was hard, and
it took no thought to do it well enough. No worry about rains or no
rains, making a crop or selling it, the baby's croup, the mule's spavins,
or a hundred other things which kept a man from his rest at night. Just
take up a shovel and take up the dirt, eat your three squares, and pocket
your cash money.

The longer he stayed, the more his thoughts turned also to Gad,
wondering if the boy was standing up to his responsibilities solid and
true. Sam knew his eldest son. He knew that Gad was restless and
stubborn, always following some spark of an idea that kept him looking
for something more. If he caught a mess of bream, he wished he had
a turtle. If he shot a rabbit, he wished it were a buck. He always yearned
for what he didn't have. What he held was never enough for Gad, and
it made him just a bit mad at the world. Not like his mama, not like
his brother. Lem was a gentle boy, at heart, though he did his best to
hide that heart around his brother. Lem would likely be the one to
take on the farm when Sam was done with it, he knew. Gad might be
content to come back to it, after he'd wrestled down a few of his bigger
dreams. But not until then.

At night, Sam sat with Henry and Hamp, playing cards or telling
tales, and it seemed to him that he was only dreaming. His real life
was still going on without him, a six-day ride home to the south, where
May slept alone under the soft worn quilt her mama had made. Each
night that passed without her, he wondered if the money was worth
it. Finally, he could not pass another night in that fashion.

After two months of work, Sam was so aching to see his family and his own rocker chair, that he leaped at the chance to join a wagon going south toward home. Henry and Hamp were willing to keep shouldering their shovels, but Sam wanted to see that the house still stood upright. He told the crew boss he'd be back, and he hitched a ride as far south as the Withlacoochee. From there, he walked the rest of the way along trails which seemed to him to be easier to follow than he would have guessed. More and more settlers were passing through, he saw, and the land was giving up to them in subtle ways. He saw less game in his travels, heard fewer gators bellowing in the nearby swamps, and he knew that man was the reason.

He walked up the narrow, rutted road to his homestead late in the afternoon near ten days after he set out from the Canal Company, and as he approached his house, he listened hard for the sounds he had missed. His ox lowed in the nearby field when he spied him, and he felt like putting a finger to his lips to shush the beast, for he wanted to surprise May, if he could. But then the hounds began to bark, racing round the corner of the barn as though to tear him apart for trespassing. When they got to him, they mauled him happily, jumping up and whining, pawing him all over as though to reassure themselves that he was returned, and he looked up to see Gad and Lem racing toward him, screaming, "Pa! Pa!" Sure enough, Mattie and May instantly appeared on the porch, and he broke into a trot.

Lem and Gad reached him first, throwing themselves onto his legs and shoulders just as the hounds had done, and Mattie squealed happily, skipping down the steps to squeeze into his embrace. He looked over his children's heads to see May standing there, her face shining with pleasure. After a hug and kiss for each, he gently put them aside and went up the steps as though courting her for the first time.

"My May," he said softly, folding her into his arms. It was good, he thought then, that the children should see them love each other. That way, they would expect no less in their own unions. May's cheeks were wet when they drew apart, and she stroked his mouth gently, gazing into his eyes. "Near 'bout the longest two months a' my life," she smiled.

"Me, too," he murmured, kissing her right before the children.

Mattie giggled and the boys whooped, for they had rarely seen him be so affectionate in broad daylight. But then they were on him again: "Pa, did you make lots of cash money?" Lem called out, tugging on his sleeve. "Did you bring me somethin' from up there?"

"Pa? How long you fixin' to stay, Pa?" Mattie called, slipping his other hand onto her shoulder and holding it there, patting him as she would one of her dolls. "You home for good, Pa?"

"I 'spect you'll be wantin' to see the mule, Pa," Gad said importantly. "I feel sure he's near to lame, an' I told Ma so jus' yesterday."

Sam glanced at his eldest son with a grin. He looked inches taller in just two months, or perhaps it was because he was holding himself with such dignity. Newfound dignity. The time had been good for him, that much was evident.

"Is that so, son?" he answered Gad. "Well, I reckon we best look into that problem then. I cain' hardly expect you to do the work of a growed man without no mule, can I?"

"No, Pa." Gad grinned proudly. "Welcome home." He put out his hand with a jaunty air.

Sam took it and shook it soberly, feeling a twist in his heart. His boy had grown more than inches in his absence.

But then the tumult of his arrival swept him inside the house, and it was a while before Mattie and Lem would let him go long enough for him to inspect the place as he was yearning to do. He and Gad walked around the homestead as dusk was settling on the land, and even Lem, who would not be left behind, knew enough to let them speak without interruption.

"The well go good?" Sam asked as they walked the back edge of the field.

"Yes, Pa," Gad nodded. "But we used up near most of the salt pork, an' Ma says four of the hens stopped layin'. I reckon we best eat 'em up."

"Or let ol' Buck at 'em," Sam said. Buck was the rooster, always desperately eager to get at May's setting hens.

"I done that," Gad said. "But they still ain' layin'. An' Lem says one ol' biddy's jus' as evil as a cottonmouth—"

"Near pecked me to the bone!" Lem spoke up.

"Then into the stewpot she goes." Sam laughed.

They walked over the field, and Gad told Sam all the details of what had happened on the farm while he was gone, with Lem piping in whenever Gad would let him contribute. The mule was going lame, sure enough, and though Sam was not pleased to see it, he was proud to know that Gad had sense enough to see the problem while it still could possibly be helped. "Keep a warm poultice on that hoof," he told Gad, "an' make him rest it for a week. We'll see, can he heal up on his own."

"Yessir," Gad said.

"I'm proud you did a good job whilst I was gone," Sam said. "Guess you nigh put me out of a job."

Gad grinned. "Mama missed you sore."

"Well, then. Maybe I ain' gonna be turned out to pasture jus' yet." Sam cuffed the nearest capering hound. "I think we best go get some meat soon, boys, since your mama's nigh out of pork."

The boys danced as much as the hounds at the prospect of a morning hunt. When they had calmed down, Gad told Lem, "Go on to the house an' tell Mama we gonna need rations for the hunt, Lemmy. I need to talk to Pa private-like."

"No, I ain' gonna—" Lem started to protest, but Sam glanced at him and without a word, the younger boy ran off.

"He's a good boy," Gad said seriously when he was out of earshot. "He been a big help."

"I'm proud to hear it," Sam said, keeping the smile from his mouth.

"Pa, I want to go with you when you go off next time," Gad said. "Jus' for a short spell. We's comin' into cool weather now, an' the crops don' need much mindin'. If we get good meat stocked up, Ma and Mattie and Lem won' need me—"

"No, son," Sam said. "I cain' go off an' leave your mama and sister with Lem. You know that—"

"Pa, Mama don' need me round here, ask her! Not once the crop is in an' the smokehouse is full. An' I jus' got to get off this place an' see what men is doin' that ain' behind a mule!" he finished passionately. "I want to make my own cash money—"

"No, son," Sam said. "I'm rueful that you ask me, if you want to know the truth. I am proud you can take care of your family. I thought you understood how important that job is."

Gad looked down and pushed his fists in his pockets. "If it's so blasted important, why don' you stay here an' do it, then?"

Sam whirled on his son, astounded and instantly angry. He had never heard that tone from one of his children before. He held his tongue while he waited for his anger to wither enough to be able to speak without striking the boy. "Son, don' make me 'shamed of you. You done a good job. Now, you got to keep doin' it."

"Yessir," Gad said glumly.

"We won't talk about this again. An' I don' want to hear a' you takin' this out on your brother or sister or mama, son, jus' 'cause you got a notion to go wanderin'.''

Gad shook his head. "Nossir."

Sam was somewhat mollified. It was not so long ago that he could remember how secretly pleased he had been to wave his family good-bye and take off for parts unknown on a stranger's wagon. He patted his son's shoulder roughly. "Good. I know it ain' easy, bein' a man."

"Better'n bein' a girl," Gad said ruefully. "Mattie's pleased to spend her whole life jus' stayin' in the house or on the porch. She don' even care 'bout goin' huntin' or fishin' or traipsin'—"

"I got me two fine sons and a fine daughter," Sam said as they neared the house. The lanterns were on inside, and the smoke was curling softly out of the chimney. He knew that within, Mattie and May were busy cooking up a homecoming meal fit for a squire. "I'm a lucky man."

"Yessir," Gad said quietly as they went up the porch. "I will be too, one day."

* * *

Sam was home for only a week, seven short days which seemed to fly by. And then he was walking back up the road, while Mattie wept and May waved from the porch. Gad hated to see him go and hated even more that he couldn't go along, but at least now his father was absent, he was once more the man of the place.

There was some comfort in that, Gad told himself, as he turned the mule out to pasture and noticed that he needed a good brushing. Something to put Lem to, he thought. The boy has to grow up sometime.

He turned from his task when he heard a commotion in the chicken yard. There was Lem, backing out from the henhouse, his eggbasket over his arm. The hens were still putting up a racket, even as he left the yard and pulled the gate shut behind him. "Oh hush!" Gad heard him holler at the chickens, and he turned to go up to the porch.

He got to the house about the same time his mother appeared to take the basket from Lem's hands. "What in the world's ailin' those hens?" she asked him.

"They hate me," Lem glowered. "Mama, why cain' Mattie get the eggs?" He kicked angrily at the front stoop.

"Ain' no cause to blister the boards 'cause the hens pecked your pride, boy," May said mildly. "Mattie's got more'n her share, helpin' me do all the cookin', the cleanin', the mendin', and the washin'. If you want to take her place at the wrench pot, then she can swap you for the hens."

"No ma'am," Lem said glumly, dropping his head. The wrenching pot was one of the hardest jobs, though it only came once a week. Once the clothes were boiled in the harsh lye soap, they had to be wrenched and stirred and wrenched again in boiling water to get the soap out. It was hot work and impossible to do without scalding your hands at least once. Mattie wept sometimes over her red, boiled hands, maintaining that no beau would ever want to hold them, as ruined as they were from washing. Lem didn't have to think very hard to know that hens were better than hot water, any day.

As his mother took the basket and looked within, she asked, "They ain' layin' any better?"

He shrugged. "No ma'am. An' you'd think they got gold under them, the way they fight."

She smiled, ruffling his hair. "Tell your brother I said you could wear Pa's smithy gloves the next time you fetch 'em."

Gad came round the porch and said, "Jus' recollect where you got them, boy. Pa comes home an' finds them lost out in the coop, an' he'll scour your hide."

"How come I got to take orders from everyone on this place?" Lem shouted all of a sudden. "Even the danged chickens tell me what to do!" He stomped off in a fury then, toward the barn, swiping at the crape myrtle bush as he went.

May sighed as Gad shook his head. "It's hard on him, with your pa gone."

"It's hard on everybody," Gad said. "He needs to grow up."

May smiled. "He will, in his own time. Jus' as you did, son. Be a little easy on him."

"That won't make him grow up any quicker."

"Not quicker, maybe, but the right way. He deserves a chance to do it in his own time. You did."

He smiled, in spite of his determination to be somber. His mother was talking to him as she might to a grown man. He felt taller, stronger, and somehow more capable of patience with Lem and all the other inconveniences in his life. "He's gonna make it fine," he said then reassuringly to her. "Don't you worry 'bout it, Ma."

"I won't," she said, squeezing his shoulder.

Mattie called then from within. "Ma! I need the eggs for this batter!"

"Oh Lord," May hummed, now more to herself, "I clean forgot. Mattie's makin' up a cake for supper tonight."

"How come?"

She grinned. "No special reason, 'cept she wants to. I think she reckons, when a beau comes callin', she better be a good hand at bakin'."

He snorted. "She needs the practice."

"Now, don' you tease her, Gad," his mother warned him quietly. "She's got to find her own way, too, jus' like you an' Lem, you know. Some day, she'll be havin' a husband—"

"Poor sod!"

"An' when she does," his mother overran his words with a warning glare, "he'll be the luckiest man in the county. An' I want you to tell her so."

"Aw Ma—"

"It's what your pa would say," she murmured. "There's more to bein' a growed man than orderin' the stock an' your little brother around, son."

"Yessum," he said reluctantly. "If it's fit to eat, I reckon I can say so."

"That's my Gad," May said, whisking inside with a smile.

Two days later, when Mattie needed more eggs, Lem went once more out to the henhouse with his basket, muttering under his breath and already in a fierce mood. He had gone to get his father's smithy gloves, the gloves Gad wore when he had to shoe the mule or fix the fence, only to find them far too large for his hands. He knew he would never be able to pick up the eggs in such cumbersome gloves, much less transfer them safely to the basket without breakage. So now he was right back where he was before: at the mercy of the blasted hens.

He slammed the chicken gate as he went inside, as though to warn the stupid birds that he was in no mood to be trifled with, and a fluff and flurry of down and feathers and chicken dirt rose up when the gate scraped on the earth, making him even madder. He wiped it off his pants and bent down low to get into the dark coop, holding his nose against the musty stink inside.

The stupid hens always tried to lay as far inside the coop as they could; not a one ever chose the near boxes by the door. Consequently, they were crowded together on every perch, some of them half-in each other's boxes, others precariously nesting on small boards up near the rafters of the low-slung coop. The light was dim, the air filled with dust and feathers and the acrid smell of droppings and heat and old shells. The biddies liked nothing better than to somehow escape their prison and set their eggs to chicks, but Mama wanted no more chicks. It was the eggs she wanted.

He crouched lower and moved as slowly and carefully as he could, trying to be invisible and quiet among the hens. In a flash, they would erupt in a squawking flurry, flapping up around his nose and head, making him have to swat at them and burst from the coop in a fury of failure. He just wanted to get the eggs and get out.

Back in the rear of the coop, three hens sat eyeing him haughtily. Two of them were good layers, and the third was a ruined old biddy who should have gone to the block the month before, as far as Lem could see. She sat her nest day and night, but all she ever produced was an evil temper. She was the one he hated the most; she was the one who could peck with lightning speed and unerring aim on the same sore spot every time.

He bent down lower, moving his feet and crooning to her, knowing that his attempts to calm her were likely futile, but hoping that, this time, she might let him approach without pecking so viciously. She squawked suddenly, and the rest of the hens were instantly alert and poised for an uproar. He froze, and in the moment of silence, he heard a rustle down at his feet, where his hands were dangling low. He glanced to one side, just in time to see a huge rattler coiled along the sideboard of the coop, his yellow eyes glinting in the dim light. Before he had time to shriek or move, the snake struck him hard, high up his arm between his wrist and elbow. He screamed then, and the chickens erupted in a cloud of flapping, running, squawking birds, and he screamed again, screamed for his life, scrabbling out of the henhouse as fast as he could, knocking the snake off of his arm against the wood door as he fell out into the dirt, writhing in pain.

He heard the door slam, and his mother call to him worriedly, and he heard feet come running, Mattie screaming for Gad, and his mother shouting to Mattie to keep back. The rattler had flowed under the henhouse through a hole which he could not remember seeing before, looked no bigger than a rathole, and the burning in his arm was so hard, so bad, and he tried to tell his mother, as she bent over him, that the snake was under the henhouse, but he could not speak, could barely breathe, and he wondered why it was his mother's face looked so large and white. He closed his eyes then against the pain and let his mother's arms enfold him.

Gad came running around the barn, glancing first to Mattie, who stood outside the henhouse shrieking and pointing at the ground away from Lem who was sprawled on the dirt, with his mother at his head. "It was a rattler got him!" Mattie cried as he went inside the yard, and he gasped when he saw Lem's arm, already swollen large as his leg, red and dark and ominous as a hurricane cloud. His mother was ripping at her skirt, tearing a long swath of cloth, which she was tying above Lem's elbow.

"It were a big one," his mother said, her voice high and fearful. "He passed out, thank the Lord, else he couldn't take the pain. Help me get him inside." She took Lem's shoulders, and Gad took his legs, and they awkwardly managed to get him up the porch and into cabin, placing him on his bed.

Now Lem's arm was more swollen still, and his mother said to Mattie, "Loosen that tie just enough, sister, so that he don' lose that arm. Gad, put the kettle on, we be needin' to boil some cloths to pull the poison." She opened Lem's eyes and examined them quickly. "It's movin' fast," she murmured, when she saw how yellow and red-rimmed they were. "I got to cut him quick."

She went to the kitchen and took up her carving knife, the one she used to debone the chickens. Directing Mattie to hold tight to the binding on Lem's arm and Gad to hold the basin under his brother's wrist, she cut two swift slices in her son's arm, running the direction of his bone from his wrist to his elbow, opening up the flesh as calmly as she might have opened up a plucked fowl. The blood did not spurt, as Gad had expected, but oozed thick and ugly and slow from Lem's wounds, as though it were reluctant to come from his body. The blood was dark, and the flesh around the cuts already looked sick and ghastly.

"Will he die?" Mattie asked fearfully, looking away from the blood.

"Don' know, sister," May said quietly. "Not if I can help it."

"Was he a big 'un?" Gad asked.

"I didn' see him good," May said, "but must a' been, for Lem to swell up so fast. He went under the coop, likely been there a spell, festerin' those hens. No wonder they wasn't layin' proper." She was pressing on Lem's arm rhythmically, trying to force the poison out of the tissues. Each time the blood welled, she pushed it into the basin. "It ain' good blood, that's certain. The poison's already thickened it like molasses."

"Does that mean it got to his heart?" Gad asked.

"Don' know. I 'spect so. Mattie, come and do jus' what I be doin', an' I'll go make the poultice—"

"Ma—" Mattie moaned, with wide eyes and pale face.

"Ain' no time for faintin' fits now, Mattie, don' you dare do it," May said sharply. "Jus' take Lem's arm an' push the blood out like I tole' you!"

Mattie took her mother's place without another word, and Gad patted her on the shoulder as she did so. "He's gonna make it fine," he said gruffly to his sister, though he did not feel half the assurance he pretended. He had never seen a boy look so sick as Lem did, with his face puffed out and glistening with sweat, his mouth pinched and fallen in like an old man's and his eyes blue and green round the edges as though he were already dead and in the grave. He could not believe that a body could live and look so sick.

His mother was measuring herbs into the steaming kettle and ripping cloths frantically, as though the sheer speed of her movements would somehow reach her son before the poison did and halt its deadly tide through his body. Mattie was still moaning quietly, probably did not even know she was doing it, Gad thought, and Lem, poor Lem, kept his eyes shut fast.

Gad concentrated as hard as he could on his brother's arm, willing the poison to go away. Lem's flesh did not look like skin and bone anymore, but some strange, bruised fruit, shining and grotesque and near to bursting with evil juice. As he stared at what had been his brother's arm, he heard Mattie gasp, and she let go of his arm suddenly, making him almost drop the basin. He glanced at her and then at Lem: his brother's eyes were flickering. "Mama!" Gad called. "He's awakin' up!"

May came quickly, a hot cloth full of foul-smelling herbs in her hands, her brow furrowed and anxious. "Lem? Lem, honey, can you hear me?"

Lem lay silent. His eyes moved slowly back and forth under his lids, as though he were watching his own life roll past like a river. But he did not speak, nor did he open his eyes to his mother.

"He's gonna be like this for a spell," May said reassuringly to Gad and Mattie. "I seen it once before, when Mister Jim Ray got bit over to Palatka an' we was at meetin'. They come in an' out for a spell, whilst the poison fights the body, but then they wake up. Don' you worry, this boy's a lively one. He ain' gonna slip away on us."

But Gad did not believe her. For the first time in his life, he realized that his mother was saying something that she likely did not believe herself. He could see the doubt in her eyes, could smell the fear coming from her body. Lem might die, and she knew it. He forced the sobs down in his throat and pushed his voice out louder than he'd intended. "Don' you worry none, Mama," he said manfully as he might. "Lem's a good fighter."

For five days and five nights, they waited for Lem to die, half-fearing to believe he might not. Mattie whispered to Gad that she had heard that children always died of snakebite. "Mama says no, but I heard tell," she told him, her eyes swollen from weeping. "An' he ain' but a little thing, even if he is loud," she added. "He ain' strong like you, Gad."

"I ain' so strong," Gad said, still pleased that she thought so. "Lem's jus' as big as I was, at his age."

Mattie shook her head mournfully. "He ain' neither. He's a good boy, but he ain' like you an' Pa; he's more like Mama an' me. He ain' strong, he's only gentle an' good." Her eyes welled up again. "He's gonna die—"

"Don' say that again," Gad said fiercely. "Lem's gonna make it, an' Pa's comin' home soon, an' we'll be jus' like we was before!" He suddenly could take no more pity on her tears; he had seen too many of them over the past five days. "Now get some more water, Mama's near out."

She hung her head and obeyed him just as she might her father's will. He was part-perplexed, part-proud of his new status, and he wondered if he would be able to live up to what everyone seemed to expect. If Lem died, he'd likely never get off this farm, he told himself. Mama and Pa would want him to stay on until he rooted there like a chinaberry. Well, he just wouldn't, he told himself, frowning fiercely. Lem would make it, and he would take over the place when he was big enough, and that was just how it had to be.

Finally, at the end of nearly eight days, Lem opened his eyes again, and his face began to look less ghastly. He had endured convulsions, what must have been intense pain, judging by the look of his arm, and high fevers, sweatings which poured off him like a working mule, and he had slept through it all. When he opened his eyes, Gad happened to be sitting near him, sponging off his bare legs and belly as he had ten times since Lem had been struck.

Something made Gad look up, and there Lem lay, staring down at him as though he had no idea who he might be. "Mama!" Gad called loudly to where she was on the porch, sweeping. "Lem's awakin' up!"

The door slammed open and May came in swiftly, pulling close the little cane chair she had vigiled in so many nights. She smiled down at Lem and touched his cheek. "You comin' out of it now, son," she said.

Lem tried to speak, but his mouth could not seem to get around the words.

"I reckon you got a powerful thirst," May said calmly. "Gad, get your brother some cool water."

Gad leaped up to fetch it, reluctant to miss what might be the most important moments of the last many days. He stopped to holler out the door to the sweet-potato patch, where Mattie was hoeing the rows. "Mattie, come quick! Lem's awakin' up!" At least he got to be the one who spread the news. She dropped her hoe and came running.

When he handed the glass to his mother, he saw that she was weeping. He realized that it was the first time he'd seen his mother weep since Lem had been struck. She put the glass to Lem's lips and helped him sip at it. He struggled and choked and slobbered at first like a newborn lamb, and then he finally took a good drink between his lips and kept it down. He sighed deeply, his eyes flickering.

"Son, you had a hard spell," May was saying firmly, "but you come out of it, thank the Lord. You beat that ol' rattler, Lem."

He turned wondering eyes to Gad and Mattie, who stood to one side of him staring at him in wonder. Then he looked down at his poor, ugly arm, still horribly blackened and swollen, still barely recognizable as human flesh, and he tried to scream, but it came out as a strangled groan.

" 'Tis where the serpent struck you," May said, stroking his head comfortingly. "But you past the hard part now. You'll heal up good as new."

Lem took more water and finally cleared his throat and his lips enough to speak. His words came slowly, painfully, as though he were coming back from the depths of some dark, cold place into the sun, blinking like a bewildered owl. "Mama," he said first, then he looked again at Gad and Mattie. "Mama, it were a big snake."

May smiled, wiping her eyes. "Yes, son. It were that, indeed."

"My arm hurts fearful," Lem moaned, trying to move it.

"Likely, it's gonna hurt for a spell longer," his mother said, taking his hand and holding it still. " 'Tis where you took the poison."

Lem closed his eyes again, pale and weak.

"Son, can you sit up an' take some good broth?" May coaxed him. "Your body needs it, son."

Lem did not answer, but May went and got a cup of meat broth she had on the stove, moved him so he was sitting up higher, and coaxed him to take a few sips. He immediately retched and vomited on the bedclothes.

"That's fine, son," May said as though he had done a brave thing. "That's your belly tellin' you it means to fight this poison a mite longer. We'll try again later—"

"Pa," Lem said faintly. "I want Pa to come."

Gad glanced at his mother and saw Lem's words hit her hard. She patted Lem's good arm. "I know, son. An' I 'spect he will come, soon enough. When he comes, he'll be so proud of how you beat that ol' rattler—"

"Pa!" Lem began to weep. "I want my pa!" as though he were a child of three.

May took him in her arms and rocked him, crooning to him quiet words of comfort which Gad could scarcely hear. He moved away from the bed and stood at the window then, staring out at the fields. If he could have willed it, his father would have been walking down the road toward the little house right then. But, of course, the road was empty. He could never be his father. Not to Lem, not to Mattie. Not to the world.

A month passed, and Lem was finally up and around, though he could scarcely use his arm and hand at all. His mother reassured him that both would heal, but as the time passed, he seemed to gain little strength in either. He could not grip well with his fingers, and his thumb would not work at all. When he tried to hold a fishing pole, he had to do it with his left hand, for his right was mostly useless. When he had to pull Caleb's harness, he had to use his bad hand, but it could do little more than steady his left, for he had no strength in it, no firmness of grip. But at least he ate and ran and laughed through the fields, with his old hound dog following after him as ever, Gad thought. He might never be a whole man, but he was still a boy. Still his brother.

And then his father came down the road again, and time once again stood still. He held Lem long and hard when he heard of his bout with the rattler, and of course, by the time Lem told it, the serpent was taller than the mule and near big around as his leg. Sam told his children he was proud of them, each and every one, for the way they had stood

together and saved their brother. And then he embraced May and held
her for a very long time. Gad heard him say, "I'm so sorry you had to
go through it alone."

His mother murmured something in his father's chest, but Gad did
not wait to listen. He went out on the porch and sat in the big rocker,
the one he had used since Sam left home. Gad waited for him to come
and hear what else had occurred on the homestead in his absence.
"Alone," his father had said. As though he had not been here at all.
Gad felt the rise of anger in him, but he pressed it down.

Finally, Sam came out on the porch and sat down alongside him in
his mother's rocker. He glanced at Gad and said, "Seems like you had
quite a time of it whilst I were gone."

Gad shrugged. "It were bad for a bit, but Lem's gonna be all right.
Likely, he won't never be so good with that arm, but he's still young
yet. I took him out soon's as he was able an' found a good one. Near
eight feet, if he was a foot. I let him shoot him right through the head.
Then I told him to cut his rattles off—"

"He told me. He showed me the rattles. Must a' been a big one."

Gad nodded. "So he's gonna be all right."

"And you? You gonna be all right, too, son?"

Gad looked up at his father. "Pa, you fixin' to take off again?"

Sam thought for a moment. "I was fixin' to. If you think you can
take care of things around here for a spell longer."

"They payin' you good?"

"Yes," Sam nodded, "but it's more than that, I reckon. They figure
to do a grand thing to the land, son, an' it's a good feelin' to be part
of it. They gonna drain the whole swamp an' make it easy to take the
cypress an' the turpentine, an' make good farmland out of it. Think
of it, Gad. The houses that wood will make, an' the ships an' such
which will use that turp, an' the men who will make crops where right
now, nothin' but rattlers can live—"

"An' you're helpin' do all that?"

Sam nodded. "An' I want to keep doin' it. Can you carry your burden
a few more months?"

"I been doin' it, ain' I?" Gad asked, his voice a little rougher, a little
more angry than he had intended.

"Yes, you have, son. You have been doin' it. I reckon if I was here,
I couldn'a done no better with Lem an' your mama and Mattie."

"That rattler would have bit him, even if you was here," Gad said.

"That's a truth."

The two of them sat side by side in silence for long moments, Gad rocking back and forth faster than his father. Finally Sam asked again, "So you think I can leave you in charge a mite more?"

" 'Course you can, Pa," Gad said, struggling for his thoughts. "But I don' want to do this my whole life, you know?" He looked up at his father with a plea for understanding. "Maybe 'tis all right for Lem an' Mattie, maybe not. But I got to do somethin' else. Whyn't you stay on here, an' let me go in your stead? I can dig a canal good as the next feller—"

"No," Sam said. "I cain' let you go that far all by your lonesome, son. Your mama couldn't stand it. I can go, an' whilst I'm gone, you can hold things together here. But I cain' let you go, an' even if I did, they wouldn't take you on. They want men, Gad, men with shoulders bigger than mine, truth be told. You ain' growed enough yet."

"I'm growed enough to take a man's part around here," Gad said scornfully.

"An' I'm proud of you for doin' it," Sam said. "But you cain' go 'long with me, an' you cain' go alone."

"Guess that means I got to bide here."

"Guess so."

Just then his mother stepped out on the porch, glanced at the two of them, and said, "You men solve the problems of the world?"

"Jus' this corner of it," Sam said amiably.

"If I was really a man," Gad said gloomily, "I'd be doin' what Pa's doin', an' goin' off to make my own way." He got up wearily, and said, "Long's you're here, Pa, you best come look at that corner of the barn. I think we got to stave it up, or it's gonna come down in the next storm."

Sam rose and followed him off the porch, and May stood, watching them disappear around the corner of the house. There was something new in her son's walk, something she had not had the time to notice before. He strode wider now, with a more determined step. He had lost the little bounce and skip he had as a boy, a step so distinctive that she had thought he would carry it all of his days. But it was gone now. She sighed and went back inside, wiping her hands out of habit, though they were already dry.

*   *   *

Among the denizens of the swamp, one of the most curious of all the beasts also formed one of the most perilous alliances. This creature lived in the deepest part of the lakes and streams, was the fastest swimmer,and had one of the sharpest beaks. It disliked and distrusted land and only came ashore to lay its eggs or, occasionally, bask in the sun. And of all the other beasts it could partner with, it chose the alligator as its ally. It was *Trionyx ferox*, the Florida softshell turtle, and a surprisingly fierce protector of its own domain.

This June afternoon, a large female softshell, Onyx, was hunting for crayfish in her pond, unusually relaxed considering she had just laid her second clutch of eggs for the year in the nearby sunny, sandy bank. She was larger than her mate, whom she had not seen since he'd covered her two months before. She had a nearly circular, pancake-shaped carapace, which was covered with soft, leathery skin instead of the horny scutes of her other turtle kin. She was dark brown and had the distinctive ridge of her kind along the margin of her shell, with numerous blunt tubercles on the edge nearest her head. She had, also, a beautiful yellow band from her eye to the base of her lower jaw, and she was more than a foot and a half across.

Onyx had feet which were paddles, fully webbed, with three claws each. Her snout was tubular, a perfect snorkel when she was submerged. Her long neck and her sharp beak made her a formidable predator, but she was, of course, second in rank to the other ruler of this body of water: the female alligator which nested on the other side of the pond.

Together, they formed a strange pair. Of course, the alligator could have severed her in seconds with its huge jaws, could have done so even if her shell were of the hard variety like her other turtle cousins. Softshelled and large, she was certainly easy and worthwhile prey— but the alligator never threatened her. Not even when she nested so close to the alligator that she could hear the great beast's breath at night.

Onyx could not know, nor did the alligator understand her own tolerance for the closeness of the softshell, but it was because their eggs were laid in similar clutches in the same environment, and the eggs of the softshell often were taken by raccoons and minks, leaving the eggs of the alligator untouched. Their very nearness made the partnership work. The difference was that the alligator's babies took years to mature, and she only laid a single clutch each year or perhaps every two years. Onyx laid as many as three clutches a year, and so her eggs and her offspring were more numerous and expendable. In this way, one generation was sacrificed for the survival of another, even of a different species.

But of course, the turtle and alligator knew only that they tolerated each other's nearness and had done so since the later evolvement of their reptile brains. Sometimes, Onyx was drawn to sleep closer to the alligator than prudence would have dictated, for over generations, her anxiety was quelled when the larger, more ferocious beast was nearby.

Now as Onyx sought the crayfish, she kept one eye on the basking alligator, something she did for different reasons than did most denizens of the pond. She sensed the alligator's growing hunger. So did every other creature within range. She knew the alligator would hunt soon. But her response to that sensation was altogether unique. Slowly, she swam nearer and nearer to the beast as it hung in the water, with only its eyes and great snout protruding above the surface.

Onyx took some trouble to maneuver deftly to the side of the alligator and let her shell brush against its leg; as she did so, she bubbled copiously, directing the rising bubbles to move up and against the alligator's underbelly. Then she moved to the front of the alligator, so that she could be clearly seen. This was her customary approach, a mannered response she had evolved and one which she never varied. The alligator's eyes followed her carefully, but the beast did not move in the water.

From the edge of the pond, a small scaup waddled into the water followed by her eight ducklings. They were getting quite large now, but they were quieter than most ducks. The female gave a guttural scolding call to the ducklings, and they tightened their ranks. The alligator gave no signal save a slow lowering into the water so that nothing showed of its body above the surface.

Onyx slid behind the alligator, careful to keep well back from its tail. The alligator was barely aware of her presence, she knew, and could knock her so hard that her shell would split, with no clear intention of killing. Once she was wounded, she would be prey, however, and the alligator would take her as easily as it would anything else in the water. Onyx stayed below the surface until the alligator was close to the scaup, keeping low and quiet.

When the alligator was close enough to see the scaup's webbed feet moving underwater, Onyx rose to the surface behind the scaup, close to the rear duckling. Of course, the scaup turned to see what threatened her brood, whistling a shrill alarm. In that moment, the alligator lunged to the surface from behind and beneath the duck, took her in one swift mouthful, and fell back into the water with a resounding crash of spray.

Simultaneously, Onyx grabbed the rear duckling by the leg, pulled it under and snapped it in two, then lunged for another duckling, severed it, and then two more ducklings while they panicked and scurried for shore, squawking loudly. In the space of a few swift moments, she had eaten most of four ducklings. The alligator rose to the surface once more and took two more before they reached shore.

As Onyx busily patrolled the surface, scavenging remaining scraps, the alligator lazily swam to the other shore and began to clamber out onto the bank. Now it would bask, Onyx knew, with its mouth open and its eyes near-shut in the sunlight.

She clambered out of the water alongside the alligator, plodding by the creature's open jaws with impudence. She knew she could be incautious now, for the alligator was fed and sun-lazed. She found her favorite personal basking rock, a flat, partially submerged platform in the shallow water close to where she had laid her clutch of ten spherical eggs. They were hard-shelled, unlike herself, and probably would be eaten within a few nights by raccoon, weasel, wild boar, skunk, fox, or bear. Then she would lay another clutch, and then another, if need be. Meanwhile, the nest of the alligator might remain intact. It was a partnership she did not fully comprehend, but it kept her world a place of balance.

* * *

In 1895, news came to the canal camp that Captain Jackson had died. Suddenly, they said, of a stroke. Some of the men murmured that someone must have finally told him that his efforts, long called "Jackson's Folly" by the locals, were never going to alter the swamp enough to make the water run where it would not. Likely, they said, the news stopped his heart right then. Sam could remember a day clearly when one of the crew bosses called up to Jackson as he sat on his horse watching them labor, "Captain! If we is fixin' to run the water to the Saint Marys, why is it all runnin' the other way to the Suwannee?"

The men had laughed then, glancing warily up at Captain to see how he took the jest, but it was nothing they had not spoken of together over their fires. They were digging so low, they were opening up springs which flowed back into the swamp, not in the direction they wanted them to go. They laid bets on which waterway was the strongest, which one would ultimately claim victory over the swamp. No one would take odds on the Saint Marys, these days. Most everyone believed that the Suwannee was too strong, not only for the Saint Marys, but also for Captain Jackson.

Sam heard that Captain Jackson hired a government man to advise him before they started digging, and the man told him that it would take three hundred miles of canals to drain the swamp completely. The sheer largeness of the number dazzled him. He could not recall if he had ever seen three hundred of anything together in his life, much less miles.

Sam was amazed that a man would take on a task that might take him more than his entire life, *two* lives, and he was humbled by the sheer bravado such a dream demanded.

"I ain' studyin' on being no expert," Henry said when they heard that particular tale, "but they been diggin' a year, they say, an' we ain' gone three miles yet. At this rate, Hamp here might even have hisself a gal a'fore they finish."

Hamp had cuffed him then, for it was a commonplace between them that like most young men, Hamp wanted a woman more than he wanted a new shotgun, but he wasn't likely to find one in the swamp. Leastwhys, his father said, not one who would put up with the likes of him.

But then the dream of altering the swamp forever died, right along with the man. When the news came that Captain Jackson was dead, the men put down their shovels, picked up their sacks, and abandoned the diggings at the rate of more than a hundred a day. In five years, they had dug twelve miles of canal and six miles of drainage ditches, but the money was gone and so was the powerful will which had pushed it along. Even the most stubborn of them knew well enough that with Captain gone, no one else would take up the yoke.

And so the dollar-a-day bonanza was over. Sam came home, hitching a ride with first one wagon, then another, until he found himself back on his own porch, rocking in his own chair. Mattie climbed up on his lap that first night and nuzzled her head under his chin like she used to do, her favorite position. But after a brief spell of comfort, she shifted uneasily and finally stretched out her neck with a grimace. "I don' fit no more," she said sadly. "I got too big."

He pulled her braid gently. "You ain' never gonna be too big for this lap," he said.

"Yes I am, Pa," she said. "I cain' do this no more." She stood up and smoothed her apron gracefully. "I ain' a child, Pa. I be a growed woman nearly." She flushed and looked away as she fingered her braid.

He was hit by a hard sadness. May had not told him, but of course it must be so. Mattie had come into her womanly times while he was absent. He sighed and leaned back, gazing out over her shoulder, seeing now how much taller she was than when he had left.

Lem's arm and hand would never be the same. Wasted flesh which would never grow to be larger or stronger than a ten-year-old's limb. And Mattie would never be the same, never again be his little girl in her first blush of innocence. Gad would never be the same, either. Forced to manhood before his time, he was stronger and leaner than he'd been, more hooded around the eyes, and he spoke with less joy and lightness in his voice than before. All these things had happened in his absence, Sam realized. Near four years of his life and the lives of his children. He'd traded it all for a dollar a day, a tent, and all the beans and johnnycake he could eat. By the time he gave thirty dollars for a new mule and twenty for that new stove May hankered for, he could hardly claim he was a rich man. Right now, looking at his lovely daughter and knowing what he had missed in the past years, he felt downright impoverished.

It had seemed so proud. So important. To change the land, to alter even the flow of the waters. But they had made little headway, and he knew that what they had done would be swallowed up by the swamp within a few years, as though they had never been there at all. Men were fools, he realized in that moment, fools in the face of what God made to run 'long just fine without their meddling. He felt now almost ashamed that he had ever even lifted up a shovel in support of such a plan. And when he looked into his daughter's face, he knew he had been a fool as well.

I made a poor bargain, he thought, gazing at Mattie. "Come an' rock with me, anyways," he said. "You ain' never gonna be too old for that, at least."

She smiled sadly and took May's seat next to him, moving for all the world like a younger version of May.

He could have wept then, but the day was too brilliant with sunshine for such waste. "So. You ain' a child no more, then. Does that mean I got to start runnin' lovestruck beaux off my porch like addled bucks?"

She giggled, "Oh, Pa, don' tease me."

Now that sounded more like his Mattie. "Your mama's set on goin' to meetin' next week," he said. "I s'pose you mean to go 'long?"

She widened her eyes in surprise. " 'Course I do, Pa! I ain' never missed meetin' yet."

"Well, it's gonna be different now, Miss Mattie," he said softly. "All the boys is gonna see a pretty gal where a little girl sat a few years past."

She sniffed and tossed her braid over her shoulder for all the world like an experienced flirt. "Let them look, then," she said archly. "I don' care what they do."

He laughed delightedly at her spirit. "Oh, I reckon you'll come to care all right, Miss Mattie. But I'm proud to hear you plan to give them a run for their money."

May came out on the porch then, drawn by the sound of his laughter. She smiled at them both curiously. "Mattie, don' pester your pa to death. He only jus' got home—"

"Don' shoo her away, honey, we're talkin' 'bout whether or not she should come to meetin', next—"

"Pa!"

" 'Course she's comin', don' rile her, Sam," May said calmly. "But a'fore then, you better study on teachin' your daughter to dance a few steps."

"Dance!"

"She's gonna be asked, an' less you want some young buck to teach her, you best do it yourself." May chuckled at them both and went back inside.

"Dance?" Sam said to Mattie in mock horror. "You fixin' to dance at meetin' now?"

"I guess so, Pa," she said shyly, her face flushed again.

"Well." He thought for a minute. "You best call Gad, then."

"I ain' dancin' with him, Pa!"

"Not for dancin', for makin' somethin' we can dance to, Miss Mattie. Tell him to bring his mouth organ an' come a'runnin'."

And so in the middle of the day, the chores were forgotten, the heat was ignored, and the family gathered on the front porch to listen to Gad make a rickety effort at "Ol' Dan Cotton" and Sam show Mattie how to execute a do-si-do.

A month later, Sam stood at the sidelines of a circle of dancing partners, May leaning against him, and they watched as Mattie danced those same steps with a stranger. From the time they had arrived, she was glanced at, gazed at, gawked over, and finally sought out by quite a few of the young men at the meeting. Even those, Sam thought, who were too old to be romancing a girl of such tender years, asked after her the moment she stopped whirling by. At first, he had glowered at each of them but when May pulled him away and murmured, "You look like a sour ol' razorback. Let her frolic a bit," he subsided. Content now to only glare at those young men who were clearly ten years her senior, he still had much to do to keep her in view.

The music was deafeningly impartial, however, and after a few rounds, May pulled him out to the circle himself. Now he had a new and startling view of his daughter, as she danced by him on the arm of a boy a full head taller than himself. She no longer looked like his baby Mattie gal, now she looked like a young woman. She tilted her head back with abandon, her hair flew round her shining, radiant face, and her arms and shoulders looked like they were attached to a spine which was meant to move and work and be embraced by a man—

He pulled his stare away from her almost painfully to see May's rueful grin. "She's growin' fast," May said.

"She's already *growed*," he moaned softly. "How did that happen?"

"Like it always does," May chuckled. "Inch by inch, day by day."

"Too fast." He shook his head.

"She don' think so. Neither does that Hebard boy." May nodded at them as they whirled by. "She can do better, I reckon."

He stared at his wife, amazed. She was already thinking of a prospective mate for their daughter; he had not even accepted the idea that a boy might hold her hand at meeting. Was this one more thing women seemed to understand better than their menfolk?

Lem stood on the edge of the happy crowd, watching the dancers with a shy smile. A few of the young girls glanced his way and then off to other boys. He stood as he usually did these days, with his bad arm tucked tightly behind him, self-conscious of the withered, shrunken limb.

May murmured, "That boy looks like a lost lamb. Ain' no gal gonna take up with him like that."

"He's too young to be studyin' on gals anyhow," Sam said briskly.

"He ain' too young, he's too small. Leastwhys, he looks small with his arm tucked back like a broken wing." She pulled away from her husband and went to her son, smiling gaily. "Come on an' dance with your ol' mama," she said pertly. "You ain' got no better offer so far."

Sam stood back and watched while May tried her best to coax her young son out into the circle of dancers, but he only ducked his head, shrugged his shoulders, and faded back into the crowd.

She came back and took Sam's arm once more, still smiling. She moved him into the dance and only when they were away from Lem did her smile falter. "He ain' never gonna be whole, if he don' forget that arm," she said. "My poor little crippled boy—"

"He ain' no cripple," Sam said. "You got to stop babyin' him, is all."

"I don' baby him." May's jaw went hard. "I see the way the gals don' look his way. He ain' blind, Sam, an' he ain' stupid." Her eyes softened, and she sighed. "He ain' happy, neither."

Just then, from the edge of the crowd, a small explosion of anger
and sharp movement drew their eye. Some of the dancers stopped
turning, and a girl cried out, shrill and excited. Sam turned to see Gad
down on the ground, pushing his way upright and swinging his fist at
another boy all in the same motion. He dropped May's hand swiftly
and stepped through the gathering bystanders.

Sam reached his son just in time to see his swing miss the mark,
and he snatched his boy by the shoulder before he could swing again.
"Here now," he said roughly. "What's amiss?"

Gad's eyes were wild, and he snorted and puffed, out of breath and
trembling, panting too hard to speak.

The boy who had ducked his ill-aimed blows said, "She ain' dancin'
with him. She don' want to, nohow, an' she be spoken for—"

He was a tall young man with a pale face and corn yellow hair, older
than Gad and still holding on to his dignity. The girl behind him peeked
over his shoulder at Gad as though he were a rabid dog.

"She ain' spoken for 'til *she* says so!" Gad shouted then, finally
finding his voice. "You ain' her pa!"

May came to Sam's shoulder then, and she said softly, "Did my boy
insult you, honey?"

"No ma'am," the girl said quietly, ducking her head now that she
saw so many folks watching her.

Gad huffed, "I asked her polite, an' this rascal pushed his way in
where he ain' wanted—"

"He is wanted," the girl said then, blushing.

Gad goggled at her, his face crestfallen.

"Looks to me, son, like you picked a filly what's already branded,"
Sam said easily. "Sometimes, it ain' always easy to see, in the heat a'
the moment—"

Gad jerked himself out of his father's grasp and stalked off, shouting
back over his shoulder, "Take her then, you cockle-headed fool! Take
her an' welcome!"

Sam smiled at the young woman. "I guess you jus' gonna have to
forgive that boy, miss. He ain' used to being 'round gals much, 'specially
ones as pretty as you—"

"Needs a good thrashin'," the boy said stoutly.

Sam's eyes cooled and his voice turned to steel. "Yes, well, I'm sure
we all got better things to do than stand 'round here. May?" He took
her hand then, and Mattie's, too, for she had come to the edge of the

crowd in time to see her brother stalk away. When they were a bit away from the throng, Sam said, "Mattie, get Lem an' come on now. We got to be gettin' back home."

"Oh, Pa!" she moaned. "Gad ruined everthin'!"

"Hush now, Mattie. Mind your pa now an' run get Lem. Come on back to the wagon soon's you find him." May pushed her gently in the direction of a few old men who sat under a patch of shade. Lem was standing near them.

"Let me tend to him," Sam said quietly to May.

She looked at him for a moment silently. Then, without a word, she turned and went to wait by the wagon.

Sam found Gad down at the creek, wiping his face off on his shirt. He had obviously been weeping, but he made a good display of dignified indignation when he saw his father approach.

He started to speak, but Sam held up a hand to silence him. "I don' want to hear it," he said coldly. "Get on now, up to the wagon. We're goin' on home."

"Fine by me," Gad said huffily.

As they walked past the straggling folks and the bustle and noise of the dancers, now clumping noisily with happy feet as though they had never been interrupted, Sam said, "You shamed me, boy."

Gad glared up at him defiantly. "She spoke to me first, Pa. I was watchin' her, an' she came up an' spoke right in my face."

"What she say?"

"She asked what I was lookin' at! I told her, an' next thing I know, that fool came up an' put his hands on my chest—"

"So you swung on him. At meetin' with your mama an' your sister right there to see."

"Pa, he started it—"

"Don' look to me like he started it, boy. Don' look to me like she started it, neither. Looks to me—an' I 'spect to most everybody who was watchin'—that ol' Gad Craven don' know better than to stare down another fella's gal right in front of that fella's nose."

"Pa, he got no right to keep her from dancin' if she wants to—"

"He got whatever right she give him. You ain' growed near big enough to be making battles over some gal, anyhow. You look like a bear cub out there, swattin' at a gator. That boy was two heads taller—"

"An' not a one o' them got a brain inside," Gad snapped.

Sam kept his smile from reaching his mouth. "I don' want to hear 'bout nothin' like this again, boy. Pick yourself a doe who ain' got a buck already tailin' her."

"Yessir," Gad said sullenly.

"An' 'specially when your mama an' your sister is there to see. You hear me?"

"Yessir."

"An' son," Sam added as they neared the wagon. "Next time, pick yourself a boy whose arm's 'bout as long as yours. You won' be in the dirt quite so quick."

"She weren't much nohow," Gad said lightly then, when he knew his mother could hear.

"Gad, I don' like to hear you talk like that," May said quietly. "If she were good enough to fight for, she be good enough to speak kindly of when the fight's lost."

Gad flushed angrily and climbed up in the wagon. Lem grinned at him, and he snapped, "Don' you say a word!" to his brother.

Lem's face fell. "I weren't fixin' to, Gaddy," he said timidly.

"Son, you best settle in an' keep your peace, 'tis a long ride," Sam turned back to say to Gad.

"Yessir," Gad said sourly.

Mattie spoke up from the rear of the wagon where she was sitting high, still flushed and jubilant from her victory. "Weren't it wonderful, Ma?" she called out. "I can still hear the music—" She turned and gazed yearningly back to the clearing where the meeting was still going strong.

"Yes, it were wonderful," May said patiently.

"If you was female," Gad muttered.

"I saw lots o' folks who weren't female havin' themselves a rollickin' time," Mattie said, tossing her head. " 'Course, they weren't fools, neither—"

"That's enough, Mattie," Sam said. "Let's have a little less jawin' an' a little more peace."

The wagon fell silent then, and they creaked up the road. After they had been driving for a bit, May said quietly, so the children could not hear her, "What did Gad tell you?"

"Nothin' that made it tolerable," Sam murmured. "Jus' that the gal gave him the eye."

" 'Twon' be the last time that happens," May said.

"Likely won' be the last time he gets riled over it, neither. I think we got ourselves a rooster spoilin' for a good tussle most every wakin' moment."

May sighed. "An' another lil' ol' cockerel who cain' hardly fly strong enough to keep hisself out of trouble."

Sam just put his arm around her shoulders and pulled her close, letting the rocking of the wagon soothe her as much as his touch. "They'll be grown and gone soon enough," he whispered. "Might as well enjoy them whilst we got them."

She put her head in the crook of his neck and closed her eyes, letting the heat and bulk of his body calm her nerves.

On a warm day in May, a wagon pulled down the rutted road to the Craven homestead and four men got out, halloing to the farmhouse, careful to keep a way back from the porch until they determined their welcome. Lem and Gad's hounds leaped at the men, barking and yelping with lolling-tongued glee, and Sam came round from the side of the stable to see what all the fuss was about. He was just in time to see Lem come from the coop and Gad from the tanning shed.

May and Mattie were already on the porch, waiting for the men to make their introductions. It was the custom for the women to keep back inside the house until their menfolks had either recognized the newcomers or made their acquaintance and ascertained their business, but Mattie had the door opened before May could call to her to stop, and so there the two women were, smiling and nodding to strangers before Sam had a chance even to see who they might be.

The older man came forward, taller than Sam and leaner, putting out his hand with one motion and doffing his hat with another. "Wes Dobbin!" he called jovially. "These here are my boys, Joseph, Andrew, and Jacob. Their mama liked big names, an' they grew to fit 'em!"

It was obviously a joke the man used often, but Sam shook his hand, laughing politely and gesturing his own boys forward. As he introduced Lem and Gad, noticing that he had to call Lem to come from behind twice. Mattie and May came down the steps to meet the callers eagerly.

"We don' see strangers often down this road, Mr. Dobbin," May said cheerfully. "Please do step in an' rest yourselves. Mattie, go fetch some cold cider from the springhouse, an' you, Lem, fetch me a slab of bacon—"

"We surely don' mean to put you out, ma'am," Wes Dobbin protested. "We jus' hoped to set a spell an' clear the dust from our throats."

"Come on, come on," Sam said. "The womenfolk won' be happy

'til they drug out every piece o' gossip you heard in five counties. You're in for it now, Dobbin.''

Laughing, the two older men went inside, May following behind them. Gad stood and sized up Dobbin's three sons. Joseph was the tallest, older than him by a few years. Andrew was probably about Mattie's age, and Jacob might be a year or two older than Lem. Hard to tell, Lem seemed so short and spavined, these days.

"Y'all wan' to sit out on the porch," Gad asked politely. "It's cooler out here anyways."

Joseph said, "We come from Tampa. Nearly five days on the road."

"If you wan' to call it that," Andrew scoffed. "Ain' no road a'tall, most o' the ways. You all sure live a far piece out."

"Yup, we like it like that," Gad said stoutly. "We been here since dirt, an' I run it, mostly."

Joseph looked Gad over with new respect. "Do tell? How big is it?"

"Nigh fifty acres," Lem said quietly, coming now up on the porch and setting down among them. "But only half put to plow."

"You do the plowin?" Jacob asked, eyeing Lem's arm and hand.

"He got struck by a rattler," Gad said quickly. "Almost died, but he's a tough one. Lemmy, tell 'em how big it were—"

Lem dropped his head, shy now and silent that someone was looking at his withered limb.

"Nigh to six feet," Mattie said pertly, coming out with tin cups and cold cider. "I nursed him for more'n ten days."

Andrew looked up at her and smiled. "You done a good job. Six feet would kill most any man."

Lem smiled gratefully at him, but Andrew didn't see it. He was still gazing at Mattie.

Mattie smiled warmly at him, put his cup gently into his hands, and turned away with a flounce of her hair.

"She's thirteen," Gad said, though no one had asked.

"She's a beauty," Andrew said softly.

"Plenty think so," Gad said airily. "But Pa says she's too young for courtin'."

The door opened again, and this time everyone came out on the porch, May carrying a small plate of corn cakes for the boys and Mattie carrying the cider. There was a brief shuffle for rockers and sitting space, and then Sam said, "Tell my boys what you told me 'bout the doin's up to Waycross."

"Well, we ain' seed it, but we only heard," Wes began, "but talk's all over the state, so's I reckon it's true. Some ol' company out o' Georgia done bought up all the swamp to the north, an' they're fixin' to log it an' make a fortune. Cypress, they're after. Call themselves the Hebard Cypress Company. An' they say they took near three hundred thousand acres offen poor ol' Captain Jackson's canal company."

"Hope they have better luck with it than he did." Sam chuckled.

"I think they mean to," Dobbin said, nodding his head. "They already got a mill up over to Waycross, fixin' to run more'n one hundred thousand board feet a day."

Gad whistled in amazement.

"It's steam-drove, like a locomotive. They say you can hear the whistle more'n ten miles off."

"They hirin'?" Gad asked eagerly.

"Not that it matters much to us," Sam said quickly. "We got all we can do to keep our own place in shape."

"I heard tell they's hiring more'n fifty men a day," Wes Dobbin said. "Folks say there's goin' to be a regular town, right in the middle of the swamp, with houses an' hotels an' shops an' suchlike. 'Course I ain' seen it myself—"

"Miss Mattie, these cakes are good," Andrew said then. "Did you make 'em your ownself?"

She nodded shyly.

"Mattie's a fair cook," May said gently. "Better'n her mama, leastwhys."

"You should taste her pies," Lem said approvingly.

"I'd like that," Andrew said, and his eyes never left her face.

"So what's doin' in Tampa?" Sam asked suddenly. "Y'all come a long ways down a bad road."

"We's headin' south," Wes Dobbin said. "We was hopin' to inflict ourselves on your generosity for one night, ma'am"—this to May—"an' then take ourselves out a' your way. This porch'd be jus' fine for us, an' we got cash money to pay for our horses' feed."

"No need for that," May said. "You stay, an' welcome."

Sam glanced at the wagon. Two horses pulled it and another two were hitched behind. "Lem, Gad, go get those fellas out a' harness an' over to the stable. Get 'em watered an' fed good."

"Boys, you do the unhitchin'," Wes Dobbin called as his three lumbered up off the porch. "I'm mighty particular 'bout my stock," he confided to Sam. "I always take along two extry, so's to rest the two pullin'."

"A good plan," Sam allowed.

"Well, I don' break down so often as some." Wes grinned. "Now you asked after doin's in Tampa—"

The boys led the four horses round back of the house, and once they got them to the stable, Mattie came in with an apron full of corncobs. "You can give 'em these," she said to Andrew, offering him the whole lot.

"Those are for Mama's Rhodies," Lem started to say, but he stopped and thought better of it. Obviously Mattie had a reason for what she did. Anyways, Andrew took them from her hands gladly.

"You got land south?" Gad asked Joseph.

The older boy nodded. "Pa's got fifty acres, an' we're fixin' to get more. It's cheaper the further south you go, you know."

"I didn' know that," Gad said. "Cain' be no cheaper than swampland up north."

"Likely not, but at least you can plow it. We heard those ol' boys who surveyed the swamp for the Hebard Company had a time of it. Took 'em more'n a year jus' to mark the boundaries, workin' twelve hours a day, sleepin' on logs up out of the mud in the swamp, an' wadin' through the water up to their necks, draggin' that survey chain. They say they were lucky to make a mile a day."

Gad whistled low. "But they's payin' well?"

"Most likely. If you can get on at the mill, the work'd be steady an' good, I reckon. But you got a good place here." He grinned at Gad. "You ain' fixin' to go stomp some swamp, is you?"

Gad shrugged. "I cain' stay on my pa's land forever."

"Don' know why not," Andrew said, still fixed on Mattie. "Looks like a good piece to me."

"I got other things to do with my days," Gad said stiffly.

"Oh, pay him no mind." Mattie laughed. "He's a sour ol' pup, an' there ain' nothin' round here pleases him much."

"He's a blind man, then," Andrew said meaningfully.

Mattie flushed and turned to go back to the house.

"I'll walk you back," Andrew said politely.

The two of them disappeared into the dusk shadows.

"She spoken for?" Joseph asked bluntly.

"Not yet," Lem said quietly.

"I 'spect she will be, soon." Joseph watched them move closer to the house, their two silhouettes walking in tandem.

Gad scoffed. "She's jus' a child."

Joseph grinned at him knowingly. "You been stuck on the farm too long, boy. That peach's ripe for pickin'."

The next morning, when Lem rose and looked over at Gad's bed, it was empty. He hurriedly pulled on his boots and went out on the porch where the Dobbin boys were still scattered about in their bedrolls. Gad was not there, and nobody else seemed to be stirring. Lem stepped lightly over the sleeping forms, shushed the hounds, and went out to the barn. It was still shut up; no sign of Gad about.

On a hunch, Lem opened the stable door and went to where the Dobbins' horses were tied up with Sam's two mounts. Caleb and Black were there. But only three of Dobbin's horses were dozing in the fresh straw. The fourth horse, a large gray, was gone. So was his harness and blanket.

Lem sank down in the straw and gazed at the empty stall, his mind a sudden, cold blank. His heart was beating high and wild in his throat, and his fingers in his good hand trembled. Gad was gone. He knew it as surely as he knew that his arm would never come back. Gad was gone for good.

* * *

On an early-summer morning, a small, solid gray creature no more than four inches long was patrolling her burrows with her usual speed and vigor. She had a short tail, short dense fur, and five clawed toes on her fore and hind feet. Her eyes and ears were so tiny as to be almost hidden beneath her fur, yet her hearing was quite acute.

She was *Blarina brevicauda*, a short-tailed shrew, and she was nothing at all like a mouse, which she vaguely resembled. Brevi had a long and slender pointed snout, much more pointed than that of a mouse. She had a continuous row of needle-sharp teeth, much sharper and used less for gnawing than for biting. She had two more toes than mice, who had only four.

But these were not Brevi's main distinctions when compared with mice, moles, and her other small mammal cousins: Brevi was a fighter.

Like most of her shrew kin, Brevi was exceedingly active and nervous, with such a high metabolism that she had to feed every three hours, both day and night, resting only for short intervals between her meals. Her energy output was higher than any other mammal's, exceeded only by that of the hummingbird, and so she had to eat twice her weight each and every day. Her meals were not particular. In fact, Brevi would eat anything she could find near her one-inch burrow tunnels, including roots and leaves, mushrooms, mice, worms, any sort of insect, any carrion or decayed kills, or even small mammals if she could catch them unawares. Like a bat, Brevi had a high-pitched squeaky voice which she used constantly in echolocation, so she could not depend on the element of surprise in her hunt.

Brevi had, instead, a most ingenious and unusual way of feeding herself. When she found something, anything, living which she thought she could swallow, she bit it viciously, aiming for the throat and face, paralyzing it almost instantly with a poison in her saliva. Once her victim could not move, she worked like a small engine to drag it to her burrow, where she could eat it slowly, often while it was still alive. In this way, she devoured snails, centipedes, beetles, other shrews, mice, moles, and anything she thought she could overpower. If the prey was too large to pull into her small burrow, she quickly used her sturdy snout as well as her powerful forefeet to excavate a bigger hole which would connect her to her underground runways. Then she pulled and pushed and worked until she got the paralyzed creature down into the dark earth, covered them both up so that no other hunter could steal her cache, and ate in speedy solitude.

Brevi was two summers old, and she had already been mated once. Her mate marked his territory close to hers with secretions from glands on his hips and belly, and other males hunting mates rarely disturbed her. Once, a young, inexperienced male had blundered into their territory, and Brevi had called to her mate in high-pitched anger. He had hurried to defend her nest, attacking the intruder fiercely. After being bitten severely, the young trespasser rolled over on his back in the submissive posture. Brevi's mate then stopped the attack and retreated, as was their custom, so that the intruder could crawl away alive.

Brevi enjoyed the excitement of the battle, and she was eager to rush forward and bite the strange male herself, but she did not do so. When her mate came back to the burrow, she ran her small paws over his entire back and haunches, smelling him for the stranger's scent, growling at him and squeaking as though she might battle him instead. But he turned and pinned her down with his shoulder, and she quieted. Her union with her mate was permanent, as were matings with most of her kind. He would likely father her young until one of them perished.

And once fathered, he would leave her to her solitary burrow and be as unwelcome as any other intruder.

Now Brevi came to the surface of the earth, searching more intently for food. She had not eaten in two hours, and her hunger was high.

She rolled over a small stick of fallen wood and found two earthworms entangled in copulation. She ripped one apart quickly, swallowing it whole and bit the other one to stop its escape. The worm was instantly paralyzed and unable to flee. Brevi dragged the worm to the entry of her burrow, stuffed it inside, and turned to continue her hunt. Very soon she would have to descend again to her young, a litter of six blind, pink, and hairless kits which waited for her to nurse them. She must cache more than a single worm for her next feeding.

Brevi hurried into a patch of trampled grasses and discovered a hidden burrow under a fallen cypress. She saw that the tree had been chewed by some gigantic beast nearly around its middle. Dying from the inside out, the cypress had finally collapsed. But what was more interesting was what was hidden beneath this large death. Brevi stopped and sniffed the ground carefully. Under the tangled cypress branches, she saw the telltale signs of nesting mice. She suddenly forgot her waiting litter for the moment.

She sent a flurry of squeaks down the burrow, listening for the echo which would tell her if it was occupied. She heard, with her tiny ears, the responding bounce of warm bodies down in the hole, and she instantly descended, following the echoes of her squeaks in the strange darkness until she came upon the mouse's nest, left while the mother foraged just as she was foraging. She quickly devoured four of the tiny, squealing mouselets, all of them hairless and blind as were her own infants. Then turning with two more in her mouth, she raced back to her burrow. She cached the two now-dead mice with the worm and hurried down to her nest, where her litter waited.

The moment the tiny babies sensed her approach, they set up a high-pitched cry which could only be heard by ears sensitive as her own. She threw herself down among them, exposing her tiny teats for them to nurse. This was the only time she was quiet, this the only place she would rest. She gave them what they needed, pushing the largest aside when he had surfeited, that the smaller might have his share. She was a careful if inconstant mother, often driven from her litter by the demands of her own belly.

A month after her discovery of the mouse nest in her territory, she took her young to the place of the fallen cypress, that they might see the hunt and experience the finding of prey for themselves. She had left three mouselets alive, and she knew that even if the mouse mother had moved them, she likely had not abandoned the burrow completely. It was as good a place as any for her young to begin to kill.

She hid her youngsters at one end of the burrow under the branches and she went to the other end of the burrow to flush out the mice. As she moved toward the long mouse tunnel, she heard a scraping noise and she turned around, her heartbeat already accelerating to more than a thousand beats per minute in fear.

A long yellow rat snake was approaching the mouse tunnels cautiously, drawn by the same prey Brevi hunted. As the snake moved forward, flicking its long forked tongue at the still air, Brevi squeaked in terror, a signal which also told her young that danger was near. Instantly, the weanlings each grasped with its mouth the base of the tail of its closest sibling, forming a chain of tiny shrews, end to end. Brevi scuttled quickly to her children, and the youngster closest to her took hold of her tail. They hurried away in a long caravan, looking from a distance like a moving small snake.

As Brevi looked back at the fallen cypress, she could no longer see the yellow rat snake. It had disappeared down the mouse hole. Whatever was within would walk the belly of that snake within the hour. She did not turn back again, but raced back to her own burrow, dragging her young behind her to safety.

* * *

It took Gad more than five days to reach Tampa, even though Dobbin's horse did his best. He got lost twice on the trail to Fort Brooke, wandering once to the east and once to the north before finally finding the right path again, spending one fearful night close enough to deep swamp that he could hear the boom and bellow of alligators on all sides. The horse was so nervous, Gad had to hobble him and tie him to a tree as well, for fear he'd run off in the darkness. By the time he reached the settlement, he was already out of the salt pork and biscuits he'd stashed in the saddlebags, and his blanket was torn and wet clear through.

He spent all of the four dollars he'd taken from his mother's cash money jar on rations in Fort Brooke, pushed on to Tampa, and got as far north as the Withlacoochee before he got lost again. This time he wandered nearly a day before he could ford the river, trying to keep to the west and out of the deeper swamp. A man in Tampa told him to keep to the coast, find the Suwannee, and follow it up to where the Hebard Cypress Company was working. It sounded simple enough, but once away from home, nothing was simple at all. Even supper required a good deal of effort and thought, and he almost turned back many times and gave up his plan.

But when he thought of his father's face, Gad kept on going. Better to be lost than to have to turn tail and slink home again like a suck-egg hound. Somewhere a few miles up the Suwannee, he lost Dobbin's horse, having tied it too loosely when he sat down to catch some bream on the eastern bank. He set out on foot then, for he knew it was impossible to make it back without a horse. He could only go on.

After more than two weeks, he finally reached the central part of the swamp up the Suwannee, and he could hear the shriek of the saws and smell the burning of the timber before he reached the logging camp. He began to pass large stretches of land which were stripped of trees and flattened by the great wagon roads of the company crews.

He arrived at the crew boss's tent hungry, weary, and mostly barefoot. Within two days, he had a job, half of a cot he shared with another bucket boy, and a bellyful of camp food. He was amazed at how that full belly made everything else easy enough to stomach.

The Hebard Cypress Company had one mission to accomplish, and everything which supported that goal was good; anything which stood in the way was unnecessary. The mission was to take out the heavy timber of the swamplands and turn it into cash money, and not a man on Billy's Island, the site of the company's main camp, had a doubt that Charles Hebard of Charles Hebard and Sons Lumber Company of Philadelphia would accomplish that mission, if he had to hire every man in the state to do it.

Gad worked on a crew which was at the task from sunup to sundown, fifteen miles into the depths of the swamplands, slogging through muck and whatever dry hammocks they could find. He was a bucket boy on the girdling crew, fetching water for a troop of ten men who went through the woods and girdled or ringed every tree their bossman told them to cut. By hand, they cut through the bark and the sapwood of every marked tree, leaving it to die as it stood. Gad brought the water and also held the sap buckets which kept the rosin from miring their saws so fast, dumping them and then holding them for long hours again, moving from cutting to cutting. In a week, he was upped to girdler and some other poor fool, younger even than he was, held the heavy buckets.

Behind their girdling crew came the logging crews, which harvested the trees girdled by earlier cuts. If they ran out of girdled trees, they simply took down the ones closest to them. Using huge crosscut saws, they felled timber for twelve hours a day. Skidder crews operated the steam-powered skidders which had cables running out for more than a thousand feet in all directions into the swamp. The logs were hooked to a trolley, which ran on overhead cables, and hauled to flatcars. The railroad crews had laid down and were running more than thirty-five miles of track into the swamp interior.

Gad was grateful he was not hired out to that crew. They had to lay the track on twenty-foot pilings which they drove deep into the muck as much as fifteen feet below the surface. Then small-gauge engines screamed and puffed their way into the swamp and dragged the flatcars out to the mill. The men on that crew got paid two dollars a day, but they earned every penny, between snakes and varmints and mosquitoes.

The woods were bristling with the shriek of steam engines, the buzz of saws, shouting, profane men, and the crash and roar of falling timber. It seemed to Gad that there was not a quiet moment from the time he opened his eyes to the time the last lamp went out in camp. He would not have believed there could be so many trees cut so fast, but the men moved like a swarm of ants in and out of the woods, crawling over fallen timber, cutting it to haulable lengths, and dragging it to the flatcars, then back again for more loads. At first, there seemed to be no order to it, but after a week, Gad saw that he was a cog in a machine, and he put his mind to being the best, that he might soon get out of the crew altogether. The train engineers made more than two dollars a day. It seemed to Gad that such a berth was the best place for him.

Gad was paid a dollar for every twelve hours he worked, paid on Saturday night, for six days of labor. With his six dollars, he was then set loose with the other two thousand men to enjoy his Sunday of rest as best he might.

There wasn't time to make it out to Hebardville, the bustling town which had sprung up around the main company mill. Gad heard it had its own school, two churches, gaslights, and a post office. A few of his crewmates also boasted that Hebardville had the finest whores this side of Waycross, Georgia.

Gad wasn't sure what a whore was, but his bunkmate was proud to educate him fast enough, and so within a month, he knew more, he reckoned, than his father did about such things. He told no one he was only sixteen. They did not ask, and he did not offer. So long as he could girdle the trees, no one seemed to give a damn.

On Saturday night, Gad followed the crews to the hub of the logging settlement, Billy's Island. It was an old homestead, farmed by the Dan Lee family way back when, but the Hebard Company took it over and turned it into a bustling crew town. Billy's Island was out in the middle of the swamp, fifteen miles from the nearest real village, but to Gad, it looked big as Tampa. When he first arrived, it had still the remnants of the old homestead intact, and just to look at the falling farm buildings and the sagging fence lines made him feel lonely and homesick. But within the year, the house and barns were torn down to make room for the workers' families. The next year, a hotel and a large company store were built, and by the time Gad had worked for Charles Hebard nearly five years, there were streets laid out with shade trees, telephones, a doctor, a vaudeville theater, a school, and a pretty schoolmistress.

But Gad wasn't interested in the pretty schoolmistress. Of the six hundred inhabitants of Billy's Island, the one who caught and kept his eye was Dorrie Slipper, the redheaded cashier at the Hebard Hotel.

He was twenty, he was as hard-muscled as he was ever going to be, he was a crew boss now at a dollar and a half a day, he had cash money in his pockets, and he had a girl. He still thought of his mother and father, of Mattie and Lem and the old place with soft longing every so often, but such thoughts never brought water to his eyes anymore. He had told himself often enough, when he left, and for the next five years, it was get out or get stuck. Those were the choices, he saw it clear then and he hadn't altered that view much over time.

But staggered fence lines of the Dan Lee homestead, straggling lines of rotting wood which nobody maintained and nobody heeded, still reminded him of a long wooden porch with two rockers, of an old barn with the smell of hay and the solid contentment of chewing stock, of a rooster which crowed in the early swamp light . . . of his mother.

No doubt by now, Miss Mattie had a beau, likely even a husband, he told himself. Ol' Lem was probably still walking behind ol' Caleb, plowing the same acres over and over. And Pa was likely spending the better part of each day in one of those rickety rockers.

Most times, he thanked God he wasn't in the other one. But some evenings, when the wind was soft from the swamp and the smell of cooking drifted through the boardinghouse and upward to his small raftered room over the parlor, he wished he could see the old place again. Wished he could shake Lem's good hand and slip him ten dollars. Wished he could apologize for not saying good-bye.

But there was nothing he could say, he knew, to make up for the fact that he slipped away without a farewell. And on a stolen horse, in the bargain. He had been on Billy's Island long enough now to hear many men tell their tales of how they came to be fifteen miles into the deepest swamplands in the state. Most of them had left something behind in a hurry. Some of them were dangerously silent when the subject came up, and Gad knew that like as not those boys hired on to get away from more than a plow. He was no worse than most of them, he figured. But no better, neither.

The times he felt best about his life and what he left behind were when he held pretty Dorrie in his arms, either smuggled away up in his small raftered room or out in the woods on some tangled path of bowered hammock. Dorrie lived in the hotel, and Charles Hebard frowned on female employees fraternizing with the crew. Guests in female quarters were strictly forbidden, lest Billy's Island get a worse reputation than Hebardville.

And so Gad had only an hour or two with Dorrie in the evenings and Sundays, but he told himself that was plenty. Tell the truth, likely the best times were when he got off by himself, off in the woods away from the noise of the crew and the shriek of the steam engines. Then, with the silence of the swamp all around him, he could almost imagine himself a boy again, with his whole life before him, shining and perfect as a new-laid egg.

He missed his brother, he missed his parents, he missed his old hound dog. But he guessed this must be what it was like to be a man. Having some, missing others, and rising to the work whistle every day for a dollar.

Gad had been keeping company with Dorrie for about a year, when she began to speak of more than long walks on warm evenings and the pleasures of his lumpy boardinghouse bed. His first hint that things between them were not going to go on this way forever was when she up and told him one night that Bobby May asked to take her to the vaudeville show on Saturday night, next.

He raised his eyebrows and said, "I don't know no Bobby May. What crew's he on?"

"Oh, he's a skidder," Dorrie said casually. "But he's gonna be a team boss soon."

"Yeah? Well, so's Miss Aster." Miss Laura Aster was the full-bosomed, gray-haired widow lady who ran Gad's boardinghouse with a soft voice and an iron glare. "So, what's he doin' sparkin' my gal?"

"Oh, he don' mean no harm," Dorrie said airily. "He's a good man. An' he asked real polite." She looked up at Gad innocently. "I ain' sure if we had any plans for that evenin', so I told him I'd have to let him know."

"What do you think? 'Course we got plans. Since when ain' we got plans on a Saturday night?"

"Well, you ain' asked me," she pouted prettily.

"I ain' asked you. You an' me been keepin' company now since the Thanksgivin' dance, an' now all of a sudden, I got to ask you? You want to go to the vaudeville show with this May fly?"

She swung her hand which was in his, making their two arms circumscribe great loops. "Oh, he's all right, Gaddy. He takes a girl serious, leastwhys."

"How you know that?"

" 'Cause he asks so polite. I can tell. Mister May is lookin' for more than a Saturday-night gal."

"Well, bully for him. I need to suggest to the boy that he look elsewhere than at the cashier window at Hebard's."

"Well, *you* don' take me very serious," she murmured in a soft complaint.

"I ain' polite?" he asked indignantly.

"Oh, you're polite enough, but you never talk about the future none. An' you never ask me proper anymore. You just reckon, good ol' Dorrie, she's gonna be there, no matter what." She turned to him with her chin a bit higher. "Well, what if good ol' Dorrie was to study on somethin' else sometime, Gaddy? What 'bout that?"

"Like what?" Now he stopped and faced her, his mouth tight with exasperation. When Dorrie got like this, it was better to stop the train rolling down the track while it was going slow. Once it picked up speed, it would bowl down an ox.

"Well, a girl's got to think on her future," she said petulantly. "A girl wants a place of her own an' her own pots to cook in. Maybe even a bit of a garden, so's she can have some flowers or somethin'." She looked up at him appealingly. "Maybe even some kids, Gaddy. An' a man who comes home to her every night, an' not just on Saturdays."

He took her hand again and began walking silently. This was a conversation he had dreaded, but of course, he knew it would come sooner or later. If Dorrie were a smarter gal, it would have been sooner.

He glanced sideways at her bosom, resting high and full in her light, cotton frock. She wasn't a smart one, Dorrie wasn't, but she was pretty enough, and she had a ready laugh. And once he managed to maneuver her under him, she made him sweat and buck, all the while whispering to him secret pleas and demands which made him forget the six days of hard labor he'd just had and the six more he faced once Sunday was past.

He didn't want to lose her, but he surely didn't want to say what she wanted him to say, just to keep her. And kids! He felt like he was still a kid himself. Where did gals get such notions?

"So this May fella's lookin' for a marryin' kind of gal, and I'm not? Is that what you're sayin' to me, Dorrie?" He thought if he acted indignant enough, she might just back off.

She said calmly, "I don' know what you're lookin' for, Mister Craven. I jus' know you ain' askin' me to go to the vaudeville show these days. I don' know what else you ain' askin' me to do."

Perhaps Dorrie was a bit smarter than he'd thought. He turned suddenly and pulled her into his arms, hoping that his embrace would soften her. It usually did. But instead his body betrayed him, and his nether parts reared up and acted like they hadn't touched a woman in a month instead of a week. Naturally, she felt his response and giggled, pulling away. She knew she had the upper hand. "You're gonna miss me when I'm gone, Gaddy," she teased him.

"Where you goin'?" he asked a little roughly. "Not with any damn-fool skidder, not if I got a word to say about it."

"Oh you got a word to say about it," she smiled. "Leastwhys, a little word. But don't wait too long to ask me, Gaddy. A gal cain' wait forever, you know."

"So I hear," he said, nuzzling her neck. "A man cain' wait forever, neither, Dorrie. Why do you make me beg you?"

" 'Cause you do it so nice," she murmured, twisting her body against his in a way which made him moan involuntarily. "I'm crazy 'bout you, Gaddy."

"I'm crazy 'bout you, too, Dorrie," he said, trying to hold her still and kiss her all at once. He knew that if she said anything else, he'd likely agree to it now. He could only pray she wouldn't press her advantage.

"I think we should get married," she said then, quietly.

He groaned and buried his teeth in her neck, half in passion, half in exasperation. Why did they always have to say the one thing which should not be said?

And she was still talking!

"I know you ain' ready yet," she was saying methodically, as though they were not nearly making love on a public road, "but you will be soon, I hope. 'Cause I cain' wait forever to think 'bout the future."

"I wish you'd think more 'bout tonight," he said, trying now to fondle her full bosom through the light cloth, "an' let the damned future take care of itself."

"Gaddy!" she protested in mock righteousness. "Don' cuss 'round me, it ain' polite!" She tried to push him away with another delicious giggle.

To stop her talking, he pressed his mouth over hers, held down her hands, and, making a masterly effort, tried not to think about what this might cost him in the nights to come. "Dorrie," he said, almost gasping, "I ain' against marriage. I just ain' quite ready yet. An' if you keep torturin' me this way, I'll likely keel over dead before I ever get to the altar."

"Oh, my poor Gaddy," she murmured, kissing him now in the way that inflamed him. "Dorrie's not goin' to tease you anymore, sweet lamb. She's gonna give you what you want, she promises."

Before she could change her mind, he hurried her back to the boardinghouse, up the creaky stairs in the rear, and behind the door of his cramped little room. She allowed herself to be drawn to the bed only reluctantly, as though she had no idea how she got there or what he had in mind. Of course, this only made him more crazy with desire, and naturally she knew that.

In some part of his mind, Gad was cursing her and all women, even as he was loving her, even as he was loving her ways. He wondered vaguely if all women acted as Dorrie did. Had his mother teased his father so unmercifully? Did little Mattie know how to make a man beg like this? And then he put all thoughts of mother and sister out of his mind, as Dorrie was once more under him, moving like liquid heat.

Gad got used to the long hours and the exhausting work in the swamps after a year or two, but he never got used to rising before dark and jumping in the crew wagon before he even had a chance to clear his bowels, much less his eyes in the morning.

Now he knew what his father had endured. He wondered that the man had been able to do it, so much older than he was now. But as he kept with the crew and began to get used to the rhythms, he found that the labor had some compensating factors besides just the pay.

The swamp was a haunting place, now that his eyes were old enough to appreciate what they saw, so much more than it had been when he was just a boy. It was constantly changing, always destroying itself and rebuilding, in a way he had never noticed when he lived on the outskirts of it, on acres which were level and tilled.

As if by some grand design, teeming hosts of grasses and sedges, shrubs and water plants, grew almost without cease, filling in the swamp with their decaying bodies as they died and gradually making water into cushiony bogs—bogs which tortured the men as they stepped into them, for they looked like solid land until they were asked to bear any weight.

And, of course, they would be solid land, someday. They were the babies of the swamp, bogs that would someday grow to be the solid pinelands that the crews were stripping of trees now.

As Gad walked through the swamp, moving from one point to another, he often had to go around peat bogs, places where the narrow, barely moving water was filled with a pungent black mass which was in the process of completely blocking the stream. Sprawling atop it, like little orphans, were white and yellow lilies and tiny-flowered spikes of neverwets or golden clubs that the black mass had thrust up in its own rise out of the water.

Gad thought of the rising, growing peat bogs as the great pumping heart of the swamp. He often got out of his canoe and touched his boot onto the stuff carefully, just to see if it could hold him. It never could. His boot always went in as far as he would let it sink. It was pure peat, a mass of organic matter that had risen from the bottom of the prairie to the surface and, in rising, had stranded all the water plants floating above it. He always ended up trying not to lose his balance, half-awed, half-disgusted at the muck of the stuff, for it seemed to be the slimiest mud in all God's creation. But, in fact, he discovered that the peat only looked like mud: as did so many things in the swamp, it looked like something it was not. Actually, if he got it on his clothes and then washed it off, it never stained and cleaned up quick. Not like the mud round the homestead at all.

The peat was just one example of how the swamp was always changing, always killing itself off just to be reborn again. It was gas, forming down below the peat in huge amounts by the decay of sunken, dead vegetation trapped under itself, that lifted the peat up high. The loggers called this a blowup. The floating peat bogs could be more than a hundred feet long and germinate seeds faster than cow piles. And then they could break off, drift with the currents, and lodge at the edge of the prairies where they'd make new grasses, shrubs, and finally, trees.

The blowups and the batteries were a first stage, so far as Gad could see, of the swamp making itself over. The crowding of plants into every available piece of ground began the process of turning muck and water into someplace a man could, eventually, stand upright. Some of the peat islands were grassed, places where waterfowl could stand and scan the water for hunters. Others were covered with low shrubs, swamp-loving button bushes and other upstarts. The oldest islands—the loggers called them houses when they were dry and firm enough to use as campsites—were dotted with trees and on the verge of turning into even larger cypress bays, tracts of more than twenty acres where the mighty trees could flourish.

And once the cypress grew tall, the loggers took them down, reversing the process that the swamp was always starting again someplace new. It seemed to Gad that the swamp was as eternal as God. It had its own rhythms, its own laws, and its own sense of time. They took down timber as fast as they could find it, and still the numbers of trees seemed to stretch on forever. They could never cut it all, he knew, not if Hebard hired every man jack in Florida and took the rest of his life paying them.

The animals were fewer, of course, far fewer than he remembered on the homestead. But it might be, he told himself, simply that he wasn't hunting much these days. He rarely saw the numbers of deer and black bear and ducks and whooping cranes he recollected at home, and those he did see were more skittish.

All except the wild boars. Those piney woods rooters, as the boys called them, were the most dangerous animals in the swamp, so far as Gad was concerned. He'd seen wild boars take on and kill a bear in pitched battles, and they thought nothing of dispatching diamondbacks and swallowing them whole. His father never hunted them, because a man always risked losing even his best dogs when the boar turned to fight at the end.

But in this dense swamp, the boars were even more numerous and fearless. They feasted on the roots of the wampee plant, a bulb so hot it could burn a man's throat to the bone. The old-timers said it must make the boars drunk, and even meaner than usual, because they stood so long in the shallows digging for roots that the water softened their hooves, and they could hardly walk. When the crews came on them, they stood their ground, lowered their tusks, and squealed in fierce anger.

Gad got so he just went around them and left them the ground, rather than try to chase them out. Better to come back another day than risk a man's leg over a stand of trees.

It was markedly easier to get lost in this part of the swamp, even after Gad had been there for years. At home, he was able to find his

way through the labyrinthine waters by noticing the small differences
in the growth of bark on trees, or the nests of the osprey, which usually
kept themselves about four miles apart. Find a nest and then another,
and you could tell how far you had traveled.

But here, the landmarks, if there were any, were very hard to note.
He learned to be an even better navigator than he had been as a boy,
for it was easy to get confused, even more easy when the territory was
new almost every week. Many on his crew were ex-swampers, men
who had lived in the swamp and made their living from it. They were
straightforward, practical men, and they shared a common pride in the
fact that they figured nobody else could master this world like they
could.

They knew, most of them, to listen to birdsong for clues to the
weather, to the hoot of the barred owl that signaled when the animals
began to feed at dusk. They knew that the chattering of woodpeckers
in the open pinewoods told that the fish were biting, and the humming-
birds could lead a man to honey just as fast as bees. And with all that,
if they didn't stay in hollering distance from each other, he could reckon
to lose a man a week to the swamp, while the poor sod wandered until
he could find his way out or stumble into another crew.

What they knew best, of course, was the trees and how to cut them.
They gave Hebard his money's worth, Gad liked to tell them on Saturday payday, and any man who wouldn't best hire onto a different crew.

Saturday night was something to look forward to all week. At least
Gad had gals on his arm, most of the time. In fact, he soon got the
reputation for being quite a ladies' man with the rest of the crew.
"Young buck," they called him jocularly, or "Gad-abuck," when they
were feeling frisky. The closer it came to Saturday night, the more he
heard that name.

Dorrie Slipper had not been on his arm for a month or more, when
Gaddy decided to go to meeting on Billy's Island one Sunday. Generally,
he avoided the large, open field where the meeting was once each
month, for the sun was hot, the folks usually snakebit by religion, and
the preaching long and sanctimonious. But this Sunday, he was without
gal and without plans. Gaddy strolled over to the meeting grounds with
his best hat and high hopes.

As he approached the place where folks came to listen to the word
of four different preachers under the hot, stifling tent, he thought of
his sister, Mattie, and how she had blossomed that meeting into a

dancing filly, right before their eyes. He also remembered, dimly, the gal who had grinned at him, causing him to take a swing at the tall swamp-boy next to her. But he was older now and wiser, he told himself. There weren't no gal worth fighting over, not when there were so many willing and eager to take his arm and accept his attentions.

He sauntered into the midst of more than a hundred people, many of them milling toward the meeting tent, and he could hear over the hum of the arriving throng, the calling of the preachers to the faithful, already exhorting them to penance before they even took their seats. Of course, it wasn't the preaching Gad came for, and he suspected most of the men who clustered at the rear of the tent, languidly leaning against the poles and watching the crowd, felt as he did. It was the gals which drew them, the gals who gazed up at the preachers with great wide eyes of youthful hope and smiled tremulously when they caught the gaze of one of the men at the edge.

Gad was leaning with some of the others, keeping his hat at just the right tilt, his mouth in a serious pose, when he saw her sitting in a gaggle of gals to the right of the preacher's box. She was dark-haired and luminous, her skin pale as cream, her cheeks faintly pink with the heat. Small tendrils of dark hair had escaped from the pile on top her head and curled in dampened twists down her neck. She wore a blue dress with a wide white collar, red stitching around it, and she was beautiful.

Gad stared at her, suddenly alert to every nuance of gesture, every breath of air which might come from her side of the crowd. He lifted his head slightly, as though he might actually scent her on the wind. She was talking to a friend and when she laughed suddenly, a low, private sound of delight, he was struck with a wave of longing so powerful that he almost swayed into the tent, as though drawn by a hand at his collar.

He moved without thinking so that he came closer to her, and from that angle, he could see that she had a slender body, long graceful arms, and no rings on her fingers at all. Unadorned by either jewelry or paint, she seemed to shine like a white mushroom against dark soil. Now he could hear her voice.

"I don't care," she was saying to her friend. "It seems to me that Mister Grady's got more on his mind than your best interests these days."

"Well, why shouldn't he?" her friend answered blithely. "He's a man, ain't he? I never seen one yet that thought of nothin' else save his ownself."

"If I thought that," the woman said thoughtfully, "I should never have a single thing to do with a one of them. I'd go be a nun in a convent."

"You'd miss out on all the fun," her friend giggled. "Shush, now!" she gestured to the makeshift stage where one of the preachers was hauling his girth up to speak. "This here one's supposed to be quite a workup."

Gad moved closer still, hoping that he might hear her speak again, might catch a glimpse of her heart and soul somehow by her words. But she was silent now, watching and listening, leaning forward with her mouth slightly open in concentration, a thin film of moisture on her cheeks, rocking slightly back and forth as the preacher began to shout his welcome and beckon them into his spell of exhortation.

Gad was barely aware of the noise from the makeshift stage or the buzz and murmur and loud purr of the crowd. He was more aware of the fly which seemed about to land on the girl's right shoulder, and the movement in and out of her back as she breathed. The color of her dress was like the sky, the detail around the collar a bright red, like the red fruit of a cassena tree.

He wondered vaguely why he had never seen her on Billy's Island before. Surely he must have seen every eligible gal for miles around. She had to be new in town, he realized. And as such, she would quickly capture the attention of every man who would want to have her for his own. He knew that if he did not stake his claim fast, he'd have no chance at all.

He waited impatiently, watching her, as first one preacher and then another got up and stoked the crowd for signs of life. It was hot, the flies buzzed unmercifully, and ladies wilted on all sides, their soft talcum scent rising up like decayed fruit. At some point, only about two-thirds through the meeting, she turned and whispered to her companion, stood up abruptly, and made her way down the aisle, fanning herself with a pure white handkerchief and smiling apologetically to those she had to squeeze past.

He was there when she came out of the tent, and he waited while she patted her brow.

"It's mighty close in there," he ventured courteously, doffing his hat. "Them preachers put out plenty of hot air."

She glanced over at him and appraised him quickly, taking in his new vest, his shoes, and the way he held his bowler all at once. He stood up a little taller and smiled as encouragingly as he could.

"Yes," she murmured, beginning to walk away toward the tables where the ladies were setting up box lunches and lemonade under the trees.

"My name's Gad Craven," he said, moving a little closer. "I don' 'spect they be servin' yet, but if you like, I can get you somethin' cold at the hotel an' bring it back for you. You could just wait over there in the shade."

She turned and looked at him more fully now, her eyes bewildered. "Have we met, Mister Craven?"

"No ma'am," he said, standing up forthrightly. "But I figure you must be new in town, an' I'm just tryin' to welcome you proper."

She smiled ruefully. "You figure I must be new in town. That means you must know every young lady on Billy's Island, and since you don't know me, I must be new. Is that the way of it, Mister Craven?"

He was taken back by her quick assessment and turned his bowler around and around at the edge with nervous fingers. "No ma'am," he said meekly. "I don' know every gal in town. But I reckon when I saw you, I sure enough need to know this one."

She tilted her head and smiled again, this time more kindly. "Well, I thank you for your kindness, Mister Craven, but I feel sure I can manage quite well."

She turned from the tables then, and he had the distinct impression that he had made her swerve from where she wanted to go. He watched her walk past the meeting tent, past the clustered group of wagons and drays and hitched horses, and up the long walk toward town. He followed her at a discreet distance, trying to look as though he had other places to go and important business to tend.

She never looked back at him once. He was relieved, of course, for he did not wish to look like a fool, but he was also disgruntled. She was so completely unaware of him, so unconcerned about his presence. Even a doe would look around to see if she were followed, he thought. Her walk was smooth, unhurried, but possessed of more dignity and self-containment than was usual in a woman of her years. He thought, this one is going to be a handful.

She turned past the hotel, to his surprise, and went into a small white house two blocks past the center of town, a house set back on a yellowing swatch of dry grass, banked by profusions of blue asters. He waited until she was inside, and then he strolled by, glancing at the window which faced the street. She was not watching him from within, at least not so he could see.

He turned and went right to the window at the hotel which served as the post office for Billy's Island. The clerk behind the counter was a bespectacled old man who knew everyone within five miles.

"Mister Harper," Gad asked, "who lives at that white house with the blue asters just past the hotel?"

"The one with the window facing the street?" the old man asked, taking off his glasses and wiping them thoughtfully.

"That be the one."

"That's Miss Delma's house," he said, bobbing his head vigorously. "Can't miss those blue asters. Though I 'magine, they're all but eat up in this heat—"

"Miss Delma? Do she have a daughter?"

"Lord no, Miss Delma's a spinster-lady, Gad-abuck," Harper chuckled. "You must 'a seen her niece."

Passing right over the rather discouraging fact that even this old man knew his nickname, Gad said, "That must 'a been her. Tall gal with dark hair an' pale skin? Kinda slender, with a blue dress—"

"Well, I don' know as I place the dress, but the rest sounds close enough."

"What might the lady's name be?"

Mister Harper came closer, put on his spectacles, and looked him up and down. "This ain' no lonely hearts meetin', Gad-abuck. This is the United States Post Office. If you want to know the lady's name, you best ask her your ownself."

Gad leaned forward on the counter and grinned at the man, assuming his best air of boyish camaraderie. "Ah come on, Mister Harper. Ain' you never seen a lady you just got to speak to or die? Just one time? I can tell by lookin', she won't give me the time of day, lest I can call her by her name. Just give me a hint. I don' need to know her Christian name, just how to 'Miss' her proper."

The old man shook his head stubbornly. "If I give it to one, I got to give it to every blamed buck that come in here, sniffing around every gal in town. I got a policy, Mister Craven. And it's the same policy of the United States government. Everybody's got a right to privacy."

"Yessir," Gad said, pulling his elbows off the counter reluctantly. He turned to go. Then he thought of her dark hair and her graceful walk and he turned back one more time. "How 'bout if I study on that idea, Mister Harper? How 'bout if I come back here an' discuss it like a politician? Then you think maybe you could see your way clear to telling me her name?"

Mister Harper chuckled then, wiping his hands on his leather apron. "Gad-abuck, you got more spunk than most, I give you that. I tell you what. You come back here 'bout four o'clock sharp an' you bring your ears 'long with you, an' could be, you could just figure out what you want to know all by your ownself."

Gad grinned and slapped his fist on the counter jubilantly. "Thank you, sir! Thank you, Mister Harper! I be back at four o'clock!"

"I don' doubt it a bit," the old man said laconically, shaking his head.

At quarter to four, Gad arrived at the counter again, waved at Mister Harper, and sat down to wait. Sure enough, right close to four, he saw her coming. She had changed out of her blue meeting dress into a softer, lighter frock, something she might wear to gather flowers in the garden or dust the parlor or maybe just take a walk to town to pick up the mail. As she stepped inside, she saw him right away, nodded to him politely, and went to the counter. He saw that she saved her smile for Mister Harper.

"Afternoon, Miss Georgia," he nodded, handing her a small stack of letters. He never glanced at Gad.

"Good afternoon," she said softly.

As she turned away from the counter, Mister Harper asked, "Have you heard any news from your mother? Missus Freeman was always pretty regular, writing your aunt."

"Yessir," she said nodding. "She says the humidity in Atlanta is so horrid, she's near give out."

" 'Tain't no better down here," he said, nodding wisely. "Tell her, she's better off stayin' put. Most folks are."

"I'll tell her," she said, stepping out the door with never another look in Gad's direction.

Gad waited until she was out of hearing, leaped up out of his chair, and said, "You are a prince, Mister Harper! A genu-wine prince!"

"Just don' let on to the rest of 'em you heard it here," he gruffed. "An' don't pester the poor woman to death!"

"I give you my solemn oath!" Gad said, hurrying out the door. Georgia Freeman, of Atlanta, a splendid name for a splendid woman.

He raced around the corner just in time to see her stopped at a haber-
dashery store and bend down, looking at something in the window. He
slowed to a stroll.

She did not glance up as he went by, but he could tell that she had
seen him. She straightened and began to walk toward the small white
house, and he followed, this time at less of a distance than before.

Suddenly she turned to face him, her chin high. "Sir, do you intend
to follow me all over Billy's Island?"

He bowed, doffing his bowler. "If I have to," he murmured politely.

She turned on her heel and walked a little more quickly.

He continued to follow.

"Really, I wish you wouldn't—" she turned and began to protest.

"I can' help it," he said softly. "Please don' break my heart, Miss
Freeman."

"Well, there's certainly nothing wrong with your hearing," she said
sourly. "I can't say the same for your good sense."

"I think I got better sense than most in this town," he said. "I saw
you, I knew right off that you were the one woman I want to marry,
an' I be doin' my best to make that happen. To me, that seems like
the best sense of all." He was amazed at himself. He had no idea he
felt that way, but as he said the words, he knew them to be true. He
had never spoken so seriously to a woman in his life. To his relief, she
did not laugh. Neither did she run away.

She took a long moment, gazing at him. "You don't know me at
all," she said finally. "But you have decided you want to marry me.
How do you know I'm not already betrothed?"

"You don' wear no ring," he said. "Besides, any man you were wed
to be a fool to let you go away from him to someplace like this."

Now she smiled. "I suppose you're right about that much, at least.
Billy's Island is hardly paradise."

He smiled softly. "It can be. If you got the right companion by your
side."

"And you're that—companion?"

"I mean to be, if you'll let me try."

She laughed lightly. "Sir, I don't even know your name, and you've
already proposed to me. I would say you're trying, whether I wish you
to or not."

"My name is Gad Craven," he said firmly, taking a small step closer
to her. "I be boss of the girdlin' crew. I'm twenty-two, fit an' healthy,
an' my family farms to the south herebouts." He hesitated, dropping

his eyes. "If you want me to quit pesterin' you, just say the word, Miss Freeman."

She waited a long while before she answered. He never raised his head. "I can't encourage you, Mister Craven," she finally said gently. "I mean no offense, but I also mean not to marry."

"There ain' no one else?"

She shook her head.

"Can I take my chances?"

She smiled ruefully. "I would say, you've done plenty of that in your life. You're probably not going to stop now."

He stepped up to her side and offered her his arm. "I be honored to walk you home, Miss Freeman."

"You may," she said, not taking his arm. "But I won't invite you in."

"Maybe 'nother time."

She chuckled, moving ahead of him with a quick pace.

For a month, Gad courted Georgia lavishly, spending all his money and his time to prove to her that he was sincere in his efforts to win her. She never budged from her first position that he was not to be taken seriously, not even when he spoke again and again of their future together. She only invited him to her aunt's home twice, both times for a short and stifling tea which hardly showed him, he knew, to his best advantage.

On the other hand, she had finally allowed him to kiss her, however briefly, and he could only hope that this trespass meant she at least considered him a possibility. She was of a different cut than Dorrie, much more dignified and mature. Surely she wouldn't allow such a liberty if she didn't care for him, would she? If she didn't think he was serious?

He pondered the soul of woman—most particularly, this woman—over and over in his small, crowded room. He had never offered to take her to his chambers, for he knew that she would consider them beneath her. Her aunt kept a tidy home, at least what he could tell from the parlor. Her husband had been on a steam crew and had died four years back. She stayed on, Gad guessed, because of the house. So the family was not rich, that much was apparent, yet they seemed secure enough. Georgia was clearly head and shoulders above his own family, but he told himself that this would not matter once they were married. He wouldn't be a girdler forever. He told her this so often that she nodded and completed the sentence for him. And then she would smile up at him sideways with that slight tilt to her chin that told him she was teasing. He wanted to take her in his arms right then and kiss her on the public street, but he knew better. Georgia Freeman was not a gal; she was a lady.

And a lady was exactly what Gad Craven wanted.

Always before Georgia, Gad had rubbed raw against the boredom of Billy's Island, cussing the place every Saturday night because there was so little to do. Now he was glad there were few distractions and only one vaudeville house to go to, for it made the long walks he liked to take with Georgia through the woods more acceptable.

At first, Georgia had little appreciation for the beauty of the swamp, but once he took her out in his canoe, she began to see more than those sights which only dry land could offer. Now that it was autumn, the swamp took on an almost ghostly quality, and often the mist fell onto the water even before dusk, making all outlines illusive, all shapes indistinct.

He liked to paddle her to the largest prairie near Billy's Island, a broad grassy swampland where the air brightened and the mist glowed. Marigolds bloomed in yellow clusters and the stately cypresses were shrouded in mist. It all looked permanent, unchanging, and motionless. But Gad knew that every plant, every flowing ripple of water was part of the struggle to transform the swamp from water to land and then back again.

This was the swamp's quiet time of the year. As he paddled, he said to Georgia, "See there, you cain' hardly find a single frog now. A month ago, they was thick through here."

"Where'd they go?"

"Under the mud, gettin' ready for winter. All the pig frogs an' the cricket frogs are diggin' their holes already, an' the others will soon enough. In a few months, you won' see a one. Fish, neither. They be down in the peat an' the muck, goin' all quiet-like with the cold."

"It's hardly a winter," Georgia said. "Compared with what we have farther north."

Georgia had traveled to Boston and New York to visit relatives, and he bowed to her expertise. But when it came to the swamp, he was not afraid to tell her what was so.

" 'Tis winter enough for these varmints. Wait 'nother two months, an' you can spy whole flocks of robins comin' in from the north, an' nary a frog nor a gator to be seen." He paddled nearer to a stark, dead cypress which reached into the gray sky.

"Is that one the girdle crew took?" she asked.

"No ma'am," he shook his head. "That one was took by fire. Likely ten years ago or more. See that nest up top?"

She peered upward, shading her eyes, and nodded.

" 'Tis osprey. Won' be 'nother one for four miles or so. That's one way not to get lost, watch for the osprey nests."

"I hope I don't have to worry about it one way or the other," she murmured.

"You don't," he said firmly. "I never got lost in this swamp yet."

"Why'd you come here, Gad?" she asked.

He grinned. "To make a fortune, of course."

"Same reason they all came," she said ruefully. "Only one I see's making a fortune is Charles Hebard."

"Oh, I'm makin' my share," he said with more confidence than he felt. "Hebard pays good wages, better'n most. So long as the trees hold out, the money's good."

"What happens when the cypress are gone?"

He laughed. "Then the sun'll drop in the swamp, an' we'll all melt down to mud." He reached over and plucked a fallen leaf off her shoulder. "Don' you worry none 'bout that, Georgia. The old-timers say these trees go all the way to the sea in both directions an' halfway through Georgia. They'll still be cutting cypress when I'm an old man like my pa."

He turned the boat expertly in an eddy. " 'Sides, I ain' fixin' to bide here much longer. I'm studyin' on goin' north an' findin' me a piece of land which ain' wet half the year. Maybe raise some stock, maybe put in orchard trees. Think you'd like that, Georgia?"

"Depends," she said evenly.

"On what?"

"On who my husband may be. If that's what he wants to do, and he's making me happy, then I'll do whatever he thinks will make *him* happy."

She said it so gracefully, with such logical repose, that it seemed to him the finest statement of equity in a relationship between a man and a woman that he had ever heard. He felt suddenly humbled before her. Georgia seemed to have figured out so many things that still confused him. "I'm gonna be that husband," he could only say quietly, with as much force as he could muster.

She smiled gently at him, trailing her hand in the water.

"Now look here," he said then, pointing to a plant that held itself high above the water. He knew, instinctively, that he should somehow change the subject and capture her admiration back again. "This here's a pitcher plant, see?" He pointed to a withered plant, reddened on the bottom and tall despite its hunched appearance. "Ever seen one of them?"

She shook her head, watching him more than the plant.

"Well, 'tis somethin'," he said jovially. "Just 'nother fact 'bout how the female's got everythin' all figured out. See, this plant eats flies an' such. When they set down on its lip to get the nectar it puts out, they get stuck an' cain' get out. The plant melts them down an' eats them."

She grimaced slightly.

"No, 'tis a miracle," he went on hurriedly, afraid he was losing her attention, "see, there be one special fly that this ol' pitcher plant won't eat. 'Tis the flesh fly. An' each summer, the female a' the flesh fly lays this big ol' egg inside the pitcher plant, the egg hatches into a maggot, an' the maggot eats the bugs that fall into the pitcher plant. They share the wealth, like. An' then just 'bout this time of year, the maggot chews a hole in the pitcher plant high up on the leaf, the pitcher plant falls over, an' makes a nest for the maggot to sleep in all through the winter."

"Sounds like the female fly gets the best end of that bargain." She smiled knowingly.

"Looks like it, don't it? But see, here's the trade-off. In the spring, the maggot comes out, but now it's a new flesh fly. An' soon as it takes off, it poll'nates the pitcher plant an' makes sure more pitcher plants will grow all season. Ain' that somethin'?"

She chuckled. "How do you know all this, Gad Craven?"

"I read books," he said proudly. "An' I listen when the old-timers talk 'bout the swamp creatures. An' my pa told me plenty; he were a book reader, too."

"I almost went to college," she said suddenly, softly.

"You did?" He was startled. She had never spoken much about her past.

She nodded. "I was planning on it for years, but my father passed right after my uncle, and my mother decided that it was more important for my brother to get his education and a good start in life. We had words." She shrugged. "So I came to stay with my aunt for a time." She smiled wryly. "Until I could develop a better attitude, my mother said."

That small confession opened up a whole wide window on Georgia's heart and soul which he had not glimpsed so far. He felt instantly angry at her mother, at her father, at anyone who had stood between her and her dreams. And yet, because of that decision, she was here with him now.

"I ain' had much schoolin'," he confessed, "but we always read books to home. My mother saw to it."

"A good mother," Georgia said, idly gazing out over the water.

Gad felt sure she was not thinking of his mother when she said that. "Well," he said, trying for good cheer, "whatever brings you here'bouts, I'm sure grateful."

She turned and looked at him pensively. "Why?"

He was taken back by her direct question. "Because I love you," he said shyly.

"You scarcely know me."

He nodded. "I know that. An' I'm sort of shamed that I love you anyways. But I do, an' that's a fact, an' I cain' seem to do nothin' 'bout it but hope that sometime, you might come to care for me, too."

She laughed lightly. "You are a sweet man."

He turned mock-gruff in a moment. " 'Course I am, gal, what'd you think?"

"I thought you were a rake," she said.

"Me? How come?"

"Oh, please. Gad-abuck? Did you think the boys in the woods were the only ones who called you that?"

He blushed and turned away. "Those times is over."

She was silent for a long moment. "Good," she finally said.

They rowed placidly over the wet prairie, with Gad showing her whatever he thought might amuse her, trying to make the day last as long as he dared. The river was almost a water garden with bands of gorgeous green mosses decorating the bases of the cypress, the dark water meandering along a course which only it seemed to fathom. The yellow flowers of some of the water lilies were still in bloom, and wood ibises and white ibises perched above them, immobile, silent, watching. It was an afternoon of great serenity.

And then a breeze came up, a cool wind which dimpled the black water and broke the reflections of the overhanging trees into thousands of dancing, circular distortions. In the middle of the river stood many small mounds, sculpted gracefully upward from the surface of the water, old cypress trunks, so colonized by shrubs, ferns, and even bay trees that they looked like miniature plant villages. In the distance, black vultures soared on the rising winds, and ducks settled like moths on the water.

"Best be getting back," Georgia said then, pulling her shawl closer about her.

"Whatever you wish," he nodded.

As they rowed back toward Billy's Island, the wind began to rise steadily, and the sky turned a strange and ominous gray-yellow toward the east. It was not a usual color for an autumn sky, and Gad began to watch it more carefully. Finally he said, "You know, we might be in for a blow."

Georgia sat up more alertly and looked about her. "You might be right," she said. "The wind is a little sharp."

"I don' like the color of that sky."

"Have you ever been in a hurricane?" she asked.

He shook his head. "None that come close." He realized that he was having to raise his voice to be heard over the wind. He began to paddle for Billy's Island with more vigor.

Georgia sensed his change of mood and sat up now completely, pulling her shawl around her shoulders as though for defense. The wind through the trees began to make a humming sound which seemed constant, rather than the usual bluff and blurred gusts of a normal squall. All of a sudden, a crack of thunder boomed, low and forbidding from the east. Gad looked in that direction and saw lightning snake rapidly to the ground.

"We be in for it, all right," he said, pulling harder on the paddle.

The wind was piling up the clouds quickly now, and they were dark on the undersides, rolling and spread out as though pushed by high, fast currents. The rain began, with little warning, and Gad cursed under his breath as he saw that Georgia was not only unprepared for bad weather but immediately annoyed by it. Now the mood of intimacy was lost between them, and he could only paddle as hard and fast as he could to get her home.

When they finally reached the settlement, the wind was blowing so hard that the tops of the trees were bent, and the howl was unmistakable.

"Looks like a bad one!" he shouted to her over the wind, struggling to tie up the canoe. Her skirts were blowing so hard that they nearly propelled her forward again into the water.

"Is it a hurricane?" she shouted back, her eyes wide and fearful.

He did not answer her; it was too much effort to try to be heard

over the wind and also secure his craft. Finally, he got the boat pulled
up high enough from the water and tied to a large oak, and then he
took her arm and began to help her to the street.

"Gad, is it a hurricane?" she cried again. "Is it?"

He turned to her and embraced her, feeling the wind push them
nearly over, sensing her trembling even over the shove of the wind,
"I think so," he said in her neck, "but we gonna be all right,
Georgia—"

As though to mock his comfort, a large palmetto branch of the tree
they stood beneath suddenly creaked ominously and ripped from the
trunk, spiraling away toward the water, twisting its lethal spines as it
went. Georgia screamed sharply, a sudden single yelp of terror, and he
took her arm and pulled her away, up the street now, where people
were hurrying for shelter, struggling with wagons and horses, and in a
state of frenzied confusion. The rain was coming down harder now,
driven nearly horizontal by the wind, sharp-edged and colder than he
could remember rain ever feeling in this land.

Her skirts were tangled and pulled by the wind so hard that they
made her progress difficult, and once he swore under his breath, nearly
ready to reach down and yank them off her. Sodden and struggling,
they came to the intersection where the hotel stood, and saw that
shutters were being pulled off the upper windows. Debris was flying
through the air, and he had to keep ducking and wincing, trying to
shield his eyes and pull her along at the same time.

Suddenly a large limb caught her full in the chest, and she cried
out, doubling over with the pain of the blow. He cried out as well,
pulling her to him and frantically checking her face, her bodice for
injury, calling her name. Now his fear was entirely for her and none at
all for his own safety, and in some part of his mind which was still
calm, he recognized that his love was now a tangible force, as powerful
in its own way as the hurricane, something which would propel him
forward and cause him to carry her with him or die in the attempt.

Finally, they made it to the shelter of the little white house, but it
scarcely seemed shelter enough as the winds blew harder with each
moment, the noise so strong it made his head ache. They wrenched
open the door and tumbled inside, and he quickly moved them away
from the windows which bulged inward with the pressure of the storm.

It was such a relief to be at least within four walls and to leave some
of the chaos outside, that he embraced her, once again checking to see
if she were injured. Georgia was gasping, almost weeping now, and her

fear made him frantic to get her to safety. Her aunt came hurrying down the stairs, wringing her hands and calling her name. The two women embraced, and then they heard the sound of a loud impact on the roof, as though a big limb had slammed into it. They shrieked and jumped apart.

"We got to get to the center of the house," Gad said. "Wisht we had a root cellar or somethin', but the middle will take this blow best, I reckon."

"Have you ever seen a wind like this before?" Georgia's aunt asked him fearfully. "Never in all my life!"

He shook his head. " 'Tis the worst I seen, but I been lucky so far." He took Georgia's hand and propelled her aunt by the elbow. "Pray that luck holds now."

They went to the middle of the center hallway of the small house and hunkered down on the floor, leaning against the wall. Georgia had grabbed her aunt's lap robe off the sofa, and she wrapped the old woman in it, trying to calm her down.

Gad was pleased to see that given someone else to comfort, Georgia was now less fearful herself. She would make a good mother, he found himself thinking, and then that thought was pushed out of his head by yet another horrible thud on the roof and an answering crash of an upstairs window.

"Oh, oh!" shrieked Georgia's aunt, and Georgia closed her eyes, pushing herself against Gad for reassurance.

"It cain' last forever!" he said as heartily as he could.

"Neither can this house," murmured Georgia against his chest.

He held her tightly. "You be safe," he said to her in her ear.

She looked up at him with the first smile he had seen since they got back to the settlement. "You're not afraid," she said.

"Only of losin' you," he answered.

"The river's coming in!" her aunt shrieked suddenly, pointing to the back door, where the kitchen stood.

Gad could see the water flowing into the lower level, pushed against the house by the rising winds.

"We still better off here," he said. " 'Less the water gets much higher."

They huddled together for what seemed an hour or more, and with each shove of the wind against the house, each thud on the roof and groan of the timbers, they started and braced for a worse blow. Finally, they could feel that the rain was lessening, and the terrible shriek of the winds began to abate.

" 'Tis passin', I reckon," Gad finally said, helping Georgia and her aunt to their feet.

They went to the door and looked out on a scene of destruction. The settlement was scarcely recognizable from what it had been only four hours before. At least half of the roof of the hotel was missing and part of an upper floor; two houses near the hotel were tilted to one side, one of them missing a roof and most of a porch. Glass and trees and brush and timber littered the roadway, and water stood high in the streets. A dead dog floated near the corner of the yard, wedged up against what was left of the white picket fence.

"My Lord," the old woman breathed. "Is it over, do you think?"

"Seems like it," Gad said cautiously. "We must a' been at the edges of it, 'cause I heard tell of worse."

"I don't think I could stand worse," Georgia said, shaking her head.

He turned to her and kissed her on the cheek. "Yes, you would. You be stronger than you think." He led them back inside saying, "Don' go outside 'til the water drains off, for snakes an' such."

While the women worked to get the water out of the kitchen, Gad went upstairs to assess the damage. Two windows broken, and a spear of cypress near three feet in diameter was wedged in a north portion of the roof, right through the outer wall. He'd have to get up on the roof to pull it out and make the repairs. But all of that would wait. He stuffed blankets in the two open windows and swept up the glass into piles out of the middle of the floor. Leaves and branches and wind debris littered the upstairs; water had drenched some of the downstairs, but they were alive and the house was standing.

He kissed Georgia again and went to assess the damage to the boardinghouse and his own small chambers. To his dismay, the whole top part of the building was badly damaged, including his own room. The boarders stood about outside the wreckage, trying to find their belongings and move aside debris. His landlady wept in one corner, consoled by the cook and two of the gentlemen who had lived there for years. Gad could see, without stumbling about the yard, that most of what he had was lost.

But to his amazement, he felt no real despair. He had been lucky, he realized, to be out of the boardinghouse when the storm struck, lucky to have a place of refuge, lucky most of all to have someone to protect other than himself and his small packet of clothing and belongings. In fact, he was aware that he had never felt more alive in his life.

He turned and went back to the little white house in something of a daze. He knocked on the door and when Georgia answered, he pulled her into his arms, heedless of the eyes of passersby and the calling voice of her aunt. "Will you marry me?" he asked, holding both of her hands as though in prayer. "I got to know right now. Marry me, Georgia."

She hesitated for a moment, and he held his breath. "I will," she said then. And she turned her face up to his and put her arms round his neck, kissing him unabashedly.

* * *

The hurricane which struck Billy's Island was not the largest to ever hit the region, nor was it a direct hit. However, it did enough damage, caused enough flooding, that the creatures which lived on the edges of man's encroachment into the swamp felt the pressures it created. Water was muddied and fouled; debris blocked the hunting paths, and small vermin had been flooded from their burrows. While that meant easy hunting for the larger game, such prosperity was short-lived, for the vermin immediately stopped bearing litters, even abandoning nests, as they self-regulated their populations so that more breeding pairs could surivive.

A moon after the storm had passed, those animals which depended on good hunting to thrive were hungry. Within two moons, they were desperate.

One creature, in particular, found her territory even more empty than usual. She was Felis, *Felis concolor*, a female mountain lion in the prime of her breeding life, and she had the misfortune to be teaching her four young to hunt in a season when the game was as scarce as she had ever known it to be.

Felis was five years old, yellow and tawny above with white overlaid with buff on her belly below. She was unspotted, with a long tail with a black tip. The backs and the tips of her ears were dark, as well as her two whisker patches on her upper lip. She was more than six feet long and weighed nearly two hundred pounds. Large for her sex, she was fearless and aggressive, especially when it came to guarding her cubs or her territory. These days, she had to be so, for man was coming closer and closer to that region she called her own.

She watched the men come into the swamp, saw them as they cut the trees, set their fires, and brought their horrid machines and noise closer and closer to her den. She moved it twice, each time watching to see what direction they went. They seemed to go all directions at once, and she lay in the upper branches of well-leaved trees, her ears flattened in hate, as she watched their invasion.

But she could not leave the swamp. She feared that if she abandoned her territory and went to the south, as many of the larger hunters had done, she would surely perish. And so she waited, hoping that the men would take their timber and go.

Felis was a superb hunter, and well equipped for the game. Her body was long and sleek and powerful, her short head with small rounded ears and eyes that faced forward were ideal for the binocular vision and depth perception so vital to her success. Her night vision was unequaled by any other hunter: in the day, her pupils contracted into vertical slits; by night, they expanded to fill her eyes, while a layer of cells behind her retinas absorbed even the dimmest light. Felis moved so confidently in the dark, using her sensitive whiskers to gauge spaces through which she could pass, that she sometimes took prey even away from the owls.

When she caught her meal, her molariform teeth with their well-developed shearing edges and her long-fanged canines were perfect for tearing flesh. Her rough tongue, with which she groomed her fur and the fur of her cubs, was also good for rasping meat from bones. At the end of her five-toed forepaws and four-toed hind paws, she had retractile claws. She kept those withdrawn to keep from blunting them when she hunted, but when she needed them, they were instantly saber-sharp and extended to snatch and slash prey. In short, she was the most effective killer in the swamp, save possibly the larger venomous snakes. She rarely went hungry and had few enemies save man. She knew a confidence which few large predators experienced, and the loss of that surety pleased her not at all.

Felis had been mated by the same male which covered her two years before. She had no idea where he was now, nor did she care. She knew that males could cover more than twenty-five miles in one night, and so he could have come even from outside the swamp. It did not matter. He had come into her territory once she was in season; he followed her scent markings, tree scratchings, and scat droppings until he found her in the winter. For two weeks, he courted her, hunting with her and sleeping next to her side. Then he disappeared, hurried along by her snarls and growls as he came too near. Her season was finished. She was a solitary female, and she wished that solitude back again.

But it was short-lived. In one hundred days, she gave birth to four new cubs in her maternal den, a hollow she dug under a huge cypress ringed by boulders and well up from the flood line. Her kittens were born blind and helpless. They would stay with her two years. She would not know solitude again for at least that long, but neither would she have to tolerate another male in her midst, for none would intrude so long as she was with cubs.

Now it was time for her cubs to learn to hunt. And she knew that this litter would have a harder time than the one before it.

Felis could not know it but her kind was soon to disappear completely from the swamp. Once widely adapted to hilly northern forests, mountainous and semiarid terrain, and subtropical forests, the mountain lion or cougar or catamount, as her species was called by man, had been driven from every place it once thrived. Once the most widely numbered cat in the Americas, her kind was now hard-pressed to keep territory, and almost extinct in many areas where they had ranged freely before. Because Felis and other mountain lions needed isolated, game-rich land to roam, their litters were becoming fewer; their kittens often did not survive.

Felis could not know that her time in the swamp was doomed. She could only know that it was threatened. But tonight, her cubs must be shown the hunt. This imperative was all that concerned her for now.

Felis signaled the cubs to follow her out into the dark swamp, something she had often done before but never for the hunt. She let them follow her quietly up a game trail she often used to good success, and she hid them in tangled brush within sight of the water hole. Hissing them to silence, she then hid herself on the other side of the water hole, to watch and wait.

She knew that the deer often came this way early in the evening, most particularly since man had crowded other watering places to the east. She had a good sense that tonight she would be successful, and as she waited, her eyes gleaming in the dark, she kneaded her claws thoughtfully in the soft mud.

A noise from the upwind game trail froze her still, and she raised her nose to the night air. Deer were moving closer. She inched her haunches under herself more deliberately and poised herself to full alertness. The cubs were silent and invisible, as she had trained them. The night was loud with the noise of insects and frogs. The hunt had begun.

Silently, carefully, two deer came down to the water hole, moving deliberately, with careful steps through the soft mud. Two does, Felis saw instantly, and one of them heavy with fawn. This one would be slower. This one was her choice.

The deer stood and watched the water, their ears flicking back and forth for danger, their noses busy with the breeze. Felis was downwind from them, but she knew that the slightest noise would send them leaping to safety. She could outrun a deer on clear ground for short distances, but this was not clear ground. Her best chance was to leap on them as they came forward, not to try to catch them as they ran off. She tensed, still as stone.

The deer now moved forward carefully, one standing guard while the other bent her head to drink. Felis moved her legs slightly, tensed to leap. She was within thirty feet of the closest deer. She could leap more than twenty feet if she had a good takeoff. The mud would be to her disadvantage, but so it would be for the deer as well. She waited until the deer changed places, the one heavy with fawn now drinking, her head down to the water.

With a hiss and a snarl, Felis leaped from hiding, and with one bound, jumped onto the drinking deer's back, biting it savagely in the neck and simultaneously gashing it in the belly with her sharp claws fully extended. The other deer bleated and fled, crashing through the brush, and the wounded deer was borne heavily to the ground with Felis upon her, kicking and slashing and biting relentlessly.

In moments, the deer was dead, and Felis took her by the throat and dragged her well away from the water. Alligators watched from the depths and the sides of the water, she knew, and were not afraid to come and try to steal her prey. She uttered a shrill, piercing whistle, signaling her cubs. They tumbled from their hiding place, growling and hissing in reply, falling on the deer with cheerful gusto, sniffing at her bloodied neck, and lunging at her nose as she panted with exhaustion.

Felis did, then, something she might normally not have done, she growled her cubs away, pushing them firmly to the sides of the carcass, not letting them near the food. They whimpered and watched her, bewildered, as she cut the deer into great chunks of steaming, bleeding meat. She ate some hurriedly, gorging herself without regard for the cubs. Then she took a large haunch and dragged it farther still from the water. This, she would cache somewhere close to her maternal den, for those times when the hunt would not be so successful.

After she had eaten her fill, only then did she allow the cubs to approach the carcass once more, even purring as they worried the meat and scrapped over small fragments of flesh, bone, and hide. They could digest the flesh now, she knew, and her milk was almost gone. Even the heavy feeding of deer flesh would not bring it back. But she also knew, with some mysterious knowing which would help preserve her kind, that she must somehow live, even if her cubs died. She would protect them to the death against any enemy, any predator, even against their own father. But she could not protect them against lean times if she herself perished in them. She would feed first; they must take the leavings.

*   *   *

The seasons passed more quickly for Gad now, and it seemed to him that the swamp had changed in some perceptible way that he could not put a name to but knew in his senses. It was not only that the hurricane had changed the lay of the land. Waters which once flowed were now stagnant; other blocked channels were now open; trees which had towered over low scrub had fallen, new ones sprang up to take their place. But what Gad sensed was that for him, at least, the feeling of antiquity in the swamp, of immortality, had altered.

He knew that his own sense of immortality had altered as well, and marriage to Georgia had changed him, diminished him in some way, as the hurricane had changed the swamp. They were married soon after the storm; she was delivered of their first son a year later. He was quickly a husband, a father, and no longer a youthful Gad-abuck, all in the space of what seemed to him to be seasons rather than years.

He was so different now in his perception of himself that he scarcely recognized the boy he had been more than fifteen years before. He felt smaller, in that Georgia took so much of his life, his consciousness, and also somehow larger, as though he were now a part of the rhythms of life and unconfined by his own mind and heart. When his two daughters were born, one after the other in two hot summers, he no longer could say where he left off and his family began. They were within him and without him, and he was somehow the larger for it as well as diminished as to who he had been.

He could remember so clearly how passionate he was once, with Georgia, how she returned his touches with the same fever. There was a time . . . was it so very long ago? . . . when he could make her shudder simply by running his fingers lightly down her arm or her back, shudder and turn to him, her face uplifted for his kiss even as she was turning, her eyes closed, already taking him inside her even as they stood together, clinging with only their fingers touching. And there was a time, he knew it was not so very long ago, when she could make him groan, involuntarily, could make him twist and turn in painful joy, by simply moving her hand up his thigh, simply insinuating her fingers into the inner, dark spaces of his groin, hinting at what she might touch next. There was a time when they would spend so many hours in their bed that they were giddy with a sense of power, exhausted and triumphant, convinced that no two people had ever loved as they loved each other now. And it must be true, they told themselves, for if others knew such ecstasy, how was it that the world still turned, that men went outside their bedrooms to make a living, that meals were ever prepared and floors swept?

He could remember it all as well as he recalled the slant of his father's porch, the feel of the plow under his hands, even though it had been a long time since he'd felt either.

After ten years of marriage and fatherhood, Gad sometimes walked the swamp trails alone, noticing that the timber was thin, the swamp was less richly wild and primeval, and knowing that he, too, had been civilized somehow. It made him at once sad and also content, but he no longer felt the strong sense of shouting joy and abandoned freedom when he walked the woods. In fact, he scarcely ever felt those emotions at all anymore.

Georgia was a fine wife, a good partner, and an excellent mother, just as he had known she would be. She never turned him away, although she also rarely seemed to match his passion for their union. Still, he was so used to her keeping him at arm's length in her heart, that he no longer yearned for more than she could give him. He used to wonder what happened after that first daughter was born, what took her so far from him that she could not find her way back. But he no longer wondered much about those yearnings anymore. He thought of contentment instead of joy.

Georgia saved most of her passion for the children, yet he could hardly resent them. Thomas was a sturdy boy, bright as a penny and full of charm. The two girls, Tess and Elizabeth, were sweet, quiet, and as lovely as their mother. Tom, Tess, and Bess were at once such upheavals in his life and also his foundation. He sometimes thought of himself as a tree, planted in one place, thinking the world was nothing but sunshine and birdsong, and then suddenly ringed by a brick path. His roots would eventually move the bricks aside, but not before they had changed his growth forever.

In time, he thought of his wife less and his children more, his children less and his job more, and somehow of himself in the spaces in between.

The men were gradually dwindling on the crews, for there was less and less work to do. The cypresses were thinned, the crews had to go farther and farther from their camps, and the fast promotions of the earlier years had been replaced by layoffs of those least necessary to do the work which remained.

Gad had finally reached his goal of engineer on one of the smaller lines to the west of camp, but now the locomotive sometimes sat idle, waiting for enough timber to be cut to warrant the trip into the swamp.

Used to be, Gad spent most of his working hours hearing men brag about the size of the trees they cut and how fast they cut them. Now men spoke of other opportunities to the north, in Georgia, to the east, in Saint Augustine, to the south, on cattle ranches near Ocala, or even out of the state altogether.

When Thomas said he wanted to be an engineer just like his father, Gad told him, "Better get some schoolin', boy. When the cypress runs out, so will the work."

Billy's Island also was running down, like an engine starved for fuel. The movie theater, which had replaced the vaudeville house, was closed, the marquee empty of letters and the ticket box window broken. The hotel still welcomed guests, but the Saturday-night dance tradition had disappeared. The school, where Georgia taught English and penmanship to twenty-seven children, was still full of shining faces, but the men no longer played horseshoes in the park, and the Sunday meetings had been cut to one every month, instead of every week.

Georgia and Gad talked often about what they should do and where they should go. She enjoyed the quiet of the town and her teaching responsibilities, but she wondered aloud who might court her daughters on Billy's Island. The men who were left on the crew were those with no gumption, she said, men who had no other skills. She did not include Gad in that category, of course, because she knew he was staying for her sake. But those others . . . she wasn't at all sure she wanted sons of such fathers as husbands for her girls.

Privately, Gad thought such concerns were more than premature, they were almost obscene. Elizabeth and Tess were barely girls yet, as far as he could see. They were still children, and he frowned and grumbled when they showed any interest in boys at all. He could still remember his great discomfort when Mattie began to develop and become less his baby sister than a young lady, and he was certainly not looking forward to that evolvement in his own household. Good old Tommy, he had no head for such as that. Give him a trail to follow, a stick to smack against a tree, or a ball to throw, and he was happy. Billy's Island would be good enough for him, no doubt, for many years to come.

At night, he would hold Georgia and say things like, "I could get work in Tampa, I bet. Or maybe in Gainesville. Plenty of fellas left for there, an' none of 'em come back, at least."

"Doing what, though?" she asked softly, nestled against him tightly, her backside curved to his belly. "They're not logging cypress, that's for certain."

"No, but they got trains runnin'. I could get a job as an engineer."

She said nothing. Both of them knew that a berth as an engineer on a small backwoods line which ran from the swamp to the mill was not going to translate to a job on a regular commercial train route. Gad knew timber and how to cut it. He knew the swamp, and he knew how to work with men in its most tangled depths. But those skills would not take him far in the growing cities of Saint Augustine or Tampa.

"Well," he said finally, "one thing's sure. This place is gonna dry up an' blow away when the cypress is gone. Wisht I knew when that was gonna be."

"The only way to predict the future is to create it," she murmured.

"That somethin' you tell your schoolkids?" He chuckled.

"Yes. And they're smart enough to believe it."

"Oh I believe it well enough," he said. "I just don' know what to do 'bout it."

"You'll figure it out in time," she sighed, patting his hand. "Now let me get some sleep. Unless you want to teach twenty kids long division tomorrow morning."

He groaned, rolling over. "Rather rassle a gator."

"If you're in the mood to wrestle," she purred, dropping one hand over his hip, "I have a better idea."

He turned back again to her, reaching gently for her breast. "Thought you needed all you got for long division."

"I'm a woman." She chuckled softly. "I can change my mind."

A few months later, Gad was walking down the main street of Billy's Island. Another shop had closed its doors, a haberdasher this time. As he stood by the darkened window, lamenting the end of things, he saw a man go by who looked strongly familiar. He turned and watched the man from the rear for a moment, suddenly calling out, "Lem! Lem Craven!"

To his amazement and delight, his brother turned and faced him, his eyes wide with surprise. "Gaddy?"

Gad took his hand and pumped it up and down happily. "My God, boy, what you doin' on Billy's Island? You growed six feet! An' your arm looks damn good, damn good! Is Ma an' Pa with you? How's Mattie? Jesus, boy, 'tis good to see you!" and he pulled Lem into his arms with joy.

Lem pulled back and gazed into his face with wonder. "Gaddy! I never thought to see you ag'in in my whole natur'l life."

"Well, 'tis me, boy! In the flesh! Why, I been bossin' crews here on Billy's Island since I hightailed it off the homestead. I got me a wife, Lemmy! Three kids, too—when you get in town?"

Lem appeared dazed, pulling back finally from Gad's embrace and grinning shyly. "Gaddy, I swannee. Why, I wouldn'a knowed you, to look at you. We give you up years ago. Why'd you never write? Ma an' Pa waited for word for so long—" He frowned then, suddenly indignant. "That weren't right, Gad, to take off like you done. You ought to be whipped, breakin' Ma's heart like a no-good—"

"You're right, Lemmy, an' I been kickin' myself every day since I run off. I should a' writ, should a' come back, leastwhys to say I was all right, but I was shamed." He noticed how quickly he slipped back into the old ways of speech, the same rhythms of Lem and his past, how fast he abandoned the better grammar he'd learned over the years from Georgia. But he needed to reach his brother's heart, and as he said the words, he knew them to be true. "I couldn't go back, Lemmy," he added, dropping his voice and his head. "Not after the way I left."

Lem looked away, embarrassed. After a long moment, he slapped Gad on the shoulder with his good hand. "Hell, I know, Gaddy. Sometimes, families is like a noose 'round a man's neck. Sometimes, they's a life raft. But it ain' for me to judge."

"Ma an' Pa, they's well? An' Mattie?"

"They ain' gettin' younger, but neither am I," Lem said wryly. "Mattie's got herself a brood a' six—"

"Six kids!"

"Yessir, our Mattie don' let no grass grow under her, that's for certain.

Pa says she's a better breeder than his milch cow." Lem laughed, shaking his head. "But come an' hear for yourself."

The two brothers walked toward the hotel, past it, and onto the side street where two small boardinghouses still took in trade, less expensive lodging than the hotel could provide. As they walked, Gad learned that his father was in town to see about buying some old equipment, wagons, and stock that Hebard was selling off, and his mother had come along to "see the sights," as Lem told it, having heard that Billy's Island was the closest thing to a city that the wilderness could provide. Tampa was a sight to see, Lem said, but they'd heard tell that Billy's Island was more of an amazement, being out in the middle of the woods and yet having every modern wonder known to man.

"Well, I don' know 'bout that," Gad said wryly. "The island done already seen its boom times. Wish't you could 'a seen it in its heyday—"

"Cain' believe the movie house is closed down. Ma most 'specially wanted to see that," Lem said.

"You stayed on the farm all this time?"

Lem shrugged. "Pa's gettin' too bent to work much, though Ma's still spry." He added, with some defensiveness, "It ain' a bad life."

"Never said t'was," Gad said evenly. "Jus' weren't for me."

"Well, you made that clear enough."

They walked on in silence for a long, awkward moment. Finally Gad said, "See your arm's 'bout good as new."

"Not nearly," Lem shook his head. "But I get by."

"Ain' never took a shine to no gal?"

Lem smiled, a ghostly wisp of a smile. "A few."

Gad wanted to ask more questions, but they were at the boarding-house door now and he hurried forward to the chamber door on the bottom floor where Lem led him. They knocked, and when Sam opened the door, Gad stood back, suddenly shy as when he'd been twelve.

"Look who I found!" Lem said loudly.

Gad stepped forward into the little room. His mother stood by the window with a garment in her hand, an open bag on the bed. His father stood back from the door with a look of pale amazement.

"Hey, Pa. Hey, Ma," Gad said softly.

"Oh my Lord!" May whimpered, dropping her hands to her side and swaying against the window. "Is that my Gad?"

Gad went to his mother and took her in his arms. She began to weep, and he felt his own cheeks wet with tears. He pulled away then, trembling with emotion he scarcely knew he had. He met his father's eyes, downcast and suddenly ashamed.

"Gad," his father said gently. "We 'bout give you up, boy."

Gad nodded, unable to speak.

His father gathered him into his arms, arms which were frail and bent but which felt to Gad, in that moment, like the strongest tethers on earth. "Praise God," his father murmured. "He must a' brung us here for a purpose this trip."

"He were jus' standin' on the street," Lem said happily. "Big as life. An' I 'bout walked past, never knew him a'tall. 'Til he called out my name, an' I turned, an' there he be!"

"Gad, you all right?" his mother asked, anxiously pulling him close again and patting his cheeks with wrinkled hands. "How come you never writ us, son? Where you been all these years?"

Gad hugged her again and then pulled her down on the bed next to him, suddenly mindful of her fragility. "Been right here, Ma, the whole time. Never got farther than Billy's Island, though I kept threatenin' to, every year. Ma, I got me a wife—"

"Three more gran'babies, Ma!" Lem crowed.

"You have three?" May asked faintly, clutching his arm. "Where's your wife?"

"Right here in the big city, Ma!" Gad laughed. "Why, we cain' hardly tear ourselves away, it's such a hustle-bustle."

They laughed then, helplessly, for somehow the ridiculousness of their long absence from each other and accidental encounter on the main street of Billy's Island hit all four of them at the same time. When May had finished wiping her eyes and rocking with the pleasure of the shared mirth, she said, "I want to see these gran'babies right now."

Within hours, they were all seated round the small kitchen of Gad's little house, and May had pronounced Georgia's three babies near the prettiest she'd ever seen, and Georgia had congratulated May on her excellent judgment and discerning eye. "Them two is thick as fleas already," Lem grinned across the table at Gad, jerking his head at his mother and Georgia.

Georgia was coaching Bess on her recitation of the Lord's Prayer for Gran'ma, and Tess was warming up for her performance of "Dixie." Thomas stood as close to his grandfather as he could, alternating between looking manfully disinterested in the progress of the women and stealing glances at the old man's wizened face when he thought he was unobserved.

"I should a'made the trip home long ago," Gad admitted. "Guess I jus' lost track of the years."

"That happens to each of us," Sam said, nodding. "It goes a little faster when you get to be my age, but they still slip by, willy-nilly. You done any figurin' on what you gonna do when the timber's run out?"

"We talked 'bout it enough," Gad said. "But we ain' got no plan yet."

Georgia cast him a quick look at his grammar but said only, "I imagine we'll need to make some decisions soon as the school year's over."

"We was surprised to see the changes in the land when we come," Sam went on. "An' it only took six days to get here. They been cutting far south as Ocala, an' not jus' cypress, neither. Big stands of oak been taken down, some so big I wouldn'a thought men could pull 'em out."

"Why, Pa, those engines'll cut down most anythin' with roots," Gad bragged. "Ain' a tree too big to cut an' carry out, with steam power."

"I guess that's true."

"You should think 'bout selling off your own timber," Gad said, leaning forward eagerly. "It's a cash crop, same's corn, but worth one hell of a lot more at the mill. You an' Ma could sell off cuttin' rights an' not have to plant again for the rest o' your lives."

"I ain' doin' that much now." His father chuckled wryly. "Lem's workin' the fields, an' he's takin' care o' things good."

Gad turned to Lem. "How you do it all with that arm, Lemmy? Don' it pain you none?"

"I manage," Lem said, a little stiff.

"Well, I guess we all learn to do that well enough, eh?" Gad said cheerfully. "Anyways, if you was to sell off the timber off the place, you wouldn't have to worry 'bout next season's crops nor the season after that, neither. Maybe more. An' you ain' takin' no use from those trees, anyway. Ain' like they's fodder nor fuel. Cypress ain' good for nothin' but buildin', an' you got all the house you need right now, ain' that so?"

"That's purely so," Lem said slowly.

"Well, then! Say the word, an' I set you up with the gentlemen who can turn that timber into cash in your pockets. Pa, what you say?"

"You sayin', you come all the way south to cut it, Gad?" May looked around then.

"No ma'am," Gad shook his head. "But I'd get me a finder's fee from them that would. An' you all would get the cash money for somethin' you don' need anyhow."

"I cain' see me allowin' clear-cut on my land," Sam said mildly. "Ain' nobody else doin' such, far as I can see. Leastways, none of my neighbors."

"Well, that don' mean you cain' be the first," Gad jumped in. "When they see how much you got for those trees you ain' usin' anyways, they might see the sense to it, I reckon."

"Maybe," Sam said reluctantly. "But I cain' see me allowin' it."

"Ain' no clear-cut, Pa," Gad said, a little impatiently. "The crews come in an' take only what they got to take, jus' the cypress an' maybe some oak. You got more trees than a hound's got fleas, an' they's nothin' but a hindrance when you want to put more land to plow, ain' they? Why not get cash money for them now?"

"I reckon not," Sam said, shaking his head.

"Why not?" Gad asked indignantly.

"Jus' ain' somethin' I reckon I need to do," Sam replied patiently.

"What 'bout Ma? You figure on keepin' her out in the swamp all the rest a' her days? Maybe she'd like to move closer in town, see her gran'babies more. Maybe 'tis time to give it up, Pa."

"Maybe," Sam said evenly. "Guess I'll know that when the time comes."

"Time's here," Gad said. "Prices for timber is high now, Pa. Might be, in a year or two when the cypress is gone, the crews go on elsewhere. Then you cain' give timber away, an' you missed the boat."

"Maybe."

Gad rolled his eyes and thumped his hands on the table. "Well, I cain' say no more—"

"Jus' as well," Lem said quietly.

"But I'm tellin' you, it's a foolhardy thing to let good cash money go a' wastin', when folks'll pay dear to take that timber off your hands, timber you ain' got no use for nohow. Nothin' special 'bout Craven cypress, there's plenty in the woods still for them to get for free—"

"Swamp's got a use for it, I reckon," Sam said mildly. "Anyways, if they got so much of it, they don' need mine."

Gad shook his head in resignation. "Pa, you out of touch with progress. Folks need houses an' houses need timber. It's downright un-

American to waste it, standing there an' rottin', when it could be makin' you a rich man.''

"That's enough now, Gaddy," May said pleasantly. "Your pa give his answer, ain' no sense in wallopin' him with your words no more."

"You right 'bout that, anyways," Gad said with small disgust. "Might as well wallop his ol' mule, get as much satisfaction."

"Get more," Lem said with a smile. "Leastways, that ol' mule giddup in a straight furrow *most* a' the time."

Sam just grinned. Nothing Gad said seemed to rile him; nothing Lem said was an affront. This must be what it's like to come to the end of a life, Gad thought to himself. Nothing much matters, nothing's worth fighting over or getting excited about. He shook his head again with distaste. Nigh to dying before your time, looks like, he thought. Old man's getting feeble in his mind.

That evening, when the children were in bed and Georgia had shown Lem and his father to their room, Gad sat up with his mother and talked quietly over the past. Their two heads together in the pool of lamplight at the table were alike as two coins, Georgia thought as she passed them on her way to bed, herself. The old woman's hair was lightened by age to nearly the same hue as Gad's, and she wore it up close on her head, so in profile, they resembled each other greatly.

"Good night, Mother," she said softly.

"Good night, dear," May called.

"Gad, check on Thomas before you come up," Georgia called, trailing up the stairs.

"Yes, honey," he called out softly. Then to his mother he said, "She's wonderful with them."

"I can see that," May said. "So are you, son."

He sighed and leaned forward candidly. "I don' know how you did it, Ma. Way out there in the backwoods, not a spit of help, no neighbors, an' three kids to raise an' school an' clothe. I never thought much on it, 'til I had my own."

She smiled. "Some of the best years of my life, those early ones. I was blessed." She took his hand lightly. "Still am."

He gazed at her for a moment. She was still lovely, in his eyes, but he could see how much smaller she had gotten in the past years. She was no longer even middle-aged. His mother was old now. Old as some of the ancients who sat on the benches on Main Street and watched life pass them by. Old as his father, though she did not look as bent as he. "How's Pa?" he asked. "He looks like his joints are painin' him."

She nodded. "Your father always had a barrel chest. Big man,even when he was young. His legs have a hard time carryin' that much, I reckon. They 'bout give out."

"He do much about the place anymore?"

"Sits, mostly, on the porch an' tells Lemmy what he should be doin'." She smiled. "Like Lemmy don' know."

Gad sighed. "He looks so—old, Ma."

She patted his hand. "That's the way he's s'posed to look, son."

He looked into her face. For the first time in his life, he felt like he could really see his mother. Not as his mother, not as the woman who kept all their lives in order, but as a person, a young girl, a woman, a wife, an old woman. He thought, for a moment, he could see all at once what she must have been like as a child and also how she would look when she was dead. The planes of her face were narrow and etched more sharply now, the long line of her nose more severe. Her skin was stretched over her cheekbones, thin and taut and pale, and in the furrows of her mouth and over her lips, there were scores of lines, many of them deep and shadowed. She was an old woman. She was his mother. She was somehow a stranger to him and yet also the person who knew him best of all in the world. His heart ached with love and shame, mixed together. She had given up her whole life to care for him and his brother and siser and father—given up her beauty, her youth, her freedom. And he had not even thought to write and say he was alive.

He dropped his head. "Ma, I'm sorry I run out on you."

"I know, son," she said softly. "No sense frettin' over it none, though. You had wings, an' you had to fly. Lemmy, he never had wings. That boy's got roots, same's his Pa." She peered at him. "You more like me, I reckon."

"But you never flew," he said, surprised.

"Thought of it once or twice, but never could do it. Never could leave your pa. But I don' blame you for doin' it, son. You had to take your life your ownself, lest your pa take it up for you."

Gad was silent, watching her mouth move, watching the brightness of her eyes in the lamplight. It seemed to him that he had never really known his parents before this time. Always, they were only a collection of small quirks and personal foibles: funny ways of speech, the way they chewed their food and held their forks and said his name and walked and whistled and sang, and a hundred other private details of their souls which were not their souls at all but only those parts of themselves which he could see, which they would allow him to see.

But now, after years of separation from them, he could see them as simply people. His father was an elderly man; his mother was an aged woman. They had each made choices in their lives, choices he had come to despise, in the case of his father, until all he could see were the choices instead of the people. Now that he was making choices himself, choices which he had no doubt that Tom would someday come to question, he saw the terrible beauty in their lives. He could see that beauty now in his mother's face.

Perhaps, Gad told himself, the only way he could finally leave his home, take to that lifeboat and sail away into his life, was to do so on the waters of his father's choices, over the wind of his mother's voice. Without them, there was nothing to run from and, without them, there was nothing to go home to after all.

"Ma, how old are you?" he asked gently.

"I taught you better manners than that, Gaddy," she teased him lightly. "You don' never ask a lady her years, you know better."

"Fifty?"

"Not quite," she said firmly. "An' I feel young as I did when I had no more'n forty years on these bones."

He smiled and patted her hand. He was closer to thirty than forty. He knew there was a time when he would no longer have her; indeed, there had been so many years now when he had not had her—and yet, he always knew she was there, in the back of his heart. The time would come, sooner perhaps now than later, when she would be gone. And then, with her would go his past. With her would go the one person who had always been on his side, who always believed in him, who always would take him back, no matter how he might have transgressed. He had no doubt that if he were arrested for murder, his father would be shocked and dismayed, his brother would be outraged, his sister would be frightened for him. But his mother would never believe it. She would go to her death insisting that he was innocent. Because he was her son, her firstborn, and nothing would ever change that until she was in her grave.

"I love you, Ma," he said.

"I know that, Gaddy."

"I wisht things had been different."

She chuckled softly, a low, liquid sound of compassion. "Ah, son, they never are. They're always jus' the way they're s'posed to be, I reckon."

More months went by and the crews dwindled down to less than half what they had been when Billy's Island had been a humming, bustling center of cypress harvest. The rumors said that Hebard would soon be releasing two thousand men, and Gad knew in every place of his soul that he would be among the two thousand.

"We should get out of here before then," he told Georgia the night he heard the rumors for the third time. "Once they hit the streets, it's gonna be tougher to get work."

"I can leave in two months," she said. "School's out then—"

"We cain' wait two months," Gad said shortly. "If I got to pound on doors from here to Saint Augustine with every man jack in the woods, I ain' gonna find nothin' that pays much."

She touched his shoulder softly, patting him for comfort. She knew that when Gad was worried his grammar suffered. "We've been hearing rumors like this for months," she said. "Perhaps you won't be released in this bunch."

He shook his head. "Georgia, I'm tellin' you, I can feel it comin'. I'm gonna be cut this time, an' when I am, we won' hardly be able to get a wagon to move us out, much less a job to move us to. Now, I think we should pull up stakes an' head to Ocala. I heard tell there's jobs there, an' they surely need good teachers, too. You can get a job, same's here—"

"Not in the middle of the term, I can't," she said. "And what if you can't find work right away? Then we'd have nothing at all."

"Then I'm goin' on," he said firmly. "You can follow after with the kids when you get 'round to it."

She sat back, alarmed. He had never spoken to her in such a tone, never mentioned a separation of even one night in all their years of marriage. "Why, Gad—"

"I mean it, Georgia," he said, standing now and running his hand through his hair anxiously. "I ain' gonna wait for the axe to fall. I mean to be gone 'fore the week is up."

The woods were dry, so dry that the men were warned to keep sparks from the parched patches of grass. The last rain they had was many months away and the water levels were down low enough that men could walk on the dried bed of the watercourse north of Billy's

Island. Both Minnie's Lake and Big Water were almost dry, and boat travel was impossible.

Gad wandered along the fringes of the swamp that summer and saw countless fish trapped in pools that were slowly sinking to mudholes. As the water fell, each pond was covered with the tracks of raccoon, otter, opossum, fox, and herons. The fish were dying off in such numbers that the stench of their rotting bodies made the smell of the swamp nigh unbearable in the heat.

And then as the drought went on, the hunters became the hunted, for the fish were gone, the frogs were buried in mud, and the shallow prairies were teeming with resident and immigrant alligators.

In November, another thousand men were laid off, and Gad still had a job. But a crew working on the southeastern edge of the Okefenokee collecting turpentine decided to light a campfire to ward off the chill, not realizing that even though some rain had come, the peat was dry enough to burn. A mule switched its tail into a bucket of turpentine, then into the campfire. It ran with its tail ablaze into the woods, a living torch setting fires as it raced in terror. Within hours, the flames were gorging on the swamp, higher than the tallest canopies, pushed toward Billy's Island by winds which helped them leapfrog across the narrow waterways.

What was left of the town mobilized for flight, but the winds shifted, and the flames moved into the western part of the swamp. The smoke was so thick over Billy's Island that Gad could not see a light in a neighbor's window at midday. Within two days, he could no longer see flames, only great pillars of smoke rising from the smoldering peat in the distance. When a wind rose, an occasional fire would break out again near town, for the whole underside of the peat bog was hot, and men raced to put it out before it could spread.

But there was no putting it out. They could only wait for the rains to come again and smother the fire in the deepest bogs.

People left Billy's Island by the wagonload then, for they knew that once the fires were out, they would find few trees left to harvest. But Gad still had a job, of sorts, and Georgia was determined to keep the school open so long as there were any children left to teach.

When the fire was still burning to the north, Gad opened the door one late afternoon to see his father standing on his porch.

"What in the world are you doin' here, Pa?" Gad looked over the old man's shoulder, half-expecting to see his mother and Lemmy trailing behind. "How'd you get through the swamp?"

"It ain' bad to the south," his father said, shaking his hand and stepping inside. "I come to see if you was all right. We heard tell of the fire down to Tampa."

"Come in, Pa," Gad said, pulling his father inside with a sense of relief. "You come all this way jus' to see if we was burned out?"

"Your ma was frettin', Gad, an' I was, too, when I heard tell how bad it were. They say more'n three hundred thousand acres is wiped out."

Gad stopped, his mouth open in amazement. "That many? I ain' heard that!"

"That's what they're tellin', down to Ocala."

"But Ma's all right?"

"Your ma's all right, an' so's Lemmy," his father nodded. "Last we heard, Mattie's doin' jus' fine, as well. But I come to talk 'bout you, Gaddy. You an' that good wife you got an' those young ones. An' not jus' 'cause a' the fire, neither."

Gad took his father into the kitchen and made him comfortable with a cup of coffee. He was glad, for the moment, that the house was empty. He looked at his father closely as they settled down together. From the rear, no doubt a casual observer would know they were related, simply by the sameness of their shoulders and the set of their heads. His father fiddled with his coffee for a bit, speaking of his trip up and the burn, and finally he said, "Your ma an' I been talkin', an' we finally put it to Lemmy, an' he agreed. I been thinkin' on buyin' 'bout thirty acres to the south, that ol' pasture John Dreyfuss worked for years, been lyin' fallow for nigh four years an' more. You 'member it, son?"

"Cain' say's I do," Gad said.

"Well, it butts our pasture, an' it's right good land, to my thinkin'. I talked to Dreyfuss, an' he's willin'."

"You need more land, Pa?" Gad asked, still confused.

"Only if you be willin' to come home an' help farm it," his father said. "So I reckoned to come an' ask you plain. I was studyin' on it, even 'fore we heard 'bout the fire. But when we heard, my course was plain."

Gad stopped and stared at his father. "You want me to come home?"

"If you be willin'," the old man repeated. "Lemmy needs the help, an' your ma an' I would be proud to have you. You could put up your own house an', when the time comes, the land would be yours an' your brother's."

"I got a job, Pa," Gad said, a little stiffly.

"I know, son. An' if you think it's what you want, then I surely understand. But if you could see your way clear—"

"An' Ma wants this?"

He grinned. "What do you think?"

Gad returned his smile, ruefully. "What did Lemmy say?"

"Lemmy would welcome the extry hands."

Gad fell silent, feeling somehow angered and bewildered all at once. "I got a job, Pa," he heard himself say again.

His father said nothing.

" 'Course, I 'spect they be layin' off more men next month, an' maybe me, in the bargain. Timber's nigh gone, an' the wages ain' worth what we're cuttin' these days. Got to think of overhead, you know," he said importantly. "I still got a job, naturally, since I'm engineer, but plenty a' boys won' be seein' no pay come this time next month."

His father nodded. "This fire ain' helped none. But even without it, guess the trees won' hold out forever," he said softly.

"No," Gad agreed. "Seems nothin' much does."

Sam Craven smiled. "Guess sometimes, it seems so."

"An' you say, Lemmy reckons this is a good idea?"

His father was silent for a moment. "Lemmy's a good lad, an' he's a good farmer, too. But no man can plant more'n forty acres all by his ownself."

"So you came all this way to ask me if I want to come home," Gad murmured. "Jus' like I ain' hardly been gone a'tall."

"Well, I come to see if you is safe. But I would'a come, no matter. This fire jus' give me a reason to come now."

"You come to offer me a place," he said.

"That's 'bout the jist of it," his father said. "Will you think on it?"

Gad reached across and took his father's hand and shook it. "I thank 'ee, Pa. You come a long ways to see if we was makin' out. I thank 'ee for it."

"But you ain' gonna consider it," his father said.

"I ain' said that." Gad grinned suddenly. " 'Tis a right generous offer."

"Don' say no right off," his father said. "Give it a good study, 'fore you do."

Gad laughed then. "Say no? I mean to say yes, Pa, if Georgia's willin'. I think it's nigh time we left Billy's Island an' come on home."

Sam Craven stood up suddenly, his hands flat on the table, leaning forward into his son's face. In that instant, Gad could see the youth that was still there in his father's expression, the power in his body. His father's grin spread; wide and disbelieving, slow and infectious. "You mean it, son?"

"I do. 'Course, I cain' speak for the wife, but I know she's not partial to city livin'." He chuckled. "An' we got her at a disadvantage. Less she wants to live in a burnt-out bog an' breathe peat smoke for the next six months. I daresay, she might be willin' to see her way clear—"

"Your ma don' want to press her, son," Sam said. "Only if she could be happy—"

"We'll talk to her together," Gad said, slapping his father on the shoulder and pushing him down again in his chair. "Hell, she cain' stand up 'gainst us both, I reckon."

To his satisfaction, she did not even try. Georgia came in, saw his father, and seemed to guess all at once what he had on his mind. She embraced the idea of moving south to join Gad's family as much as if she had thought of the idea herself. In a flurry of happy bustle, she sent Sam Craven back to tell the family that they would be there in a month. Then she closed up the school, packed up their furnishings and belongings, put the little white house up for sale, and shushed any misgivings voiced by the girls with a solid sense of knowing comfort.

"Do you think we're doin' the right thing?" Gad asked once, in a night-ache of self-doubt.

"I do," she said firmly. "And if we change our minds, it's not as though we'll be buried up to our chins. If we want to go someplace else, we will. Maybe Tampa, maybe Fort Myers. But for now, this is what we need."

He stroked her arm softly. "Will *you* be happy?"

She smiled. "Will you be there?"

"I'm plannin' on it."

"Then so am I."

As they traveled the long miles by wagon down to the homestead, Sam held the reins lightly and let the mule choose the trail. Gad sat alongside him, grateful that his father had come to fetch them. The children dozed or talked or tusseled among themselves in the rear of the wagon, and Georgia sat among them, keeping peace.

Gad was amazed at the destruction he saw as they traveled. The very earth itself seemed burned to its core, and smoke still streamed slowly up out of the deeper peat bogs, as though they might burn through eternity. The landscape looked like a scene from hell.

As they followed the river south, they came out of the area of the fire and into the region of piney woods, with its sand scrub, its longleaf, slash, and black pines, into the darker region of live oak, water oak, the laurel, the red bay, and sassafras and sweet gum. And all around them, in the distance, Gad could see the tall canopies of cypress looming. It was a relief to see that somewhere, the cypress still stood.

Gad thought of all the things he had seen in the swamp, all the places he had wandered on the river. He recalled one summer night when a huge orange sun sank behind a great rookery of egrets and herons on Chesser Prairie. The colors of the sun had fused into the stillness of the waters, and the prairie had been luminous in anticipation of the dark velvet of night. He remembered one time when ibises passed over him in hundreds, so low that he could hear their wings rustling like silk being shaken. He could feel, rather than see in his mind's eye, a night that he and Georgia had walked over the trail by the river, and the moon was rising, its great white eye appearing through the locked branches of cypress and pine like a giant pearl caught in a woman's hair.

The swamp would be in his blood, he knew, so long as the river and his blood flowed. It did not matter where he went, he would feel its great heart beat until his was stilled forever.

"You know, Pa," he said to Sam as they rode along, "the old-timers tole' me that the trees went all the way through Georgia. Think that's true?"

His father nodded. "I used to think they'd be cuttin' cypress forever. But now, I wonder."

"Me, too," Gad said softly.

"I ever tell you 'bout my ma?" Sam asked.

"Not much."

"Well, not much's 'bout what I recollect. But I guess I got more of her in my blood than I thought."

"What you mean?"

Sam shrugged. "I jus' never had no need to leave the swamp, you know? Or to cut the timber or change it much. Seems like even if a man was to give me cash money for them trees, I still couldn't cut 'em down. I heard tell the Indians was like that." He chuckled. "Guess that's the breed blood in me."

Gad thought for a moment. "Well, I guess I got the same blood in me, somewheres." Then he sighed. "Ah, Pa, I don' know what's right no more, I swannee."

"Sure you do," Sam said softly, "an' you're doin' it." And then they lapsed back into silence, each in his own thoughts.

They drove south to Tampa and then on the trail east for home, and finally Sam said, "You know, Lemmy's made quite a few changes in the ol' place since you left."

Gad knew that his father had waited to begin this conversation until they neared the old homestead. "That so?" he asked mildly. "Like what?"

"Well, I reckon you can see for yourself," Sam said. "But anyways, he done all the work you goin' to see."

"You tole' me he put in some new crop."

"Besides the corn an' the cotton an' sweet taters, now we got sugar cane, some peanuts, watermelons, an' peaches."

"That's good," Gad said. "Maybe we should put in some orange trees; I heard tell the Indians used to plant 'em."

Sam nodded. "An' they did good, I reckon." He thought for a moment. "Maybe," he said slowly. "We see what Lemmy says on that."

Gad took a deep breath and let it out carefully. "So you tellin' me, Lemmy's got to be my boss."

His father hesitated a long moment. "Not your boss, surely. But he knows the land, son. He's earned the right to his say-so."

Gad looked all about him, at the deep canopy of trees, at the marsh on both sides of the thin pathway the mule walked, at the vast expanse of wet prairie which spread out before them, through which the wagon must trundle on what dry land was there. It looked altogether different than it had when he last passed through, somehow smaller and less amazing. But no less beautiful for its diminishment in power. The trees would always be here, he realized. Changed, just as they were changed, but always here, at least in the hearts of those men who valued them.

"You gonna be content, son?" Sam asked then, glancing over at him.

"Don' know," Gad said honestly. "Guess I'll figure that out as I go."

To his surprise, his father chuckled. "Just like the Good Book says. Even the lilies of the field, they make it up as they go 'long."

"Hell, Pa." Gad laughed then, feeling for an instant less a son and more a comrade in a mutual struggle. "I been doin' that all my life!"

* * *

When they pulled the wagon down the road, up to the old house, Gad was pleased to see the hounds burst off the porch and caterwaul up to the mule, to see new cypress shingles on the roof, to see the golden corn standing tassel high in the near fields, old memories, some of them polished up for company. He had no doubt that Lem had shingled the roof, that Lem had plowed the field, and now he came down off the porch after the dogs, calling to them to get down with the voice of authority. It was Lem's show, for all that his brother still ducked his head and blushed like a boy at company.

The children hopped down from the wagon as though they had not been riding for six days, and Georgia stepped down eagerly, beating the trail dust off her skirts and righting her bonnet. From the front door then came May, calling and waving, and right behind her, to Gad's surprise and joy, came Mattie, bounding down the steps as happily as one of the children.

When hugs and welcomes had been exchanged all round, the hounds shushed, and the mule tethered, they gathered in the little room which Gad recalled from his earliest memories. The room was suddenly so small with so many heads and sets of shoulders, eager laughter, and the rise and fall of voices, each trying to be heard. Gad sat down in a chair, briefly wondered if it belonged to his father or to Lemmy, and then resigned himself to taking someone else's place, no matter where he stood or sat.

"Mattie, you all growed up!" Gad said, pulling her to his lap.

She laughed becomingly and pulled away, slapping his hand and settling her skirts. "Gaddy, you ain' changed a bit, I swannee. Always did have a hand for the gals—"

And then she realized what she had said before Georgia, and she flushed miserably, murmuring, "Sorry, Missus, I don' know what made me say such a thing—"

Georgia impulsively hugged her. "Don't you worry, little sister. I made that old hound dog chase me hard before I caught him, and so I know what a rascal he was."

"I'm proud to say, I been stump-broke good, however." Gad winked at his wife. "Mattie, how many youngsters you got, anyways?"

She shook her head ruefully. "Too many, an' you be seein' them for yourselves in a few days, iffen you got a mind to get back in that wagon. We look forward to makin' you welcome."

They talked for a bit and then Gad pulled his father and Lem outside to give him a view of the place. He knew that by the time the men came back to the porch, the women would have worked out their pecking order, exchanged their courtesies, and become fast friends. He suspected Georgia wouldn't have it any other way.

As they walked to the stable, Gad said, "The place looks fine, Lemmy. I can see you done real good for yourself."

Lem cast him a quick glance.

Sam said, "He done it for all of us, Gaddy. Jus' as you could a' done, if you had stayed."

Gad said, "I know that, Pa. I don' mean nothin' by it."

Lem stopped and faced his brother then, and his face was stolid and firm. "Gaddy, I'm right glad you come, but I ain' gonna listen no more 'bout how I done had it so good an' you got cheated. You left, an' I stayed. You chose your way, an' I chose mine. You got a wife an' younguns, an' I got a mule an' forty acres. I ain' sayin' that's good, an' I ain' sayin' that's bad, but facts is facts. If you think you made a sorry trade, well, I'm sorry for you. 'Tain' no more to say on it."

Gad stared at his little brother for a long, silent moment. "You're right, Lemmy." He smiled ruefully. "Sometimes, it's hard for a man to have his kid brother tell him what's so. But you ain' no kid no more, an' neither am I."

"No, I ain'."

"Well," Sam said slowly. "Now we got that settled, think we can get on to the barn?"

Sam walked behind his two sons, watching as they started out striding apart and slowly fell into step, their bodies moving closer unconsciously, walking in rhythm. He looked up at the canopy of tall trees around him, at the line of trees which marked the boundary of his land and the lands which still belonged to the swamp and its creatures, and he smiled peacefully. Everything had changed, yet nothing had changed at all. And that, likely, was how it was supposed to be in a man's life.

Epilogue

"The Seminole War may now be considered at a close."

(General Andrew Jackson, 1818)

"I cannot see that any danger can be apprehended from the miserable Indians who inhabit the peninsula of Florida."

(General Alexander Macomb, 1829)

"I promise you that I will soon put an end to the war in Florida or perish in the attempt."

(General Richard Keith Call, 1836)

In 1976, the Indian Claims Commission found for the Seminoles, and on April 27, awarded to those who still survived sixteen million dollars in reparations for the three illegal wars fought against them by the United States government. The award was meant to be distributed evenly among the descendants of all those Indians living in Florida on September 18, 1823, the date of the Treaty of Moultrie Creek. The award was divided four ways: to the Seminole Nation of Oklahoma, whose ancestors were deported from Florida, to the Seminole Tribe of Florida and the Micousukie Tribe of Florida, both federally recognized tribes descended from the original Florida Seminoles, and to the remaining Seminoles in Florida who still refused tribal affiliations of any kind.

The most recent survey showed 1315 Seminoles who were due $12,167 per person. However, the United States government could not decide upon any equitable means of distributing the funds which were so divided, and so the monies remained undelivered more than fifteen years later. American history books record the Seminoles as the only Native American tribe which never gave in to United States "assimilation."

As for the woodlands and its many "dark meanders," the fate of the region seems to have been determined not by man, but by the swamp, itself.

The Okefenokee has survived all sorts of trials, resisting Captain Harry Jackson's efforts to drain it, living through the loss of more than half a billion board feet of trees, and the hunting or decimation of more than three-quarters of its wildlife. Left alone, the swamp eventually replaced much that was taken from it, even thriving in its isolation.

Later in the century, the government attempted to drain the swamp again and open it up to cultivation by means of a canal across the top of Florida which would join the Atlantic and the Gulf of Mexico. When that failed, a scenic highway was planned to let tourists race from the western side of Big Water, past Minnie's Lake, and across Billy's Island. Finally, the swamp defeated that attempt as well. And then in 1960, the Suwannnee River Authority, under the auspices of the Army Corps of Engineers, attempted to build a dam on the river to help irrigate nearby agriculture and prevent flooding. But that plan, too, was soon abandoned as a disaster. The porous limestone of the region proved to be an engineering nightmare, and the bulk of the dam, half-finished, had to be removed. Remains of that final attempt to tame the Suwannee may still be seen on the banks of the river, but even those piles of debris will soon be gone, as the river wends its way as it always has, unperturbed, to the sea.

The swamp, indeed all swamps, are reminders that man is hard-pressed to know what is best for the wild places of the planet. The Okefenokee, the Suwannee River, and the deep swamplands around it are bold victors in the contest between man and nature, as we continually try to wrest the earth around to our own notions and, in this peculiar place, repeatedly fail.

In the swamp, man is subdued. The sounds of the earth, of its creatures, overwhelm his voice and compel him to give way, fall back, and relinquish control. The swamp, like its native inhabitants, simply refuses to obey the rules, and in that defiance, embodies the best nature has to offer.

Bibliography

PART ONE

The single book which was most helpful to me in learning the ways of the Seminole, most particularly the history of Osceola and his people, was Lucia St. Clair Robson's *Light a Distant Fire* (Ballantine Books, NY, 1988). Though fiction, this work is replete with authentic, accurate research, Seminole vocabulary, and a vivid portrayal of the Florida wilderness. For those interested in reading more about Osceola, I highly recommend Ms. Robson's work. Other works which added to my understanding of the Seminole and early Florida were:

Bell, Vereen, *Swamp Water*, Little Brown & Co, NY, 1941.

Brown, G.M., *Ponce DeLeon Land*, DaCosta Printing Co, Jacksonville, FL, 1895.

Cotterill, R.S., *The Southern Indians: The Story of the Civilized Tribes Before Removal*, Univ. of Oklahoma Press, Norman, OK, 1954.

Harper, Francis, and Delma E. Presley, *Okefenokee Album*, Brown Thrasher Books, University of Georgia Press, Athens, GA, 1981.

Josephy, Alvin, M., Jr., *The Patriot Chiefs: A Chronicle of American Indian Resistance*, Penguin Books, NY, 1989.

Kersey, Harry A., Jr., *Pelts, Plumes, and Hides: White Traders Among the Seminole Indians, 1870–1930*, Florida Atlantic University Book, University Press of Florida, Gainesville, FL, 1975.

Littlefield, Daniel F., Jr., *Africans and Seminoles: From Removal to Emancipation*, Greenwood Press, Westport, CT, 1977.

Martin, Sidney Walter, *Florida during the Territorial Days*, Porcupine Press, Philadelphia, PA, 1974.

Mays, Louis B., *Settlers of the Okefenokee*, Okefenokee Press, Folkston, GA, 1975.

McQueen, Alexander S. and Hamp Mizell, *History of Okefenokee Swamp*, Charlton County Historical Society, Folkston, GA, 1926, 1992.

Meanley, Brooke, *Swamps, River Bottoms and Canebrakes*, Barre Publishers, Barre, MA, 1972.

Mulroy, Kevin, *Freedom on the Border: The Seminole Maroons in Florida, the Indian Territory, Coahuila, and Texas*, Texas Tech University Press, Lubbock, TX, 1993.

Peters, Virginia Bergman, *The Florida Wars*, Archon Books, Hamden, CT, 1979.

Polseno, Jo, *Secrets of a Cypress Swamp: The Natural History of Okefenokee*, Golden Press, Western Publishing Co., NY, 1976.

Russell, Franklin, *The Okefenokee Swamp*, Time-Life Books, NY, 1973.

Sneve, Virginia Driving Hawk, *The Seminoles*, Holiday House, New York, NY, 1994.

Weisman, Brent Richards, *Like Beads on a String: A Cultural History of the Seminole Indians in North Peninsular Florida*, University of Alabama Press, Tuscaloosa, AL, 1989.

Wickman, Patricia R., *Osceola's Legacy*, University of Alabama Press, Tuscaloosa, AL, 1991.

Wright, J. Leitch, Jr., *Creeks and Seminoles: The Destruction and Regeneration of the Muscogulge People*, University of Nebraska Press, Lincoln, NE, 1986.

Wright, J. Leitch, Jr., *The Only Land They Knew; The Tragic Story of the American Indians in the Old South*, Free Press, Macmillan Publishing Co., NY, 1981.

PART TWO

For those interested in reading more about the Civil War in Florida, I would recommend Shelby Foote's superb trilogy, *The Civil War, a Narrative*, (1963, Vintage Books Edition, 1986). His perceptive account of the Battle of Oulstee was my primary source, although Not Black's account of the battle was, of course, my own.

Kent Nerburn's *Neither Wolf nor Dog: On Forgotten Roads with an Indian Elder* ((New World Library, 1994) is one of the more eloquent statements of Indian perceptions I have read, and I recommend the book to anyone interested in an Indian version of how America was formed from original Indian lands and spiritual values.

PART THREE

Those books most helpful in this last part of the novel were:

Brockman, C. Frank, *Trees of North America*, Western Publishing Company, NY, 1968.

Hopkins, John M., *Forty-five Years with the Okefenokee Swamp: 1900–1945*, Georgia Society of Naturalists Bulletin no. 4, pp. 1–75.

Matschat, Cecile Hulse, *Suwannee River: Strange Green Land*, Literary Guild of America, NY, 1938.

Mays, Louis B., *Settlers of the Okefenokee*, Folkston, Okefenokee Press, GA, 1975.

Morris, Willie, *North Toward Home*, Yoknapatawpha Press, Oxford, MS, 1982.

Wright, Albert Hazen, *Life Histories of the Frogs of the Okefenokee Swamp*, Macmillan, NY, 1932.

Afterword

Besides those other writers whose works were of enormous benefit to me, there are other more personal sources of support and joy in my life whom I would like to thank here. My excellent agent, Roz Targ, has shepherded this as well as all my other works with diligence. My editor, Ann LaFarge, has graced each page with her eye for eloquence and grace, smacking my hand when I grow tedious. My family, of course, has seen me through ten books now and surely has every reason to yawn at the announcement of each new title, yet does not. Instead, they clap as thunderously for the last effort as they did for the first. My daughter, to whom this book is dedicated, is a wellspring of wonder and delight to me, and when I weary of the writing, I remember that one day, long after I'm gone, she may read these words and glean a bit of her mother's soul herein. That hope makes me work a little harder, a little better. I have a host of friends who add love and beauty to my life: Sandy and Judy, Chris and Steve and Jo and Kelley and Suzi, Vicky and Dee, Sharon and Gail, and too many more to name here. My daughter's father, my once-spouse, co-parent, and friend, Bill, still has the grace and love to applaud my efforts and stand up to my failures. And Jack, my dearest heart, makes me sparkle within and without. To all of them and my readers as well, I leave these words

There is a place within me
Which only you have reached,
A wild and secret garden
Whose walls had not been breached.

A landscape somewhere near my heart
Where only you have walked,
A courtyard hid behind my lips
Where only we have talked.
A body turned to fields
For your hands alone to till,
A flesh aflood with reservoirs
For only you to fill,
A mind which stores as souvenirs
Each ingot you assayed,
And eyes which keep in view
Forgotten boundaries you surveyed.

All I'll own at my life's end
Is what my soul recalls.
Our past constricts to tiny rooms
Down narrow, empty halls.
And after all the homes, the lands,
The graves in which we sleep,
Memories of love are all
The real estates we keep.